Paul David Gould is of mixed-race heritage and grew up on a council estate in Huddersfield. He studied Russian at the University of Birmingham, and spent four years in the former Soviet Union, where he made his start in journalism. His experiences of work, life and love in Russia have inspired *Last Dance at the Discotheque for Deviants*, his first novel. He works as a sub-editor on the *Financial Times* and lives with his husband in Brighton.

Paul David Gould

LAST DANCE AT THE DISCOTHEQUE FOR DEVIANTS

unbound

First published in 2023

Unbound
c/o TC Group, 6th Floor King's House, 9-10 Haymarket, London SW1Y 4BP
www.unbound.com

This is a work of fiction. Names and characters are the product of the author's
imagination and any resemblance to actual persons, living or dead,
is entirely coincidental.

Text design by Jouve

A CIP record for this book is available from the British Library

ISBN 978-1-80018-220-2 (paperback)
ISBN 978-1-80018-222-6 (ebook)

Printed in Great Britain by Clays Ltd, Elcograf S.p.A.

1 3 5 7 9 8 6 4 2

For my beloved LAURENT,
with heartfelt gratitude for his support, patience and,
above all, for loving me enough to marry me

IN MEMORY
of my 1990s disco-going Moscow buddies
CHRIS GEHRING (murdered, 1997)
MARCUS MALABAD (deceased, 2020)

and ANDREJS ZAGARS (deceased, 2019),
who enabled my escape to Latvia

With special thanks to the following people for their generous support of this book

BOOKSHOP PATRONS

Dave Butko
Tom Dillon
Mark Gamble
Mrs Jay-Shelley Heathfield
  BaMA
Russell Mackintosh
Webster T. Mudge
Fr. Mulligan

Jervis Pereira
Melaney Pereira
Dino Sicoli
Mike Tomaino
Jaclyn Turner
Paul Turner
Tina Turner

PATRONS

Tony Aitman
Robert M Atwater
Debbie Elliott
Mike Griffiths
E Hall
Emilia Leese
Garry McQuinn
John Mitchinson

Tom Moody-Stuart
Jackie Morris
Matthew Newman
Elewa Otengi
Christoph Sander
Matthew Scott
Toni Smerdon

A NOTE ON RUSSIAN NAMES

All Russians have a middle name, a *patronymic* formed from their father's first name – hence Ivanovich means 'son of Ivan', while Ivanovna means 'daughter of Ivan'. Other patronymics include Mikhailovich, Sergeyevna, Borisovna and so on. When you use someone's patronymic after their first name, it's an expression of courtesy or of respect for their age or seniority. The tone is akin to addressing someone as 'Mr' or 'Mrs' (which in Russian are archaic words and almost never used, except sometimes for foreigners).

Russians also use *diminutives* of first names to indicate affection. Konstantin becomes Kostya; Dmitry/Dima; Galina/ Galya. But younger people never address each other using patronymics, so characters in their twenties, such as Kostya and Dima, use only each other's first names or diminutives. The older characters would expect to be addressed more formally (Tamara Borisovna, Stepan Mikhailovich, Galina Sergeyevna).

Pronunciation of Russian names:

Dima — *DEE-ma*
Oleg — *al-YEG*
Valery — *val-YAIR-i*
Borisovna — *ba-REES-uv-na*
Gennady — *gi-NAH-di*
Voronezh — *va-RON-yesh*
Igor — *EE-gor*
Kirill — *ki-REEL*

FEBRUARY 1993. Moscow

Dima

One week, three phone calls. That's all it takes for him to realise he'll never see his boyfriend again.

Wait ... His '*boyfriend*'? Nah, make that his *would-be* boyfriend ... Truth be told, he'd wanted to end it with Kostya, hadn't he? And as for even referring to Kostya as his 'boyfriend', he'd prefer to say they've just been 'seeing each other'. Goofing around, that's all. Like he told him, last time they met, 'Kostya, we live in Russia. Men can't have *boyfriends* here.'

But this one week changes everything. Ending it with Kostya is no longer in his hands, only words snatched from his mouth to evaporate like breath in the freezing air. Just one short week in this long, long winter ... It's been months since the first snowfall, yet still Moscow's sidewalks lie armour-plated with ice − ice now worn smooth by the feet of its shuffling, swaddled masses. And with no let-up in the blizzards laying siege to the city, fresh snow is piling up outside the window of the bedroom he's rented these past two years.

It's a room he's always shared with Oleg, his 'partner in

crime' – that being an English expression they'd picked up from bootleg pop videos. This one's from that early 1980s song by Wham! that Oleg keeps playing. Last night, as the pair of them were getting ready to go out, they danced to it on the painted floorboards between their two single beds, and argued over which one of them looked more like George Michael and which of the British pop duo they most fancied.

Tonight though, Oleg's gone out cruising without him; he's not in the mood to hang around that seedy metro station again, trying to catch strangers' eyes in pursuit of yet another one-night stand. Besides, it's bothering him (uncool as it would be to admit it to Oleg) that Kostya hasn't phoned. It's been a couple of weeks since their showdown outside McDonald's. At first, he felt sure Kostya was just sulking. Let him sulk, he thought, he'll be on the phone soon enough, wanting to kiss and make up – I mean, the boy can hardly keep away from me.

Ever since they met at the end of October, Kostya has phoned him nearly every goddamn day, and begged to come and sleep over at least twice a week. Look, he'd told Kostya, he needed to 'cool it', but now – now that the phone calls have stopped – it comes as an affront. *I'm* the one who decides when I've finished with a guy, he thinks, not the other way around.

Still no call from Kostya. After a few days, he catches himself jumping up whenever the phone rings. But the calls are usually for Valery Ivanovich, the elderly widower who's rented out his spare room to him and Oleg: calls from Valery's daughter, reminding the old man how he has to move out, now he's no longer fit to look after himself.

Only one call that week is for him. For a second, as he

recognises Yuri's voice down the phone, he thinks: forget Kostya, I've got Yuri. Tough, sexy Yuri, muscly and smouldering. OK, so Yuri can be a little *controlling*, he thinks, but he does look after me ... This call, however, isn't one of Yuri's more 'intimate' summonses – it's simply to remind Dima of the shoot he'll be in that week and what gear he should wear for it.

The waiting becomes unbearable. He decides to phone. It's been a while since he called; last time, though they'd never even met, he got such a frosty reception from Tamara Borisovna – God knows what Kostya's mother could have against him, but in all the photos Kostya's shown him she looks such a sour-faced prude. Anyway, since Oleg's out, he'll ask Kostya round tonight. Or suggest they go ice-skating in Gorky Park again. A little flirting, he thinks, and I'll have Kostya eating out of my hand – I can pull any guy I want, so it shouldn't be difficult.

He gets the answering machine. '*You've reached Konstantin Krolikov and Tamara Borisovna Krolikova in Moscow. We can't come to the phone, so please leave a message.*'

Try to sound casual, he tells himself. 'Hi, Kostya. Good evening, Tamara Borisovna. Dima here. Hey, Kostya, it's been a while. How about getting together? Tonight even? Or this weekend? Let's go ice-skating again – you liked that. How about it? Call me. Bye.'

No one phones back.

Two days later, when he calls the second time, the same. *We can't come to the phone* ... What? Why can't they just say, 'We're not at home'? Or wait ... what if they *are* at home but deliberately not answering? Maybe Kostya and his mum have one of those number display gadgets, like the one Yuri uses to screen incoming calls? Is Kostya avoiding him? So much for the boy he thought he had eating out of his hand . . .

I won't have him ignoring me, he thinks – I know, I'll conceal the number I'm calling from . . . And out he heads to the payphone down by the vodka kiosk. It's dark on the street, the concrete of apartment blocks tinted yellow in the glow of street lamps. He looks up at the hundreds of windows, blind black squares by day, but now blazing with warmth as people hunker down with tea or vodka at their kitchen tables. Give it an hour, he thinks, and that'll be me and Kostya. He'll be round here in a flash, soon as I've called.

He keeps his warm woolly cap pulled down tight over his ears, but once inside the phone box, as he removes his gloves to dial, his fingers shrivel in the cold. His breath mists up the inside of the booth, blurring his view of the line for vodka outside: men with red faces and missing teeth who swear and spit and stomp their boots in the snow. The queue lengthens, creeping towards the payphone. They look to him like *bomzhy*, homeless rough sleepers.

This time, the dialling tone gives way to the sound of a phone being picked up at the other end. His frozen fingers force a fifteen-kopeck coin into the slot.

The voice that answers is barely a whisper. 'Doctor? *Please*? Doctor, is that you?'

'*Allo*? Tamara Borisovna?'

Silence down the phone.

'*Allo*?' he persists. 'Tamara Borisovna? Can you hear me? It's Konstantin's friend Dmitry, I'm calling from—'

Still a whisper: 'Who?'

'Dmitry. A friend of Konstantin. We've spoken on the phone before—'

'*Dmitry?*' She sounds dazed. '*Kakoy Dmitry?*' What Dmitry?

He glances at the lengthening line for vodka. The booze-addled *bomzhy* are shuffling closer, rowdier by the second. 'We've never met, Tamara Borisovna, but me and Kostya—'

'Kostya? Oh, Kostya, Kostya ... my Kostya ...'

Her voice caves in – like it's fighting for breath or something – and all he can hear, crackling down the line, is a sort of heaving, distant and strangled. He covers his other ear, trying to block out the howling of the wind and the ruckus in the vodka queue.

'Tamara Borisovna, I don't understand. Is something wrong?'

He catches another voice in the background, in the same room – not Kostya's voice but a woman's voice – and before he knows it this other woman, whoever she is, has grabbed the phone.

'Young man,' she says, abruptly loud and clear, 'this is no time to be calling. Leave Tamara Borisovna in peace and don't phone here again.'

She hangs up. The dead tone drills into his ear. Slowly, disbelievingly, he lets his hand, now numb with cold and still clamped to the receiver, drop limp and frozen to his side.

Tamara Borisovna

They were told to be at Paveletsky Station two hours before their overnight train. That's how long it could take, she seems to remember hearing, for them to go over all the paperwork and to be sure of an appropriate space in the baggage car. In the end, the inspection took a cursory twenty minutes, and for most of those two hours the inspector's office remained closed. For 'technical reasons', it said.

So she and Galina simply had to wait, choked by the stench

of damp and train fumes, perched on the trunk she'd never properly unpacked during her time in Moscow. She sits in a daze, numb and stupefied at the indifference of the comings and goings brushing past her, of the voices echoing across the public address system. Every half-hour, Galina scuttles over to the station buffet, fetching cups of acrid black tea for her to warm her hands on.

Night has fallen by the time they're ready for boarding. The platform is covered with patches of snow and ice. She forces herself to watch as two railway porters approach, wheeling what looks like a wooden crate. 'Make way!' the porters call in their quaint sing-song cry of '*do-RO-gu! do-RO-gu!*', a call that disperses the crowd of fur hats and padded winter coats huddled alongside the waiting train. People do make way, thankfully. They don't stare, not too much. In the dark, that wooden box could pass for almost any other cargo.

She buries her face in Galina's shoulder. Thank God for her dear old friend rushing up to Moscow to be with her. That old saying, *It's times like these you find out who your friends are*, keeps circling round her head. She wishes she could stop thinking it. Not that she isn't grateful, rather that her gratitude brings none of the solace offered by that circling homily. The sobs come. Quietly this time, not like earlier. Galina's so strong now, she thinks, it's years since she went through this herself. Another wretched adage comes to mind – *Time's a great healer*. No one's said *that* to her yet. But then she's hardly spoken these past few days.

More fur hats and quilted coats bustle past, people dragging suitcases, some of them on sledges, people puffing out steam as if imitating the trains. In their hurry to board, they pay her no attention, she's invisible. Lucky them, she thinks. Oh, to be one of them, to be anyone but her. By now the two porters are reversing out of the baggage car, their cart empty, the fragile cargo loaded, along with her trunk, inside that windowless space.

*

It would've cost a week's wages to get a compartment to themselves, so she and Galina end up sharing with two young men in their twenties, about Kostya's age. Mercifully, the boys – *malchiki*, Galina calls them, being all motherly and taking charge – cease their honking and sniggering as soon as she pokes her head in. Thank God they've quietened down, she thinks. Still, the boys show the proper respect, giving up the more comfortable lower berths and stepping into the corridor to let the women change out of their street clothes.

She doesn't bother though: this custom of changing into pyjamas and slippers on night trains is all well and good for going on holiday or for visiting loved ones. But not this trip. As Galina hangs up their coats, she sits by the window, twisting her hat in her hands. The radio babbles away. Funny how the radio's always on in these trains, turned down low, like the lighting. She feels Galina slide up beside her and touch her arm. She stares outside, confronted with her reflection staring back at her, eyes downcast, cheeks pale and lined under limp, dark hair that she was once proud to call 'curly'; hair that now straggles past her face.

Snow is falling. It looks like ashes drifting earthwards, fluttering in the lights of the railway yard. From unseen loudspeakers, departures and destinations are barked out like orders in a prison camp – destinations far from Moscow, places that are dull and provincial but less intimidating. Places with ties, like her own hometown, twelve hours south of here. The train jolts into motion: another step on this unbearable journey, and another wave of sobbing brims up inside her. Not here, she thinks, not in public. But she can't stop herself. *Let it all out*, she'd told Galina all those years ago.

The door slides open. She sees the two boys, about to come back in. They freeze at the sight of her, a woman old enough to be their mother, convulsed and sobbing. Let them see me, she thinks, what do I care? Apologising, the boys retreat back into the corridor.

Jamie

There's always some busybody telling him how his coat's too thin for a Russian winter, and bloody hell, they wouldn't be wrong – not today. Mind you, this was his own bright idea, so here he is, freezing his balls off, stood outside the Moscow Conservatory on a February afternoon. A few yards away, beneath the statue of Tchaikovsky, he sees bunches of flowers, frozen in the snow. That'd be a good sign, he thinks, folk still coming to leave flowers when it's minus fifteen.

He's chosen a day marking the centenary of Tchaikovsky's death and can see by the pile of flowers spilling well beyond the base of the statue how much the Russians revere their beloved great composer. So it's gonna take a hell of a nerve to go up to total strangers and ask them the kind of questions *he* has in mind . . .

His Russian is good, they tell him, good enough to turn on the charm. And he's got his spiel worked out: 'Excuse me, may I bother you a minute? – *Izvinitye, vas mozhno na minutku?*' followed by: 'I see you're laying flowers in honour of Tchaikovsky . . . Ah, yes, of course, the centenary . . . So tragic, his early death . . .'

And then his killer question: 'If Tchaikovsky were alive

today, d'you think people would be more accepting of his homosexuality?'

He came up with it himself, this idea for a story (*story*, he reminds himself: don't call it an 'article' if you wanna be a proper journalist) about Russians' primitive attitudes towards homosexuality. There's even a gay 'scene' of sorts in Moscow these days, but it's tiny and underground, hidden away out of fear. Which makes him sometimes wonder why the hell he came back to Russia instead of staying put in England. Still, his pitch had gone down well with his editor: 'Sounds like a great *story*,' Bernie said, before sending Jamie out to canvass opinion on the street.

First up, a housewife: two shopping bags and a headscarf tied under her chin. He waits until she's laid her bouquet and picked up her bags again. For a minute, his charm works, and she fairly gushes with pride: 'Tchaikovsky? Oh, we *worship* Tchaikovsky!'

But when he poses his 'killer question', her smile vanishes. 'A *gomoseksualist*? Why must you soil his name with that *filth*? You foreigners! No respect for our culture.' And with that, she's off, stupid cow, shouting back over her shoulder how 'shameless' he is.

Next, some old codger in an overcoat and wolfskin hat. The same questions and a similar response – 'Homosexuals? Perverts! Ought to be castrated' – only this time, the old git actually spits in the snow near his feet before storming off.

Then there's that kind-looking couple in mittens and fur hats who remind him of Mum and Dad back home. But they frown and shake their heads: 'We'd probably disown our son if he was gay.' Even the culture vultures emerging from the Conservatory's lunchtime recitals tell him that they think *gomoseksualisty* are 'sick' or 'in need of help'.

9

A whole hour he's been stood on this street corner and that's the most sympathetic comment he's heard. Honestly, he thinks, I despair of the Russians. So bloody backward – like *peasants*, some of them. So much for the hopes of change and enlightenment dawning across Russia, along with *glasnost* and foreign travel and McDonald's and the rest of it.

Giving it up as a bad job, he sets off on the long trudge through the snow back to the office, his hands now numb and buried in his pockets. All this talk of Tchaikovsky has turned his thoughts to Kostya, the first Russian he'd truly made a friend of – now there's a proper Tchaikovsky fan for you. All that drama – right up Kostya's street. He really should get in touch ... Back in the days when they hung out together all the time, Kostya had once made him sit through the finale of the *Pathétique* Symphony. He can still picture Kostya's faraway gaze and his eyes welling up with tears.

I know, he thinks, I'll phone this evening from work. Maybe Kostik can help me with my story. It'd flatter him to be interviewed – it'd be an excuse for getting back in touch too. That's what I'll do, I'll call him tonight.

★

That rancid whiff of boiled cabbage, infiltrating the office as it does of an evening. A smell that makes him gag in every block of flats he's been to in this bloody country; the smell of suppers being cooked in the apartments downstairs. Means he's working late again.

The *Moscow Herald*'s office is on the top floor of a squat five-storey block built in the 1950s. It's a far cry from the swanky business centre where the *Moscow Times* has set up shop – now *that's* where he should be working, a reporter for a *respected* English-language newspaper. Then he could work his way up, become a correspondent for one of the British broadsheets.

His eyes wander around the converted Soviet apartment, all wood-effect lino and faded flowery wallpaper. The smaller room serves as an office for Bernie, the forty-something American who co-founded this expat weekly and runs it on a shoestring; crammed into the larger room are the desks of three more reporters, piled high with paper, and that of the *Herald*'s secretary Larisa. The others have gone, and the lamp on his desk casts a solitary pool of light. Even the teletype machines that churn out endless news from Tass and Reuters have fallen quiet.

He picks up the phone and dials Kostya's number. It's been so long since they spoke that he feels his heart rate quicken. Deep breath now as he prepares to put on his matey, chatty voice. But there's no reply. Not even the answering machine. That's odd, he thinks, thought they had an answering machine, Kostya and his mum . . . He lets it continue ringing, then hangs up. He can always try again tomorrow.

He turns back to his computer. All he's written so far is his byline. *By James Goodier.* The cursor blinks, bright green against the dark, blank monitor. He slurps his tea, a good strong English brew, not that weak crap the Russians drink – though he'll need more than one cuppa to keep him going if he works late trying to get something written.

But what, Bernie would ask, is the *angle* of his story? The news that Moscow, a city of nigh on ten million people, now has one poxy gay disco a week? That's up from none at all just a year ago, mind. Or is it the homophobia spouted by most Russians, like those people on the street? No, that's just the tip of the iceberg; they were only a random bunch of passers-by. What he should focus on is the hard-core hate brigade, the gangs of gay-bashing thugs. Now *that's* the story he should be writing.

It's almost a month since he last went to the 'Discotheque for Sexual Minorities'. 'What a name!' he recalls saying to Artyom, his boyfriend for the past year. 'It's like calling it the "Discotheque for Deviants".' The venue had been the canteen of the Red Hammer Cement Works, a tram ride beyond the last metro stop – the point being that these discos were 'underground'; they were *meant* to be hard to find. They even changed venue from one week to the next, with the location kept secret until the big night.

Somehow though, a gang of thugs had got word and lain in wait outside, armed with baseball bats. He didn't witness the attacks himself – he and Artyom were safely inside – but he did see two of the guys who got beaten up. One of them staggered in, his face bloodied, his shirt ripped, and collapsed, clutching his sides, howling in pain. Cracked ribs, he heard later. The other, that ginger-haired boy he recognised from a party at Artyom's, had to be carried in by the hired security guards, unconscious. Both were driven away in an ambulance.

After that, the security guys had locked everyone inside, where they'd hunkered down until daybreak, sipping vodka at the canteen tables, under siege and in no mood for dancing. He eventually fell asleep on Artyom's shoulder, and it was almost light when they woke and left for Artyom's place.

He recalls spotting Kostya at the disco that same night, a while before the attack. Not that they spoke ... Kostya – his 'Russian best mate' in happier times – had instead skulked past, pretending not to see him and Artyom as they smooched on the dance floor. Was Kostya still there when those guys got beaten up? Did he know anything about it? And had he been safe there on his own? There'd been no Dima at his side that time, nor the time before. Come to think of it, he's not seen Kostya together with Dima since the disco before New Year ... On *that* occasion, Kostya's mood had been nauseatingly bubbly; he'd made a point of swanning up to them, hanging off Dima's arm, batting his eyelids, all chatty. Dima had barely nodded at them. What a knob. He doesn't half fancy himself, that Dima, with his fake leather biker jacket and his black-market Levi's. Jeez, Kostik, what're you doing with a tosser like that?

★

Things haven't been right between them since he – followed by Kostya – relocated to Moscow. Down in Kostya's hometown of Voronezh, where they'd met back in the autumn of 1989, things had been so different. That had been on his year abroad, he and two dozen other Brits on a language course at the local university. Most of the Russian he learnt wasn't in those stuffy Soviet tutorials though – no, it was at student dormitory parties, great pile-ins of debauchery and vodka, of pirated pop music and empty bottles rattling down corridors of peeling lino.

Look at me, he used to think. Me, a lad from Manchester, and one of only a handful of Westerners in this provincial hole, twelve hours by night train from Moscow. It made him feel intrepid: a foreign correspondent in the making. Every indignity, every privation, had been a tale to tell. And although his phone calls home needed to be booked in advance at the telegraph office (*booked* – like, how primitive was that?), once he got through to his mum, how he loved to regale her with his stories of food rationing, the lack of hot water in the dorm, the cockroaches, the toilets you had to squat over.

But he'd had a regular bolthole too, a haven of sanity where he'd flee all that noise and filth, the cockroaches and squatty toilets. And that was Kostya's family home, a modest fifth-storey flat on the other side of Voronezh. One night a week he used to sleep over there, having wolfed down a huge dinner conjured up by Kostya's mother. God knows how she did it, 'cause there was bugger all in the shops. And at every meal, she'd insist on giving him and Kostya the same lecture: '*You'll both have to find wives to cook for you one day . . .*'

Meanwhile Kostya's father Gennady would crack open his Crimean wine and bombard Jamie with questions about the West. Later, he and Kostya would stay up, talking in Kostya's room until the small hours, sharing his bed – sleeping top-to-tail, though – discussing politics, *glasnost* and the changes sweeping across Russia. They never discussed future wives or girlfriends. They didn't discuss boyfriends either. And then, eventually, they would fall asleep, barely touching one another.

Tamara Borisovna

Her head is squashed against the mothball-smelling pillow, and her pillow is squashed against the lowered window blind. *Cl-clunk, cl-clunk*, goes the train, rumbling into the night. Opposite her, Galina is asleep. One of the young men in the top berths is snoring. She sits in the dark, upright, having not bothered with the bed Galina made up for her, the starchy sheets and itchy blankets stretched across her bunk.

She can't believe she's slept at all, having barely managed to sleep a wink these past few nights. Not since the call from the hospital, since hearing the news that no mother should ever hear. There's another of the phrases echoing round her head: *No mother should ever have to . . .* Stop, stop, she thinks. It's true, though: no mother should ever have to bury her child. So why her? If only, please, God, she could turn back time, even these few wretched weeks.

'*Natural causes*,' was all the hospital would say. They told her not to blame herself, said she could have counselling. Counselling? What good would that do? That won't bring him back. '*Oh, Kostya, my Kostya . . .*' She hears herself repeating a name she's whispered down the years – at his bedside while he slept, the times he came home from school close to tears, when she'd opened his letters from the army, and that day she'd got him out . . .

The news had hit her like a body blow, disbelief taking the form of actual physical pain. She was winded, unable to scream, scarcely able to breathe. She had collapsed against the display cabinet, breaking several plates, and slid slowly to the floor. There she had stayed, whimpering, curled up in a ball. It took her hours to drag herself back to the phone, to call Galina, to find the words. Who was she now – a bereaved mother, an *ex*-mother? There were words, she thought, for orphans and for widows, but not for her, not for a parent robbed of a child.

She fumbles in the dark and quietly slides open the door. The half-lit corridor is empty; the whole carriage must be asleep. The train trundles through a clearing in a forest: *cl-lunk, cl-clunk . . . cl-clunk, cl-clunk*, a sound she once found so comforting. Outside, the railway banking slopes down towards a field of white – icy blue in the moonlight – and flurries of falling snow blur the blackness of the trees. The train arcs round a bend and a chain of lighted windows curves into view, reflections rippling on the snow. A trail of footprints crosses the field. She thinks of children's stories of wooden houses, of bears and wolves, of hunters brewing tea from a samovar. Stories she used to tell Kostya.

Someone's edging along the corridor towards her, from the toilets, a young man in a red tracksuit with the word 'Sport' across his chest. Not 'Nike', not 'Adidas', just 'Sport'. He has floppy hair, and dark eyebrows that rise in greeting. He stops to enter his compartment – the same compartment as hers. It's one of the two boys.

He turns to her, gesturing at the door. 'Sorry ... were you waiting to go back in?'

She stiffens, shaking her head. In the silence, she again hears *cl-clunk, cl-clunk* ...

'Oh,' the boy says, 'I just thought—'

'I can't sleep, that's all.' Leave me alone, she thinks, please don't ask questions.

'I see ...' The boy hesitates, but presses on. 'I'm sure you'll sleep better when you get home, eh?' A pause. 'That *is* where you're going, right? Home?'

Home, she thinks. Where's home now? Not Moscow – Moscow was never home. She looks at him – he seems a nice boy, a bit like Kostya, only more sure of himself.

'Yes,' she manages. 'Voronezh.'

'Oh, me too,' he says.

She doesn't answer, looking down at the carpet and letting the silence hang.

The boy shrugs, taking the hint. 'Well ... err, goodnight then.'

He smiles awkwardly and slides open the door to their compartment. She turns back to the window and presses her nose against the glass. Peering into the night outside, she scans the length of the curving train, looking for the one carriage that casts no light on the snow, the windowless baggage car carrying the coffin that contains her son.

Jamie

He hears one of the teletype machines chatter into life and glances at the roll of paper inching out of the Tass feed. In the past hour, there have been three short news bulletins in Russian, one of them barely four lines long. The shortest ones can be the worst though, like the ones announcing the dissolution of the Soviet Union at the end of 1991. Just his luck to be stuck in the office as some big news breaks.

Cup of tea in hand, he gets up from his desk to check what Tass is reporting. The first bulletin simply announces a press conference, the second is a statement from some junior trade minister, and the third—

He feels his grip slacken, feels the cup slip from his hand . . . Yet even as it shatters on the lino, he stays frozen on the spot, not stooping to clear it up. Instead, he stays standing as he reads the bulletin a second time, a third time, then a fourth. No, it can't be, he can't have read it right – it's this Russian text, he must've misunderstood it. Perhaps, if he keeps re-reading it, he hopes, some different meaning might surface from the Cyrillic type swimming before his eyes . . .

A 24-year-old man who recently died in the Moscow suburb of Khimki has been named as an employee of an American trade organisation in Moscow. A hospital statement blames 'natural causes' for the death of Konstantin Krolikov – a diagnosis confirmed by both police and medical authorities, who insist that post-mortem procedures were followed to the letter.

2

THREE YEARS EARLIER

MAY 1990. Voronezh

Kostya

Oh, Jamie ... the mess I made of that rehearsal! Wasn't it embarrassing enough, without knowing you'd been watching? I'd invited you in the hope that you'd be proud of me, so I stood there on stage, my eyes scanning the rows of seats in the darkness beyond the footlights, and thinking: is Jamie here yet? When you finally showed up, twenty minutes late, a crack of light distracted me as a door opened and I saw your stooped figure creeping towards a seat near the back.

It's not like I had a big part: I was a mere understudy, offered an unexpected chance when the actor playing Eric fell ill. You know, Eric Birling in *An Inspector Calls*. I showed you I'd even been working on my own translation of the play, remember? I'd read it in Russian – as *Vizit Inspektora* – so many times that I knew entire scenes by heart, and when we rehearsed Eric's confrontation with his father, I decided I'd give *my* translation a go, right there on stage, instead of the standard text.

It was the first time Arkady Bogdanovich had seen me act. As artistic director of the Voronezh Youth Theatre, he'd treated me well, encouraging me to write programme notes and design posters on top of my day-to-day job in administration and ticket sales. Maybe, one day, I'd be made assistant director. But, as you saw, I blew it.

'Stop, Kostya!' he called from the front row. 'Stop. What're you *doing*? You've changed the meaning of Eric's words. Why've you done that?'

I edged forwards into the unforgiving glare of the footlights, and started explaining how my translation was closer to the English text: in the original, you see, Eric tells his father he shouldn't have fired the factory girl, the one who's been found dead – whereas in the Russian version he accuses Mr Birling—

Arkady Bogdanovich drew his hands down his face and sighed, loudly enough for his assistant director and other actors to hear. 'Kostya, you wanted a chance to come out from behind the scenes,' he said. 'I'm giving you that chance. Now let's do the scene again. But remember, theatre can be just like life: if you want the part, you've got to stick to the script.'

★

When I was little, barely turned eight years old, Papa built me a toy theatre for my birthday. He'd made it in a workshop at the factory where he was the chief engineer and kept it a surprise until he brought it home. It was half a metre wide, with footlights and curtains, even a revolving stage. Papa was particularly proud of the revolving stage, with the little handle you cranked to turn from one scene to the next. 'Look at the gears underneath,' he'd say, as he turned the handle. 'That's engineering, that is.'

But Papa was to be disappointed by my lack of interest in gears or wiring. What I loved was the make-believe, the stories, the characters: I would make cut-out figures of princes or knights, princesses or wicked witches, and there I'd crouch, moving them around on that tiny stage. I played with it for hours on end, long after Papa tired of watching. I played at theatre more than I ever played at soldiers or cosmonauts. And now I wanted to do it as a grown-up.

★

But my services as an understudy were no longer required. The actor playing Eric made a full recovery and Arkady Bogdanovich lined up another understudy, just in case. He never asked me to audition again.

I did, however, sit in on dress rehearsals for *Vizit Inspektora*. To watch, not to offer any opinions. And there, when the curtain went up, was the same old backdrop they'd dusted off from last season's *Uncle Vanya*. Russian country estate, English industrial city – who'd know the difference? No one in Voronezh anyway.

No one, that is, except you and the other British students. You see, until you appeared, I'd never met anyone who'd even *been* to England, let alone come from there. '*Provocation and lies!*' they used to warn us at the compulsory Young Communist meetings of my teens. '*Beware of fraternising with Westerners – don't be tempted by their jeans and hamburgers. Don't let them poison you with capitalist propaganda!*' But the year we met, that message had softened: it was the fourth year of *glasnost*, a time when banned books were being published and political prisoners set free. And once I'd met *you*, I stopped being impressed by Arkady Bogdanovich's Party-sponsored trips to Czechoslovakia. I had a friend from the West, and *glasnost* meant I could practise my English with you without being accused of 'fraternising'. The Young Communists even invited your group for tea and cake; we were officially *allowed* to be friends and could invite foreigners to our homes. Better still, foreigners could invite *us* to the West.

Jamie

Poor Kostya, embarrassing himself on stage. Just as well he didn't get offered the part ... Bless him, he knew his stuff – anything to do with theatre, classical music, the arts – but his acting was so, well ... *wooden*. He didn't live and breathe the part, he just held himself stiffly, frowning with concentration and striking melodramatic poses like he was in an opera.

Of course, he couldn't *tell* Kostya he was 'wooden'. He'd have to say, 'Good on you for trying.' Kostya would no doubt ask him to look over the text of the play, and he'd have to nod along and say, 'You're right, Kostik, your translation *is* closer to the original.'

But all he could think of that afternoon was getting out of the theatre and getting some grub down him. He'd never felt so hungry, so much of the time, and that summer in Voronezh there was no food in the shops. Bugger all. Folk back home, they didn't believe him – he'd be on the phone to Mum or his sister Lisa, and he'd say, 'Look, I couldn't even find spuds yesterday', and they'd say, 'Get away with you, our Jamie, you must be getting fed somehow.'

And he was. He'd sussed out, for example, that the Youth Theatre buffet always had an under-the-counter supply of smoked salmon, served on bread with a sprig of dill. Bloody dill, the Russians put it on everything. Still, once he'd discovered that, he was there every other day. Which is where he met Kostya, manning the box office with that coy, blushing smile of his. He'd soon twigged that Kostya must be gay as well. But what a closet case. He wasn't sure if Kostya realised it himself – or would have admitted to having a crush on him. Before long though, he started getting invited home, to Kostya's parents' flat. Most weeks he'd sleep over too, and Kostya's mum would lay on a feast, seeing as they had a guest, an English boy no less. It was the best meal he'd get anywhere in that godforsaken town, so he'd be daft to refuse. Plus, Kostya would get upset if he didn't go. It was soon part of their weekly routine.

★

Shortly after Kostya's botched outing on stage, he'd called in at the theatre to find Kostya back in the box office, processing paperwork from the Ministry of Culture. It was a warm evening in late May, and he'd dressed the way he would back in England: like he was off out on the pull. Hair close-cropped on the sides, but gelled and spiky up top. His Soul II Soul T-shirt with his old denim jacket thrown over it. And on his feet, those battered off-white Converse All Stars. He could see Kostya's eyes running up and down him in what looked like awe.

He enjoyed that, teasing Kostya a bit. And not only Kostya – he also liked getting a rise out of the locals. As the pair of them strolled through the evening sunshine to the trolleybus stop on Lenin Square, he noticed how folk stared at him. Especially the babushkas, shaking their heads and muttering. But he'd attract envious looks from young Russian guys too. Not surprising, with the gear some of them had on: synthetic slacks and brown slip-ons like their dads wore. It brought a smirk to his face. Kostya was smiling too, he saw, walking a little taller, proud to be seen with him, literally rubbing shoulders in that warm, leafy light of summer.

Kostya

Later that night, as was our weekly custom, we ended up in bed together. Only kidding – what I mean is, we *shared my bed*, carefully positioning ourselves top-to-tail. We never did anything, you know, *intimate*. How could we, sleeping under the same roof as Mama and Papa?

For dinner, Mama had made that garlicky carrot salad you liked so much, followed by salmon – only the tinned stuff, mind – with new potatoes from a neighbour's allotment. 'Tamara Borisovna,' you said (flattering her like you did), 'with all the shortages and rationing, I don't know how you manage to rustle up a feast like this.'

Mama blushed, her habitual modesty act. 'Oh, you just have to know the right times and places to queue . . .' She never mentioned how she used her job at the library to get hold of banned books for a local Party bigwig in charge of food supplies. People did each other favours, you see. Papa was in jovial spirits too, about to set off to Leningrad for some engineering conference. He plied you with wine, and you were more tipsy than usual.

Perhaps that's why our conversation took the turn it did. Me, I'd wanted to talk about *An Inspector Calls*. Was my translation closer to the original? Was Manchester anything like the town in the play? But no, we didn't talk about that in the end. My questions weren't life-changing, nothing that would turn our friendship upside down. You, it turned out, had far more searching questions to ask.

We sat facing each other from opposite ends of my bed, me

in my pyjamas, you still in your Soul II Soul T-shirt. Even in semi-darkness, well away from my bedside lamp, I could see you were distracted, your eyes wandering over the theatre posters on my wall. Many of them were from my student days at the local arts academy, but the one that caught your eye was from a Bolshoi performance of *Swan Lake*. Had I been to see it?, you asked.

'No,' I said (I'd only been to Moscow four times in my life). 'That's a present from Arkady Bogdanovich. He went to see it at New Year.'

'Why didn't you go, Kostik? You're the biggest Tchaikovsky fan in town!'

I sighed. 'You can't get tickets to the Bolshoi unless you've got connections. Or unless you pay in dollars. Besides, where would I stay overnight in Moscow?'

You didn't answer. Instead, still not looking at me, you asked, 'Do Russians these days ever hear the *truth* about Tchaikovsky? You know, what with openness, *glasnost* and all that?'

'Truth?' I hadn't cottoned on to what you meant. 'What truth?'

Now looking me in the eye, you said, 'About him being homosexual.'

We spoke in Russian that night, and that word *gomoseksualist* made me freeze. It was a word that never reared its head in polite conversation, a label stubbornly fixated on two men's carnal *activity*, rather than on their love. As for Tchaikovsky, yes, there had long been rumours about his doomed infatuations. Remember seeing me close to tears as I played you the finale of his *Pathétique* Symphony? That, I somehow knew, was his unmentionable love expressed in music – and an omen that presaged his suspicious death.

I mumbled something about having heard the rumours and thought that'd be the end of it. But no. It wasn't Tchaikovsky you wanted to talk about. It was me.

Leaning closer, you held my gaze and said, 'Noticed how your mum keeps telling us we'll need to find ourselves *wives* one day? Every time she cooks for us, she brings that up.' A pause. Your eyes searched mine. 'So d'you think you ever will?'

My throat was dry, my voice small and apologetic. 'I guess so,' I muttered. I tried for a casual-looking shrug. 'One day ... I suppose it's a matter of time—'

'You've never had a girlfriend though, have you?'

I was dumbstruck. How did you know? How could you tell? I know Mama once nursed hopes for me and Zhanna, my best friend at the arts academy, my cinema-going confidante. I miss Zhanna. She was a punkish blonde who would drag me to student discos and even get me to dance. But she wasn't a *girlfriend* ... Mama's hopes finally crumbled when Zhanna met some boy at the university, abruptly got married and then left Voronezh for good.

You took my silence as a 'no', then said, 'Let me tell you something, Kostik. *I've* never had a girlfriend either.'

I stared at you. You were smiling – like you were happy about it.

'Oh,' I heard myself reply. 'Maybe you've just not met the right girl yet ...'

Not met the right girl yet. Those words again. That well-worn excuse I'd felt obliged to trot out year after year ...

You shook your head. 'No, Kostik. I tried telling myself that. Right through my teens. But there's only so long I could kid myself. Sooner or later, I had to face up to the truth.' A heartbeat. You were still smiling. 'I tell you Kostik, I'm *gay*.'

Although you kept your voice to a whisper, you used a word that echoed in my head like the clanging of a bell – *goluboy*, Russian slang for 'gay', a word every bit as tainted with suspicion and contempt as *gomoseksualist*.

I was silent. Still whispering, you pressed on: 'It's not been easy for me, this past year in Voronezh. Sure, there's a few good-looking Russian lads around, but you can't be too careful here, it's so backward, this country – the racism, the homophobia—'

'*Gomofobia*?' It was a word I'd never come across.

'You know,' you said, 'an aversion to homosexuality.'

But wasn't it normal, I protested, to feel some degree of aversion? After all, it was an aversion I felt myself. Surely *gomoseksualizm* wasn't natural?

'Natural?' you said, chuckling. 'If the human race lived "naturally", we'd still all be cave dwellers! Anyway, Kostik, it *is* natural, for me.' A pause. 'What about you? Isn't it natural for you?'

That moment was as if you'd taken my hand and marched the two of us towards the edge of a cliff. Like we were ready to shut our eyes and jump. Except our eyes were wide open, your gaze holding mine as you strode ahead, magically defying gravity and hovering in mid-air. As you invited me to follow and step off that cliff edge, you – unlike me – were oblivious to what people would think.

'I'm scared.'

'Scared of what, Kostik?'

I swallowed. Should I tell you what I'd endured in the army all those years ago? I never talked about it. Not yet, I thought, and simply said, 'Of turning out to be one of them.'

Your eyes widened. 'One of *them*? Try saying "one of *us*".

There's some Russian slang you should know: *nashi* – ours, one of us. You knew that, didn't you?'

But no, I didn't. Even you, a foreigner, were more clued-up on Russian subculture than me. I reached for another well-worn answer. 'I know I'm ... *different*. It's just that I'm not ready' – the cliff edge reappeared in my head – 'to take that leap.'

Different, I told you. By 'different', I meant being unable to join in when boys at school boasted about fancying girls. It meant feigning interest, fending off questions and watching my schoolmates, one by one, as they got themselves girl-friends, then wives, then children. Then came conscription. Compulsory military service. Being 'different' in the army barracks. When every day, every waking hour made me nauseous with dread, not knowing when the next fist would knock the wind out of me, or the next glob of spit would hit my face.

I'd kept telling myself, as I entered my twenties, that I was a 'late developer', that a girlfriend would one day save me. Mama eventually grew tired of asking if I was 'courting'. And now, at the age of twenty-one, I was running out of excuses.

These thoughts took only seconds to etch themselves on my face. You thrust your face into the lamplight near my end of the bed.

'Yes, it *is* a leap,' you said. 'D'you think it was easy for *me*? Growing up gay on a working-class estate in northern England—'

'*England*?' I said. 'This is the Soviet Union, Jamie. *Gomosek-sualizm* is against the law. I'd get arrested, ostracised, lose my job, my parents would kick me out—'

'What're you gonna do then? Pretend to be straight?' Your voice, no longer a whisper, was getting louder. 'I've tried that, tried it for years, but fuck it, Kostik, I like *men*, I get crushes on *men*, I get turned on by—'

'Shush!' I pointed to the wall separating my room from Mama and Papa's.

Your reply was one I'll never forget. 'You think your mum doesn't know? Mums *know* this kind of thing.' You nodded, as if this was meant to reassure me. 'They just do.'

Silence. Maybe you were right. All those hints from Mama about finding a wife . . .

'You don't have to *live* in this country,' I said, accusingly. 'A year in Voronezh, it's some big adventure to you. But when you go home to the West, I've got to carry on living here. I can't take that leap like you did. Why should I?'

'What's the alternative, Kostik? Find some girl who'll marry you for appearances?'

'Maybe,' I said. 'Maybe that's what I'll have to do.' I grappled for some way to throw you off my scent. It was 'only a phase', I insisted, there was time to grow out of it—

'I used to think that,' you said. 'But I didn't "grow out of it". Come on, Kostik, you're twenty-one. If you're anything like me, you'll have been having *feelings* for years.'

'Feelings?' I said. 'I don't *want* those feelings. I just want to be—'

'What? Normal?'

Our to-and-fro seemed to go on for hours. As I sat up in bed facing you, I was shivering. I pulled the bedclothes around my shoulders for warmth, wanting to hide under them. I knew you'd say this condition *was* normal, or that there was no such thing as 'normal'. Eventually you reached over and squeezed my thigh through the bedclothes. It was almost worth all the questioning to feel your touch. As I sat trembling, your hand felt warm and protective.

Your voice was gentler now. 'All those lads you knew at school, Kostik – like you say, they're all married by now. And they're your typical *muzhiki*, only interested in football and beer. You know you're not like that.'

Silence. You leaned a little closer from your end, your hand still on my thigh. 'Kostik, can I ask you something?'

Still shivering – but with a quick glance at your hand – I nodded.

'Are you attracted to me?'

I managed – God knows how – to reply without a flicker of hesitation. 'No, Jamie!' A forced laugh. 'Of course I'm not!' That should deflect you, I thought. That should get you off my case. The last thing I wanted was any further questioning.

My quick response seemed to do the trick. 'I'm sorry, Kostik,' you said. 'I shouldn't be pushing you, you're not ready for all this.'

And with that, you removed your hand from my thigh. As soon as you did, I missed your touch. It felt like I'd lost out on something; I'll never know what.

We looked at each other a moment longer. I was tired, I told you – couldn't we talk about this some other time? You sighed and slumped back onto your pillow.

'Sure,' you said, a whisper in the semi-darkness, distant from the glow of my bedside lamp. 'But don't forget, I'm going back to England in just over a month.'

★

Within minutes of my turning out the lamp, you had fallen asleep. Not me though. It was already getting light outside, so

I could see the dark spikes of your hair scrunched up on your pillow and one bare arm protruding from under the bedcovers, lean but sinewy, with soft, strokable hairs running up to your elbow. You looked so boyish, so vulnerable, nothing like the streetwise lad who had swaggered by my side across Lenin Square the evening before. I studied you for a moment or two more, then I lay watching the light of dawn filter across the ceiling.

I couldn't sleep. You were right: I *did* have feelings for other boys. I always had. And not only for you, Jamie. I didn't call them 'crushes' of course, not in my schooldays, but now I could see that's exactly what they were.

When I was fifteen, there was a boy in my class called Vasily. He was handsome, popular and – something I could never be – *cool*. I was desperate to be Vasily's friend, or at least to be seen with him. He was always surrounded by a gang of lads, hanging on every word and laughing at all his jokes. Whenever I was near Vasily, I would laugh at his jokes too, even if I didn't understand them. I tried to laugh louder than the other lads, hoping he would notice me, but then they'd look at me as if to say, 'Who asked you?'

One day, in class, I read out a poem I'd written. Afterwards, Vasily slapped me on the back and said, 'Nice one, Kostik!' He called me Kostik! Me, who usually got called by my surname. 'Did you like it, did you like it?' I gushed, like a puppy wagging its tail.

Most days it wasn't like that. Most days Vasily had his gang with him. I'd watch them sloping off to smoke in the alley between the schoolyard and the Lenin Print Works next door. Most days he didn't notice me, much as I tried to catch his eye. Once, grinning hopefully, I waved at him as he and his gang rolled by. Waved! How lame of me. Later, three of his gang cornered me in the locker room and taunted me for 'waving like a little poof'.

I never saw Vasily around Voronezh any more. Rumour had it that he'd joined the KGB or ended up in prison. I wondered how he was, if he even remembered me.

*

Hundreds of us crowded round your train that late June evening, necks craned, standing on tiptoe. It felt like half the university had turned out. And all congregated at one carriage: the one taking you, along with the other British students, up to Moscow for your flight back to England, back to the West.

It had been a hot day, and even at 8 p.m. it would be another two hours before the heat relented. Papa was away on business – Leningrad again – but Mama was there at my side, all flustered in the flowery summer dress she'd put on for the big send-off. It was sleeveless, exposing her pale, blotchy arms and making a pitiful match with her tea-coloured stockings. Not that she stood out among the local women, all dressed like her and fanning themselves, or the local men in their cracked brown sandals and grey socks sticky, like mine, with sweat.

How liberated you looked, you British kids: girls in skimpy miniskirts and Dr Martens, boys in torn jeans and T-shirts of rock bands I'd never heard of. Your clothes were mismatched and never ironed, but none of you gave a damn; you didn't dress to please your elders.

Ten minutes earlier, everyone had posed for photos. *Look*, they'd say, *this is us with our Russian friends*. And I'd say, 'This is me with my English friend Jamie.' You had one taken with both me and Mama, and another that was just you and me, our arms round each other. I wondered how that one would turn out, how soon I would get to see it.

As I gave you a lingering goodbye hug, you'd pressed a folded piece of paper into my hand. When I read what you'd written on it, it took my breath away.

But it was time for you to board. Remember that train conductress, the *provodnitsa*, in her uniform and make-up all smudged by perspiration? 'Step back from the train if you're not travelling!' she barked, unmoved by the emotional separations she presided over, and slamming the door shut as she signalled ahead. Ignoring her shouts and threats, your group were opening windows and leaning out of them right along the carriage. All the British girls who'd had Russian boyfriends that past year were wailing and in tears. The two girls who'd dated those African students wept openly too; even their love was less taboo than mine.

A voice from a loudspeaker announced that the night train to Moscow was ready to depart. That night train – though I didn't know it at the time – would eventually take me away, and Mama too, carrying us to a new, unforeseen life ... Then, from the same loudspeaker gushed the lush, sentimental music they played as trains were leaving: a wistful murmur on woodwind and cellos that built to a chorus of violins washing over the platform. I bet you found it all too corny.

It had the desired effect though. On cue, those of us who were not yet waving started to wave, and those who were already waving now waved harder, brandishing hats, handkerchiefs, bunches of flowers. There were cries of 'safe trip!' and 'come and visit!' and 'please write!' The rusty green bulk of the train lurched forwards, and the waving and shouting intensified. In concert with the rest of the crowd, Mama and I found ourselves shuffling, then trotting, then running along the platform, swept up by some shared hysteria.

Your head appeared out of a window, but too far along for me to read your face. I ran a little faster, leaving Mama behind and jostling people as I ran. Then you moved, re-emerging at another window closer to the back of the carriage, your head crammed between two others. You waved, and even blew me a cheeky kiss.

'*Do svidanya*, Jamie!' I called. There was a lump in my throat. '*Do svidanya!*' Goodbye, until we next meet . . .

The train gathered speed, your face grew smaller and smaller, and the crowd reached the end of the platform. We had nowhere left to run. Our exotic friends were headed for the West – but us, this was as far as we could go. Some of us kept waving as the tail end of the train rattled by. *Cl-clunk, cl-clunk*, it went, the sound now diminishing along with its shrinking form, trembling in the heat. Dust settled on rails that glinted in the evening sun. The waving stopped and, as one, we shambled, subdued and silent, back towards the station.

Mama stood waiting for me. She offered me a sad little smile and stroked my hair like she used to when I was a child, lifting my chin with a finger so that our eyes met.

'*Ne grusti*, Kostik,' she said. Don't be sad. 'Didn't Jamie say he's coming back next year? Besides, there'll be a new group of English students in September.'

I didn't reply. I didn't want Mama to see me close to tears – or did I? Surely *someone* sensed how bereft your departure would leave me. But then I remembered the piece of paper you'd given me, and I was able to smile back at her. My hands shook as I unfolded it and read it again. Your note was scrupulously phrased, in faultless Russian, in the long-winded clauses beloved of Soviet bureaucrats, yet there was no mistaking what it meant to me:

I, James Goodier, a citizen of the United Kingdom, resident in Manchester and a student of Russian at the University of Birmingham, hereby invite my friend Konstantin Gennadyevich Krolikov, a citizen of the USSR resident in Voronezh, to visit the United Kingdom . . .

It was already stamped and notarised by the local KGB. Oh, thank you, Jamie, thank you! Your invitation meant I could apply for a visa and get on a waiting list for those coveted overseas travel tickets. It meant I could get permission, for the first time in my life, to set foot outside the Soviet Union.

And that you and I could be together again.

3

FEBRUARY 1993. Moscow

Dima

He slumps against the inside of the front door, shivering and unexpectedly out of breath. At his feet, he watches the snow melt off the soles of his lumberjack boots, forming tiny pools on the lino. His fingers are still numb from being clamped to the receiver at the phone booth. He stares, panting, willing them to thaw out.

From the kitchen comes the sound of Valery Ivanovich coughing, the phlegm-choked hacking of old age and decrepitude; he hears a chair scrape against the floor, the running of a tap, a glass of water being poured. Then a woman's voice, more of a hiss than a whisper: 'Papa, the state of you! You'll have caught pneumonia, going out today! That's why you need to—'

Blyad, he curses, it's Alla Valeryevna, Valery's daughter. She's been round a lot lately, badgering the old fella into giving up his flat to move into a nursing home. The last thing he wants, right now, is to get accosted by her.

Kicking off his boots, he dives into his room and sinks onto his bed, still fully dressed. The bed sags. It always sags, especially whenever he's got some guy in there with him. But it will never, after tonight, sag under the weight of him and Kostya squeezed up tight together. Not if he's understood right ... Over and over, he replays Tamara Borisovna's voice in his head, her son's name spilled out in a fit of sobbing. He didn't actually *hear* her say Kostya had died – but what else could she have meant? *Don't phone here again*, that other woman said.

He stares at the ceiling, grey and shadowy from the street light outside, then across at Oleg's side of the room, where another single bed is wedged between the wardrobe and the bulbous 1950s-style radiator. On his room-mate's side, tell-tale patches remain on the mud-coloured wallpaper where Oleg has taken down all the pictures he'd torn from Western magazines, adverts for Coca-Cola, BMWs and Nike trainers. All that's left is a poster of Jean-Claude Van Damme, bare-chested and striking a martial-arts pose; that was a present from him to Oleg. His own wall looks equally sparse: last night, he took down his poster for *My Own Private Idaho*, leaving only a photo of his mum and one postcard of Latvia, the homeland he'd abandoned to pursue a supposed 'film career' in Moscow.

Some 'boyfriend' he's been to Kostya. Sure, he'd warned Kostya not to fall in love with him, told Kostya he might not stick around in Moscow forever. Yet he catches himself wishing he could turn back time ... Just over a fortnight ago, the two of them had been queuing to get into McDonald's, feet stamping in the snow, faces pink with cold and framed by woolly caps. Yes, the grey knitted cap that Kostya pulled right down to hide his thinning hair. Not that he looked Kostya in the face – that day, he'd avoided his eye, glancing impatiently at the queue stretching round Pushkin Square. He'd hoped to break it to him gently, his plans to leave; maybe over tea at home. Instead it had all burst out there and then, on the street, their breath billowing in the cold and Kostya's eyes red and watering. Kostya, poor boy, wanted them to find a flat and live together, like a couple. And he'd played along, knowing he'd need a roof over his head once he left Valery Ivanovich's. But his heart wasn't in it. No: he wanted out of Moscow, back home to Latvia. His 'film career' here has been a sham. Besides, now that Latvia's an independent, post-Soviet nation, this could be his chance to get citizenship.

His thoughts churn. Could he have kept Kostya 'on hold', at least until he'd got settled back in Latvia? If they'd kept dating a while longer, might he have prevented Kostya's death, whatever caused it? No: it would've been best if they'd never met, that's all, if he hadn't 'rescued' Kostya that night outside the Bolshoi. Kostya would have been better off with a guy more like himself, someone with an education and a job, not a film school drop-out.

I can't stay here, he thinks, I won't be able to sleep anyway. Should he call Yuri? Yuri has 'connections'; they could look into what happened ... But the phone's in the hallway and he doesn't want to run into Alla Valeryevna. He listens, hoping she'll be gone soon, then hears the daughter's voice grow more distinct as she emerges from the kitchen. 'You'll get round-the-clock care there, Papa,' she's saying. 'Mark my words, you'll be better off than here.'

He hears her going into the toilet and locking the door behind her. Right, he thinks, now's my chance. In a flash, he's out of his room, pulling on his boots as he leaves. Forget phoning Yuri. It's Oleg he needs to talk to.

*

Outdoors, it's nudging minus twenty. Too cold to be loitering outside the Bolshoi Theatre; too cold to be smoking on that park bench by the walls of the Kremlin. That leaves one place he can be sure of finding Oleg: down inside the metro station at Ploshchad Revolyutsii.

He rides the metro in one of the emptier carriages so he can get a seat and try to think clearly. But his thoughts race like the stop-start of the train, roaring through pitch-black tunnels, then halting and startled in the glare of each station. Thoughts of Kostya's face, the last words he heard him speak, that final time their bodies touched.

Arriving at Ploshchad Revolyutsii, he hurries along a platform lined with sculptures of soldiers and sailors bearing arms, defenders of Soviet power. He spots Oleg leaning against a statue of a crouching machine-gunner, his coat slung over his arm, all the better to show off his faded body-hugging denims, and his thumbs hooked in the pockets of his jeans so that his hands frame his crotch. At every corner, he can see other young men loitering just like Oleg, affecting to look casual and clearly in no rush to catch a train. The commuters hurrying past those arches of dark red marble are oblivious to the hook-ups being traded right under their noses. But not Dima. He spots a young man sidling up to Oleg as if to ask him for a light, then an exchange of nods and grins, and sideways glances to check that they aren't being observed.

Any other night, he'd allow himself a smile of recognition. It's a little ritual, a game he and Oleg often play; not only here, but also at other pick-up grounds like the square outside the Bolshoi or the park by the Kremlin – how many times has he worked that block, strolling back and forth past the same park bench? They look out for each other, 'partners in crime', making sure they've rehearsed their coded questions and keeping an eye on one another until it feels safe to go off with a stranger. Every night he's out looking to get laid, there's the risk of getting beaten up. The law's no protection – in fact, most beatings he's heard about have come at the hands of the police, deploying undercover officers to entrap the *goluboys*. And yet something about these forbidden hook-ups, that clandestine man-on-man action, keeps him hungry and going back for more ... If it came to the worst, his teenage stint in the coastal patrol had taught him how to fight. It's a world he'd always kept hidden from Kostya.

Recognising the leer on Oleg's face, that twinkle in his dark, heavy-lidded eyes, he barges in before his room-mate can disappear with his newfound shag-buddy. The smiles fall from their faces, and the young stranger, cursing the pair of them, flounces off towards the other end of the platform.

'*Blyad*, Dima!' Oleg glares at him. 'What the fuck—'

'Oleg, I need you. Something's happened.'

'Can't it wait? I was in with a chance there—'

'No, Oleg!' He hears himself sounding sharper than he meant to. 'No, it can't wait.' He looks around and lowers his voice. 'It's about Kostya.'

'Lover Boy? What now? Wants to marry you, does he?'

'Oleg! I'm serious.'

He's not used to talking like this with his room-mate. Banter and teasing, that's their thing, comparing notes about who they've shagged, trading gossip about the closet cases they've seen out cruising. With a sigh, scarcely believing the words coming out of his mouth, he tells Oleg about Kostya's mother breaking down on the phone. It can only mean one thing.

Oleg frowns, more puzzled than sympathetic. 'But he wasn't ill, was he?'

He shakes his head. Kostya often looked sickly and run-down, but when they last saw each other he wasn't showing any symptoms of a life-threatening condition.

'Could he have been in an accident then?'

He shakes his head again. 'I don't think so. This other woman came on the phone – she'd have said, wouldn't she, if Kostya had been run over or something?'

'Guess she would,' Oleg mutters. He pauses. 'If it was an *accident*, that is.'

He searches Oleg's face. Under that greasy dark hair, the squinty-eyed mischief he knows so well has given way to a frown directed not at him but towards the creaking escalators and the station exit, towards the city outside. He sees Oleg flinch.

'What are you thinking?'

Oleg drags his fingers through his hair. His brow is furrowed. 'You weren't at the disco the week before last, were you? The night of the ambush?'

He wonders why Oleg has brought this up. 'You told me about it,' he says, warily. He tries to ignore the unease stirring in his gut. 'What's that got to do with Kostya?'

Oleg pinches his lips together. He looks like he doesn't want to say more. 'I saw him there that night. Alone. Without you.'

Dima feels the colour drain from his face, that chill rising from his gut to his cheeks.

'I can't be sure Kostya got beaten up—' Oleg sounds hasty, like he's regretting his words. 'I mean, I didn't see him after the attack. Maybe he'd gone home. But a few of our boys took a beating. I saw two guys being taken away in an ambulance – blood pouring out of their noses, cracked ribs. The doormen said it was some skinhead gang, with baseball bats and shit.'

He keeps shaking his head, more in denial than certainty. 'No, no, not Kostya. He isn't the type—' He halts, stumbling over the word 'isn't': the present tense, as if Kostya were living and breathing still, not just a memory, now existing only in the past tense.

'C'mon, you didn't even know he'd gone to the disco without you,' Oleg says. 'Though that's nothing compared with what he didn't know about *you*.'

His head-shaking stops. It's true: he'd kept Kostya in the dark about his 'film career'. On arriving in Moscow, he'd fancied himself in a patriotic war movie, the type churned out by the state film studios. He had the required looks – Slavic, square-jawed, blue eyes – that should have landed him a part as a young soldier. But as the collapse of the Soviet system sent living costs sky-high, he could no longer afford to be a student, so he'd dropped out of film school – too theoretical for him anyway – and set his sights on earning money: modelling or pop videos, that kind of thing. All he'd told Kostya was that he was 'auditioning'.

He looks up. A skinny guy in a grey trench coat is ogling him from the platform opposite. The face is familiar – another of the guys he'd bedded while he was dating Kostya – but he can't recall the name. Misha? Slava? Whatever.

Oleg squeezes his arm. 'I'm sorry, Dimik,' he says. 'I didn't realise you *cared* that much.'

He hangs his head. Cared? Let's face it, he's always acted like he didn't. Looking up again, he sees the skinny guy in the trench coat winking at him.

'Let's go home, Oleg,' he says. 'I don't feel like hanging around here any more.'

★

As they travel back on the metro, he struggles to disentangle his memories and imaginings, from Kostya's tears outside McDonald's to this scenario that Oleg has planted in his head, of Kostya on a stretcher, bloodied and broken, ribs cracked by those thugs ... Tunnel after tunnel, the rattle and roar of the train gives him an excuse not to talk, and he sits at Oleg's side, neither of them looking at each other until they reach their stop.

The flat is quiet, and he can hear Valery Ivanovich snoring in the room next to theirs. The daughter must have left a while ago, thank God. Heading straight for his bed, he undresses, dumping his clothes on the floor and stripping down to his boxer shorts, the black silk ones that Yuri, in one of his better moods, brought him from Finland; the ones that Kostya always found such a turn-on ... Under the sheets, his sagging single bunk feels lifeless with cold. It'd been so warm whenever he had Kostya in here with him (usually when he'd got rid of Oleg for the night); a tight squeeze, yes, but warm, a warmth that Kostya will never bring him again.

Oleg perches on the bunk and squeezes his arm. They keep talking, but end up going around in circles: the same questions, the same lack of answers. What happened to Kostya? And why did it have to be just as he was ending it with Kostya? After an hour, he can see Oleg's sympathy starting to flag; then, stifling a yawn, his room-mate goes and flops on his own bed.

He lies there, staring at the ceiling. Poor Kostya. That trusting nature is what makes him – no, he remembers: past tense now – what *made* him so different. Kostya wasn't like Oleg,

42

certainly not like Yuri, and nothing like the half-dozen guys he'd 'had' when he was dating Kostya. They may have been better-looking, those guys, better in the sack, but they were jaded, they'd done the rounds. Kostya, though, had a faith in human nature and an *enthusiasm* for stuff, stuff like Tchaikovsky and Chekhov or perfecting his English.

Silence from the other side of the room. 'Oleg?' he whispers. 'You still awake?'

A grunt, bordering on a snore. 'Uh?'

'Oleg, you've gotta help me. I've gotta find out what happened to Kostya.'

*

First thing is to phone Tamara Borisovna again. It'll be intrusive, that can't be helped, so he'll have to brave her tears, possibly her anger too. He'll tell her what a good friend Kostya was; then she might let him take her some flowers. Maybe, if he can get to see her, she'll tell him what's happened – and that might set his mind at rest.

The next day, once Oleg's gone, he picks up the phone in the hallway. No point trekking to the phone box now. He peeks into Valery Ivanovich's room to make sure he won't be overheard, but he's fast asleep. He takes exaggerated deep breaths and dials. This time, he'll claim to be a friend of that British guy as well – what's his name? Jimmy? Jeremy? That should help. Kostya was always wittering on about his special English friend and how he'd charmed his mother.

The answering machine again: *'You've reached Konstantin Krolikov and Tamara Borisovna Krolikova in Moscow . . .'* Hearing Kostya's voice on tape sends a chill down his spine; the normalness of it, the pedantry of including 'Borisovna' in his mother's name and spelling out 'in Moscow' to clarify that they haven't always lived here. And what else is there about Kostya's voice? That nerdiness: he can picture Kostya scripting and redrafting and recording the message, taking great pride in it as if were the text of a play.

But he doesn't leave a message. Instead, he redials straight away, knowing that no one will answer but feeling a need to listen to Kostya's voice once more. It might be the only way he's ever going to hear it again.

★

He tries calling the following day too. This time there's no answering machine. And three days later, when he phones once more, there isn't even a dialling tone.

★

It's almost midday when he wakes. Days after the news, he still feels hung-over, his head still reeling. He rubs his eyes and sees that Oleg's bed is empty, sheets all messy and thrown back.

The phone rings. He leaps up out of bed. Could that be Tamara Borisovna? No, wait, it can't be – he didn't leave her a message, let alone his number. But then, maybe, just maybe . . . Still hesitating, he hears the drag-shuffle, drag-shuffle of slippers on the hallway floor as Valery Ivanovich heads for the phone. He strains to listen in.

'*Allo?*' A pause. 'Speak up, I can't hear you!' Poor doddery, half-deaf Valery Ivanovich . . .

He hears coughing and wheezing, then hammering at his door. 'Dmitry! It's for you!'

'One second!' He pulls on the grey hoodie and tracksuit bottoms that Yuri gave him after a shoot last winter and sticks his head out into the hallway. Valery Ivanovich is shuffling away, stooped and wrapped in a tatty brown cardigan with holes at the elbows. Just before the kitchen, the landlord stops and turns.

'Sounds like that boss of yours.' He pauses and gestures towards the kitchen. 'Kettle's boiled – will you have some tea?'

'Uh, all right then. Thank you, Valery Ivan'ich. *Spasibo*.'

He waits for the old man to disappear into the kitchen and picks up the phone. '*Allo*? Yuri? I was gonna—'

'Dmitry, what the fuck? You're meant to have been here half an hour ago.'

Oh, no . . . Today's shoot. It's completely slipped his mind . . . 'I'm sorry, Yuri, I should've called earlier, I'm not well—'

'Not *well*? Caught something off someone, have you?'

Yuri's tone hits him like a slap in the face; he's usually more accommodating, at least with his 'favourites'. 'Aw c'mon, Yuri, I think I might have the flu—'

'Enough of the sob stories, Dmitry. All I want is for you to get that gym-toned arse of yours here *now*, all right?'

Shit, he thinks, what's gotten into Yuri? 'OK, OK,' he says. 'I'll be there soon as I can.'

'I'll give you an hour.' Yuri hangs up.

Just then, Valery Ivanovich calls from the kitchen. 'Dmitry! Tea!'

He groans. It'll take at least forty minutes on the metro to get to Yuri's. 'I'm sorry, Valery Ivan'ich,' he calls from the hall-way. 'I have to go. I'm late for work.'

Again he hears the drag-shuffle of the old man's slippers, and there he is, at the door, heavily veined hands trembling as they cradle a mug of tea. Not any old mug but Dima's favourite mug. Valery Ivanovich squints up at him; the eyes that meet his are watery and plaintive, yet not without a glimmer of insistence.

'I've made you tea – won't you at least drink it?'

It's unexpectedly appealing, the idea of drinking tea at the kitchen table with the old man who'll soon be his ex-landlord. He knows only too well that Valery Ivanovich, frail and lonely as he is, rented that room out to him and Oleg for the feeling of safety, for the reassurance of having two male lodgers under his roof. And since he hasn't a clue about the rental market, the rent they've been paying him is peanuts.

'OK, Valery Ivan'ich,' he calls. 'Another minute or two won't hurt.'

Feeling a shiver of regret, he realises that he'll even miss Valery Ivanovich once he gets bundled off into a care home. He casts a glance back at his room, at the bags he and Oleg have started to pack. They've been hoping to move in together somewhere – but now, out of the blue, another thought flashes across his mind: how might things have turned out if he still had the option of shacking up with Kostya?

★

Unlike last night, there's no hurry for him to undress. He pauses at the side of the bed, head lowered, eyes fixed on some point on the floor. Most of the room is in darkness, but in the lamplight his features are orange-tinted, accentuated by ripples of shadow.

Slowly, deliberately, he pulls off his T-shirt. It's black, tight-fitting, with sleeves short enough to show off the tattoo acquired in his coastal patrol days, an anchor and chain that rises and swells on his right bicep. He crosses his arms over his midriff to unpeel the T-shirt from the waist upwards and flings it on the bed. His chest glistens, pectorals pumped up from the gym. Then, button by button, he unfastens his Levi's, revealing his new briefs with lettering round the waistband – the latest fashion, he's heard. His thighs are muscly, covered in blond hair. He steps out of the jeans and leaves them crumpled on the floor. Keeping his eyes lowered, he hooks his thumbs into the waistband of his briefs and—

'Cut! Stop right there! Dmitry, this isn't working for me.'

The lights come on. He blinks in the overhead glare, abruptly exposed in the middle of a room that's bare except for the bed – and except for the guy with the video camera, the technician operating the sound and the orangey light, and the cassette player, which continues to spool, spewing out pseudo-erotic Soviet electronica.

'And switch that crap off, will you.'

Someone hits the stop button. He grabs his T-shirt and holds it to his chest, cowering behind it, not managing to put it back on before the man who has just spoken turns on him. A man the same height as him, but ten or so years older, dark, stubbly, bloodshot and wearing a silky blue tracksuit with 'Everlast' emblazoned across the chest, part of his habitual boxing kit. He eyeballs Dima, inches from his face, oozing vodka breath and violence.

'Something wrong with you today, Dmitry? Your mind gone elsewhere, has it?'

'I'm sorry, Yuri,' he mumbles, eyes down, unable to meet Yuri's glare.

'We don't have all day to get this scene right – filming, shooting retakes. Time is money, Dmitry. My money. I pay you to look *sexy*, don't I?'

He swallows, eyes flicking to one side to seek out a sympathetic look from Edik, the cameraman. Edik looks away, at the floor.

'But, Yuri, I was trying to look moody ... You know, sultry, pouting—'

'*Pouting*? You call that pouting? Know what I see? I see you looking like you're about to top yourself. Mean and moody, yeah, let's see that. But not fucking miserable, right? I could easily cast some other lad in this part. That'd give you something to look miserable about.'

Yuri licks his lips, throwing a glance at Edik and the soundman. 'And another thing,' he lunges for Dima's groin, cupping a hand around his balls, 'what's the matter down here? You don't usually have trouble getting it up.'

Yuri half-turns towards Edik and the sound guy, expecting a laugh. They nervously oblige. As Yuri's hand tightens on Dima's balls, he looks up, trying to stare back. But there's a coal-fired menace in those eyes, and his gaze drops to Yuri's Adam's apple, to the chain around Yuri's neck, the dark chest hairs beneath his unzipped tracksuit top.

This isn't so different from that first time, he thinks – that advertisement on the school noticeboard for 'short-film auditions'. He'd replied to the ad and found the auditions being held at Yuri's gym, where Yuri had come straight from his boxing class, kitted out in silky shorts and Adidas boots. The 'audition', it turned out, consisted of acting out a locker-room fantasy, also not that different from so many he'd played out in his head before.

His pulse, already speeding, quickens – and then, unbidden, he feels a stirring, then a stiffening down below. 'That's better, my boy,' says Yuri, giving his cock a squeeze through his briefs. 'Let's see if you can keep it up. Edik – from the top.'

★

He's been paid in dollars for this afternoon's shoot. Not bad, considering the temper Yuri was in. Other times, depending on Yuri's mood, he gets paid in roubles and clothes – Western gear like jeans, trainers, his lumberjack boots. All part and parcel of the 'job', he tells himself, a job where usually he can switch on the sex appeal with a mere grin.

As he makes his way back to the metro, he slips and stumbles on ice that's hard to see in the lengthening shadows of dusk. He feels almost dizzy with the questions about Kostya that have plagued him throughout this afternoon's shoot. What if Oleg was right? Could Kostya have been beaten up during that ambush? Did he end up in a coma, on life-support? And could he, his 'rescuer' from that night outside the Bolshoi, have saved him?

He passes the Olympic pool complex. Until recently, he'd be swimming lengths four times a week here, keen to stay in shape for Yuri's shoots. I should get back in the pool, he thinks, it'd help me sleep at nights . . . Besides, it'd be an excuse to buy those Speedo trunks he's had his eye on. Anything to lift his mood.

Across the road in the Olympic Penta Hotel, there's a hard-currency shop where he could buy those Speedos, right now, with his dollars. He decides to go for it, swanning past the doorman with an entitled swagger, like he's a guest here – although once out of the cold and dark, he finds himself inside a class of hotel where Russians like him rarely get to tread: rooms at $300 a night, a jazz pianist tinkling away and a bar where he could blow his afternoon's earnings on a couple of cocktails. He strides through a lobby buzzing with chatter in English, full of businessmen in suits and long-legged women in heels and short skirts. The shop is at the other end.

Something catches his eye. Just before the shop is a table with piles of newspapers for the taking. There's the *Moscow Times*, the *Moscow Tribune* – both published in English, he realises, to be read by the Western business types schmoozing in the hotel lobby. Wait a minute, didn't Kostya say that his friend, that smartarse British guy, worked for a newspaper like this, one of these new, *glasnost*-driven English-language titles?

He tries to remember the guy's name – 'Jimmy' or something. Perhaps *he* would know what happened to Kostya; after all, he's a journalist. He doesn't have a phone number for him, but this might be a way ... Grabbing a copy of the *Moscow Times*, he flicks through the pages, his eyes darting from one byline to the next, deciphering the English as best he can. There's an Oliver, a Jenny – no, that's a girl's name. How about the *Tribune*? Nope, no Jimmy there.

He is about to abandon the idea and go spend his dollars on those Speedo trunks when he spots a third pile of newspapers: smudgy print, cramped layout, cheap paper ... who'd want to read that? The *Moscow Herald*. Worth a look, though. But as soon as he picks up a copy, he spots a man in hotel staff livery approaching, no doubt to check his ID, ask if he's a guest, then throw him out. He folds up the newspaper, stuffs it in his rucksack and heads for the exit.

4

TWO YEARS EARLIER

JANUARY 1991. Birmingham

Kostya

I kept my eyes closed, like you told me to, and waited at your side while Sanjay and Wag wheeled the trolley ahead of us. Davy, your third housemate, hung back at the cigarette kiosk. When I opened my eyes, you were looking at me as if to say, 'So? How about this then?'

It was my second night in England and my first time in a Western supermarket. I was open-mouthed, gawping like an idiot. Exactly as you knew I would be. The colours, the choices, the decadence and temptation piled high in every aisle . . . In the Soviet Union, we thought we had it good when the *gastronom* stocked three types of sausage. But here I counted seven brands of deodorant, twenty varieties of breakfast cereal and toilet paper in five different colours.

You wanted me to be impressed, to keep saying 'wow' at everything. But what I felt – a word you taught me – was 'gobsmacked'. I felt, as my eyes roamed those brimming shelves, like I'd been smacked in the face, hit by the truth of the deprivation we endured in my homeland: the queues, the rationing, the untouched stacks of tinned fish that babushkas would feed to their cats. *Glasnost* could come as a shock. After generations of being taught that the West was wrong and the Soviet Union was right, the new openness had brought a trickle of admissions. Maybe we got this wrong, maybe we got that wrong, maybe there are things we could learn from the West. But when I set foot inside that branch of Sainsbury's, it was as though some great lie had been exposed. Now I saw the truth: you greedy thieving capitalists could feed your people, and we sharing egalitarian communists couldn't.

*

Barely a week earlier, Mama had seen me off from the station in Voronezh. She had cut a solitary figure, there in her winter coat, the lamplight throwing her shadow across the snow lying thick on the platform. So different from last summer's big send-off for *your* overnight train – except that Papa, again, was away at another of his conferences. As the train set off, they broadcast the same farewell lament over the loudspeakers, violins soaring and swooning as snowflakes swirled under the station lights. Mama shed a tear. She hugged me tight, begging me to be careful over there in the big bad West. I hadn't seen her weep like that since she got me out of the army.

It had taken months to save up, get an overseas passport and apply for a visa from the British embassy, and once on board that night train, I collapsed and slept all the way to Moscow. Over the next three days, another train carried me across Ukraine, a familiar landscape of snowy plains and birch forests, through the mountains of Czechoslovakia, then over the Iron Curtain into the West. I was sleepless that night, peeking through the blinds for a glimpse of autobahn or Frankfurt's neon lights. The following evening, I boarded the ferry in Hook of Holland.

It was night again when I arrived in London. Lugging my suitcase off the train, I spotted your face at the end of the platform, pale and tiny among the knot of waiting people. I ran, as much as my suitcase allowed, and threw myself at you, jumping for joy. We hugged and laughed. But your eyes were red and bleary, I noticed; my last-minute telegram meant you'd had to drop everything to meet me, and within half an hour of boarding the coach to Birmingham, you fell asleep. I, however, was buzzing, mesmerised by the traffic. Trucks roared past, labelled not with their cargo (no plain old 'oil' or 'timber' like Soviet trucks), but emblazoned with 'Sainsbury's' or 'McDonald's', the names of their capitalist owners writ large.

Later, crossing Birmingham on one of your funny double-decker buses, we passed street after street of small redbrick houses squeezed side by side – 'Victorian', you called them. It was a house like these that you shared with Davy, Sanjay and Wag. Inside, its windows rattled in the wind, and I could see patches of damp. Not that any of you cared for what Mama called *poryadok*; you lived amid unwashed plates and discarded beer cans – a freedom denied to my Voronezh ex-schoolmates, all now married and living under the same roofs as their mothers-in-law.

But forget *poryadok*, I was with you! On our first morning in England, my joy was mirrored by the sunshine, the lawns and playing fields of your university campus verdant and glowing, even in winter. In your shops, people smiled at me; on your streets, they said sorry if I bumped into them. It all made my homeland look like a place that had been ravaged by war.

Jamie

Christ, Kostya, he thought, stop asking me questions every five sodding minutes, will you. Why this, why that, why the other. And one question Kostya kept repeating: 'How can you want to go back to Russia again when you've got a country like England to call home?'

He couldn't resist pulling Kostya's leg. 'You're right,' he said. 'I'm gonna call it off—'

'No!' Kostya's face went visibly pale. 'I mean, *I* want to see you back there, it'd be fantastic for *me*, it's just that if I had the *choice* between living here . . .'

With a sigh, he put down his copy of *The Master and Margarita*. He still hadn't read the book and was supposed to be submitting an essay on it that week. 'Kostik, I want to be a journalist, a foreign correspondent. The best way for me to do that is to base myself in Moscow. I've got bugger all prospects if I stay here.'

A few years back, when he'd started university, he'd thought: I'll show 'em. I'll show those lads at school who took the piss, those neighbours who told me I should know my place. Just watch me when I'm on telly reporting for the BBC. Since then, however, he'd cottoned on that his degree in Russian was no guarantee of that career; it wasn't, he tried telling Kostya, like Soviet universities, whose agriculture graduates got dispatched to collective farms whether they liked it or not. If he was to get into journalism, his time was better spent writing for the student newspaper rather than swotting for essays on *Dr Zhivago* or *The Master and Margarita*.

'But those are novels that were banned for decades!' Kostya

protested. 'People have waited a generation for the freedom to read them.'

He opened his desk drawer and showed Kostya the pile of rejection letters for jobs he'd already applied for. He was proud of it, that pile, in a bolshie kind of way.

'No one'll give me a job for knowing all this bollocks about Bulgakov or Pasternak,' he said. 'That's life under capitalism, Kostik. Out there,' he nodded towards his window, 'it's a market for jobs. And on that market, I'm nothing more than a product on a shelf.'

*

If Kostik had got his act together and made it to England last summer, they could have stayed in Manchester, at Mum and Dad's. Instead, Kostya pitched up during the term before his final-year exams, following him around the university campus by day and bedding down on the floor of his room at night, the time he usually got around to his coursework.

Still, he'd hoped to impress Davy, Sanjay and Wag. *Look at me, I've got a mate from the other side of the Iron Curtain.* That was cool, cutting-edge stuff then, what with the cold war barely over. All the Brits who'd been in Voronezh were riding that wave, handing out invitations. Instead, it made things awkward with his housemates. They'd be down the pub or shooting the breeze at home when he'd notice Kostya's face take on that lost, left-out kind of look. He'd have to step in and translate, trying to explain Wag's wisecracks or Davy's sarky put-downs. Sanjay, bless him, had more patience, telling Kostya that he was studying to be a doctor, and asking him about Soviet health-care. But Kostya went and put his foot in it, didn't he, unable to believe that someone Indian *and* gay could be a doctor in Britain.

'Bloody hell, Kostik!' he said, teeth gritted. 'You can't say that kind of thing here. This isn't Voronezh, you know.'

Later, he'd regret snapping at him. But Kostya's image of England was outdated, straight out of Agatha Christie. It was time he showed Kostya a different side to Britain, a happening, down-and-dirty Britain that might loosen him up. It'd be a good way for them to spend time together as well – but without having to do too much talking.

Kostya

A week after my arrival you announced, over hamburgers in the students' union, that you were going to take me to a gay club. *Club*? I thought, trying to swallow a chunk of burger stuck in my throat. Like *gomoseksualist*, the word 'club' made me think of something covert and cultish. 'A gay *club*? What's that?'

The next night I found out. We set off very late – not until almost 9 p.m. – and although it was January, you dressed much the same as in Voronezh last summer, in Converse trainers, new ones this time, a denim jacket and a T-shirt proclaiming 'The Stone Roses', whatever they were. You'd spent over an hour getting ready, hogging the shower, spraying yourself with Lynx deodorant and gelling your hair up into spikes.

'Gotta look my best,' you said with a wink, 'if I'm gonna pull.'

I didn't know what you meant by 'pull', and nerves made me hesitate to ask.

My hair had started to recede by then. No amount of gel would transform those thinning locks into the sharp, cheeky style that *you* sported; no way could I pull off that pseudo-rebellious look that was the default style of all those British boys who caught my eye. You'd taken me to buy jeans, the only ones I could afford being cheap and stiff, and I wore them that night with my 'trendiest' shirt, wide-collared and patterned with brown flowers. But then, I wasn't trying to impress anyone; all I wanted was to have a good dance with you.

'Wait till you see this club, Kostik,' you said, swigging beer from the tin you'd brought onto the top deck of the bus, then wiping your mouth on the sleeve of your denim jacket. 'First time I went there, I was like a kid in a sweet shop.'

Most nights, you went on, the Powerhouse was a straight venue, but tonight was Gay Night. The club was tucked beneath a concrete underpass similar to one in a Soviet city – only unlike any Soviet city, there was a big neon sign above the doors – and outside a queue of men and boys stood shivering in jackets as light and flimsy as yours. Young people in England didn't bother to dress warmly for winter, I noticed. No babushkas to tell you off, I suppose, only the doormen, arms folded and faces stony to distance themselves from the clientele.

Once inside, my ears were pummelled by the pulse and grind of 'Vogue', our favourite Madonna song on that tape you'd recorded for me. I squinted in the dark but, as you steered us to the bar through a thicket of faces blitzed by strobe lights, I felt your arm around my waist; for a moment, as you bought us each a beer, it felt like we truly were together.

It was too loud to talk though, so you turned to survey the dance floor, one hand clutching your bottle, the other in the pocket of your jeans, your head nodding to the beat. I followed your gaze. The crowd consisted entirely of men and boys, some younger than us, possibly teenagers, their hair floppy or outlandishly spiked; some were older men with moustaches and waistcoats. Mostly they crowded around the edge spectating, while those on the dance floor shimmied self-consciously, as if they knew they were being given a score. Hardly anyone was dancing together. Instead, men danced alone, eyes roving from side to side, yet feigning a lack of interest.

I felt you tug at my elbow, then your breath hot in my ear. 'Let's go and dance.'

Grabbing my hand, you dragged me towards the dance floor. I didn't offer any resistance: there was a twinkle of invitation in your eye that seemed to say, 'Me and you, we're out dancing, we're celebrating.' So we left our beers and pushed our way through to a spot where I hoped I wouldn't be too visible.

They were playing 'Killer'. You know, that track by Adamski & Seal that was on the radio all the time. I remember you beaming at me as your head bobbed and your body swayed to the beat, that infectious *dum-dum-dum, dah-dum, dum-dum*. I did my best to copy your moves, but found my feet clomping one way, then the other, and my hips jiggling in what I took to be enthusiasm. I must have looked embarrassing – in fact, I'm sure I did because before long your eyes stopped meeting mine. Even then you'd started to drift away ... And four or five tracks later – by which time the dance floor was packed, a sea of uplifted arms waving along to Kylie Minogue – I'd lost sight of you altogether.

I squeezed past people to get off the dance floor and wandered around looking for you. 'Excuse me, sorry,' I kept saying, though it was too loud for anyone to hear. I found myself up-close to two young guys whose lips were glued to one another's, and apologised again. A few older men winked at me. I nodded back politely the first couple of times, but soon learnt to avert my eyes so as not to encourage them. An hour must have passed this way. When I checked my watch, it was nearly midnight. I went back to the bar and bought a bottle of Coca-Cola, just for something to do with my hands – no wonder so many men here felt the need to smoke or grip beer bottles right by their crotches.

Then I spotted you. I wasn't sure at first because it was so dark, so crowded, and so many other boys were wearing that same uniform of T-shirt, jeans, spiky hair. But it was you. You were sprawled, face-down, across a bench, on top of another boy, your mouth locked onto his and working away like you were chewing, devouring his face. 'Snogging' – that was the word, another word you taught me. I couldn't see much of the other boy, except his jeans, with your hand groping inside them.

For a moment, I stood and watched. I wasn't the only one: you had a small audience of men standing there, pulling on their cigarettes and leering. Your words came back to me, the ones about being 'on the market', 'a product on a shelf'. I could hardly tap you on the shoulder and say, 'Jamie, I've been looking for you', so I wandered back to the dance floor, dazed.

Shortly after that, I left. I didn't bother to tell you I was going. Taking a taxi would have been too expensive and I couldn't find the bus stop, but I remembered the route – the roundabout, the car showroom and the mosque that we'd passed on our way – so I decided to walk. Before I'd got as far as the mosque, it had started to rain.

My thoughts ran backwards and forwards, round and around, always ending up back at the same place. How could you do this to me? Were you simply being 'like a kid in a sweet shop'? And me, why didn't I know better? Why did I cling to the hope of being special to you? Perhaps it was my own fault, all those months ago, for denying my attraction to you. I could hardly lay claim to you now, could I? You were free, and so was I. But free to enjoy what? Alone, I walked the glistening, orange-lit streets of Birmingham all the way to your house, the rain plastering what was left of my hair to my skull.

★

It was 2 a.m. when I got back. I was drenched and didn't have a key. How embarrassing to be ringing the doorbell, waking your housemates at this hour. As if I wasn't already a burden to them. But it wasn't Davy or Sanjay or Wag who opened the door. It was you. Turned out you'd taken a taxi and passed me somewhere along the way.

'Kostik, thank God you're back!' You gave me a hug, over-doing it as if to compensate for your behaviour. 'Mate, I was worried sick,' you were saying. 'And look at the state of you – you're wet through! You didn't walk all that way, did you?'

Yes, I told you, I did. In the rain.

Without a word, I slung my dripping coat over your bike in the hallway and stepped past you. You followed me to the kitchen, insisting all the while how worried you'd been, that you'd looked all over the club for me before giving up and hailing a cab.

'Why didn't you say you wanted to leave, Kostik? I would've come with you.'

I wasn't good at confrontations. Turning my back on you, I gripped the edge of the worktop, fixing my eyes on the toaster and wishing it was that first morning after I arrived, all sunny and you making me beans on toast.

'I could see ...' I inhaled, trying to find the right words, then exhaled sharply, 'that you were otherwise occupied.'

'What? That lad at Powerhouse?' You gave a little laugh. 'Don't say you stormed off because of that! It was just a snog – I wasn't gonna bring him home or leave without you.'

I looked round. You were shaking your head as if I was being unreasonable. 'Look,' you said, 'didn't I come rushing back here as soon as I realised you'd gone? Come on, Kostik, don't be so daft. Let me get you a towel, and we'll put the kettle on.'

As you opened the drawer, you added, 'Anyway, I can see that lad some other time. I've got his number, if I feel like meeting up. I probably won't bother though.'

That, I think, was supposed to make me feel better. Instead it shocked me to hear you talk about that boy – whoever he was – like some disposable plaything.

'You *won't*?' I meant to strike a sarcastic note, but my words came out all quivery, more like a plea for reassurance.

'Nah, probably not. Now stop being so daft.'

Standing behind me with the towel, you began to pat my hair dry. Part of me wanted to let you look after me, drying my hair, making me tea, but I snatched the towel from you and sank onto a chair to take off my shoes. My feet were soaked and my socks stank of damp.

I draped the towel over my head, staring at a coffee stain on the kitchen lino, then found myself asking, 'So what's his name?'

'That lad at the club? Andy, I think. Does it matter?'

'You haven't fallen in love with him then?' As soon as the words were out of my mouth, I realised how melodramatic I sounded.

Your response was half-laugh, half-snort. '*Fallen in love?* Course I haven't!'

If your denial handed me a split second of relief, it was a relief marred by my having given away so much of my feelings. Even so, I blurted out, 'Then why did you abandon me?'

You sighed: part apology, part exasperation. 'I'm sorry if I've upset you, Kostik,' – sorry *if*, you said, as though there were any 'if' about it – 'I'd had a few bevvies and I got carried away. Being around all those lads on the pull – as I said, it's like being a kid in a sweet shop.'

That line again. I stopped towelling my hair and for some reason recalled our trip to the supermarket. All that choice and availability on the shelves, all there for the taking.

You carried on talking. 'The reason I took you to a gay club was to show you the kind of life you *could* be living. It's like *glasnost*. Freedom, choice, losing your inhibitions – that's what's on offer once you get out of the closet—'

'*The life I could be living?*' I stopped staring at the lino and looked up at you. 'It was my first-ever time at a gay discotheque and you abandoned me so you could – what's the word? – go on the *pull.*'

'Jesus, Kostya! I'm here now, aren't I? Don't you think you're over-reacting?'

'I'm not over-reacting, I was ...' The word *jealous* formed in my mouth, but instead I said, 'I was nervous and needed you by my side. I wanted us to dance together.'

'We did dance together, didn't we?' You crouched down to look me in the eye and put your hand on my knee.

Your hand. My knee. 'Yes,' I muttered, blushing. 'But I mean for longer than that.'

You looked puzzled. '*Longer*? What, like all night?'

I shrugged. 'Yes, like all night.'

You stood up and leaned back against the fridge, letting out another sigh. 'Kostik, the whole point of a gay club is you're free to go off and dance and flirt and, yeah, have a snog with any lad you fancy.'

'But I didn't *want* to go and dance with any old lad. There wasn't anyone else I fancied, apart from—'

That was when I admitted it to your face, that I was attracted to you. Yet after all my caution and denial, you didn't seem fazed. You didn't budge from leaning on the fridge.

'We're not like *boyfriends* though, are we, Kostik? And I'm not looking to settle down in some cosy relationship. After all, I'll be off to Moscow once I'm done with uni.'

Yes, Moscow – we might still have Moscow . . . I looked up again. 'And would you be looking for a relationship . . .' I hesitated, wondering how to put it, 'with *someone* there?'

Shaking your head, you gave a half-smile, directed not at me but at some point over by the kitchen sink. 'I doubt it. I'll be going there to build my career, not to make a home. But if I'm in Moscow, I could still visit you in Voronezh, couldn't I? We'll still be friends, right?'

I nodded. I managed a smile too, a small one. If that sounds like our showdown just fizzled out, I guess that's right, it did. There was no confession of love, no dramatic rejection, only a sense that settled on me, as consoling and woolly as the fluffy towel wrapped around my shoulders, that I would muddle through. As I said, I was no good at confrontations.

★

We didn't go to Gay Night at the Powerhouse again. But we did go to the theatre. As luck would have it, *An Inspector Calls* was on at the Birmingham Repertory. It was the first time I'd seen it in English. 'My treat, Kostik,' you'd insisted, and all evening you were attentive and generous, even affectionate.

On the bus home, I thumbed through my theatre pro-gramme feeling strangely subdued. The play had unsettled me, its drip-by-drip revelation of betrayals building up as if behind the wall of a dam, never confronted until the dam has burst, until the guilt of those responsible comes to haunt them, even while their victim is silenced by death.

It also shook me to be reminded of my month-long absence during Voronezh Youth Theatre's busy season. How could I convince Arkady Bogdanovich of my ambition to become a director now I'd missed that? What, I asked you, should I do?

'You should go for it, Kostik,' you said. 'But aim high. And why stay in Voronezh? Why don't you look for theatre work in Moscow?'

Yes, I thought, why not? Especially if *you* were going to be in Moscow too. We could support each other, you in journal-ism, me in theatre. We could even share a flat in Moscow, like you shared a house at university.

The following evening, you and I strolled back from the campus to your house. It was a starry night, and I was testing your knowledge of the constellations. There was a frost – nothing like a Russian winter though – and we were looking forward to a curry to warm us up.

On our way in, we passed the open door of Davy's room. He was strumming on his guitar, earrings rattling as his head nodded in concentration. Sanjay must have been upstairs, and

Wag was in the living room, watching television. As soon as he saw me though, he stood up and switched it off. Under his floppy red fringe, he looked pale and uneasy.

'Kostya,' he said, 'your mum phoned.' Then he added: 'From Russia.'

Mama? Phoning here? Why? I'd called her twice already since I arrived.

'What did she want?' I asked, knowing that Mama's English was unpractised, hardly capable of sustained conversation.

'She wants you to call her.' A pause. 'She sounded upset.'

I looked at you. You nodded towards the telephone. 'Don't worry about the bill, Kostik. I'll go and put the kettle on.' You slung your coat on the sofa and went to the kitchen.

Wag left the room too, as if mindful of a need to give me privacy. I sat by the phone, eased off my coat and started to dial. My hand gripped the receiver, knuckles turning white as I waited for the connection that would bring me Mama's voice from the other side of the Iron Curtain, more than three days' train journey away. It would be past 9 p.m. in Voronezh.

I heard the dialling tone, then '*Allo*? Is that you, Kostya?' It was surreal to hear her voice while I sat next to Wag's abandoned mug of tea and last week's edition of the campus newspaper, left open at an article you'd written.

'*Allo*, Mama? I got your message. Is everything all right?'

She went quiet for a second. Then I sensed a muffled, halting sound coming down the line. I realised she was crying.

'Mama, what's wrong, what's happened?'

The sound of sniffling. 'Kostya, I'm sorry to ask this of you.' A pause. The silence throbbed in my ear. 'Can you cut short your trip and come home?'

'Come home?' But I still had two weeks left on my visa ...

Two weeks to be with you, in England. I didn't say that, of course. I just asked, 'But why?'

Her voice started to crack again. 'It's Papa. Some young woman he's met in Leningrad. He says he loves her, needs to be with her ... Kostya, he's leaving us.'

5

FEBRUARY 1993. Voronezh

Jamie

The cemetery is on a slope running down to the river, and beyond the huts and dachas huddled by the riverbank he can see the wind ruffle the surface of the water. Snow has settled on every roof, every pathway, every grave, softening all edges, muffling every sound; all he hears is the wind and the cawing of crows in trees etched black and thorny against the sky.

He's missed the funeral by three days. Three days that he's spent scouring the Russian press for clues, calling hospitals, the police and the now-vacated flat that Kostya and his mum rented in Moscow. He's even tried Kostya's old Voronezh phone number, although he knows full well that new tenants moved in the year before last. And here he is, back in the town where they met only three years earlier, shivering at the side of Kostya's grave.

The headstone is modest, almost apologetic. Just like Kostya, he thinks. No verse, no engraved likeness of the deceased, only Kostya's name and the dates of his birth and death. A hurried job too, he guesses, some factory-issue slab with space for

Kostya's twenty-four years to be compressed into a handful of hastily stamped letters and numbers. A bouquet of white lilies, frozen and brittle in the snow, lies beside a framed black-and-white photograph. He recognises it as the picture Kostya had taken on his graduation from the academy of arts: not smiling, of course – that wasn't the done thing in Russia – but with his eyes to one side, soulful and quizzical, a portrait of a would-be thespian.

Artyom hands him his bunch of ten white carnations. 'In Russia,' Artyom reminded him when they bought the flowers from a babushka outside the church up the hill, 'it's an *even number* for bereavements.' To think, all those times he'd taken flowers to Tamara Borisovna, always making sure he bought an odd number ... He takes off his fur hat and crouches to place the carnations in front of the photograph.

Poor Kostik, he thinks – that loyal, trusting softie who wouldn't hurt a fly. All his interests and passions cut short, leaving just a buried corpse and a makeshift grave. He feels a lump sticking in his throat, then a scene from an old film slips into his head: Scrooge's vision of Tiny Tim's grave in *A Christmas Carol*. If only this grave were as it was in Scrooge's dream, nothing more than a premonition, an omen of something he could prevent.

If Kostya had been ill though, why didn't he tell him? How many months is it since they last spoke? He thinks of what he owed Kostya, how he never got to say goodbye.

He feels Artyom's hand on his shoulder; it's decent of him to come down to Voronezh, supporting him like a boyfriend should. He looks up at Artyom in his long black leather coat, his ponytail draped down the back, the 'bohemian' look of his art school cronies. Artyom gives him a smile, permission for him to drop his brave face and have a little cry on Artyom's shoulder. But he turns back, picks up the photograph and brushes off its dusting of snowflakes. Kostya's sideward-gazing eyes appear to refuse to look at him.

The silence behind him is pierced by a shout – an older woman, it sounds like. 'Young man!' she's yelling. '*Molodoy chelovyek*! What are you doing there?'

He puts down the photograph, stands and turns. A woman in her late fifties, with curls of henna-dyed hair marshalled under a fluffy woollen beret, is waddling towards them, looking, in her quilted winter coat, like an overgrown hen.

'What are you doing, touching that photograph? Have you no respect!'

Jesus, he thinks, some interfering old busybody, that's all I need. 'This,' he shoots back at her, jabbing his finger towards the grave, 'was my *friend*!'

He hears that word, *droog*, echo off the tombstones, hanging in the air. The woman looks him up and down, her eyes grey and unblinking, bulging out of puffy pink cheeks. She looks at Artyom too, a flicker of disapproval as she takes in his ponytail and earring.

'Your *droog*?' She puts her shopping bag on the ground.

'Yes, and this,' he jerks his head towards Artyom, 'is my *droog* too.' That word again, a 'male friend' in Russian: the same word whether he means Kostya or Artyom – almost as if the language itself can't express, let alone allow, the idea of two men being lovers.

'I see,' she says. 'And who are you?'

'Who's asking?' He stares back at her – now realising that she looks vaguely familiar.

'I've come to clear the snow from Konstantin's grave.'

A sigh. 'His mother's too upset to be coming here doing it herself—'

'You know Tamara Borisovna?' He frowns, wondering: where have I seen this woman before? 'But the Krolikov family,' he says, 'they used to invite me to their home all the time. Did we ever meet there, by any chance?'

'Of course.' She sniffs. 'I remember now. I thought I detected a foreign accent. You're that English boy, aren't you?'

That English boy? Anyone'd think he was a spy or saboteur or something. Is that how Kostya's mum sees him? He replies, 'That's right. I spent a year here as a student,' and offers her a handshake. 'My name's James and my *droog* here is Artyom.'

'Galina Sergeyevna.' She shakes hands, limply, the way Russian women do.

'Pleased to meet you,' says Artyom, curling his lips into a lazy smile.

'Humph.' Galina Sergeyevna takes a small brush out of her bag, turns her back on them to bend over the grave, and busies herself brushing away the snow. Two of the crows caw and take wing, flapping past them towards the church.

He glances at Artyom, then asks, 'Tell me, how is Tamara Borisovna doing?'

'Badly. What do you expect?' Galina doesn't look round from her brushing.

'Of course, it's a shock.' He hesitates. Try not to sound intrusive, he tells himself – or just plain trite – then adds, 'I didn't hear how Kostya died. Do you know, by any chance?'

'What difference does that make now?' She keeps brushing, still not looking round.

He shrugs. 'It's a reasonable question, isn't it? Was it illness? An accident?'

Galina straightens up but still doesn't look at him, facing down the hill instead. She looks as though she's trying to pluck some answer out of the wind blowing up across the river. She sighs, wisps of steam around her mouth. 'That's not for me to say. You'd have to ask Tamara Borisovna.'

'I only want to offer my condolences. Can't I see her?'

Galina turns sharply back to stare at him. 'See her? Young man, she's traumatised. Far too upset for visitors and being asked questions.'

He persists. 'But we've come specially, all the way from Moscow. I would've been here for the funeral, but it was too late – I only found out a few days ago.'

'Well, I'll tell Tamara Borisovna I've seen you.' Galina puts her brush away in her bag and turns to leave. 'I'll be sure to pass on your respects.'

'Wait – is she still here? She's not at their flat, I tried calling.'

Galina shakes her head. 'No, she's not. Not any more.'

'So where could I—?'

'She's staying with me, all right? In my spare room. But she doesn't want to see anyone. Believe me, there's nothing like a mother's grief.' She pinches her lips together. 'I should know.'

'I'm sorry, *izvinitye*.' He finds himself doing that typical Russian shrug, more pleading than incomprehension. 'It's just that Tamara Borisovna was always so hospitable to me. And Kostya came to stay with me in England, you know.'

'I know. He was very excited about that trip. Gave him ideas, it seems.'

Gave him ideas – what does she mean? He's on the point of asking, but Galina puts a hand on his arm and looks him in the eye. 'Listen, young man, please, no questions about Kostya – promise?'

He nods, swallowing his need for answers. 'You mean—'

'Come with me and we'll go to my flat. On your own, if you don't mind.' She gives Artyom a look that's more wary than apologetic. 'And only for five or ten minutes, no more. I warned you – she's in no fit state for an interrogation.'

Tamara Borisovna

Her hands tremble as she stands the newly framed photograph on her bedside table. It's a copy of the portrait she placed at Kostya's grave, and next to it a candle flickers in the lengthening shadows of a winter afternoon. In the middle of the room sits the trunk she's brought down from Moscow, still not unpacked. It's mostly Kostya's stuff in there – his books, diaries, tapes, photo albums. There's a load of her own clothes she hasn't unpacked too. What's the point? Might as well keep wearing the black dress she's had on since the funeral.

She sits on the floor, on a cushion, tempted to simply curl up on the rug and stay there all day. Yet somehow she summons up the strength to rummage through the trunk. All these books of his, what should she do with them? Especially the ones in English, the E. M. Forster and J. B. Priestley. No one's going to want those, are they?

She opens a photo album and something falls out – Kostya's train tickets for London two years ago and a programme for *An Inspector Calls* at some theatre in England. Inside the album, she recognises the photo she took of Kostya and Jamie that hot summer evening when the English students were leaving: the two of them with their arms around each other's shoulders,

Jamie grinning and Kostya fighting back tears that he thought she couldn't see. Turning the page, she sees pictures of England that Kostya showed her some time ago, those redbrick houses and the university clock tower. There's at least a dozen photos of Jamie, more than she realised, some that Kostya hadn't shown her − Jamie leaning against a car with three other boys, one of them Indian-looking, another with earrings; then Jamie with his feet up on his desk; Jamie wearing nothing but a T-shirt and boxer shorts . . .

She snaps the album shut. Her thoughts begin to spin. That English boy. How Kostya used to witter on about him. All these photos . . . and all those invitations for him to sleep over, that happened almost every week. Then those late-night conversations they'd have in Kostya's bedroom. The first time her son invited Jamie to their home, she'd found him so *forward*, impertinent almost, with his firm handshake and the way he nodded and smiled at her and held eye contact. She'd never met a young man quite like him. Soviet boys weren't talkative, they were gruff or sullen, deep-voiced or meek.

It's too much to take in. Putting the cushion under her head, she lies down on the rug. I want to fall asleep, she thinks, right here. She closes her eyes, tight, but then opens them and finds her gaze wandering around the room. She feels like an intruder, trespassing here in the bedroom of another mother's dead son − a room she's seen dozens of times, enough to know that Galina has kept it exactly as Viktor left it more than twelve years ago.

Across one wall spreads a map of the USSR, still intact, a union that the Soviet national anthem hailed as unbreakable. Unbreakable, she thinks − humph, look at it now, the crumbling 'brotherhood of nations' that she was raised to love . . .

By the bed is a poster of the Soviet ice-hockey team at the 1980 Olympics in Moscow. Elsewhere, scattered across the mustard-yellow wallpaper, are posters of T34 tanks and MiG fighter jets.

The only things Viktor didn't leave on the walls himself – items Galina has added since he left this room for good – are an Orthodox cross and, below that, a photograph of Viktor, aged twenty-one, in the uniform of a Red Army sergeant. Like Kostya's portrait, it is framed, black-and-white and unsmiling. But unlike Kostya's day-dreaming gaze, the eyes of the young man staring across the room at her now are disdainful and steely.

Viktor had served in Afghanistan, keen to play his part in the motherland's fight against the Islamist threat on its doorstep. That's what Galina believed too, just the way it was reported on the news. Until February 1981, the day that telegram arrived from the Ministry of Defence. *Respected Galina Sergeyevna*, it said, *in his selfless defence of the motherland, your son has made the ultimate sacrifice*. It didn't say Viktor had been killed by a roadside bomb; Galina had had to find that out for herself, years later.

Back then, it was *her* turn to hold Galina's hand, organising the wake and being the shoulder to cry on.

Within two years of Viktor's death, Galina had lost her husband Artur to vodka. And although Viktor was awarded a hero's funeral, the truths uncovered by *glasnost* spurred Galina to get out campaigning with the Mothers for Peace, brandishing their 'Bring Our Sons Home' placards outside the local military headquarters. Galina even travelled up to Moscow once to protest outside the same ministry that had professed its condolences to her.

She stares back at the photograph of Viktor. When he was fifteen or so, he had come to Kostya's tenth birthday party and, clearly bored by all the children's games, boasted how he preferred to play soldiers. She'd overheard him sneering at Kostya's toy theatre too – '*That's for girls*,' he'd said. She shudders. If Viktor had lived, he'd have thrived in the Russian army. God knows, he might even have become one of Kostya's tormentors.

★

Her son's call-up papers had arrived in October 1985. Military service was compulsory, so there'd been nothing she could do – though she feared, deep down, that he might not even survive it. 'It'll toughen him up,' Gennady tried to reassure her, 'he needs to learn to stand up for himself.' She wasn't convinced though, and after Kostya had been packed off with a busload of acne-faced boys to a barracks near Volgograd, she spent the next three months poring over every one of his letters, knowing they were censored, trying to read between the lines.

Autumn had turned to winter before Kostya's first weekend of leave. When the big day came, she had prepared a homecoming feast – four courses, Crimean wine, her best china dinner service – and invited Galina, the couple from next door and one of Kostya's school friends, she can't remember who. But in answer to their questions about army life and his new 'comrades', Kostya had only mumbled and stuttered. 'Come on, it'll make a man out of you,' Gennady insisted, again. 'Never did me any harm.'

That was when Kostya had rushed out to the bathroom. Even now, she recalls the noise of his retching and vomiting as it invaded the embarrassed silence at the table. 'Might be the food,' one of the neighbours had ventured, 'too rich for him after army rations.' Later that night though, she was kept awake by the sobbing from Kostya's room, a muffled sound from which she knew he had his head buried in his pillow.

She wasn't naïve and could imagine what had happened to her son in the army – since Gorbachev had been anointed Soviet leader, his policy of *glasnost* had encouraged stories of beatings and abuse to come out into the open. Even Galina had worried, knowing what bullies like her own beloved Viktor had been capable of. In fact, it was Galina who'd told her about Dr Milyukov, and urged her to make the trip to his clinic near Moscow. Once there, the consultation had been for show: what sticks in her mind is the image of the doctor counting the roubles she'd stuffed into the envelope, locking them in his safe, then writing out the certificate that branded Kostya psychologically unfit for military service. It had cost her three months' salary – plus a month of Gennady's – and she knew the doctor wasn't issuing certificates out of the kindness of his heart. Even so, to her, it had been worth every kopeck.

★

She had saved her son from the army, only for him to live, what, barely another seven years? Worse still, she can't tell anyone – not even Galina – how he died.

After they had brought Kostya's body down from Moscow, Galina had arranged for him to be clothed in white in a proper coffin, not the temporary one used for the train journey. For the next three days, she had looked at her son lying there in Galina's living room until the day of the burial. It was a tradition that felt to her like torture, as if he were in a coma, or even just asleep and might rise, blinking, from that white-swaddled slumber.

Gennady had travelled down from Leningrad – alone, thank God, without his fancy woman. But at the funeral they stood apart, she and Kostya's father, barely able to meet each other's eye as the coffin was lowered into the ground. When she did steal a glance at her ex-husband, he looked shaken, no doubt about that, but something else was written on his twitching lips and downcast eyes, something other than regret. Was it shame? she wondered. Shame that Kostya didn't die a 'man', like Viktor?

She had seen Gennady only twice these past two years, for the purposes of their divorce and retrieving his belongings from their flat. This time, at the funeral, his face was as red as his eyes – he'd needed a drink to allow himself tears, she suspected. '*Our son, our son . . .*' he'd sobbed, making as if to hug her. She had turned away, rejecting his embrace. 'Yes, *our* son,' she spat. 'You should've thought of that when you left us.' They didn't speak again, and Gennady soon left, absent from his own son's wake at Galina's flat.

The floor is hard, too hard to be lying here all afternoon. She picks up her cushion, staggers to her feet and limps into the room where the wake was held three days earlier. It has a fold-down bed where Galina sleeps, but doubles up as a living room – as it did that day when six of them had crammed in here around a table laid with a white cloth and Galina's best cutlery. Among the guests, with their pungent white lilies and faces of practised solemnity, had been Arkady Bogdanovich from the theatre and an old school-friend of Kostya's with his new wife. She wanted to invite Zhanna, the girl she had once hoped might make a wife for Kostya, but she didn't have an address or phone number for her in Rostov-on-Don.

All afternoon she had been incapable of saying anything

beyond 'thank you for coming'. What *could* she say? Was there any point trying to assign blame? Meanwhile Galina had bustled about making tea, pouring the tea and filling the silences with offers of more tea. With or without Galina's choreography, the wake was a dance of quiet sidesteps, of clinking china and sympathetic nods: a dance executed on tiptoe by every one of its performers.

The lilies are still here, their scent stagnant and sickly, petals littering the tablecloth. But she's alone with her terrors now – the guests, for all their professions of support, aren't people she can phone up and say, 'Help me, I need to talk'.

She hears the front door opening. Galina's back. Wait, she must have someone with her because she's talking in a low voice, whispering in that way people do when they think they're being discreet. It's too late to scurry back and hide in Viktor's bedroom; she just hopes Galina and her guest will sit in the kitchen and stay there, leaving her alone, and not come to look for her. But looking for her is precisely what Galina is doing: she hears her shuffle down the hall towards Viktor's room, knocking on the door and calling her name.

She sinks into the armchair. Please, no visitors, no asking her how she is, no asking how it happened. What do people expect her to say? I'll pretend to be asleep, she decides. But before she can close her eyes, before she can attempt to blank it all out, she glimpses Galina at the door with someone behind her, indistinct in the dimness of the hallway.

'Tamara, dear, forgive me,' she says. 'I met someone at the cemetery who wanted to see you. I've told him he can't stay long, but he has come all the way from Moscow.'

Galina steps aside, no doubt off to the kitchen to make tea again, and now she sees her unwanted visitor. That English boy. Her mind reels back to Kostya's photos, and here he is, the object of her son's infatuation, tiptoeing into the room as if he's stepped out of that photo album. She stares and her mouth drops open; then she blinks, clamps her mouth shut and looks away, both hands gripping the arms of the chair.

She can barely speak – but Jamie does it for her, saying, 'Tamara Borisovna, I'm so, so sorry …' There's nothing she hasn't heard repeated and rehashed these past few days, the condolences, the apologies, the protestations of disbelief. Only there's that impishness of his too, that impertinence that British youths seem to exude. He's crouching down to meet her eye, reaching to touch her shoulder. She glances up at his face, not so much listening as registering the words she's heard all week and recognising the same old facial expressions, the downward-turned eyebrows, the pleading eyes. He's got a nerve.

She speaks. 'He would still be alive if it weren't for you.'

The English boy stops talking. His hand falls from her shoulder. Look at his face, that pained expression that he's probably been rehearsing all the way from the cemetery; she sees it turn wide-eyed and dumbstruck.

'You corrupted him, you and *your sort*,' she continues, now glaring at Jamie, her hands shaking while still gripping the arms of the chair. He stands, retreating from the presumptuous intimacy of crouching at her side. She sees him look towards the door as if hoping for Galina to come to his rescue.

'But please, Tamara Borisovna, please,' he's saying, stuttering *pozhalsta, pozhalsta*, as if that'd win him any indulgence from her. 'What's this got to do with Kostya—'

'You know what I mean,' she hisses. 'You led him astray, encouraged him, didn't you?' As the words come pouring out, even as she hears how biblical they sound, she adds, 'You and others like you, you led him into temptation.'

'Temptation?' He repeats the word as if he doesn't understand its meaning.

'Yes, temptation. Putting ideas in his head, corrupting him.'

She sees Jamie's ruddy-cheeked glow drain from his face, but all she wants right now is for him to shut up and listen as her rage spews forth.

'Do you think I didn't hear the kind of conversation you had with my son? "Mums know these things", you said. Well, you're right, we do. Kostya was a late developer, that's all. I wanted to find him a girl to marry – what right did you have to go *recruiting* him? Was it that trip to England? Or these new "friends" in Moscow? All I know is he got tainted with this Western *disease*, and now he's not here for me to—'

She has felt the tears building as she speaks, an undercurrent propelling her anger; but now the tears interrupt her flow and suddenly she can't go on. Jamie stands, frozen, by the door. She turns away from him, head in her hands, her body heaving. Apart from her sobbing, there's silence, then the clatter of teacups being dropped on the kitchen table as Galina comes hurrying back. She hears an exchange of whispers out in the hallway, then Galina's voice, loud and firm, saying, 'No, young man, I think you'd better be going.'

6

FEBRUARY 1993. Moscow

Dima

Above his head looms a line-up of black-and-white portraits, a gallery of Soviet film stars, all of them stern, all of them looking down on him. Their jaws are clenched, their faces proud and righteous. He scowls, reminded of how he's forced to scrape by in black-market porn videos while arse-lickers like these made it big by toeing the party line. *People's Cinematic Artists of the USSR*, declare the stern block capitals beneath.

Tonight, however, he sees those stony faces under a barrage of disco lights – orange, green, purple, red – and booming out of the speakers across the cinema foyer comes the *thud-thud, thud-thud* beat of last summer's big hit, 'Rhythm Is a Dancer' ... They were playing that song the night he met Kostya.

This Saturday the Proletariat Cinema, where Kostya once dragged him to see *Moscow Doesn't Believe in Tears,* is the latest venue for the 'Discotheque for Sexual Minorities'. But after the ambush a couple of weeks ago, he can feel the cranking-up of nerves about keeping this disco secret; a new phone number had been circulated by word of mouth, and he and Oleg had to wait until Friday night to call up and hear the recorded message giving directions.

With one hand in his jeans, the other clutching a cigarette, he stands off to the side of the dance floor, scanning the faces as they pass. He's clocked at least five guys cruising back and forth to give him the once-over. Plus two invitations to dance that he's turned down, one of them from a guy he shagged before Christmas.

In the flicker of the disco lights, he watches a huddle of heads bobbing awkwardly at the far side of the dance floor, well away from the doors, as if wary of the dangers lurking outside. Yet apart from the week-to-week switch of venue, little has changed from his first disco with Kostya. The same Soviet décor, all murals and enforced public-spiritedness. The same playlist of Western hits with trashy Russian pop thrown in. The same faces too – after all, there's nowhere else in Moscow for them to go. Only no Kostya. Not tonight, not next Saturday, not next year, not ever. He stares at the shaking hips and shimmying shoulders of the dance crowd, thinking: how can they carry on like nothing's happened? Don't they *know* one of us has died?

Pulling on his cigarette, he paces round the dance floor, past the box office and over to the entrance to Screen 1, where the cinema café is being used as a bar. As he expected, that's where he finds Oleg, already reeking of vodka.

'Give us a smoke, Dimik!' Oleg bellows in his ear, over the music. They're playing Dr Alban, 'It's My Life': another Western hit that had given him the chance to show off his dance moves in front of Kostya, singing along as if its lyrics proclaimed his attitude to the world.

Frowning at Oleg, he takes his Marlboros from inside his biker jacket. 'Did you find them?' he asks.

Oleg leans in to light his cigarette and inhales deeply, tipping his head back. 'One of them, yeah. Igor, he's called. He's over there, other end of the bar.'

He looks. Igor is a much older guy, probably in his forties, and the type he rarely fancies, with an unbuttoned silk shirt and a 1970s-style moustache; stringy hair spills from beneath the bandage still wrapped around his balding head. As Igor turns towards them, he notices a spasm of pain cross Igor's face and an arm wrapped protectively around his abdomen. Must be where they broke his ribs. They walk over to Igor and they shake hands as Oleg asks the barman for three glasses of vodka.

He offers Igor a Marlboro, a transaction that on most nights would form part of his chat-up routine. But Igor shakes his head, and he puts the cigarettes away, reaching into his other inside pocket for a photo of Kostya. It's one Kostya gave him, pictured on a spring day about three years earlier, smiling coyly under a tree heavy with blossom. Here, his hair is thinning less, and he's wearing a cream-coloured shirt with a big collar and a pattern of brown flowers.

Stubbing out his cigarette, he lays the photo on the bar, choosing a spot where there's more light, taking care to place it away from Igor's glass of vodka.

Igor shakes his head again. 'Sorry, I've never seen him before.'

Dima persists, leaning closer, getting a noseful of Igor's cheap cologne. He's forced to raise his voice over the music. 'Please, bro, take another look. It's important.'

Igor raises his voice too. 'I don't recognise him, OK?' He downs his vodka. 'I only saw one other guy and that was Kirill, in the same ambulance as me. He's not here tonight, I don't think. Too scared, I'll bet.'

He gives Igor what he hopes is a sympathetic nod, and gestures at Oleg to order more booze. 'It's just that we think Kostya here' – he holds the photo under Igor's nose – 'might've been beaten up that night as well—'

'Listen.' Igor turns and interrupts him. 'I was outside getting some air. Before I knew it, I found myself surrounded. Five or six of them, there were. They knocked me to the ground, started laying into me. One of them had a baseball bat, another must've been wearing steel-capped boots. All I could think of was how to get away from them. So I'm sorry, I didn't *see* who else they were kicking the shit out of—'

As the words catch in Igor's throat, Oleg passes Dima another shot of vodka, which he puts in front of Igor. Shit, he thinks, is that what happened to Kostya? Kicked and beaten, lying in the snow? Steel-capped boots, baseball bats? Cracked ribs, vital organ failure?

Igor manages to carry on. 'Next thing I knew, the gang had scarpered and the security guys were carrying me inside. I must've passed out then. When I came round, I was in an ambulance – just me, Kirill and the ambulance crew.'

'And this Kirill?' Oleg asks. 'Can you put us in touch with him?'

More shaking of Igor's head, bandage, stringy hair and all. 'No. Never met him before. And like I said, he's not here tonight.' He swirls his vodka round, staring into the glass.

Dima hears himself blurt out, 'Kostya and I were seeing each other, right? He had plans for our future. But no one can even tell me how he died. It was after *this* attack though. Didn't you *see* him at all? If not here, not in the ambulance, then in hospital? Anywhere?'

'I'm so sorry.' Igor drops his head, then flinches again,

clutching his ribcage. 'I didn't realise.' He puts down his vodka and lays a hand on Dima's arm. 'I didn't hear anything about anyone being *killed*.' A pause, then he removes his hand. 'It wouldn't surprise me though. Not in this country. God knows how many of our lives have been claimed by homophobia.'

Jamie

Jesus, that reek of boiled cabbage again. Dried fish today too. Halfway down the stairs from the office, he sees a garbage chute has been left open overnight, a stinking cavity in a wall painted half sludge-green, half flaking whitewash. Holding his nose and trying not to look, he pulls his furry hat down over his ears.

Two days have passed since his trip to Voronezh. The first day back, he phoned Bernie to say he was too ill to come to work. Although not strictly true, he hadn't slept a wink on the overnight train up to Moscow. Even now, his ears ring with the words of Tamara Borisovna's accusation – Kostya, she said, *would still be alive if it weren't for you* . . . He had *led Kostya astray*, she said, *recruited* him, tainted him with that *Western disease*. She didn't say the word *gomoseksualizm* – that, he guessed, was what she meant by 'Western disease' – yet nor had she said how Kostya actually died. He was as much in the dark as ever. It had almost come as a relief when that battle-axe Galina turfed him out of her flat; after all, he couldn't have stayed and argued with Kostya's mum, the state she was in. As he left, however, he'd managed to press his business card into Galina's hand, begging her to phone him once things had calmed down.

Western disease, he keeps thinking. But simply *being* gay couldn't have killed Kostya. Unless – he stops, gripping the stair-rail – unless Tamara Borisovna meant Aids. How though? Kostya was a virgin. At least he was when they talked about it in Voronezh. But what about these past few months, since he'd been seeing that knob Dima? Jeez, the number of times he and Artyom had spotted Dima out cruising or taking lads home from the 'Discotheque for Deviants'. Not to mention that dirty video Artyom started playing one bedtime ...

Which reminds him: he's supposed to see Artyom again tonight. Most evenings he'd be dead keen, sleeping over at the fancy apartment where Artyom's family live, in a part of Moscow that's all pastel-painted tsarist-era houses; no industry, no tower blocks. There'll be food, booze, maybe some dope. And since Artyom's parents are on a posting to the Russian consulate in New York, they'll be free to shag each other senseless in the parents' double bed. Except that didn't go too well last night. After Kostya's grave, Tamara Borisovna's accusation and a sleepless night on the train, the only thing he'd wanted was to let sleep blot it all out.

He steps outside, into a yard of parked cars. Their roofs are piled high with snow, their bodies plastered in winter mud. Beyond the car park, there's a children's playground blanketed in white, swings motionless, seemingly frozen in place, and on the far side of the yard stands another apartment block of grey curtained windows and wilting pot plants – people's homes, these: another five storeys of sludge paint and boiled cabbage.

The air's so cold, he can feel it freeze the snot inside his nostrils, a tingling sensation that even now, after three winters in Russia, gives him a little kick. Breathing it in, he turns left into a street lined with makeshift kiosks, a common sight in Moscow these days. In their icicle-laced windows, he sees fake brands of perfume, fake brands of underwear, pirated videos, Mars bars past their sell-by date and—

Wait, someone's calling his name. A Russian voice by the sound of it. Swinging round, he sees a tall figure in a ski cap, silver puffer jacket and lumberjack boots running after him . . . Oh, Christ, what's *he* doing here?

He stares at Dima, unsure of what to say. Come on brain, he thinks, switch gear, speak Russian. An exchange of muttered hellos follows, neither of them bothering to remove their gloves as they shake hands. His fingers feel crushed by Dima's handshake, his entire body almost cowering in the presence of Dima's height and physique.

Smoke from Dima's cigarette blows into his face. Look at him, that ciggy hanging out of his gob – thinks he's James bloody Dean. He coughs, pointedly, fanning the smoke away, and shivers as the wind tickles the back of his neck.

'Aren't you cold in that?' Dima nods at Jamie's second-hand overcoat, part of the student look he'd copied from Davy in his efforts to acquire a certain swagger around university.

He shivers again. Dima's bulging jacket not only looks warm but also accentuates his pumped-up torso. Smug bastard.

'I'm fine,' he says. Gritted teeth. 'But I'm in a hurry.' He makes a point of looking at his watch. 'I've got a press conference to go to.'

'You taking the metro?'

He nods, wary of Dima wanting to accompany him. 'Yeah, why?'

'I'll walk with you.'

In silence, they set off along Brestskaya Street. The cold turns their breath to steam, little clouds that disperse as they advance into them. He pinches his lips together. It's obvious why Dima's come looking for him, but he says nothing yet, fixing his gaze on the compacted snow and ice lying thick along the pavement.

When Dima speaks, his voice is subdued. 'I suppose you've heard.'

'About Kostya, yes.' It brings him to a halt, hearing himself say Kostya's name. 'I can't bring myself to believe it.'

'Me neither.'

He looks up to see Dima shaking his head and taking a prolonged, agitated drag on his cigarette. Another silence. What can he say that isn't trite, or inadequate, or that he hasn't said already? He hears himself mumble, 'It's awful', then Dima repeating the word, *uzhasno*. They each nod, still avoiding eye contact. 'There are no words,' they each say, *nyet slov*. For a second neither of them moves. He can hear their breathing.

Shooting Dima a sideways glance, he starts walking again. 'How did you find me?'

Dima pulls out a copy of the *Moscow Herald*. 'Thought you wrote for some big important newspaper. I almost missed this one.'

Screw you, he thinks. 'Oh, you read English, do you?'

Dima shrugs. 'Enough to track down where you work.' A pause while they both stand aside to let an old babushka hobble by, weighed down by her shopping bags. 'I had to come and find you though. You weren't at the last disco, and you won't return my calls.'

'What calls?'

'Three days I've been trying to reach you,' Dima says. 'Didn't you get my message?'

'I was in Voronezh, if you must know.' He turns to face Dima, to watch for his reaction. 'At Kostya's funeral.'

'His *funeral*?' Dima comes to a halt again. 'Already? You mean—'

'I mean, it's happened, it's for real.' He studies Dima's face. Is that shock? Genuine shock? Remorse even? Might 'Prince Charming' here actually feel any guilt for all his shagging around behind Kostya's back?

He sighs, deciding to relent a little. 'To be honest, they'd had the funeral already by the time I found out. All I saw was his grave—'

'His grave?' Dima takes another drag on his cigarette. '*Blyad.*'

Lost for words, Jamie resumes walking but suddenly slips on the ice; all that stops his head hitting the pavement is a swift grab by Dima, a solid steady arm cradling him inches from the ground, then hoisting him back to his feet. '*Spasibo,*' he mutters, more grudging than thankful. They make eye contact, only fleetingly but long enough for Dima to pull out a packet of Marlboros and offer him one. God, it's tempting. It'd be so easy to take up smoking again, like he did his first time in Russia – vodka, cigarettes, goes with the territory. But he shakes his head; he doesn't want Dima thinking they're like *mates* now.

'Why have you come looking for *me*?'

'Why d'you think? I wanna find out what happened to my boyfriend.'

'Your *boyfriend*? More like *one of* your boyfriends—'

Dima grabs him again, by the arm, forcing him to a standstill. 'Yeah, so I've had other guys,' he says. 'That doesn't mean I don't *care*.' Dima's breath, spiked with smoke, steams into his face. 'Anyway, wasn't Kostya in love with *you* for long enough? Didn't stop you finding yourself a boyfriend right under his nose.'

His mouth twitches, stuck for a response. It's true: he'd flaunted his relationship with Artyom in front of Kostya, knowing – but not always caring – how jealous Kostya would be. No wonder they'd barely spoken in those final months.

'But I don't know how he' – the word sticks in his mouth – '*died* though. Should I?'

'You call yourself a journalist, don't you?' Dima looks him up and down, not letting go of his arm. 'And you know his mother. Haven't you spoken to her?'

'Yeah. Briefly.' He winces at the memory of Tamara Borisovna laying into him. 'I saw her in Voronezh—'

'You saw Kostya's mother and you still don't know how he died?'

'Well, it was hardly ...' he wonders whether to tell Dima about Tamara Borisovna's outburst, then Galina's words come to him, 'hardly the time to be *interrogating* her, was it? She's *traumatised*. She's even having to stay in a friend's spare room.'

Dima lets go of his arm but gives him a 'tell-me-more' kind of shrug. 'And?'

He lets out a sigh. 'All Tamara Borisovna said was that Kostya might still have been alive if it weren't for this *Western disease*.'

'*Western disease?*' Dima's shaking his head again. 'But that's just bullshit that people believe in this country – they see *gomoseksualizm* as a sickness. It doesn't *kill* you though.'

More silence. A bus blunders past, its wheels splattering pedestrians with mud. They jump out of the way before walking on. Dima looks deep in thought, but abruptly turns to him and asks, 'Have you heard about those gangs beating up gay guys?'

'Sure I have,' he says; after all, that's a big part of the gay scene story he's meant to be writing. But then he frowns, stopping again to think. He'd been at the disco the night it was ambushed; worse still, he'd seen Kostya there. What could Dima be getting at?

'So did you hear about the incident at—'

'The Red Hammer? Yes.' He lets out a sigh, like a confession. 'I was there.'

'You were *there*?' Dima blocks his path. 'Why didn't you *say*? Did you see Kostya?'

He nods, then drops his gaze, finding it hard to meet Dima's eye. 'Yes, early on.'

'How early? What time?'

'I'm not sure. A good while before the attack.' Feeling like he's under interrogation – from Dima, of all people – he looks up. 'We didn't speak though. He was ignoring us.'

Puffing on his cigarette, Dima raises an eyebrow. '*Us*?'

Half sigh, half gritted teeth: 'Me and Artyom, of course.'

'Of course.' Dima puffs out smoke. 'So you didn't see where he got to?'

He shakes his head. 'Not later, no. Well, I wasn't exactly looking for him—'

'What, not even after the attack?'

He tries to remember. Did he see Kostya after the music was cut off and the ambulance arrived? No, all he can recall is hunkering down with Artyom, with only a snatched glimpse of that ginger boy's head on a stretcher, the crowd jostling and blocking his view.

'No,' he says. 'As I say, he was avoiding me and Artyom.'

Dima takes another long drag on his cigarette. 'Well, I *have* spoken to one of the guys who got beaten up—'

'You have?' So Dima is making his own inquiries. That

would come in useful, he thinks, if Kostya's death turned out to be part of his gay scene story.

'Yeah, he didn't see Kostya though. Only the boy who was in the ambulance with him.'

His thoughts spin as they walk on. OK, suppose Kostya *wasn't* beaten up? Suppose something else killed him, that other 'Western disease'? That'd make sense, right? Look at Dima sleeping around. Where does all that black-market gear come from? Could he – it's not impossible, even in Moscow – could he be a *rent boy*? Could Dima have Aids? It's only in the past few years, since *glasnost*, that the Russians have admitted to the existence of Aids in their pure, family-values motherland. What if Dima, even without knowing it, had infected Kostya?

He swallows, wondering what to say. They pass a kiosk selling doughnuts, the deep-fried smell lacing the icy air with grease and sugar, making him feel nauseous.

'Dima, a *delikatny* question.' Deep breath now. 'Have you been tested?'

Dima stops in his tracks. He's walked a few yards ahead before he turns to see Dima trailing behind but bearing down on him.

'*Tested*? What? You mean, for Aids?'

Oh Jesus, now Dima's acting all offended. 'C'mon, Dima,' he says, 'you sleep around. I know you do, I've seen you out on—'

Dima grabs him by the lapels of his studenty overcoat, cigarette clenched between bared teeth, and swears in Jamie's face: '*Pizdyets*! Who are you to judge? How d'you know so much about who I take to bed, unless you've been out there cruising yourself?'

Dima's cigarette smoke stings his eyes. Feels deliberate this time. 'For Christ's sake, Dima!' he says, coughing. 'Kostya's mum says he died of some "Western disease". A disease no one in this country will talk about. They're not even saying which hospital he died in. It's a possibility' – he tries to shake himself loose – 'that we can't rule out.'

Dima lets go with a shove, sending him staggering backwards into a tree. Snow falls off its branches into his face. He notices passers-by staring at them.

'You think Kostya died of *Aids*?' Dima spits out his cigarette. 'You think I infected him? If that's true, he'd have been *ill*, wouldn't he? And he wasn't. I should know – I saw him more than *you* ever did. Plus, I'd be ill myself, wouldn't I?' A pause, more angry steaming breath. 'Anyway, I never had unprotected sex with Kostya.'

He wipes snow out of his eye. 'But without getting tested, how can you be sure—'

Dima snaps at him. 'Because I didn't take him up the arse, all right? What about *you* and him, anyway?'

'Me? I never had sex with him.'

The minute his words leave his mouth, his denial sounds like an admission of neglect: of how he – whatever Dima's done – had rejected Kostya.

They continue on, arriving at Mayakovsky Square, and he glances up at the giant statue of the poet towering above the traffic. Kostya had given him a black-and-white postcard of a young, pouting Mayakovsky that he'd pinned above his desk in Birmingham – not out of love for his poetry but because Mayakovsky looked surprisingly cool for a Sov. Up ahead, the eight-lane Ring Road dips into an underpass, a stream of mud-streaked yellow taxis and the black sedans of officialdom, the stutter of Soviet exhausts mingling with the purr of the odd Mercedes or BMW. Across the way stands the Tchaikovsky Concert Hall, where Kostya once dragged him to hear that slushy Rachmaninov piano concerto.

Dima scowls at him. 'You got any other bright ideas?'

No sarky comeback springs to mind, and anyway the traffic's too noisy to make himself heard. He waits until they've crossed the road, reaching the entrance to Mayakovskaya metro station, where knots of babushkas stand selling jars of home-made pickles.

'All they're saying,' he mutters, 'is *natural causes.*'

Aside from that short Tass news bulletin, he's seen one police report saying much the same, while the Russian press have done nothing more than parrot those words 'natural causes', citing the statement issued by the medical authorities.

'That's the official line,' he adds, with a shrug. 'Came from some place in Khimki—'

'Khimki?' Dima frowns. 'That's nowhere near the Red Hammer. If Kostya got beaten up, he'd have been taken to hospital somewhere nearer, wouldn't he?'

'I guess so. But how can I find out for sure?' He looks at his watch, remembering he has a press conference to go to – and feeling relief at getting away from Dima. 'I need to go,' he says. 'Can't be late for the Foreign Ministry—'

'*The Foreign Ministry*,' Dima mimics. 'Aren't you the bigshot journalist! Well, when you've done with the Foreign Ministry, why don't you try tracking down the hospital—'

'You think I haven't been trying?' What a nerve, Dima talking to him like that. 'It's not as if they advertise in the Yellow Pages—'

'C'mon, Jamie, what the fuck is *natural causes*? You don't

know. I don't know. What else have we got to go on? Gang beatings? *Western disease*? Aids?' Dima lets out a growl of what sounds like frustration. He turns to Jamie. 'We could be helpful to each other.'

'Helpful to each other?'

'Yeah, this'd make a big story for you, wouldn't it? So if you tracked down that place in Khimki, I could go there, in person, and find out more. You'd have to make it worth my while though.' Dima winks at him. 'After all, you can't go in there as a journalist, can you, asking questions in your English accent.'

What a nerve, he thinks again. *Make it worth his while . . .* First Dima interrogates him, and then suggests getting paid to snoop around? We journalists don't pay our sources, he's about to say but—

'If you like,' Dima says, with a sneer, 'I'll tell 'em I need testing for Aids.'

Dima

Down in Mayakovskaya station, he watches Jamie squeeze into a jam-packed metro carriage, giving him a 'see you around' nod as the train clatters off into the tunnel. But rather than leave, he lingers a while: he has hours to kill before this afternoon's shoot and wishes he could skip it altogether, the way Yuri's been treating him. To think, all that time he'd managed to keep his 'arrangement' with Yuri hidden from Kostya, not wanting the boy to get hurt. Yet since Kostya's death, he's been distracted whenever he's around Yuri, unable to 'perform', and now Yuri's the one who suspects something.

Besides, Mayakovskaya used to be Kostya's favourite metro station. The pair of them had passed through here on one of their first dates, on their way to see *The Cherry Orchard* at the Satire Theatre. Truth be told, he hadn't appreciated the play at the time – all those genteel landowning twits whingeing on about loss and nostalgia – and he'd nodded off during Act II, only to be woken by a frowning Kostya digging him in the ribs.

Yeah, that was the night. It comes flooding back to him, a memory of Kostya with his head in the clouds – at least that's what it had looked like – Kostya gazing up at the station's ceiling mosaics, at those patches of sunny sky glimpsed as if through openings in the roof. He looks up, as though hoping to find the moment lingering there, preserved. The mosaics are unchanged, a vision of utopia where cherry blossom and sheaves of corn stand against the blue, where grateful citizens wave at the warplanes overhead safeguarding the motherland.

'This is all propaganda!' he'd said to Kostya at the time. 'You shouldn't fall for this, an intelligent guy like you.'

Kostya had blushed a little, turning defensive. 'I know it's propaganda,' he'd said. 'Of course I do. It's just that those mosaics, they're so beautiful . . .'

Man, that nostalgic glaze in Kostya's eyes. Sure, he recognised it too, the idyll held aloft by these ceiling mosaics with their cherry blossom and soaring skies. It wasn't that he'd ever fallen for what the Soviet state had promised him and every Soviet child – pride, security, patriotism – it was more the promise of childhood itself. The promise of happiness, of love and laughter, of Dad always being there alongside Mum and him and his little brother Petya. Promises he'd stopped believing in a long time ago.

Mayakovskaya is *his* favourite station too – more than the well-trodden Ploshchad Revolyutsii – but for a quite different reason. There's a little 'magic trick' he likes to play here, and on their way home from the theatre that night, he'd played it on Kostya. He had made Kostya stand across from him, on the opposite side of one of the many arches that ran the length of the station. Each arch, from one side to the other, was lined with ribbed chrome, and he'd pressed a coin (fifteen kopecks, of no value these days except for use in payphones) into one of its moulded metal channels. Then, with a lightning-fast upward flick of his wrist, he had sent the coin speeding along the metal channel, travelling over people's heads, right across the arch to where Kostya stood. It tinkled as it landed, leaving Kostya open-mouthed and, exactly as he intended, bewitched.

That was months ago. There's no Kostya to impress now, no Kostya to adore him. He's not even sure about Yuri any more. And his 'film career'? Is it worth staying in Moscow to 'act' in Yuri's videos?

From his coat pocket he pulls out his copy of the *Moscow Herald*. Jamie could still be useful to him, being a Westerner, a journalist with dollars to spend. What a nerve, asking if he's been tested for Aids. Sanctimonious jerk. But wait. It's true, he *hasn't* been tested. Recently though, he's seen advertisements for Aids testing, small, photocopied squares of paper pasted on walls inside metro stations. There's bound to be some at Ploshchad Revolyutsii … As long as it's anonymous – as long as they don't take his photo and hurt his chances of auditions – he *could* get tested, just to put him in the clear. If he tested negative, it'd mean he couldn't have infected Kostya. But what about all those strangers he's picked up, those nights of adrenaline-fuelled wantonness, all the times he couldn't be arsed to carry some condoms? Shit, what if he does have the virus after all? A test might be the only way to find out.

Jamie

His head feels heavy, willing him to nod off. Several rows in front of him, a Foreign Ministry spokesman is intoning the predictable government line about Russia's determination to 'guard its interests' in those pesky republics that had the audacity to split from the former Soviet Union. After a while he gives up trying to take notes and starts doodling.

He scrawls the name 'Dima' on his notepad, underlining it, etching a box around it, adding question marks. What's the deal with Dima then? Will he help him nail his story? They'd hardly spoken until today. All they have in common is Kostya.

His eyes scan the other journalists. On the front row is Oliver Rutland-Kerr, another Brit who, like him, studied Russian, but spent his student year in Russia schmoozing with diplomats. He's at the *Moscow Times* now, jammy sod. He makes a mental note to collar Oliver afterwards, ask him if there's any jobs going.

★

As soon as the journalists' questions are done, he legs it out of the Foreign Ministry – just managing to collar Oliver Rutland-Kerr before he got whisked away by his *Moscow Times* driver – and makes it back to the *Herald* in time for lunch. There's a pan of borsch, plus some meatballs and greasy macaroni cooked up by a babushka called Marusya who comes in twice a week. Without this small perk of the job, he'd go hungry most days.

Bernie is out though, as are Jamie's two fellow news reporters – 'Pushy' Patsy, a journalism graduate from Boston, and Josh Fitzsimmons, one of Oliver's private school cronies, both of whom are also chasing jobs at the *Moscow Times*.

So he finds himself at the kitchen table with Larisa, the *Herald*'s secretary. He's never warmed to her, knowing how the Ministry of Press and Information had forced Bernie to hire Larisa as a condition of opening an expat newspaper. So much for *glasnost*. Keeping his head down over his notepad, he wishes her *priyatnovo appetita* and slurps at his bowl of borsch.

After a moment, Larisa says, 'You'll get indigestion, eating in a rush like that.'

Here we go, he thinks, another ticking-off from a busybody Sov. *Your coat's too thin, you should wear a hat outdoors, don't cross your legs in public* . . . He looks up. Her eyes bulge with reproach, blinking at him out of great smears of purple eyeshadow that matches her frilly blouse. She picks at her macaroni in the cack-handed manner that Russian women imagine to be genteel and dainty, holding her fork as if it were the bow of a violin.

'Well, pardon me,' he mutters, slowing down but turning back to his notes.

More silence. Then she asks, 'What story are you working on there?'

He doesn't look up. 'Oh, just the ministry's statement on the situation in former Soviet republics. The usual stuff.'

'The Foreign Ministry? Who gave the briefing? Was it Belkin?'

His eyes flick upwards at her, his spoon hovering over his borsch. 'Yeah – why?'

Larisa dabs at her lips with a tiny paper napkin. 'I used to work for him. Before I got moved to the press ministry, before they placed me *here.*'

Here, she says, like it's beneath her. Letting it be known that she's had better jobs and she's got connections, don't you know.

An idea occurs to him. Maybe Larisa, with her ministry contacts, could access sensitive information that he can't? Maybe she can pin down the 'medical authorities' that reported Kostya's death? That way, he'd be able to take up Dima's offer to go and snoop.

He shifts to sit directly opposite her and, even though there's no one else in the office, looks to both sides and leans across the table like he's letting her into his confidence.

'Larisa,' he says, lowering his voice, 'I'm trying to get my hands on some info that the police and the authorities won't give out.' A pause. Try flattering her. 'What I need is the help of someone who's got the right *connections* – if you get my meaning.'

Frowning, Larisa picks up her fork again and stirs her congealed macaroni. Slowly, like she's playing hard to get. 'Is this for another news story you're working on?'

A thought flashes across his mind: that it might be crass of him to turn his mate's tragic death into a *story* ... Straight away, he shakes off that thought. No, he'd be exposing a tragedy or, even worse, a cover-up. Besides, 'crass' or not, Kostya was employed by an American trade organisation – as even Tass's news bulletin pointed out – and American businessmen are the very readers Bernie is anxious to reach. Who knows, an exclusive might help land him a job on the *Moscow Times*.

He nods. 'Yeah, I'm investigating an unexplained death out in Khimki.'

He looks at Larisa, expecting some flicker of recognition. But she just dabs at her lips between mouthfuls of macaroni. 'Go on.'

'I'll show you.' He takes out the little plastic wallet that holds his metro pass. Inside, carefully folded, is that Tass news bulletin, an innocuous-looking slip of paper. *A 24-year-old man who recently died ... A hospital statement blames 'natural causes' for the death of Konstantin Krolikov ...* He unfolds it, smoothing it out on the table with both hands.

Larisa twists her head to look. In the past week and a half, he has scribbled all over the bulletin – names, phone numbers, question marks, all hovering around the margins of that bald four-line statement. He's underlined the phrase 'natural causes'.

She shrugs. 'People die all the time in Russia. Alcohol poisoning, industrial accidents, you name it. Not to mention mafia hits or murders that the police aren't paid enough to follow up. I'm surprised they bothered reporting this.' She chews on her macaroni.

He recalls his own words, the wisdom he so loves to dispense about this country: *In Russia, life is cheap* ... Larisa is right, too, about the police not giving a damn. Why would they, when they can scarcely survive on their worthless salaries? They only act when bribed or threatened.

'Who would've written this?' he asks, pointing to the bulletin. 'There's no byline.'

She sniffs. 'Tass often protects its sources; sometimes it has to protect its journalists—'

'*Protects* them? All I want is to track down where the deceased was pronounced dead. Couldn't you find that out for me?'

'What d'you want, a name, a contact? Why isn't this official statement enough for you?'

'Because,' he says, 'I think the official statement's hiding something.'

He sees her eyes widen again, her purple eyeshadow seeming to flare up with them. Maybe that was too cloak-and-dagger, so he quickly adds: 'Look, the deceased happened to work in the field of US–Russian trade – that's of key interest to our readers.'

'*Hiding* something?' Larisa repeats. 'You know, Russia still has facilities that don't officially *exist*. Factories, military bases, prisons – entire towns that can be off-limits. So why not a hospital? Some of them don't even have names.'

Shit – like he'd said to Dima, *it's not as if they advertise in the Yellow Pages* ...

She pushes her half-eaten macaroni to one side and picks up the bulletin. 'Can I take a photocopy of this?'

'You mean, you'll look into it for me?'

Glancing over her shoulder, she leans in towards him. 'OK, I'll make some calls, see what I can find – just keep my name out of anything you write.'

7

EIGHTEEN MONTHS EARLIER

AUGUST 1991. Moscow/Voronezh

Jamie
A military coup. Unbelievable. He'd been back in Russia barely a fortnight when it happened. Tanks on the street, media blackout, the lot. They didn't *call* it a coup, of course: the official line from the commie diehards who'd put Mikhail Gorbachev under house arrest was that he had to step down because of some unspecified 'illness' – Mikhail Sergeyevich, they intoned, was 'unfit to fulfil his duties as leader', unfit to prevent the break-up of the Soviet Union. But try finding any actual news that day. Bugger all, just broadcasts of *Swan Lake*.

So soon after leaving cosy old England, it felt like he'd picked the worst time to pitch up in Moscow. But for a lucky break into journalism, he couldn't have chosen better if he'd tried.

*

By August, it had been over six months since that night when he and Kostya had said, let's do it, let's pursue our dream careers in Moscow. And here he was. He'd kept his side of the promise. But Kostik? The one friend he'd counted on to plug the gap left by his mates back home, where was he? Still in sodding Voronezh, tied to Mama's apron strings. So rather than wait for Kostya to pull his finger out, he'd rented a room from a lecturer called Lyudmila Fyodorovna, who'd taught Russian for a year in Birmingham.

He got straight down to looking for a job too. All the major news media had outposts in Moscow: the BBC, CNN, plus *The Times*, the *Guardian*, the *Washington Post* – that's the sort of newspaper he should be working for. On the morning of Monday 19 August, he'd set off job-hunting again, flagging down a clapped-out old Lada for a ride into the city centre. Before long though, they were stuck in traffic, and the driver launched into a sweary rant – *blyad* this, *pizdyets* that – and some bollocks about a military takeover.

Then he saw the tanks. Beneath their tracks, an entire lane of Kutuzovsky Prospekt had been ploughed into rubble, making the old Lada rattle and judder over the splintered tarmac. Another stream of *blyad* and *pizdyets* came from the driver as they overtook ten tanks in that column alone, lumbering yet unstoppable as they advanced on the centre of Moscow.

No wonder nobody had time to look at his CV. There was just one male journo at *The Times*, kindly but dishevelled with stress, who urged him to get out on the streets, to be an eyewitness and sell his story anywhere he could.

So the next night, he'd headed to the barricades. He didn't have a tape recorder and it was too anarchic for a notebook, so he found himself scripting his story in his head.

It's a scene of fires crackling in braziers, he fancied himself saying to camera. *A scene of old women – babushkas – doling out soup to*

the volunteers who've spent the day hauling steel girders and upturned
paving slabs to obstruct the tanks that are headed this way tonight.

Looking up, he saw the stars coming out and the sun setting
over the Moscow River. A few younger volunteers had broken
into song. He headed in the direction of the singing and imagined beckoning his cameraman to follow. *These brave people are*
a buffer zone between the tanks of the military junta and the resist-
ance leaders holed up in Russia's parliament building. It is from inside
this white marble edifice behind me – he pictured being on TV,
the gesture he'd make for the benefit of his viewers – *that Boris*
Yeltsin and his allies are leading opposition to the coup. Apart from
these hundreds of volunteers, apart from their flesh and – nah, scratch
that bit about flesh and blood, that's laying it on a bit thick –
apart from these volunteers, all that stands between the parliament and
the tanks are barricades built from girders, upturned paving stones and
a dozen commandeered buses.

The question is, he went on, *will the people make a difference?*
It was one thing to hope, another to report the news. Look
how it had all ended in Tiananmen Square two years earlier.
Look how many people the Sovs had slaughtered in the
purges, in the gulag. That's the thing about Russia, he loved to
tell his mates down the pub, life is cheap there. As cheap and
disposable as all the timber in Siberia.

*

He'd made his getaway down a side street too narrow for the
tanks, and from there it wasn't far to the metro.

Down on the station platform, what a sight met his eyes. If
only he'd had a camera with him, this would have made a great
picture for his story. Plastered all over the station's marble walls
were hundreds of glued or taped bits of paper, each one a bite-
size snippet of news, rumour or dissent. *Gorbachev has fled abroad,*

said one. *Gorbachev is returning to Moscow,* said another. There was *Down with the junta!* and even *Down with Gorbachev!*

He walked down the platform, taking it all in. This ground-swell of hearsay came from the people, uncensored and uncontrolled, much of it probably wrong. This from a population spoon-fed on Communist Party claptrap by the likes of *Pravda.* That was all falling apart now. Folk were hungry for news, real news. And no media blackout, no jamming of radio signals would assuage their appetite. *This* was the business he wanted to be in.

And because he was there, right place, right time, he sold his eyewitness stories to the *Manchester Evening News.* He was in Moscow for the collapse of the coup. He was there as Gorbachev returned from house arrest in Crimea. He was there as the world congratulated a new Russia that was open for business and had seen the sense of adopting a free-market economy.

Once the dust had settled, he went back to handing out his CV. With his talent, someone would surely offer him a job where he got to do exciting stuff like that all the time.

Kostya

Mama and I, transfixed in front of our television set. That's how I remember those three nights in August. If there was no news about the coup on TV, we'd try the radio. Or we'd sit watching those repeated scenes from *Swan Lake.* Either way, we hardly spoke, hardly met each other's eye. Events in Moscow made headlines around the world, the subject of international crisis talks in Washington and London – but in our little flat in Voronezh they offered us a distraction, the babble of the TV set filling a silence left by Papa's departure, papering over an unspoken pain that stretched between Mama and myself.

Six months had passed since he walked out. Six months in which, I now realise, I was forced to grow up. The world I cared so much for – theatre, Tchaikovsky, perfecting my English – was a world so distant from Papa's. And he was ashamed that I didn't complete military service. *I'd rather you'd stuck at it*, he said after I came home, my spell in the army cut short. *Other boys do – they come out as men, ready to take on the world. Still, this is what your mother wanted* . . . As for theatre, he was fine with me playing at it as a child, but scornful of my passion for it as an adult. *It's not a proper job*, he used to say.

Yet even if I didn't dwell on missing him, things were very hard for Mama. She became withdrawn and bitter, diminished and sucked dry of life. They'd never been an especially happy couple – no, they muddled through, bringing me up, going out to work and being respectable. As much as anything, it was a blow to her pride. And though I itched to be in Moscow with you instead, there was no way I could leave her alone in that state.

It took ages to reach you on the phone those August nights. Dialling, then redialling, I crouched in the hallway, away from Mama's prying ears, anxious to conceal our talk of looking for jobs in Moscow and my excuses for not being there. You sounded tetchy. I was stuck in my 'comfort zone', you said, that's why I was still in Voronezh.

Comfort? Believe me, things at home were far from comfortable. Mama and I said good morning, goodnight and what times we'd be out, not much else. Then we would go about our separate routines: me working at the theatre, Mama working at the library and drinking tea with Galina Sergeyevna – and both of us queuing for rations.

But one of those nights in August, our routine, our truce of avoidance and minimal greetings, was shattered by a terrible row.

'This military coup,' Mama declared, 'it's a good thing, if you ask me.'

She was standing near the door to the kitchen, her eyes fixed on the television. But her comments felt like they were aimed at me. 'It's time someone restored order' – *poryadok*, she said – 'time we defended the Soviet way of life. All *glasnost* has done is tear our lives apart! We used to know where we stood. We used to—'

'What, the good old days?' I burst out (and you know I hardly ever raised my voice to her). 'What was so good about them? Not being allowed to travel, or talk to foreigners? Not being allowed to *know* anything? People informing on each other in exchange for favours from the Party? Queuing gratefully for one type of fake cheese?'

I told you Mama looked shrunken and diminished – well, not during that row. She seemed to expand, filling the room like an exploding bundle of anger, teeth bared and fingers jabbing. She wanted to live in a country that didn't keep changing, she yelled. Where she could count on being paid for an honest day's work. Where she wouldn't keep being told that the communist achievements of her youth were built on sand.

I cornered her in the kitchen, gesturing at the cupboards, telling her what I'd seen in England. That supermarket, with its full, full shelves. No shortages there, I told her, I'd seen it with my own eyes. The press was free to criticise the government too—

'Listen to yourself,' she scoffed. 'One trip to the West and you're such an expert! What about the unemployment over there? What about homelessness? The gap between rich and poor? You think they know so much better than us?'

Before I could reply, I was silenced, thrown off-track by what she came out with next: 'It's that English boy, isn't it? Ideas he's been putting in your head!'

Why bring *you* into it? Did she resent my trip to England as much as that? Or had I given away too much of my feelings about you?

On she ranted, trotting out all that she held dear and was now under threat: socialism, the dignity of work, *poryadok* (again), pride in the motherland, faith in 'family values' ...

'Oh,' I said, 'you mean, like marriage? Well, how come our motherland has one of the worst divorce rates in the world? If we're so pure—'

'Don't you dare' – she prodded a finger right into my chest – 'make this about me and your father!'

I too was inflamed. Now that she'd raised the subject, I couldn't stop myself pointing out that Papa would have left us, *glasnost* or no *glasnost*; he wouldn't have stayed even if we were still living under Brezhnev—

She slapped me across the cheek. She hadn't done that since I was about thirteen. I was stunned. So, it seemed, was she. The two of us stood there in the kitchen, silent for what felt like ages, although it was probably only three seconds. And then, as she had done so often over these past six months, she collapsed in tears at the table, sobbing that it was hard enough with rising prices and food shortages and money being tight – all on top of Papa having gone. What, she bawled, were we going to do?

She had every right to worry. Papa had left us in what you would call 'deep shit'. He'd found a job in Leningrad (something else he'd arranged on the sly) and moved in with his mistress Oksana. But because our flat was in his name, Mama lived in fear of him forcing us to leave.

I had to hold her, reassure her. It wasn't easy, hugging her after what she'd just said. But I had to. Like I said, I'd done some growing up those past six months. It wasn't the first time I'd make peace with someone who slapped me in the face – figuratively, I mean – and it wouldn't be the last. I had to forgive her, to let her cry on my shoulder while trying not to cry myself, on hers. I had to tell her I'd look after her. I had to tell her that everything would be all right, even though it wasn't. It was far, far from being all right.

Tamara Borisovna

Their wardrobe looked so spacious with only her clothes hanging there, sad and abandoned, like her. That sleeveless flowery dress she'd put on a couple of times for special occasions last summer. That East German two-piece that she had once imagined to be stylish. That dark blue coat she'd asked Gennady to buy her, thinking she could wear it to the ballet. Only he hadn't taken her to the ballet for years.

She pushed the door shut. Right, that was the wardrobe done. No mementos of Gennady left in there, unless she counted the coat. There were those shoeboxes under the bed still, some of them containing photographs of him or of the two of them together that she'd removed from their frames and hidden away, not quite able to tear them up or burn them as she had vowed to the day he walked out.

That day, oh God, that awful February day ... Every time she replayed it in her mind, it was as if she were just an onlooker, not a participant: paralysed, numb and reduced to watching from the window as her husband of twenty-two years dragged a sledge with his suitcases and boxes across the snowy courtyard to a waiting taxi. He looked back once, up at the family home he was deserting, but she pulled back out of sight, recoiling as if the sub-zero wind outside was ready to take a bite out of her.

Gennady's clear-out had been as rapid and clinical as his decision to leave. Or had he made up his mind a long time ago? Either way, he didn't relent in the face of her anger. Had she really thought that *shouting* at him might make him stay? Or falling to her knees to beg? Two years this affair in Leningrad had gone on behind her back. She cursed herself for her blindness and stupidity, for not suspecting. All those 'conferences' he went away to, always insisting how tedious they were, yet never once looking pleased to come home.

When Gennady left her, Kostya had been away in England, on his 'trip of a lifetime'. How thrilled he'd been, prattling on and on about Jamie's invitation. She'd never heard him sound *that* excited about family holidays, not since he was a small child anyway. When Kostya was fourteen, she and Gennady had taken him to Sochi. There were photos in the album she'd shoved under the bed the other day: snapshots of the three of them by a palm tree, Kostya stiff and gangly at her side, covering up in long trousers and long sleeves despite the Black Sea sun. He had been subdued and distracted, not mixing with the other youths at their resort but preferring to sit in the shade reading his book.

Her son, her only child ... thank God *he* was still with her.

After all her fretting about when, if ever, he would get married, she was grateful now to have him under the same roof as her. But for how much longer? Ever since Kostya had cut short his trip to England, she could see his heart was elsewhere. He'd always been a day-dreamer, but this was different – he had even stopped chattering about the theatre where he worked and what plays it was putting on. He went out, came home, sat in his room and said he was 'fine'. Like his letters from the army all those years ago; they too had said he was 'fine' . . . All they discussed was who would go and queue for bread and who for potatoes. The gap left by Gennady's leaving, that extra space and silence in their flat, was a gap they tiptoed around until it got too much for her, the strain of keeping her head held high in front of her colleagues or gossiping neighbours.

The only times she saw any spark in Kostya's eyes, heard any animation in his voice, was when he talked about Jamie or England. Then it was Jamie this, England that – she couldn't shut him up. There was that whispering on the phone too, something about working in Moscow. The English boy was there already, having stayed a week with them in Voronezh in July. But Kostya? Find a job in Moscow? No, surely her son wouldn't abandon her too.

*

She liked order, *poryadok*, knowing where things belonged. If things were not in their place, she took pride in correcting matters. That's what made her so good at her job. Twenty years she had worked at the Koltsov Library, and her record was exemplary.

But it was trickier to impose order these days, on books even, let alone on people. The library had a few copies, just a few, of novels that had long been banned such as *Dr Zhivago* or *Life and Fate*, but they kept being returned with pages torn out, or not returned at all. And it was no use trying to fine people – they could make far more money selling stolen books.

She also noticed how no one asked to consult the Collected Works of Lenin any more. Indeed, instructions came from the city council's culture and education bigwigs to demote them to the basement floor, freeing up space for Western crime thrillers translated into Russian. She had been there the day they moved those hefty Lenin tomes, blinking and sneezing as years of accumulated dust clouded the air. She'd blown the cobwebs off one volume and marvelled at its crisp, untouched pages, as unsullied and virgin as the day it was printed – 1968, it said.

Then one morning in early September, a couple of weeks after the coup, she arrived at work to find there were no copies of *Pravda* to be arranged on the reading desks. What was going on? This was the mouthpiece of the Party, not any old newspaper. She discovered the answer soon enough from her assistant Nikolai, who sat tearing the previous week's *Pravda* into squares to be used as toilet paper. Yeltsin, he told her, had closed it down. That turncoat Yeltsin. His new government said the closure was only temporary – but still, closing down *Pravda*, whoever heard of such a thing?

Pravda was not the only thing that failed to appear in the library. At the end of that week, she joined the queue outside the window where the library bookkeeper Olga Filipovna would dispense their pay packets, thrusting bundles of cash across the counter with her sausage-like fingers. The fingers were usually all she would see of Olga Filipovna, unless she bent down and peered into the aperture, like Alice peering into one of Wonderland's miniaturised doors, and then, as she signed for her money, she'd catch a glimpse of the bookkeeper's thick spectacles and podgy arms wrapped in a grey shawl.

Today though, the shutter was down and there was an unexpected commotion from her colleagues. She stood a few feet back, reluctant to join in. She had never seen librarians being so noisy. 'Open up!' one was demanding. 'We know you're in there!' 'We'll report you!' another shouted. 'It's our money we've worked for!'

Someone was hammering on the window; it wasn't clear who. But then she saw the shutter lift, and spied Olga Filipovna's spectacles through a gap barely six inches high. Her mouth was working away, shrill with pleading. 'Comrades! Listen to me, comrades! It's not my fault! The city council has no money for us!'

The shouting grew angrier. 'Disgrace!' 'This is outrageous!' 'You promised us money last week!' She heard the shutter close again with a snap. That only made the shouting even louder, and there was more hammering on the window as her colleagues crowded round, blocking her view. 'Two months we haven't been paid!' someone bellowed.

Her elderly colleague Anatoly Vasilyevich broke free of the angry knot, bumping into her. 'You hear that?' he cried, pointing at the cash window. 'How are we supposed to live?'

She blinked at him, speechless. Two months in a row without a pay packet. Last month, instead of money, they'd been paid in coupons that could be exchanged for meat. But by the time she'd found the right places to queue, prices had risen so fast that the coupons had lost half their face value. Even if she were paid on time, hyperinflation was making cash worthless.

She looked at Anatoly Vasilyevich, with his white hair and Lenin badge on his brown suit, and put a gentle hand on his shoulder, feeling momentarily sorrier for him than for herself.

'Wouldn't have happened in Brezhnev's time,' he said. 'Tell me, Tamara Borisovna, what are we supposed to live on? How do they expect us to eat?'

She shook her head and said she didn't know. Because it was true, she didn't. Without her pay packet, she had no idea how she and Kostya were going to manage.

Kostya

So you see, I needed to earn money. Far more than I made at the Voronezh Youth Theatre. But how? Even in Moscow, a theatre job wouldn't pay much – plus, Arkady Bogdanovich had warned me, theatres up there were a 'closed shop'.

Our theatre was suffering the same money shortages as Mama's library, so when Arkady Bogdanovich called me in, shortly after Mama's salary wasn't paid, I feared the worst. He sat me down in his office, a shambolic space plastered with photographs and posters of past productions, and told me we couldn't raise ticket prices any more or people would stop coming. So, he said, digging his fingers into his temples, the theatre was seeking 'additional sources of income'.

In fact, instead of announcing that he had to let me go, Arkady Bogdanovich asked me to act as an interpreter at a meeting he had scheduled. I was flattered to be recognised for my proficiency in English. What's more, the meeting was with an American trade delegate visiting from Moscow. An *American* on business in Voronezh! Imagine how glamorous that sounded.

Arkady Bogdanovich had learnt that this American had the final say on a 'corporate sponsorship' deal for his rivals, the Voronezh Puppet Theatre, to go on tour in the States. A tour of America, picture that! The rare Hollywood movies I'd seen had imprinted my imagination with visions of skyscrapers, jazz clubs and enormous shiny cars. Not wanting to be outdone by a bunch of puppets, Arkady Bogdanovich had worked every contact possible to secure his own half-hour slot with the man from the United States Commission for Assistance to the Russian Economy, or US-Care.

The next day, Mario F. Waterson, Director, Moscow Office (as it said on his business card) arrived at our little theatre. He stepped out of a chauffeur-driven black Volga, the type of car usually reserved for Party officials. Arkady Bogdanovich was uncharacteristically nervous, grinning and nodding – and his brown suit and shapeless shoes looked so *Soviet* next to Mario F. Waterson. Here was a man who exuded the power to hand out money. He was dark-haired, about forty, and wore a linen suit that appeared to broaden his shoulders and cinch his waist. As he entered the office, he removed his tie and undid the top two buttons of his pale pink shirt, enough for a glimpse of a suntanned chest. I drank in the scent of an expensive, peppery eau de cologne. Arkady Bogdanovich, my mentor in all things theatre-related, looked so dowdy as he scrambled to clear space on his desk, those posters and photos seeming like the clutter of bygone glory.

I called our visitor *gospodin* Waterson, *Mr* Waterson, but with a smile that showed off his perfect white American teeth, he touched my arm and insisted, 'Please – call me Mario.'

He perused the posters on the wall, nodding as if in approval – something that Arkady Bogdanovich was quick to latch on to. 'You know, *gospodin* – Mario, we won first prize at the 1988 festival in Brno, Czechoslovakia—'

'Brno?' said Waterson, pronouncing it *burr-know.* 'Hey, that's the name of the hotel I'm staying at.'

'Oh, well, of course.' Arkady Bogdanovich grinned, showing rather too much of his tea-stained teeth. 'Of course, they'd send you there. It's the best hotel in Voronezh.'

'The *best*?' Waterson shot me a quick sideways frown. 'What, really?'

Once the small talk was done with, it was down to the substance of the meeting. I prided myself on my spoken English, but found it hard work interpreting between the two of them. I was used to Arkady Bogdanovich the authoritative theatre director; that day, however, he was the supplicant: grinning and shrugging and at one point offering to crack open a bottle of vodka – which the American declined with a forced chuckle.

Waterson's spiel was all applications and 'feasibility studies'. US-Care, he said, awarded grants to projects that 'unlocked business potential' or 'opened markets for corporate America'. Rather than art galleries and theatres, he reeled off a list of farms, factories and co-operatives – even the police – any organisation that was starved of equipment or supplies. True enough, thanks to *glasnost*, I had heard of collective farms that couldn't get the harvest in because they lacked spare parts to fix their crumbling machinery; I'd heard of grain being left unmilled, flour left to rot, bread that couldn't be delivered – all because of broken-down storage or transport. What the American was offering sounded like pure largesse.

However, Waterson said, he needed to see 'mutual benefits for our corporate partners': the only reason the Puppet Theatre might get sponsorship was an advertising tie-up with an

American children's TV channel. Arkady Bogdanovich, much as he 'auditioned for the part', was unable to stick to this unfamiliar script; it quickly became clear that US-Care would not be handing out grants or foreign tours or sponsorship to *our* theatre.

We accompanied Waterson out into the street, where he told us his driver had finished for the day – so maybe, if we gave him directions, he could make his own way to his hotel? At this point, I thought I saw him wink at me.

'Arkady Bogdanovich,' I said, sensing one last opportunity to make an impression on the American with the money, 'why don't I walk Mr Waterson to the Brno?'

And that, as you know, is what I did. Crossing Lenin Square, I recalled that evening with you the previous year when we headed home to our portentous late-night conversation. So much had changed since then. Still, with no time to be pensive, I made small talk about the warm September sunshine – the *babye leto*, or Indian summer. It wasn't far to the Brno and Waterson really didn't need to be accompanied, but he seemed to appreciate the gesture – or rather, to have been expecting it.

We reached the doors of the Brno, a hotel where they put delegations from other Eastern Bloc countries. I watched as groups of men in suits – grey synthetics, not linen like Waterson's – filed off the coaches parked outside.

'You speak great English, young man,' Waterson said, touching me on the arm again. 'You didn't learn that here, did you?'

Well, yes, I said – but quickly adding that I'd been to England earlier that year and telling him about your invitation. He raised an eyebrow and said, 'Ah-*ha*.'

'And what about your work at the theatre? I guess you've

quite a head for figures – bookkeeping, ticket sales, funding applications to the culture ministry. All that on top of your excellent English.'

I felt myself blush and started to tell him that while I handled that sort of work all the time, one day I hoped to be directing plays . . . Here, though, he interrupted me, lowering his voice and placing a hand on my upper arm.

'Why don't you take my business card,' he said, slipping one into my shirt pocket and patting me on the shoulder. 'And give me a call if you're in Moscow any time soon. Come see me at my office. We could sure use a smart guy like you.'

8

FEBRUARY 1993. Moscow

Dima

Of all the guys Yuri could have 'auditioned', all the ripe young
hopefuls flaunting their pecs and cocks and arses in front of his
camera, the latest – one Yuri had picked that afternoon – just
happened to be called Kostya.

That's right: 'Kostya'. Was this fate playing some sick joke
on him? Of all the boys' names under the sun, why couldn't
this one have been a Sasha or a Volodya or a Misha? Even
another Dima, for God's sake. Anyone but a 'Kostya'.

Minutes before filming, Yuri had made cursory introductions –
'Dima, Kostya; Kostya, Dima' – and he heard himself repeat the
name in disbelief, gawping at the wiry young stranger before
him: coquettish eyes, artificial suntan, about nineteen. They
even shook hands. Kostya? Sure, there's lots of guys called
Kostya; it's a common enough name. But what, if they end up
'working' together, is he supposed to call the new boy? 'Other
Kostya'? 'Kostya Two'?

Once they got down to business, of course, they didn't use
each other's names at all. 'Other Kostya' had simply smirked,

pulling down his pants to present his compact, peach-like but-tocks for the scene they were filming. He can hardly remember any foreplay or dialogue – only this tableau of Other Kostya offering his arse to him for a hard-on he couldn't produce – and he barely managed to go through the motions, thrusting his pelvis to the soundtrack of that tired Soviet electronica. His failure to 'perform' earned him another bollocking from Yuri, and they'd had to reshoot the scene from another angle to suggest – if not actually show – the act of penetration.

Thank God I didn't have to fuck him for real, he thinks. That was barely half an hour ago; the minute filming was done, he'd grabbed his coat and run for it, not bothering to check the date of the next shoot. He staggers towards the metro, blinking and squinting in the blizzard, trying to sidestep puddles deep with slush. It's been dark since five and every trace of daylight has fled, abandoning the sidewalk to the blackish-purple shadows of the Stalinist apartment blocks looming over Prospekt Mira.

In his haste, he slips on the ice underfoot, grabbing onto railings and lamp posts for support. This same old route to the metro, a route he's walked so many times, seems tonight to take longer in his hurry to get away from Yuri and his studio.

To his left, cars and buses rumble past, their lights veiled by the driving snow, a blur in the slush sprayed up behind. A trolleybus stops, and he watches men in big furry hats and women weighed down with shopping bags shove and jostle to get on board. He looks up as the trolleybus then pulls away to merge into the traffic, sparks leaping from the wires overhead. His eyes are drawn by some invisible tug of envy, a yearning to blend in among these ordinary-looking people with their ordinary jobs and ordinary marriages. And yet 'ordinary' was far from what he craved when he first came to Moscow, pumped up with the belief that he, with his looks and charm, could hit the big time, that a life transcending the ordinary was his for the taking.

★

That summer day in 1984: that's when he first felt those stirrings of ambition, of a dream he's clung onto until now. One hot afternoon, a photographer from the Party's youth magazine came to take pictures of him and his Young Pioneers volleyball team at a seaside camp near Jurmala. After the match (in which the Latvian locals beat the lads from Estonia), they'd raced down to the beach and into the waves, hollering and whooping as they splashed each other, sending arcs of water rising and glittering in the sun. To dry off, they basked on white sands under a sky so blue it was blinding. His skin, tingling with the heat, turned browner than any of the other boys and, even at fifteen, none of *them* had muscles as firm and defined as his – an observation he checked hour after hour during those blazing, often shirtless days at the camp.

The photographer, a middle-aged geezer who never stopped grinning at him, had said he wanted to capture the athleticism of Soviet youth, to revisit the spirit of Moscow's Olympic Games four years earlier. For the team portrait, he'd placed Dima in the centre of the back row, head and shoulders above the other boys. The photographer later took him to one side and got him to pose individually, grinning and bare-chested, for a full-height shot that also made it into the magazine.

That was the summer his father sailed to Stockholm and jumped ship. In the first few months, as autumn fell, Dad wrote home, promising his family they'd soon join him in Sweden, that he'd get them out of the USSR. Dad had found work on the docks near Stockholm, and even started sending them money. One day a heavy parcel arrived, containing two pairs of Bauer ice-skates – one for Dima, one for his little brother Petya. *Take him out skating,* Dad wrote. *Make sure he has fun until we're all together again.*

Only they never were together again. Dad's letters became less frequent. Applications for visas were rejected. It wasn't possible for Dad to come back either, for fear of being thrown in prison, and Mum numbed her pain by way of affairs with other sailors stationed in Riga. At sixteen, he had had to go out to work to help Mum and Petya: two years with the coastal patrols that saved him from military service – and where he got his anchor-and-chain tattoo – but that also confronted him daily with views of the seas across which Dad had sailed away.

It was years later, realising that lectures on Eisenstein and Tarkovsky were no route to an acting career in Moscow, that he answered Yuri's ad for auditions. Forget film school: *this* was his route to recognition, oiling up his chest and biceps as he and Yuri acted out locker-room fantasies of the sort that had played at the edges of his mind even at Pioneer camp.

He got paid for it too. And as well as clothes and dollars, he had Yuri's promise to look out for him, to help him make a name, maybe even in the West. On-camera, Yuri assured him, he'd get the leading roles, playing the jock other boys wanted to be – or wanted to jerk off to. Off-camera, he got the leading role in Yuri's private life, the favourite who was more than an employee. There were rides in Yuri's car and evenings at Yuri's flat, just the two of them. With Yuri, he would stop playing the lead and surrender control, kneeling to lace up Yuri's boots, nuzzling his head in the silky clinginess of Yuri's boxing shorts.

But Yuri never let him stay over. That would have been too 'romantic', that soppy scenario of morning kisses and breakfast in bed. The sort of thing Kostya had introduced into his life ... No – for Yuri, that crossed a line into being something Yuri refused to be, and that was *goluboy*, gay, queer. Yuri had done time in prison, taken up boxing, could hold his vodka. And whenever he caressed Dima's head between his legs telling him, *Good boy, that's my boy*, the message was clear: Yuri was a *muzhik*, a real man who happened to like cock. Just don't ever call him *goluboy*.

★

About a hundred metres past the trolleybus stop, a car veers towards him, skidding to a halt and spraying the kerb with slush. It sounds its horn. He looks up from his lumberjack boots, now damp from the snow. It's some flashy foreign car, a BMW. He blinks as snowflakes swirl around his head, prickling his eyes, and sees the front passenger window being lowered.

He hears his name being called. 'Dmitry? C'mon, get in the car!'

Shit, it's Yuri ... But why has he come looking for him, here on the street, on his way home? Through the gap of the open window, he sees those familiar eyes glinting in the dark.

Looking over his shoulder, he takes a step closer. 'Yuri? What're you—'

'Get in the car, Dima.'

'I don't need a lift, Yuri – the metro's just—'

Yuri bares his teeth. 'I said, *get in.*'

Too late now, he wishes he'd gone a different way. Or got on that trolleybus with all those lucky, lucky ordinary people. He lowers himself into the front passenger seat, his legs feeling heavy and sluggish, and winds up the window. Inside, the heating is on full blast, but Yuri's wearing a puffer jacket like his own, probably from the same black-market consignment, thrown over the top of a silky blue Everlast tracksuit. And all the while, he feels Yuri's eyes on him, even as they pull out into the traffic and join the procession of red tail-lights streaming south down Prospekt Mira.

For the next half-mile, until they reach the Ring Road, Yuri keeps turning to look at him, but says nothing. The air is warm and stuffy, thick with the BMW's scent of money and solidity, nothing like a Soviet car. He keeps his eyes on his lap, sensing that it's no time for small talk, yet racking his brains for something to say, a distraction from whatever reason Yuri has hauled him in. How about the car? How about flattering Yuri on his new toy?

Yuri seems to read his mind. 'So, Dmitry, how d'you like the car?'

'Yeah, cool.' He nods, relieved at having something to say. '*Krutaya mashina*,' he adds. 'Cool car. I didn't know you'd bought a new one.'

Yuri sucks on his teeth. 'Well, you wouldn't know, would you? Haven't seen much of you, past couple of weeks. Not *off*-camera, at any rate. Turning up late for shoots, running off as soon as we're done filming . . .'

He gives Dima a little shrug of mock self-pity. 'Still, get a load of this, eh? Me and my *krutaya mashina*.' His fingers pat the rim of the steering wheel in approval.

Silence. They pass under a street light, then another, and he sees the shadows on Yuri's face lengthen, then contract, then lengthen again, making it hard to read his expression.

'Wow, Yuri,' he says at last. 'Must've set you back a bit.'

Yuri gives a brief snort, not quite a laugh. '*Set me back a bit*? Well, this one's second-hand, imported via Poland. But if business keeps growing' – he turns and gives Dima a wink – 'I'll be able to afford a brand-new one soon. Know what I mean?'

Yes, he knows what Yuri means. He knows only too well. His boss's homoerotic videos are surprisingly successful – even by the debauched, anything-goes standards of the new Russia. It's still risky, still a clandestine operation but, after years of Soviet prudishness, there's clearly pent-up demand out there, not to mention Yuri's newfound 'clients' overseas.

Yuri presses the lighter on the dashboard. 'Now, how about a cigarette?'

Dima rummages in the glove compartment but can't find any cigarettes there, only a small bottle of vodka. He fishes inside his coat for his own, his Marlboros, and takes one out. Holding it between the fingers of both hands, he rolls it one way, then the other, his gaze fixed on the road ahead, past the to-and-fro of the windscreen wipers and into the blitz of snowflakes piling towards them. They're heading towards Mayakovsky Square, the opposite direction from where he lives.

'Where are we going, Yuri? This isn't my way home.'

Yuri pulls a face of mock disappointment. 'Aw, Dmitry – don't you want to go for a ride in my *krutaya mashina*? It's been a while, just you and me.'

His mouth goes dry. Most nights when they're heading back to Yuri's place, he'd ask for a swig of vodka. Tonight, somehow, he daren't. He looks over to the opposite carriage-way. A blurry mass of yellowish headlights sweeps towards him, looming up, then drifting away in the other direction – the direction he wishes he was going in.

'So?' Again, it's Yuri who breaks the silence. 'What d'you think of young Kostya?'

'*Kostya?*' He stirs, jolted from one tangle of thoughts to another, from what the fuck's gotten into Yuri, to what the fuck's happened to Kostya ... 'You mean—'

'My new boy.' Yuri grins. 'Fucking gorgeous arse, eh?'

The cigarette that he's been nervously rolling between his fingers suddenly breaks in two. At that moment, the lighter pops out, glowing in the dark. Shoving the broken cigarette back in the packet, he fumbles for a new one and presses its tip against the burning orange coil. He hands the lighted cigarette to Yuri, who accepts it without a word.

A silence. Yuri's waiting for an answer. 'Oh,' he says. '*That* Kostya.'

Yuri turns and blows smoke at him. 'Yeah, *that* Kostya.' A frown. 'Why, is there some other Kostya? One you haven't told me about?'

He coughs. 'No, Yuri, of course not.'

It's true enough too, he thinks. *His* Kostya, a boy from a world so different from Yuri's, has gone. Past tense. Exists only in his head now.

They dip into the underpass below Mayakovsky Square. The growl of slush under tyres cuts out, replaced by the *vroom* of passing cars, amplified and reverberating in the tunnel. As they emerge, back into the blizzard, he sees the Tchaikovsky Concert Hall and recalls passing by earlier with Jamie, the only other boy he knows with whom Kostya was equally infatuated.

'You see' – Yuri interrupts his ruminations – 'I wanted to try out young Kostya, build up what producers in the West call a "pool of talent". Get my drift?'

Yuri's looking at him, waiting for acknowledgement. He nods.

Yuri chuckles. 'There's plenty more where he came from – gagging for a chance to get their kit off on-camera. If I want, I could have them queuing up outside the studio.'

Is *this* why Yuri came looking for him? He eyes the car's speedometer, then the trucks and buses chugging by on one side, the cars surging past on the other. If they weren't in the middle of moving traffic, he'd be tempted to jump out and run for it.

'I'm sorry, Yuri,' he says, 'I know I wasn't performing great today, it's only—'

'I've gone out of my way for you, Dmitry.' Yuri shifts down a gear as the traffic up ahead starts to slow, red brake lights flashing in the snowstorm. 'Treated you special, confided in you. If I knew you'd stick with me, you could do all right – more money, maybe a contract. Question is, have you still got what it takes?'

What it takes? No, he hasn't got 'what it takes'. Not any more, not since Kostya. He wants out. Out of Yuri's car, out of his pocket, out of his videos. Trouble is, he has no other income, not even any show-reel to speak of – and he'll soon have to find a new place to live too.

Yuri taps his cigarette in the ashtray, shaking his head with a mirthless upward curl of his lips. 'You're having doubts, aren't you, Dmitry? What happened to that special something we had? What's the word? *Rapport*, that's it – we had a *rapport*, didn't we?'

Didn't we, not *don't we*. Like it's over already.

'If you say so, Yuri.'

'If I say so, eh?' Yuri rests his cigarette in the ashtray, using his free hand to change down another gear. Dima watches the smoke curl upwards, breaking into little eddies against the windscreen; he sees Yuri's hand shifting from the gear lever to the waistband of his tracksuit bottoms and loosening the drawstrings.

'*If I say so . . .*' Yuri returns his hand to the gear lever. 'That's the way we both like it, isn't it? I tell you what I want from you, and you do as you're told, right?'

He feels his pulse quicken and a queasiness rising from his gut. What *does* Yuri want from him? Where the hell is all this going?

'So, c'mon, Dmitry. Show me you've still got *what it takes.*'

He swallows, trying to hold down his nausea. 'I'll be on better form next time, Yuri.'

They've come to a standstill at a red traffic light: lines of cars up ahead and on both sides, headlights closing in on them from behind. Snowflakes settle in the corners of the wind-screen untouched by the whirring wipers. Now would be the time to make a run for it . . .

Yuri laughs. 'No, Dmitry, not next time.' He reaches his arm around Dima's shoulder. 'If you've still got what it takes, I wanna see it *right now.*'

Yuri's touch makes him flinch. His eyes dart towards the shadows beneath the steering wheel, and there, dimly visible in the snow-filtered street light, he sees Yuri's cock, semi-erect, getting engorged and hard. He feels Yuri's hand on the back of his neck, a caress that abruptly turns into a strangle-hold, pulling his head towards Yuri's crotch.

'Yuri, please. Not here . . .' But the grip tightens, and he glimpses Yuri's eyes, flitting from him to the traffic outside and back, and Yuri's teeth, either gritted or fixed in a sadistic grin, it's hard to tell.

'What's wrong, Dmitry? You never had a problem doing this before.'

He strains to wrest his head free of Yuri's grip, but to no avail. 'Please, Yuri,' he moans, *'pozhalsta, pozhalsta ...'* Scrabbling around with his right hand, he finds the inside door handle and tries to open it. It's locked.

'Central locking,' Yuri says. 'No getting out until I say so.'

He tries to push himself upright, but slips, his face falling into Yuri's lap, where Yuri holds him in a headlock. As he feels Yuri's bicep bulging against his jaw, he struggles to breathe, and finds his nose thrust up against the shaft of Yuri's cock, now standing proud of its nest of curly black pubic hair and giving off its familiar smell of cheap boiled meat.

He can feel vomit rising in his throat and desperately blurts out, 'C'mon, Yuri, please – let's do this back at your place.'

But Yuri tightens the armlock on his neck, taking his other hand off the steering wheel to grab his cock. 'Get your lips round that, Dima. I know you like it.'

Suddenly though, Yuri curses *'Blyad!'*, letting him go and grabbing the steering wheel.

Panting, Dima collapses back into his seat, and sees that the traffic lights have changed to green, that the traffic is advancing into the snow. The BMW revs noisily, wheels spinning on compacted ice. He slumps against the side window, its glass freezing against his cheek. His chest heaves like he's going to throw up. He starts to retch.

'Don't you dare puke in my car!'

Yuri swerves, left hand on steering wheel, right hand stuffing his cock back inside his pants, and the car cuts across a line of traffic, triggering a screech of brakes and blasts on horns from behind. It hits the kerb, throwing Dima forward against the dashboard, then back against the seat. Another bout of retching, trying not to vomit, and he hears the door unlock, a *clunk* behind his right ear.

'Go on, get out!'

He fumbles with the door handle again. His head spins. He wants to get out, yet craves the warmth of the car, the cradling of Yuri's arms. He wants to break free, yet wants to submit, to hear Yuri murmuring, *That's my boy, Dmitry, that's my boy . . .*

Yuri reaches over and flings the car door open. But before Dima even has time to get out, Yuri rams a fist into his jaw. And again, harder this time. His head reels, like it's parted company with his body. Clutching at the swinging open door, he hangs half outside the car, his face hovering above the gutter, stung by the icy air, and feels his buttocks start to slip off the car seat. Mustn't fall, he thinks, mustn't fall—

'Get the fuck out, you dirty little poof!' Yuri's taken his right foot off the pedals and launches a sideways kick into Dima's left hip, sending him sprawling, out onto the sidewalk. His rump lands on the kerb, and his head is thrown backwards, almost hitting the pavement. From the gutter, he feels ice and slush seep into the top of his boots, and down the side of his face, the dribble of something sticky.

Yuri can't resist a parting shot. '*Back at my place?* Forget it. Down there in the gutter, that's where you are without me.' The door slams shut. More revving, more blaring horns, as Yuri's car screeches back into the traffic.

Gotta get up, he thinks, gotta stand, get my foot out of this puddle. *Blyad*, it's freezing, where's my gloves? He plants his hands, bare hands, on the pavement, wincing as they burn with cold and slither on the icy ground. He hauls himself upright, feeling the squelch of a slush-drenched sock inside his left boot. Snowflakes settle on his nose and forehead. He stumbles to one side, blood trickling from his nose, and collapses against the side of a kiosk. No longer able to hold it back, he gives in to the shock and throws up.

Jamie

'Hey, Jamie, *another* late finish?'

He looks up. Bernie is silhouetted in the doorway, wearing his overcoat and clutching a furry hat. They're the only two left in the office.

'Oh, hiya, Bernie – yeah, there's a new, uh, story I wanna make a start on.'

'A new story? At this hour?' Bernie steps into the room. His face is bearded, careworn, and behind the circular frames of his John Lennon specs, he has eyes that strike Jamie as watery with regret. 'Remember, we go to *print* tomorrow afternoon.'

'Yeah, sure, Bernie, I think I'll—'

'And before we go to print, I need you to cover that American investment conference.'

He groans. More bullshit about big business eyeing up Russia's hungry consumers and cheap workforce. 'But, Bernie, there's a story I've gotta work on . . .'

Bernie peers over his glasses. 'What *is* this story then, Jamie? Moscow's underground gay scene? That's a story I'm *still* waiting for.'

He nods. 'That's the one, Moscow's gay scene. There's been a new development—'

'Well, don't be staying *too* late.' Looking at his watch, Bernie puts his hat on and heads towards the door. 'I need you fresh and alert tomorrow for a quick turnaround on that US-Russian investment story. Now, goodnight, Jamie.'

He listens for the sound of his editor's footsteps fading on their way down the stairs, then scoots over to Larisa's desk and switches on her lamp. Unlike his desk, hers is a vision of order, with neat piles of press ministry paperwork and little reminder notes lined up in a row. Taped to her computer is a photocopy of the Tass bulletin he gave her earlier, the news of Kostya's death. Alongside his scrawl of notes and numbers, she's added a couple of her own, in sloping Russian handwriting. He sits in her seat to get a better look. She's scribbled *Ministry of Healthcare?* but crossed it out, then *Ministry of Justice?*, even *Ministry of Privatisation?*

He frowns. Healthcare, fine, she's inquiring about a hospital. Justice – that'd be the police or the coroner. But *privatisation*? What's Larisa on to? Or is she as confused as he is? There's a phone number too, next to the word *restavratsiya*, 'restoration'. Picking up a pen, he's about to write down the number when the phone rings on his own desk.

Who could be calling him at the office at this time of night? He scoots back and snatches up the receiver. '*Moscow Herald*, James Goodier.'

'Hey, handsome, you gonna get here anytime soon?'

Artyom, of course … Bugger, he's supposed to go over there tonight.

'Artyom, I'm sorry, I've been held up at work—'

'Again? What is it with you and work?'

He grits his teeth. Easy for Artyom to say that, living rent-free in his parents' massive apartment while dragging out his interminable art degree. 'Some of us,' he says, pulling a face at the mouthpiece, '*have* to work for a living.'

'Chill out,' comes the reply. 'We have the whole apartment to ourselves, and I wanna make the most of it – just get here while I'm still in the mood.'

★

His head throbs, groggy after last night's booze and Artyom's home-rolled spliffs. So much for being 'fresh and alert' for Bernie . . . Yawning, he rubs his eyes. Daylight spills through the curtains and into the bedroom – Artyom's *parents'* bedroom, he thinks, feeling a kick of naughtiness. The clock on Artyom's mother's antique dressing table says 7.30 a.m. and, to his side, Artyom is asleep, mouth gaping open and still pungent with dope. His earring glints from beneath the wild brown hair splayed across the pillow.

Reaching out of bed, his hand gropes for his boxer shorts, still lying on the parquet floor where Artyom yanked them off last night. A quick sniff: they're a bit manky, but they'll have to do another day, so he pulls them on, followed by his dark blue chinos and crumpled white office shirt. That'll have to do another day too.

Looking out of the window, facing north across rooftops soft-edged with snow, he sees the golden cupolas of the Kremlin bell-towers, distant but gleaming in the winter sun. All right for some, he thinks, an apartment within sight of the Kremlin – not like his pokey one-room flat out in a suburb of identikit concrete tower blocks. Now, however, with Artyom's parents in New York for the next couple of years, maybe Artyom will ask him to move in? Or will he? Artyom's talk – especially when he's stoned – has been all about emigrating, about getting (as Artyom likes to put it) 'the fuck out of Russia'.

He shuffles into the hallway wearing Artyom's slippers,

pausing to shake his head at one of his boyfriend's 'symbolist' paintings: a jumble of red flags split by a black fissure full of neon dollar signs and titled 'Rupture of Socialism'. He pauses again at the open door to his boyfriend's own bedroom: Artyom's dyke friends Nina and Veronika are there, still asleep and heads on one pillow, Veronika's spiky blondeness buried in the back of Nina's dark bob.

In the dining room, book-lined shelves overlook a table littered with empty beer and vodka bottles, a tablecloth stained with spilt red wine. The ashtray is overflowing. It had been another of those evenings, drunken, argumentative and verging on fatalistic as they debated the future of Russia. Only this time, it was Kostya's fate that had got them all talking.

Nina and Veronika had hit it off with Kostya at Artyom's party last summer – so when he told them the news, it had drawn predictable responses of shock and disbelief: *No way ... How awful ... I can't believe it ... Such a lovely guy ... What a waste ...* Responses that he'd expected, that offered nothing new or insightful. But then the same could be said of his own input: he too had nothing new or insightful to explain Kostya's death – nothing, that is, beyond Dima's speculation about the ambush at the Red Hammer.

'That's where our friend Kirill got beaten up.' Nina put a hand to her mouth in shock. 'And we haven't been able to get hold of him since.'

'No,' Veronika added, 'he must be out of hospital by now, but he's not answering calls. He must still be in shock ...'

Ah, yes, he thought, that'd be the ginger-haired boy he'd seen on the stretcher – but before he could ask for details, Artyom had changed the subject to more general fears of gang beatings or police violence, the gay men incarcerated for their 'disease'.

'I can't see the situation improving,' Artyom had said. 'First chance I get, I'll join my parents in the States and claim asylum there.'

To which Veronika had protested, 'But, Artyom, you emigrating won't make Russia a better place to live for those of us who are stuck here.'

Whatever the threat of violence, she and Nina kept banging on about organising a gay and lesbian 'kiss-in' outside Moscow City Hall. 'If there's enough of us,' she said, 'they'll have to listen. Within ten years, we could win the same rights they have in the West.'

Dream on, Jamie had thought. Yet a part of him admired Nina and Veronika's activism. What good was it for every disaffected Russian to up and leave? And what, he wonders, would Kostik have done? He'd thought of Kostya as he lay awake the night before; if he were still alive, he'd surely want to get out too? Or would he still be tied to Mama's apron strings?

He enters the kitchen. Plates caked with dried-up sauce from the beef stroganoff that Nina and Veronika cooked last night sit abandoned on the pine table. Artyom was supposed to wash up. He sighs, rinses out a mug and switches on the coffee machine that Artyom's father brought back from Germany. As the coffee percolates and he goes to pour himself a cup, he hears the padding of feet on the kitchen lino. Two lean, hairy arms wrap around his chest from behind and he feels warm, moist kisses on the back of his neck.

'Come back to bed, Jamie, c'mon, I'm feeling horny.'

Mmmm, warm kisses on the back of his neck, he's always

liked that … He turns to see Artyom wearing a louche, lop-sided grin and a black T-shirt from a concert tour by Prince. A visible swelling stands proud beneath his paisley-patterned boxer shorts.

'I can't, Artyom, I've gotta go to work.'

Artyom plants a kiss on his lips. That taste of dope again. 'Screw work,' he says.

'I can't screw work—'

'So come and screw me.' Artyom's smile is so wanton, he's tempted to risk being late for Bernie's deadline. Maybe there's time for a quickie …

Artyom says, 'You know it's our anniversary today, don't you?'

For a moment, he's speechless. 'Anniversary?' he echoes.

Artyom pulls his hair back into a ponytail. Somehow that makes him look more sober. 'Yeah. I mentioned it last night, remember?'

He doesn't remember. Is it really a year since they met at Moscow's first 'Discotheque for Sexual Minorities'? Does this mean they're in a 'serious' relationship, that they might shack up together?

'Well, happy anniversary!' he says, kissing Artyom back on the lips. 'Coffee?'

Artyom sinks into a chair at the kitchen table. 'You didn't remember, did you?' he says, fiddling with his ponytail. 'That's why you were still at work when I called last night. What were you doing there so late anyway?'

Sitting down opposite Artyom, he reckons it's best to avert a row by coming clean. 'It wasn't so much work,' he admits. 'In fact, it was to do with Kostya.'

Artyom takes a sip of his coffee and nods at him to go on.

So he explains how he's asked Larisa to look into the reporting of Kostya's death – and how he was accosted outside work
the previous morning by Dima.

Artyom snorts. 'What, you're relying on that snoop from
the press ministry to help you get to the truth? Why would
she help you if there turns out to be a cover-up?'

A shrug. 'It's worth a try, Artyom, I'm desperate—'

'And Dima?' Another of Artyom's snorts. 'Give me a break.
We've seen him out shagging guys left, right and centre. Even
while he was dating Kostya. You know that.'

He *does* know that – yet finds himself striking a defensive
note, echoing Dima's words from the day before: 'That doesn't
mean he doesn't *care*.'

'Oh, yeah?' Artyom folds his arms and nods sarcastically. 'At
least you've got one thing in common with Dima – you both
seem to have more time for Kostya now he's dead than either
of you did when he was alive.'

9

FOURTEEN MONTHS EARLIER

DECEMBER 1991. Moscow

Kostya

'Must think he's a proper big cheese, this boss of yours,' you said, plonking yourself in Mario's black leather chair and swivelling back and forth.

That was the only time you ever came to see me at my new workplace. Not like the old days at the theatre, when you called in every week. It was shortly before you went to England for Christmas, by which time I'd worked at US-Care long enough to know when Mario would be out at one of his many long business lunches.

In those first few weeks, I used to walk into the office of my new boss and pause to drink in its top-floor view of the Moskva river looping past the white marble bulk of the Russian parliament building. *I'm here*, I'd think, I have a job in Moscow! Wasn't this what I wanted, so I could be near you? Wasn't it what *you* wanted too?

Swivel-creak, swivel-creak, went Mario's chair. 'Don't do that!'

I hissed, afraid that one of the other US-Care staff might walk in. 'Sit here instead' – I pointed to Mario's matching black sofa – 'like you're waiting for him.'

The chair rocked and creaked as you leapt out of it. 'What does he actually *do*, anyway?' you asked, jerking your chin towards Mario's enormous desk.

It was a fair question. Mario would spend hours on the phone with his feet up on his desk – a desk whose bulk and absence of clutter announced his elevated status. My own desk, out in the open-plan area, was a different story, piled high with completed application forms to translate, letters to draft, and cost/benefit reports on the cash-strapped Soviet farms and factories – even the police – that came cap-in-hand to US-Care for funding. The rest of my desk was taken up by a hulking grey IBM computer. I'd never even *used* a computer before.

But what, you'd asked me, about my big dream? The theatre? Acting? Directing? 'You haven't given up on that, have you, Kostik?'

Of course I hadn't, I told you. I could pursue that in the evenings or at weekends, I told myself. This'll be temporary, I thought, just while Mama and I needed the money.

Every time Mario called me into his office, I heard that *swivel-creak* of his chair. When he couldn't be bothered to get up, I could hear it over the intercom. He didn't even make his own phone calls. 'Can you get the embassy on the phone, kid?' he'd say, or 'Can you step in here a moment, kid?' Always 'step in', always 'kid'.

To begin with, I'd liked it, being called 'kid'; I liked getting to call my new boss Mario, not 'Mr Waterson'. But any illusion that we were somehow 'equals' was shattered that day when Mario, hurrying out to lunch with the American ambassador, sent me to his apartment to pick up his passport.

Mario's driver, Volodya, ferried me over there in a big American car, and we parked in a guarded compound reserved for Westerners. Once inside, past the steel-plated security doors, my mouth fell open at the sheer size of what must have been two standard-issue Soviet apartments knocked into one. So this was how Mario lived. He'd left the passport lying on a dining table big enough to seat twelve. *United States of America*, it said. I flicked through it, turning the pages this way, then that way, inspecting all the stamps from places I could only dream of going: Rio de Janeiro, Sydney, Barcelona, Cape Town – he had been to nearly every continent.

I lingered, tiptoeing in awe around the apartment, running my fingers along the surfaces of its sleek Scandinavian furnishings. Every inch of it had been expunged of the grubbiness of Soviet existence: no peeling lino, no scuttling cockroaches, no stench of garbage chutes. It was as if Mario – right down to his five senses and bodily functions – had to be insulated, whatever the cost, from the squalor of everyday life. Not for him the crush of the metro or the weary anger of waiting in line that we lesser mortals endured.

It was a picture you had already painted for me. In Western embassies and businesses across Moscow, there appeared to be a caste system, at the top of which were diplomats, foreign correspondents and expatriate businessmen, cosseted in their grand, rent-free apartments. They were chauffeured in Mercedes and Lincolns; they dined in dollar-only restaurants where dinner cost what Mama earned in a month; they drank in dollar-only bars and shopped in dollar-only supermarkets. I found it hard to avoid a sense of Moscow being *colonised*.

Benevolently colonised, perhaps, with all that foreign investment and new jobs – but still, anyone without dollars was
considered a third-class citizen.

I glanced into a large room with a king-size bed, its thick
white duvet crumpled and tossed aside. It faced a big TV set,
a video player and a stack of unlabelled VHS tapes. Lying
discarded on the carpet was a pair of underpants with 'Calvin
Klein' on the waistband. I was about to leave when I spotted a
framed photograph on the bedside table. It showed a middle-
aged man with blond hair and gleaming teeth, taken in what I
imagined to be Californian sunshine, with blue skies and tall
palm trees behind him. On the other side of the room, I saw a
similar framed photo, only in this one the blond guy wasn't
alone but being embraced by another—

A car horn blared from the parking lot. I looked out of
the window and saw Volodya, two floors below, standing in
the snow next to the car, smoking but pressing impatiently
on the horn through the open driver's window.

Back at the office, Mario still hadn't returned from his
lunch. But my errand did not pass without comment. 'I see
Mario's got himself another *secretary*,' said my colleague Nastya,
tottering past on her tarty high heels and smirking from beneath
her glossy fringe.

I saw Volodya return her sly smile and Sveta, the cold-eyed
blonde at the next desk, glanced up from her typing and snig-
gered. But it wasn't the smirking and sniggering that made my
stomach knot; it was the word Nastya had used – *sekretarsha*,
meaning a female secretary. Was it my voice? My mannerisms?
My inability to flirt with them? Nastya and Sveta had already
been asking me how come I wasn't married. Why not, at my
age? Didn't I have a girlfriend?

That wasn't all. Barely weeks after I started at US-Care, Mama was now following me to Moscow. I'd be living with her too, in a flat rented from one of Galina Sergeyevna's Mothers for Peace. I knew what you'd say: that I couldn't cut loose from her, I was 'tied to her apron strings'. As if that weren't enough, she'd be piling on girlfriend questions of her own.

★

I hadn't waited until I 'happened to be' in Moscow – instead I'd taken myself off to see Mario in October, within weeks of our first encounter. US-Care was based in the Mezhdunarodny Trade Centre, which you (already talking like some seasoned expatriate) called 'the Mezh'. It was the most Western building I'd ever set eyes on in Russia: tinted windows towering twenty floors up, a business-class hotel, dollar-only shops, offices with fax machines and computers.

My job 'interview' was a rehash of Mario's spiel about 'American know-how enabling Russian partners'. Instead of quizzing my aptitude, he kept saying 'what you'll be doing' – which made me realise that the job, if I wanted it, was mine. And no, I didn't say, 'This isn't what I really want; I want to work in theatre.' Instead, I followed Arkady Bogdanovich's audition advice and stuck to the script.

Dear old Arkady Bogdanovich ... he'd understand why I was leaving the Voronezh Youth Theatre, wouldn't he? But what about Mama? 'Abandoning' her after Papa had walked out? How would I break the news? Would she beg me, plead with me to stay?

Yet as you know, Mama didn't seem surprised; she must've suspected what we were planning all along. She didn't even ask if *you* had put me up to it. Instead, she took a deep breath and declared that she wouldn't stand in my way. It was only a week or so later, after long conversations conferring with Galina Sergeyevna, that Mama turned the tables on me.

Now I was the one in for a shock. After four months without a pay packet, Mama announced, she was going to quit her job at the library and come with me. She would sublet our apartment. With no salary and no husband, what was there to keep her in Voronezh?

No, Mama, I wanted to say, *please stay in Voronezh and let me get away from you.* Was this what Papa felt? Wanting to get away from her? And let me get away from the shame, the blame, the what-ifs of Papa's leaving. Let me start a new life in Moscow, with Jamie . . . But I didn't say that. She needed me, and I'd be abandoning her, no better than Papa. So here she is, 'piggybacking' on my Moscow residence permit, dragging with her that trunk of belongings – along with all the other baggage of a mother fretful about her unmarried son.

Tamara Borisovna

They're only clothes, she told herself. Don't be silly, feeling *sorry* for them. She stood at the open door of a wardrobe identical to the one she'd left behind in Voronezh, half-empty but for a few garments that were, like her, no longer loved or wanted. It was mostly winter-wear, a fur coat, a quilted anorak – of course, Irina Efraimovna wouldn't be needing those, not in Israel.

A stranger's clothes, a stranger's china dinner service – all in a stranger's apartment. 'There are flats like this all over Moscow these days,' Galina had told her the day she helped her move in. Flats, she meant, belonging to Muscovites who were finally free to emigrate, like Irina Efraimovna; or those able to move into their dachas and rent out their city apartments, often to foreigners for dollars.

There were homes disbanded by broken marriages too. Like her own: Kostya was right about Russia's divorce rates, another thing she kept hearing about, thanks to *glasnost*. At this very moment, her young new tenants would be in her long-time home in Voronezh, rifling through cupboards, frowning in distaste at the stuff she hadn't sold or taken with her.

Apart from its lighter wallpaper – and being three hundred miles away – Irina Efraimovna's flat bore an uncanny resemblance to their home in Voronezh. Kostya would still have a bedroom to himself, and she would sleep on the fold-out sofa. Its standard-issue Soviet floorplan was almost reassuring; it reminded her of the 1970s film *Irony of Fate*, where a drunken man from Moscow is mistakenly put on a flight to Leningrad and ends up in an identical flat in an identical tower block on a street with the same name. Gennady used to love that film. The apartment where her ex-husband was now shacked up with his mistress probably had the same floorplan too.

If only it were as easy as that film's running joke to feel at home in a city where she didn't know a soul. In all her fifty-four years, she had been to Moscow only a handful of times, usually just for the day. In her youth, the very thought of the capital would make her heart leap: May Day parades on Red Square, monuments to Soviet achievements, the sweep of the river past the Kremlin. Now though, all she saw was an angry, intimidating Moscow, its crowds shoving and cursing even harder than they did in Voronezh, and row upon row of destitute babushkas lining the streets trying to sell anything they could lay their hands on. And those who didn't need to shove or curse – the Party bigwigs or new self-styled *biznessmen* who never took the metro but rode in black-windowed cars – made her feel dowdy and provincial.

'I won't have you being lonely, hear?' Galina had said, wagging a finger at her. 'I'll make sure you get involved with Mothers for Peace.' Hmm, she thought, maybe she should do that, go make new friends. Can't be sitting around the flat all day. But not yet, she wasn't ready. What she needed, for her self-respect and to keep herself busy, was to find a job.

*

'So, Mrs Krolikova,' the young woman with slick blonde hair and a pale pink suit had asked, clasping her hands on the desk in front of her, 'why should Stockmann employ you?'

Why employ me? Tamara had thought. Because I need the money, that's why ... But the question, in weird, foreign-accented Russian, had been 'why *should*?' She didn't know how to answer that; there was no 'should' about it.

'Oh, you don't have to hire *me*,' she'd replied, quite innocently, 'not if you've got other people you'd prefer – young girls, I expect.'

The young woman in the suit gave a little chuckle. 'What I mean, *gospozha* Krolikova' (she'd never been called 'Mrs' before – only ever Tamara Borisovna – and 'Mrs' struck her as a rather forced courtesy) 'is what qualities can you bring to this customer-focused role?'

What *qualities*? For heaven's sake, she had run the public education section of the best library in Voronezh for twenty years. Qualities, indeed! The job for which she was being interviewed was to stack shelves and serve customers at the checkout, that's all. It was Jamie who'd alerted her to vacancies advertised in the newspaper he worked for, jobs for Russian staff at a new Finnish-owned supermarket near Paveletsky

Station. The English boy thought he was being helpful, but tactlessly added, 'It'll pay way more than you earned at the library.'

Kostya had then helped her write an application letter to some woman with a funny Finnish name at something called 'Human Resources'. Turned out it was this girl in front of her doing the interviews, one young enough to be her daughter.

She must have hesitated too long because the young woman answered the question for her: 'Well, I see from your résumé that you have a track record in end-user satisfaction. That makes a good fit with our merchandise display operations.'

What? The girl might as well have been speaking in Finnish. Tamara just nodded.

'And you have a basic command of English, which is the interface language of the bulk of our client base.' Ah, now that she understood: most of the customers speak English, that's what she means.

More gobbledygook followed about 'catering to an aspirational demographic', plus a few questions about Tamara's education and what her son was doing in Moscow. Then, to her surprise, the girl had stood up to indicate that the interview was over.

'I think,' she announced, 'we're in a position to offer you a contract.' She'd smiled and offered her a hand to shake. '*Gospozha* Krolikova – welcome to Stockmann.'

★

So much for 'merchandise display operations', she thought, massaging the small of her back at the end of another nine-hour shift. Shelf-stacking, they called it in my day.

That said, Stockmann's shelves were – she had to admit – exactly how Kostya described supermarkets in England: always full, almost overflowing with choice and luxury. It was nothing like the Soviet shops she was used to. Nothing like the futile hope that the jars of mayonnaise spotted one day would be there the next. Nothing like that stench, that rancid cocktail of dried fish and dirty dishwater. But why? Wasn't the Soviet system the best in the world? Hadn't Khrushchev promised her generation that their country would 'bury' the West?

Yet although Stockmann's shelves were always full, they also always needed to be replenished. The minute any gap appeared amid its fleshy packs of Norwegian smoked salmon or bottles of Finnish vodka (what, she wondered, was wrong with Russian vodka?), she had to abandon whatever shelf she was crouched over, wheel her rattling little trolley out to the cold store and rush back to fill the gaps. On no account could a shelf be left looking bare – there was sure to be some picky German executive or French embassy wife, complaining that they needed lobster or foie gras for a 'working lunch' or cocktail party.

One day, when she was on the checkouts, a loud American man wearing a suit and smelling of cologne asked for someone to pack his groceries for him. 'That's what they'd do in the States,' he'd said, 'especially when I'm spending a hundred dollars.' In the end, she packed his shopping herself, carefully cushioning his bottles of whisky between bags of Danish muesli. Even so, as the American left, he'd muttered something about sending his driver next time.

Kostya

Towards the end of December, by the time you'd gone to England for Christmas, I had decided on a New Year's resolution. I was embarrassed to mention it to you, in case you thought it vain or just plain 'daft'– but I felt that I deserved to spend my wages from US-Care on treating myself to something I really, really wanted.

One night after work, I was on my way out of the metro near the flat Mama and I were renting when I spotted an advert glued to the wall. *Going bald?* it asked, in big block capitals. *Don't let hair loss ruin your looks!* The advert displayed two heads photographed from above, presumably the same man, but with one labelled 'Before' and the other 'After'. 'Before' had an unsightly dome of shiny scalp between his ears, while 'After' sported a thick mane of lustrous healthy hair that could be gelled and spiked and sexy, like yours.

I slid my fingers under my woolly cap and felt the scalp where my curls had given up and only lank strands remained. I was going bald. No wonder you never found me attractive.

The bottom of the ad was cut into little strips, each with a printed telephone number, and gave an address for a hair restoration clinic at the end of the metro line. I could go there in the evenings after work and tell Mama I'd be late home, that I was meeting you. I tore off one of those phone-numbered strips and resolved to make an appointment in January.

★

But before then, Mama and I had the New Year holiday to get through. My boyhood memories of this Soviet 'Christmas' were largely happy ones: visits from friends and aunts and uncles, decorations on the fir tree and presents beneath it. Mama and Papa would have called in favours and hoarded food, so our table overflowed with roast duck and salmon, chocolates and oranges. It was a chance for Papa to play the host, waving away Mama's thrift and indulging his love of what was out-of-bounds, smoking Cuban cigars and cracking open the cognac.

The end of 1991 was nothing like that. No Papa, no decorations, none of the snugness of the home I'd been raised in. Mama put on a brave face, busying herself in the kitchen, roasting the chicken that Stockmann gave its staff for Christmas. Otherwise, the days running up to New Year were like the days of the August coup all over again, Mama and me clutching glasses of tea in front of the TV set.

When December 25 came, I thought of you. In England, it would be Christmas Day, and you'd be home in Manchester with your mum, dad and Lisa – probably burping, knowing you, after your plum pudding. Maybe you'd all watch *A Christmas Carol* on TV. Did it even snow in England, the way Dickens described it? In Moscow, it snowed for real.

As we sat in front of the television, Mama and me, I hoped to avoid a row like the one we'd had in August. Remember me telling you how she'd welcomed the coup, the prospect of restoring the nation of her youth? Well, she had no such hope of turning back the clock this time: as Gorbachev gave in to the collapse of the Soviet Union, his resignation as leader was inevitable. Out of morbid fascination, we both stayed up late to watch it all unfold. Outside, although it was six days before New Year's Eve, someone let off fireworks that banged and crackled in the night sky. From the flat above came a stomping of feet – sounded like they were dancing.

That December 25, Mama and I sat like cuckoos in Irina Efraimovna's abandoned nest. Our eyes didn't meet, staring instead at the TV set, transfixed by the sight of the Soviet flag being lowered above the Kremlin for the last time. A spotlight was trained on its sagging scarlet folds as it descended, and with it sank a vision of the nation Mama believed in. In its place rose the white, blue and red tricolour of the Russian Federation. Yeltsin's new Russia, they declared. Mama held her head in her hands. In that final week of 1991, not only were we no longer living in the home I'd known all my life: we were no longer even living in the same country.

10

FEBRUARY 1993. Moscow

Jamie

He arrives at work a couple of days later to find Larisa on the phone. '*Da, da*,' she's mumbling to whoever it is on the line, '*nyet, nyet*.' She barely looks at him as he walks in – just a flicker of her silver-daubed eyelids – but keeps her gaze lowered to her desk, where she's arranging another row of her little reminder notes.

There's no one at the other desks except Pushy Patsy, who's also on the phone, receiver cradled between jaw and shoulder. She types noisily, going 'uh-uh' every five seconds. He slings his coat over his chair, sits at his desk and looks across at Larisa again, itching to ask her what – if anything – she has found out about Kostya. But no: she's avoiding eye contact.

Suppose that's what she's phoning about right now? He tries to listen in, hunching close behind his computer and keeping one ear cocked in Larisa's direction. Her voice is lowered, a sullen babble of Russian from which he catches the odd word – *kontrakt* and *litsenziya*, 'licence', then *vzyatki*, 'bribes' ... Whoever she's talking to, dialling, redialling, asking to be connected, her tone of voice suggests they're people in positions of authority.

Eventually she puts the phone down. Now she catches his eye. She stands, adjusts her silvery blouse and totters into the kitchen. Patsy's still on the phone, still going 'uh-uh'. He waits, barely half a minute, then follows. He finds Larisa alone in the kitchen, by the samovar, dipping a teabag in a cup of boiling water. He grabs a mug from the draining board.

She glares at him and hisses, 'What's the big deal with this Krolikov guy?'

He puts a teabag in his mug and stands next to her. 'How d'you mean?'

'I mean, was he involved in bribery? Awarding contracts? Anything like that?'

'*Bribery?*' He can't believe what she's asking.

'Yes, bribery.' Larisa looks around, as if to check no one's listening in, then whispers, 'The privatisation ministry doesn't hand out business contracts for free, you know—'

'*Privatisation?*' One of the words she'd scrawled on the news bulletin ... Was Kostya caught up in some dodgy sell-off of state assets? A money-spinner that attracted criminals? After all, his job at US-Care involved handouts to cash-strapped Soviet factories and the like ...

Still, that seems far-fetched. He shakes his head. 'Nah, not Kostya—'

'*Kostya?*' She frowns. 'You mean, you *knew* him?'

Shit, he thinks, shouldn't have let that slip ... He sighs, then offers a sheepish nod.

She turns away, dropping her used teabag in the sink. 'So, this is personal?'

'You could say that.' He pours boiling water from the

samovar into his mug, drops three sugar cubes in and stirs his tea, staring into it. 'He was a friend of mine. His death's come out of the blue, totally unexplained. And I didn't hear about him being ill, I hadn't seen him for—'

Larisa places a hand on his, putting a halt to his agitated stirring. He looks at her. She pulls a sympathetic face, eyes droopy and mouth downturned. 'I'm sorry about your friend,' she says. 'But I haven't found much else to go on. All the police and the coroner say is "natural causes" – that could mean heart failure, choking, anything.'

Silence. Then she adds, '*Dzheymz*, remember you're in Russia. When people die here, you don't always get what the Americans call "closure". In our country, I'm afraid, life is—'

'Cheap?' he says, finishing her sentence. He's said it enough times himself, hasn't he, acting like the hardened expert. *In Russia, life is cheap.*

*

Dusk has fallen. Apart from lamplight on desks, the office is in darkness. Only the tapping of fingers on keyboards and the intermittent chatter of the teletype machines punctuates the quiet. It's just like the night he heard the news about Kostya.

At the desk to his right, Patsy hammers away on her keyboard, a pencil clenched between her teeth. What the hell's she working on this late? And when is she going to bloody leave? At the other end of the room, Larisa is muttering away on the phone again.

Standing up, he catches her eye as he passes her desk on his way to the loo. No good for his bladder, these endless mugs of tea. He closes the toilet door and unzips himself. Ah, the relief . . . The noise of his peeing blocks any sound from outside. Once he's done, he goes into the bathroom next door, washing his hands with scummy Soviet soap that smells of lard. Back in the hallway, he sees that Patsy is now in Bernie's office, hunched over the Xerox machine.

But Larisa has gone. That's funny, didn't hear her leaving . . . Maybe he should call it a day too. But as he lifts his coat off his chair, he spots a little envelope propped up against his keyboard. *Dzheymz* is all it says, in what he instantly recognises as Larisa's handwriting.

Dima

Only now, with Kostya dead and buried, has he bothered to pin his photo of Kostya on the wall. It's the photo he showed Igor at the disco – Kostya in his 1970s-style shirt, blushing beneath a tree laden with blossom. It's looking worse for wear after being in his jacket pocket, and he runs his fingers round its edges, trying to smooth out the creases and press it flat against the wallpaper. From the next room comes a murmur of voices, probably Valery Ivanovich's radio.

He's pinned Kostya next to the photo of his mum, a black-and-white portrait from the late 1970s. She looked so youthful then, before his dad left, head tilted to one side and a curtain of blonde hair falling to her shoulder. From her spot on his bedside wall, she looks right at him with that smile she wore every time she caught him telling lies.

Last time he was in Latvia to see her and Petya, he had bigged up his 'film career' in Moscow, taking care to omit any details. 'My future's in videos,' was all he'd told them. That time he *wasn't* lying: he'd believed it; if he earned enough on the back of Yuri's own success, he could look after them both and fill Dad's shoes. That was over a year ago. Since then, he hasn't even found a free weekend or spare cash for the train fare to go visit them again.

He sinks the right-hand side of his head into his pillow, letting air circulate around the left-hand side, where Yuri battered him. 'I've had it with Moscow,' he whispers, reaching to touch the photo of Mum. 'Can I come home?' Both photos, his mother and Kostya, seem to float from side to side, drifting in and out of focus. He lifts his head, then lets it collapse back on the pillow. With his fingertips to his face, he probes around the swelling on his cheekbone.

Looking across the room, he sees Oleg's bed is empty; a chance to inspect his injury in the mirror again. He hauls himself up, having to steady his head in his hands, and then, wearing nothing but the Calvin Kleins he wore for the shoot with that creepy 'Other Kostya', he shambles over to the wardrobe. He squints at the mirror. A bloodshot left eye stares back at him, an eye now ringed with patches of black and purple where Yuri's fist had made contact.

The *bastard*. Yuri's never been violent with him before. Macho, yeah, dominant, yeah – and sure, Yuri's always the one in charge, ordering him to his knees to give the blowjobs that Yuri seemed to expect on tap. Yuri would even summon him after a session in the boxing gym, high on adrenaline and knowing that Dima couldn't resist that cocktail of muscle, silky shorts and testosterone. But never before had Yuri left him with a physical injury.

For a second, he wonders whether his black eye excuses him from his next shoot. But no, there won't *be* another shoot. Yuri has 'fired' him, hasn't he? Dumped him, even. *In the gutter, that's where you are without me.* Those were Yuri's parting words. And as for—

The door opens. Oleg's standing there, in his slippers and pyjamas. He looks shaken. 'Dimik,' he says, 'you'd better get dressed.'

'Wh-what's happened?' He sits on his bed to pull on his tracksuit bottoms and a T-shirt – and realises, now the door's open, that it wasn't Valery Ivanovich's radio he could hear but Oleg's voice and that of a woman. A voice he now recognises as Valery's daughter. What the hell is *she* doing here at this time of day?

He steps into the hallway, rubbing his eyes, feigning an exaggerated yawn. 'Morning, Alla Valeryevna. Uh, what's going on?'

Alla Valeryevna scowls at him. A short, bustling woman in her fifties, she has severe, dyed hair and eyes that dart about from floor to ceiling in a restless search for things to find fault with. She is dressed like she's not long ago come in off the street, still wearing a long black overcoat and a silvery fur hat.

'What's *going on*?' She looks him up and down, but her glare keeps returning to his black eye. 'I might ask *you* the same thing, young man.'

'What, this?' he mumbles, waving his hand around his eye. 'Oh, I had a fall the other night. I slipped on the ice—'

'You think this is funny, do you?'

Her lips are tight, her eyes drilling into his. He sees Oleg grimace.

'I don't understand what you mean, Alla Valeryevna.'

'I mean, are you *mocking* my father?'

Mocking Valery Ivanovich? What is she talking about? 'Course not,' he says, frowning. 'Why would I do that?'

Oleg looks up and steps between them. 'Dimik, listen,' he says, 'Valery Ivan'ich has had an accident. He went out and—'

'He *slipped on the ice and fell.*' Still glaring at Dima, the daughter makes her point.

Shit. *That's* why she thinks he's taking the piss. His hand goes to his forehead. 'Alla Valeryevna, forgive me, I had no idea—'

'He's sprained his wrist and got bruising around the ribs,' Oleg says. 'I've suggested we could look after Valery Ivan'ich, at least until—'

'Father was out at six-thirty this morning to stand in line for milk,' Alla snaps. 'Which he shouldn't be doing in this wea-ther. Of course, he didn't see how icy it was, and he was carrying too much for a man of his age.'

Six-thirty in the morning? He glances at the clock on the wall: it's past ten already. Feebly, he protests, 'But you know how much Valery Ivan'ich insists on doing things himself. He values his independence.'

Her nostrils flare. 'Now *you're* trying to give me the brush-off too, like him.' She jerks her head towards Oleg. 'It's a good job Nadezhda Nikolayevna downstairs helped him back inside. If she hadn't phoned me, God knows, he'd still be out there.'

Behind Alla Valeryevna, the landlord's bedroom door stands wide open. On the rare occasions that Dima's entered the room, he's balked at the murk and squalor, curtains closed all winter and old newspapers piled knee-high from the floor. Today though, the curtains are open and pale February sun-light catches on the film of dust covering the shelves and the stray hairs on the landlord's armchair. But what hits him most is that Valery Ivanovich has gone: his bed stripped to reveal brownish-yellow stains on a mattress blistered with rips and holes; his slippers and bathrobe nowhere in sight – even his shoes are missing from the hallway. He's on the point of asking what's happened when Alla Valeryevna appears to read his mind.

'Father,' she sniffs, buttoning up her coat, 'has spent his last night in this *dump*.' She jerks her head towards Valery's room. 'As you may know, I've found him a place in a nursing home – a private one, it's certainly costing me enough – and I've decided it's time for him to take up that place. Starting today.'

'*Today*?' he hears himself echo.

'Today,' Alla repeats. 'Why wait? It's clear that he can't look after himself – and it's been a fat lot of good having two lay-about young men living under his roof.'

Oleg tries to protest. 'But we *can* look after him.' He looks to Dima. 'Both of us. We can—' Alla cuts him off again, holding up a hand and pulling on her black leather gloves.

'I'm going now,' she says, turning to the door, but looking from him to Oleg and back. 'My husband's waiting in the car. With Father. We'll be back later for the rest of his clothes and so on.' She wrinkles her nose and peers into Valery Ivanovich's room. 'Though there's a lot of stuff here that'll need chucking out.'

Dima holds his head in both hands, as if reeling from Yuri's punch to the face. He looks up to see a thin smile on Alla's lips, her eyes twitchy but gleaming, a look of victory.

'And of course,' she adds, her parting shot, 'this means you two can't carry on living here and paying, quite frankly, *peanuts* in rent.'

Jamie

That's three days in a row Larisa hasn't shown up to work. On Monday, Bernie told him she was off sick, that's all. Tuesday, the same. By Wednesday, however, he starts to worry – not least because he needs to quiz her about the cryptic note she left him, going to the lengths of sealing it in an envelope. It's all a bit 'for your eyes only', he thinks, taking it out of his desk drawer and studying it again. There's nothing more than an address, scribbled on one of Larisa's little reminder notes – but an address that doesn't quite add up: the name of a street in Khimki and, puzzlingly, the number of an apartment.

Another day goes by, then another. Still no Larisa, and Bernie on and off the phone to the Ministry of Press and Information, until one morning the editor shambles in to tell him, Josh and Patsy that the ministry has 'reassigned' Larisa to a job at another newspaper – he couldn't say where – and that they'd appoint a replacement in due course.

Oh shit, he thinks. Larisa had clearly incurred the displeasure of someone high up in whichever ministry – could be healthcare, could be privatisation – because of those inquiries about Kostya . . . Inquiries about bribes and contracts, she said. Inquiries on his behalf. He doesn't even know how to contact her to say thank you or, for that matter, sorry.

He stops by Larisa's desk. There's something sad and unfinished about her abandoned line-up of reminder notes, stuck to the desk alongside her in-tray. Her photocopy of the bulletin reporting Kostya's death is still there too, taped to the bottom of her computer screen. With a glance across the room to make sure Patsy and Josh don't see, he tears it off, takes it to his desk and slips it inside the envelope.

★

Bernie has asked him for a word before he leaves. He taps on the editor's door and steps into his office. Bernie is bent over his electric typewriter, his brow furrowed in the lamplight.

'Hey, Jamie,' he says, still typing. 'Bear with me. Just doing some late admin here – you know, press accreditation, visas, stuff I should've gotten Larisa to take care of.'

Bugger, this isn't about Larisa, is it? He sits, facing Bernie across his desk and waits. Eventually Bernie reaches behind him for a copy of the most recent *Moscow Times*, then hands it to Jamie, his finger pointing at the front-page story.

The headline reads: *Russia to maintain thousands of troops in former Soviet territories.* The byline, of course, is *by Oliver Rutland-Kerr* . . .

'*That*' – Bernie taps the newspaper with his finger – 'is the calibre of journalism we need to be producing.' He looks at Jamie over the top of his specs. 'You were at the same Foreign Ministry press briefing – how could you miss a big news story like that?'

'Oh, shit.' He draws his hands down his face and, not knowing what else to say, just mumbles, 'I'm sorry, Bernie, I've been distracted of late.'

'Distracted by what, Jamie? I'm not seeing you deliver many other stories.'

Bernie's eyes hang with a look of world-weariness, of disappointment rather than rage. Yelling at people isn't his style. Now, Jamie thinks, is the time to talk. And so he tells his editor about Kostya – about hearing of his death in a Tass news bulletin, about not knowing how he died, about the raid on the disco, not being able to pin down the relevant authorities.

Bernie leans forward over his typewriter, fingertips pressed together. 'I'm real sorry about your friend,' he says. 'I gave you time off for his funeral, right? But is this a *story* for us? We have limited resources' – Bernie performs a half-swivel in his chair, palms upturned to indicate the 1950s one-bedroom flat that is the *Herald*'s news operation – 'and only three or four reporters, so I need us focused on stories that sell the *Herald* to its mainly American readers.'

OK, Jamie thinks, time to fess up. 'Larisa was on to something,' he blurts out. 'Some trail pointing to bribery, privatisation, dodgy contracts—'

'*Larisa?*' Bernie removes his specs. 'You mean you had Larisa chasing down sensitive stuff like that? So *that's* why she's been reassigned, because—'

'Bernie, I had no choice. She's the only one here' – like Bernie, he gestures at the tiny office around them – 'who's got insider contacts high up in government ministries. We don't. Besides, isn't it – I mean, *wasn't it* – her job to do that kind of research for us?'

'Jeez.' Bernie slumps back in his chair. He lets out a sigh. 'This is a real headache for me, the Russian press ministry ain't happy ...' He draws a hand down his face. 'Still, they're gonna assign someone else – someone who'll keep tabs on us though, not "research" for us.'

'But reassigning Larisa, her being on to something fishy – isn't that precisely what makes this a story?' This is it, he thinks, I'm making a strong case. 'What's that expression? *News is what someone somewhere doesn't want reporting. The rest is advertising.*'

Bernie nods, half frowning but half smiling. 'True enough. That's what I was taught. But what else do we have to go on, apart from those thugs attacking a gay disco?'

He remembers what he told Larisa in the kitchen last week. 'You know, there *is* an angle of interest to American readers,' he says. 'Kostya was employed by a US trade organisation.'

Bernie sits up, puts his glasses back on. 'You don't mean US-Care, do you?'

He nods. 'I do. The US Commission for Assistance to the Russian Economy. Sponsors of that American investment conference—'

'Whoa, whoa.' Bernie holds up his hands, a gesture of mock surrender. 'US-Care should of course be concerned for the safety of its staff in Moscow – but we'd have a problem if your story suggests a *connection* between your friend's death and his job.'

He frowns. Has he oversold the story? After all, Kostya was a pen-pusher, not a big shot like his boss Waterson. His frown must be plain to see because Bernie leans across his desk and says, 'Jamie, we can ill afford to upset or, God forbid, libel US-Care. We depend on them for readers – and advertising.'

Dima

People scurry past him into the metro, eyes scrunched up against the blizzard, faces obscured by big furry hats. But no sign of the beer-breath *muzhik* who offered to buy his lumberjack boots. Only yesterday, the man came up to him, pointed at his feet and asked, 'How much for those?' *These?* Dima said, sorry, bro, these aren't for sale. And they weren't, not yesterday at least – he needed something winter-proof on his feet.

But then the *muzhik* offered him fifty dollars. A hundred, Dima said. They settled on seventy and the guy said he'd be back. So now he's wearing these crappy Soviet-made boots coming apart at the seams. His beloved Timberlands, hard-earned in front of Yuri's camera, stand displayed on an upturned crate on the pavement in front of him. Next to them, laid out on flattened cardboard to keep them out of the snow, are some ten-pack blocks of Marlboros and his biker jacket, the jacket he was wearing the night he met Kostya.

His teeth chatter as he beats his chest to keep warm. Thank God he's kept his puffer jacket. His first day on this patch, he took his place alongside the babushkas hawking jars of pickles and hand-knitted socks, and he managed to sell his Nike trainers – only for roubles, mind, when he should've held out for dollars. God knows, he needs the money now he's been canned by Yuri – and now that Alla Valeryevna is evicting them. Only if they forked out four times their old rent – *four times* – would she allow him and Oleg to stay. Would that be money to pay for Valery's private nursing home, he wondered, or would she just pocket it?

From where he's standing, he can see the vodka kiosk by the payphone where he made that call to Kostya's mother. They say vodka keeps you warm – it's certainly getting more takers than the babushkas' socks – and that line of red-faced men is always there, day or night. He takes a drag on his cigarette. After a year on Marlboros, this Soviet-made crap burns his throat and makes his eyes water. If only he'd listened to Kostya and quit smoking altogether. If only he still had Kostya to shack up with and keep him off the streets.

*

When he gets back to the flat, the two workmen in grey overalls are still there repainting Valery Ivanovich's room. Their banter subsides as he comes in – but not before he's overheard one of them boast that business is good, that people all over Moscow are renovating their apartments and renting them out.

'D'you reckon they'll get dollars for this place?' the younger one asks.

The older one laughs. 'Well, they'll get more than the old boy was charging!'

He coughs loudly, stepping into the room to offer them tea — not for hospitality's sake, but to remind them that he still lives here, for now. The younger guy is halfway up a ladder. 'Got any beer, mate?' he asks.

Dima shakes his head, thinking *fuck off*. He has a whole crate of beer under his bed, but needs it to sell, he needs the cash. He looks around the room and inhales: the smell of dust and pee has gone, along with all traces of Valery Ivanovich. No creaky old armchair, no yellowing lace curtains, no wilting pot plants. Even the manky patterned wallpaper is disappearing under a disinfectant-smelling white.

He wanders into the room he's shared with Oleg these past two years. On the floor sits a laundry sack of summer clothes, including the shorts that got him shouted at by a babushka when he wore them on the street last July. I'll sell those when the thaw comes, he thinks. He rifles through his wallet. In the end, the *muzhik* had turned up as night fell, but cut his offer to sixty dollars. That meant goodbye to his Timberlands.

He sits on his bed. Oleg's wall is bare, with faint patches where his posters once shielded the wallpaper from cigarette smoke. The biggest patch is where Jean-Claude Van Damme used to be. Lucky Oleg, he thinks. Shortly before their eviction, his 'partner in crime' was offered a place in a student dorm, sharing a room with three other guys; Oleg got lucky because someone dropped out of film school, like he himself had dropped out.

Next week, it's the turn of their old room to be redecorated. Then he'll have nowhere to stay. Maybe he should just go to the station and buy a one-way train ticket for Latvia.

His photos of Mum and Kostya are packed in his rucksack now, along with his poster for *My Own Private Idaho*. He unrolls it, picturing himself and Oleg as River Phoenix and Keanu Reeves, in that film star life he's never going to have. He's found a book Kostya gave him too: translations of plays by English playwrights, George Bernard Shaw, Oscar Wilde and one he's never heard of, J. B. Priestley. It's signed on the front page – *To my handsome Prince Dima, 'My Own Private' Superman, all my love, Kostya.*

I should read this, he thinks, I owe it to Kostya. He sandwiches it in his rucksack next to that photo of Mum, again catching that look on her face. Yes, Mum, I *have* been telling you lies – I don't have a future in videos, or anywhere to live, or anyone to love me—

The phone rings, loud and stark in a hallway with no hanging coats to muffle the sound. Only two months ago, he thinks, that might have been Kostya, phoning like he did almost every day . . . He hears a pause in the banter of the two workmen painting next door.

Another long ring. The older workman shouts, 'Is that for you, son?'

'I'm coming.' He drags himself into the hallway and picks up the phone just as its clatter breaks out again. '*Allo?*'

'*Allo?* Is that Dima?' The voice takes him a couple of seconds to recognise, a young man's voice, with an accent – someone who's never had cause to call here before.

'*Dzheymz?* Is that you?'

'Yeah, me.' He hears throat-clearing down the line. 'But hey – call me Jamie.'

Jamie? he thinks. Are we supposed to be buddies now or something? 'All right then, *Jamie.*' He scowls at the phone. 'What d'you want?'

'C'mon, Dima,' – the English guy's voice is low too, like he's trying not to be overheard – 'I want the same thing as you, don't I?'

'I see,' he says, thinking back to his encounter with Jamie, how the cocky little shit had all but accused him of infecting Kostya with Aids. What does he mean, *want the same thing*? Unless of course— 'You mean, this business about Kostya?'

'That's right,' comes Jamie's voice. 'You offered to help, remember?'

Help? Jamie means help to get to the bottom of Kostya's death. Help that Jamie would have to pay him for. That would be his only reason to stay in Moscow. 'OK, what about it?'

'Let's not discuss it on the phone,' Jamie replies. 'Can you meet me tomorrow? I've had a tip-off. There's a job that only you can do for me.'

11

ONE YEAR EARLIER

FEBRUARY 1992. Moscow

Kostya

Something about the treatment would always make me sleepy. I used to lie there staring at the ceiling, the fluorescent strip light humming its monotone hum and flickering in and out of my consciousness until, invariably, I drifted off. It might have been the foul-tasting herbal brew they made me drink, or the effect of the needles stuck in my arms. It might have been the electrodes taped to my head, or the gritty lotion they massaged into my bald patch.

You would've laughed if you'd seen where I used to disappear one evening a week after work. If I hadn't been too embarrassed to tell you, we would've had a good laugh about it together. Funniest of all was the 'healer' the clinic employed, a woman with a white lab-coat and frizzy hair – looked like she'd had a dose of the electrodes herself – her brow furrowed as she circled her hands around my head. 'Feel the healing energy,' she would urge me, first whispering, then rising to a chant. '*Feel* the healing energy!'

The place called itself 'Restoration' or something, and was housed in an apartment a few bus stops' ride from the last metro station on the line. The slogan on its waiting-room wall – a variation of the advert I'd spotted before New Year – was *Your Hair is Your Face*, a slogan that summed up my fears of going bald, of being ugly.

Would it work, the needles, the herbal brew, that crazy woman's 'healing energy'? Maybe, maybe not – but I was desperate for a cure and kept checking in the mirror for signs of renewed hair growth. You would have laughed *at* me, not with me. 'Kostik, they're ripping you off,' you'd have said. 'They saw you coming.'

*

The four of us sat at one end of the carriage as the metro rattled towards the city's outskirts. No one else was heading that direction at this late hour on a wintry Saturday night, so apart from me and you – and your new friends Jules and Rasmus – the carriage was almost empty, giving you free rein to joke and tease each other. It was the sort of joshing I recognised from your university house-share, all point-scoring and put-downs: which one of you would get laid, who'd be going home alone tonight.

I tried to join in. 'Let's mess Jamie's hair up!' I said. 'That'll spoil his chances!' And I made as if to scrunch your spiky gelled locks between my fingers. You recoiled, growling, 'Get off, Kostik!' and looking up and down the carriage as if embarrassed by me. The other two laughed uneasily, exchanging glances while you checked your reflection in the window.

I recognised it, that 'out on the pull' look you were wear-ing. You looked the same that night in Birmingham a year earlier, when you ditched me for a 'snog' with a stranger. I should have known this wouldn't be 'our' night out. I'd told Mama I would be at a party with you and staying the night at your place – but I could see you'd much rather be with the cool expat friends you'd been banging on about since you returned after Christmas: Jules, a copper-skinned Belgian of Mauritian parentage who worked for a law firm, and Rasmus, a tall, blond Swede employed by some furniture company opening soon in Moscow.

I gave up trying to join in and fell silent until we exited the last station. Out on the street, thick snowdrifts glistened in the moonlight and icicles knifed their way down the windows of the tram shelter where we stood, shivering. The street was deserted – it was almost 10 p.m. by now – and I gazed at the block of flats opposite, at its hive of windows, kitchens and bedrooms, little squares glowing with warmth and cosiness, and wished that I, like the inhabitants of that hive, was at home instead of this freezing street corner with you and two stran-gers. I pulled my woolly hat tight over my ears, remembering the clinic's advice that exposure to sub-zero air could stunt what little was left of my hair follicles.

Jules pulled his ski cap on too and started rubbing his hands together to warm them. 'You sure we have the right place?' he asked. 'Didn't anyone else phone to check for directions?' He gave me a smile, trying to include me. 'What about you, Kostya?'

I fumbled in my pocket for the scrap of paper I'd scribbled on earlier. 'They said catch tram number 34, go three stops, get off at Kolkhoz Street, then go down the street towards Agri-cultural Institute No. 16—'

'Jesus, could they pick somewhere more out of the fucking way?' Your words were spat with contempt from between chattering teeth; yet despite the cold, you were determined not to wear a hat – anything not to ruin your precious hairstyle.

'What d'you expect?' I said, turning to face you. 'You think they can hold a disco like this in full view, at the side of Red Square?'

'Duh, *no*,' you said, with a frown. 'But it doesn't exactly inspire confidence, does it, having to hide out here in the sticks?'

'Guys, let's just wait for the tram, eh?' Rasmus intervened. 'Then we'll follow the directions Kostya's written down and take it from there.'

Silence descended, snuffing out the banter I'd had to listen to on the metro. It was more than the chill of the moonlit night or the inky darkness pressing in from beyond the lamp-lit tram shelter – it was your mates realising how different this was from your neon-lit nightclubs. When you first told me about it, you'd sounded so *excited*, like it was something out of a spy novel, or material for one of your articles. But I could see – from the organisers' guardedness, the telephone number circulated by word of mouth, the answering machine and recorded message, the secretive directions – that this was a place on the lookout for danger.

I felt a rumble underfoot and heard a twang from the rails gleaming under the street light. You sighed with relief as the tram trundled up and squealed to a halt. We boarded at the front, near the driver, then heard a commotion: another four lads in padded coats and woolly hats had come running and got on at the back. They took their seats and eyed us down the length of the tram, intermittently disappearing from view each time it rounded a bend and its two carriages flexed inwards, then outwards, together, then apart. Soon, one of them started giggling and it was clear that they were *nashi*, our type.

I know you thought I should be excited. That this first gay disco pointed the way to the sunlit post-*glasnost* Russia that we had so often evoked in our late-night conversations. Instead, I was thinking how much it reminded me of my trips to the baldness clinic: the semi-legal activity made to disappear amid the outer fringes of Moscow, in suburbs like Strogino or Korolyov or Khimki, where Stalinist boulevards gave way to wind-blasted tower blocks, then to the forests and wilderness beyond.

We travelled one stop, then two, then three, and got off the tram, as directed, at Kolkhoz Street. So too did the giggling boys from the back. Keeping about twenty metres behind, we followed them down a road pockmarked with frozen puddles that reflected the night sky. Two of them, still wary of us, looked over their shoulders. Clearly, they'd been given the same directions, turning left through the gates of Agricultural Institute No. 16, a slab of concrete with six storeys of unlit windows, little more than rows of black rectangles. No neon, no queues of revellers – just a slogan running along the roof-top: *Forward to the Victory of Communism!*, the letters black and jagged against moonlit cloud.

'*Victory of Communism*, my arse!' you said, pointing to the slogan. 'A victory for capitalism is what this country needs.'

We watched the lads from the tram being allowed in, then I rang the buzzer for us. A panel in the door slid aside to reveal a pair of eyes. I gave the password from the recorded message and the door opened; the organisers had hired a pair of doormen in combat gear who searched us for knives and pointed us towards the cloakroom. There, we found ourselves in a queue behind the boys from the tram and, once we'd deposited our coats, we headed down the stairs in the direction of the *thud-thud-thud* reverberating from below.

It was dark and stuffy. Under stuttering pulses of red and blue disco lights, I could see that a dance floor had been set up in some sort of exhibition space, its walls lined with posters of tractors and combine harvesters. It reminded me of discos we had had at the academy of arts, with canteen tables pushed to the sides. The syrupy synths and lyrics of Soviet pop blared across the room, a sound that reminded me of dancing with my old friend Zhanna.

'Shame about the music!' you yelled, cupping your hand against my ear.

The crowd was mostly Russian boys, I could tell from their fake jeans and shiny shirts; only a handful were dressed like you, in a T-shirt and trainers. Four or five braver souls jigged and spun on the dance floor. Most, though, hovered around the edge, waiting for a crowd to hide in. So many *gomoseksualisty* in one place. I stared, trying to decide whether they looked anything like me; there was a more affectionate manner, sure, touching and kissing between those who knew each other, but also wary sideways glares between those who didn't.

I wasn't to know it at the time, but over the coming year every 'Discotheque for Sexual Minorities' would be like this. At first, the discos took place once a month, then once a fortnight, then weekly. The fear of being raided meant they switched from one out-of-the-way venue to another, from disused warehouse to factory canteen.

We stopped at the bar – a row of tables near the door – and

Rasmus bought us a round of drinks. As we stood clutching our tins of lager, you spotted one of the few other foreigners there that night and decided you needed to go and talk to him. It was Oliver Rutland-Kerr.

'You told me you didn't like him,' I had to almost yell in your ear.

'I don't really,' you turned to yell in mine.

'Then why the hurry to go talk to him?'

You shrugged. 'I wasn't *sure* he was gay. But now I've seen him here—'

'What, that makes you friends all of a sudden?'

You patted me on the shoulder, said you'd be back in a minute, and I watched you push through the crowd to greet Oliver with a hug. You weren't 'back in a minute' though, and meanwhile I'd lost sight of Jules and Rasmus. I finished my lager and felt the need for another drink, if only for something to hold, to feel less self-conscious.

There was such a crush at the bar that I couldn't catch the barman's eye. I raised a hand, but others barged in front of me, my every 'excuse me' or '*pozhalsta*' ignored. I found myself squeezed between two other boys, both of whom got served before me. On one side a dark-eyed teenager waved a wad of roubles in front of his face like a fan; on the other stood a young man about our age with long hair tied back in a pony-tail and wearing a white sweatshirt covered with the stars and stripes of the American flag. He simply raised an empty glass to the barman, who seemed to know him. Then, as his glass was topped up, the ponytailed guy tapped the barman on the hand, nodded towards me and called, 'And a drink for this young gentleman.'

He faced me and smiled. He had a broad grin, relaxed but

without showing his teeth. I caught a glimpse of a silver ring in his right ear, glinting where his hair was swept back.

'Aw, thanks,' I said. 'I'll have another beer, please.'

I opened my wallet, but he waved it away. I felt myself blush and said *spasibo*, again. He cocked his head to one side to suggest that we move away from the bar and, with one hand resting on the small of my back, steered us through the scrum of bodies and fug of cigarette smoke until we found a spot by the wall, underneath a chart about five-year plans.

As we talked, I kept mopping my forehead so it wouldn't get too shiny with sweat. But his eyes strayed nowhere near my balding pate; they simply smiled right on into mine. He was handsome, not in a laddish way like you or my school crush Vasily, but in the 'bohemian' style of the men I'd worked with at the theatre. And his ponytail – while not exactly a typical man's look – had a sort of *rakishness* about it.

I told him it was my first time here. He chuckled and shouted back, 'Ah, chill out! It's *everyone's* first time!' He swayed, a little unsteady on his feet, then leaned into my ear as if to whisper something conspiratorial. 'Or possibly *not* for some . . .'

'Oh, what d'you mean?' I was nervous and glad of a topic for conversation.

'I've heard,' he said, with a comic wiggle of his eyebrows, 'that this *isn't* the first' – he mimicked the solemn cadences of a Soviet newsreader – '*Discotheque for Sexual Minorities* in Russia. There's been one before this.'

'Really?' I should probably have tried to act more clued-up, to impress him.

'Yeah, sure.' The guy nodded confidently, knocking back his vodka in one gulp. 'It was two months ago, up in Peter.'

Peter. That's what all the switched-on types called St Petersburg, even when it was still Leningrad. Zhanna had spent a
month there, and once she was back at the academy, fired up
about the city's alternative arts scene, she never stopped talking
about it: *Peter this, Peter that* . . . Oh, Zhanna – if only she were
here tonight.

I took a sip of my beer, nodding as if I was in the know. 'I
see, in Peter—'

'You've been there, yeah?' The stranger fixed his gaze on
mine but tottered slightly and had to prop himself up against
the wall.

I blushed (not that he'd see it in that light) and offered a
sheepish smile, admitting that no, I'd never been there. I was
about to tell him I'd been to England though, thinking that
would impress him, but he grabbed my arm and said, 'Man, get
your ass up to Peter! I have friends there. My sister too. It's *way*
cooler than Moscow.' A hiccup. 'No offence, like.'

'Oh, I'm not from Moscow,' I said, before I could stop
myself. If he didn't think Moscow was 'cool', God knows what
he'd think of Voronezh.

But he just held his empty glass up before his eyes, squinted
at it and beamed at me. I beamed back and wondered whether
I should buy him another drink, though it was barely minutes since we left the bar. He bent his head close to me,
tucking his hair behind his ear, breathing vodka fumes in my
face.

'I'll tell you something else that's cool up in Peter,' he said,
putting down his glass, and taking a shiny packet and cigarette
papers from his jeans. 'You smoke?'

Anxious as I was to please this rakish, earringed stranger, I
briefly weighed up playing it cool, saying, 'yeah, sure' and

pretending I smoked. But I never had and didn't want to start, so I shook my head and told him I didn't.

He hiccupped again, waving the shiny pouch under my nose. 'This isn't tobacco.'

'Oh? What is it then?'

He flashed a toothy grin at me – then cupped his hand to my ear and half-whispered, half-shouted, 'It's grass! One thing that's so cool about the scene in Peter – it's easier to score dope there.'

My mouth fell open as I watched him start to roll up. I glanced from side to side to check if anyone was looking, but all I could see was the backs of a dozen young men, arms and shoulders shimmying against a fog of disco-lit cigarette smoke.

He must have noticed my look of concern. 'Maybe I'd better go to the toilets to roll up.' He patted me on the arm. 'I won't be long.'

He stuffed the pouch and cigarette papers back in his jeans and turned to go. Then he paused, offered me a handshake and shouted into my ear, 'Sorry – forgot to introduce myself. The name's Artyom.'

*

That's right: while you were busy schmoozing with Oliver Rutland-Kerr, I got chatted up by Artyom. Yes, *me*, flirted with, seduced ... It was a taste – albeit fleeting – of how it would be to feel *attractive*. He didn't even seem to notice that I was going bald.

It didn't last, of course. Just like you, he wasn't back in a few minutes, so I wandered down to the toilets to look for him. They were typical Soviet institutional toilets, the walls white-washed and flaking, cubicles painted sludge-green, and a stench of urine that chafed the back of my throat. I couldn't see Artyom though, so I hung around in case he was inside one of the cubicles. Instead, some older man with dyed hair and a face reddened by vodka emerged. Seeing me hesitate, instead of entering the cubicle, he puckered his lips and said, 'What's the matter, sweetie?' *Milenky*, he called me. 'Looking for some action?'

Back at the dance floor, I forced my way to the bar again. This time I caught the barman's eye and, since he seemed to know Artyom, I asked if he'd seen him. He nodded towards the tables on the far side of the room. I started to make my way over, eyes peeled for his distinctive star-spangled sweatshirt – but when I spotted Artyom, back turned to me, he was sitting with Oliver Rutland-Kerr and you, passing round his joint.

I backed away, unsure what to do. Had Artyom met you by chance, or had you been introduced by Oliver? And where did I fit in? I didn't feel able to march up and say, 'Hi, I'm with Jamie,' or, for that matter, 'I'm with Artyom.' I needed another drink, something to stop my hands fidgeting, so I fought my way to the bar once more.

Had Artyom forgotten about me already? Or had he looked for me and not found me? Maybe I *should* go and say hi . . . But no, whatever charm he'd worked on me barely ten minutes earlier now evaporated and I went back to feeling *nudny*, square and unattractive. I was of no interest to Artyom, not at the side of his dope-scoring buddies in 'Peter'.

I switched from beer to vodka, which I hardly ever touched. It kindled a warmth in my belly that spread up my back and flushed my cheeks; it was not unlike the warmth of being chatted up by Artyom. I decided I'd go back to that corner, find you all and barge in on your conversation – but that was the moment the DJ switched to the slow numbers.

I'll never forget the song that was playing. It was Madonna, 'Crazy for You'. The lights slowed down too, rapid fire giving way to a glow that bathed the dance floor, shifting lazily from orange to red. I watched as men grabbed their partners, wrapped their arms around them and swayed in time to the lyrics.

I reached the table where I'd seen you sharing Artyom's joint, but Oliver was now alone, standing with a bottle of beer in one hand, the other hand in his chinos. He was grinning in what looked like encouragement, and I turned towards the dance floor to see who he was leering at. That's when I spotted Artyom again, his star-spangled sweatshirt with the ponytail draped down his back. He was smooching along with someone who had his cheek buried in his chest and his arms around his waist.

Artyom was dancing with the very boy I'd pictured every time the lyrics to that wretched song echoed around my skull. You, Jamie. He was dancing with you.

12

MARCH 1993. Voronezh

Tamara Borisovna

Downhill from the cemetery, beyond the snow-covered roofs that descend like a flight of steps towards the river, she sees a trolleybus crossing the bridge. Snatches of its whining engine reach her ears, carried on the wind. That'll be the number 8, the bus Kostya used to take to get home from the theatre. She watches it arrive on the left bank, her old neighbourhood, then stop outside the local *gastronom* where she stood in line for her family's cheese rations.

Stop looking, she tells herself, there's no moving back, no turning back time. Thank God Galina has told her she can stay in Viktor's old room as long as she needs. She hopes Galina means it; otherwise, without Galina, she'd be homeless.

Her gaze shifts to the river. A few stray ice floes reel and bump as the current sweeps them south, towards the Don. The thaw has set in, gnawing away at the mantle of snow that has lain thick and still for months, muffling all beneath it. That white-blanketed hush feels, at least to her, *respectful* – like the white swaddling that covered Kostya in the days before his burial. There was a time, once, when she used to look forward to spring, to the patches of earth emerging from the snow like ink blots, to the tiny pink blossom softening the bare, spiny branches. But not this year. This year she wishes winter could go on and on, its long nights cloaking her with the cover of darkness, sheltering her, giving her permission to hibernate.

It's three weeks and five days since the funeral, and today's her first time here alone, without Galina to hold her hand or cradle her head. I should go out on my own, she told Galina that morning, even if it's only to tend the grave. She paces past the headstones – some taller than her, many with sculpted folds and columns, even hammers and sickles – until Kostya's grave comes into view, so improvised and unadorned that it shrinks from attention.

She adjusts her scarf, tightening it, and clutching to her chest the flowers, wrapped in *Pravda*, that she bought up the lane outside the church. And as she looks, she wishes, just as she has wished every time she's been here with Galina, for the grave not to be there, for this to be nothing but a nightmare, some extended hallucination. She shuts her eyes.

But opens them to the now-familiar sight of Kostya's black-and-white graduation portrait propped up against his headstone. Melting snow has seeped in through the frame. She picks it up and water trickles down Kostya's face. Under the glass, the photo is creased and damp. I should take it home and let it dry out, she thinks. Or bring a new one – there might be another photo in that trunk with Kostya's books and stuff. She lays her flowers, using the newspaper to wrap the leaking frame and tucking it into her bag.

Got to make myself useful while I'm at Galina's, she thinks. Can't be coming into town only to lay flowers. Keep busy, that's right, busy and useful – life has to go on, hasn't it. I'll get some shopping in. I'll buy beetroot and potatoes and make borsch. Galina'll like that.

She makes her way uphill from the cemetery, stopping to catch her breath outside the church. There's that babushka again, the one who sold her the flowers, hunched and watch-ful in her spot by the porch; she notices now that the old woman is selling candles too. What, she wonders, is the pull of something so nonsensical as religion? Why are the churches so busy? Certainty, it occurs to her – *that's* what people miss: the certainty the Party used to offer. But as she stands there, hesi-tating, she is aware too of a hankering, not for certainty but for solace; something beyond the gift of any political system.

Straightening her home-knitted beret on her head, she nods at the babushka, hands over a few roubles for a candle and walks through the porch into the church. Inside, she finds herself smothered in warmth, and inhaling wafts of sweet, smoky incense. All about her is a darkness that hides and shelters, rather like the consoling cover of a winter night, with only a muted gleam of gold where the icons catch the light of hundreds of candles. But it isn't the religious scenes she's drawn to, the images of Christ and saints and angels painted on every surface – it's the other women: knots of wives, mothers and widows, milling around from icon to icon, crossing themselves. She finds herself blending unnoticed into a sea of scarf-covered heads, all bowed in prayer. Almost all of them are women, some wrinkled and stooped, some old enough to be her mother. But where are the men? The answer comes to her straight away. Dead, of course. Lost, like so many Russian men, to war or alcoholism.

These old crones aren't so different from me, she thinks, half of them must have lost a husband or a brother or a son.

That wasn't supposed to happen with Kostya. That's all she tried to do, wasn't it? To save him. Not just from the army all those years ago, but more recently too ... She'd only wanted what was best for her son. But look at her, lighting a candle in church, mumbling a prayer to a God she never believed in. A prayer for what? For divine intervention, to undo the damage? No, she realises: what she's praying for is forgiveness.

She stays in the church longer than she planned, almost an hour, and with another nod to the babushka who sold her the flowers and the candle, she composes herself for the steep walk back up the hill. The wind hits the nape of her neck where she hasn't quite covered it with her scarf, and she shivers after the candle-lit warmth of the church. The lane climbs between rickety wooden houses stacked up the slope, so steep in places that she finds herself clinging to a handrail. A young man in a woolly ski cap passes her, heading downhill, carrying a large bunch of lilies. You don't often see that, she thinks, a man laying flowers—

'Excuse me? Hello? Tamara Borisovna? Is that you?'

Her mouth drops open. The young man isn't a young man at all but a young woman, her hair cropped short and dyed bright red, and with black jeans and those strange heavy shoes she'd seen the English students wearing. Recognition dawns: the young woman's hairstyle may have changed – after all, she was always a radical *feministka* – but the eyes are as warm as ever, their playful gleam appropriately tuned down.

'Zhanna? I didn't recognise you.'

A little nod, almost apologetic. 'Yes, Tamara Borisovna. It's been a few years.'

She stares at the young woman she'd once hoped would make a girlfriend – a fiancée even – for Kostya. When they were students at the academy of arts together, he'd talked about her non-stop, giggling and gossiping on the phone with her, inviting her to tea a few times too. But a *girlfriend*? No, Kostya insisted, they were 'just friends'. Later, Zhanna had met some older boy at the university and, despite her feminist protestations, had married in something of a hurry, moving to live with him in Rostov-on-Don. Like so many marriages these days, it hadn't lasted, and Zhanna, so she'd heard, was already divorced.

'Are you, uh, still living in Rostov?' she manages to ask.

Zhanna nods again. 'For now, yes. I'm only visiting, staying with Mama a few days.' She sees Zhanna bite her lip and offer that regretful incline of the head she's seen so often these past few weeks. 'And you, Tamara Borisovna? Please, accept my condolences.' A pause, while Zhanna gently places a hand on her arm. 'How are you holding up?'

Her eyes flit towards Zhanna's hand. How am I 'holding up'? How does anyone *think* I'm holding up? Her mouth twitches, caught somewhere between a quivering lip and a terse reply. She lowers her head, looking down at the muddy steps.

Zhanna removes her hand. 'I'm sorry, Tamara Borisovna. I can't even imagine—'

'*Nevazhno*,' she mutters: it doesn't matter. Feeling unsteady on her feet, she grips the handrail, fixing her gaze on a patch of melting snow. She pictures its minute crystals dissolving, a thaw taking place all over Russia, and shudders at the thought of that wintry blanket being eroded bit by bit. Just think of the terrain exposed below it, blackened and soiled.

She looks up. 'I've been to lay flowers on his grave.'

Zhanna nods to indicate the bouquet of ten white lilies she's carrying. 'I'm on my way to lay flowers too. It's the main reason I'm back in town.'

The two women meet each other's eye, then Zhanna adds, 'I'm sorry I didn't make it to the funeral, but I hadn't heard – until someone from the Youth Theatre told me.'

'That's kind of you, Zhanna.' She feels a catch in her throat. '*Spasibo*.'

'They miss Kostya. At the theatre, I mean,' says Zhanna. 'He loved working there, didn't he? He showed such promise.'

Such promise. They always say that about someone who dies young. *He showed such promise* ... As if the deceased had let down the people left behind. It's time to make her excuses, to get away from Zhanna, but instead she finds herself changing the subject, asking, 'What about you, Zhanna? Would you be moving back to Voronezh?'

Zhanna shakes her head. 'No, Tamara Borisovna, I couldn't, not now. I've moved on, shall we say. Besides, we wouldn't fit in—' She winces as if on the point of saying something but thinking better of it. 'We're not planning to stay in Rostov though. In fact, we're thinking of emigrating, probably to Germany.'

We? Who does Zhanna mean by 'we'? Surely she can't be married again already? More likely she's 'co-habiting', as young people call it these days. She's about to quiz Zhanna about this mysterious new man when, for some reason, she recalls how *conspiratorial* Zhanna and Kostya used to be together, all whispering and giggling, yet never any courtship.

She mutters, 'Where in the GDR are you thinking of moving to?'

'The *GDR* ?' Another little shake of Zhanna's head. 'No, Tamara Borisovna, not East Germany – I mean, it's all one country now, isn't it?'

Oh yes, she remembers, the reunification of Russia's old

enemy, all now part of that decadent West where everyone wants to emigrate, it seems. She straightens her back as if to pull herself together or to take her leave.

'Kostya went to the West,' she hears herself say, 'you know, to England' – Zhanna is nodding – 'he was so excited about it, his first trip there. Only sometimes, I wish . . .'

The words dry up. What *does* she wish? That Kostya hadn't gone to England? That he'd never met Jamie? There I go again, she thinks, trying to blame that English boy . . . She sees Zhanna's brow furrow, the young woman's face caught in a contest between a smile of sympathy and the downcast eyebrows of concern.

'I'm so sorry for your loss, Tamara Borisovna,' Zhanna says again. 'I can't imagine how hard it must be. For you, for his father, for his—' She fidgets with her bunch of flowers. 'Forgive me, but Kostya wasn't, by any chance, *attached*, was he?'

She gives Zhanna a long, wavering look. 'Why d'you ask?'

Zhanna blushes. Perhaps it's the cold on her cheeks. 'Oh, I thought he might have found someone . . . you know, someone special.'

Someone? What's with the 'someone'? Why can't Zhanna say 'girlfriend' or 'fiancée'? As if there was any alternative to a fiancée or a wife, as if . . . She looks Zhanna up and down. That short hair, the feminism, those boyish boots, the divorce – it all starts to make sense.

She grips the handrail, turning and ready to be on her way. 'No,' she says, 'he hadn't found *someone*. Or if he had, I never got to meet them.'

★

Back at Galina's, she eases the graveside photograph of Kostya out of its frame and lies it next to the identical one framed on her bedside table. Wrinkled with damp, it starts to curl at the corners. She lights a candle, as she has done every day these past few weeks. The flame flickers close to Kostya's face, and the light shows up her reflection in the glass, her eyes appearing to overlap with her son's.

What about finding another photograph? She returns to the trunk, still not unpacked after her hurried move, and opens Kostya's photo album. There are no suitable photos of Kostya though. Again, most of the ones she sees are of Jamie, or of Kostya with Jamie.

That English boy. What a nerve, turning up at Galina's flat a few days after the funeral. But then, she recalls, looking up from the album and staring at the floor, he did come all the way from Moscow. And all she did was bite his head off. Why? Was it plausible even to accuse Jamie of *causing* Kostya's death? Leading him astray, maybe; egging him on into the degenerate ways of a . . . Ugh, that word again. A word that Soviet wisdom taught her to associate with deviancy, with perversion, with a disregard for social order. A word so dirty that she finds it hard to say.

She whispers it: *'gomoseksualist'*. Then stares at Jamie's picture, at his impudent grin, messed-up hair and frayed denim jacket – not the way she'd want any son of hers to dress. Yet he defied her notion of what homosexuals were like: sickly and furtive, secretly wanting to be women. Jamie wasn't like that. She remembers him laughing it off whenever Gennady asked him how he liked Russian girls. He would converse with her in Russian too, complimenting her cooking, and regularly brought her tea from England. Whatever Jamie's influence, Kostya had at least seemed happy when they were together.

Happy together. The words converge in her head, a thought

taking shape that she's been trying to push to the back of her mind. Was Kostya *happy* when he was with Jamie? Yes, no doubt about that. But were they *together*? She thinks of that morning's encounter with Zhanna – could Jamie have been that 'someone special' Zhanna was asking about?

She snaps the album shut, flings it back in the trunk and rests her head in her hands. Forget finding a new photo, she thinks, all I want is to lie down, sleep, blot it all out. She lifts her face from her palms and stands, ready to limp over to the bed. But then her eye is caught by Kostya's diary, lying in the trunk. It has a plain red cover with '1992' embossed in silver. Every year since his teens he had kept a diary, sometimes pasting in tickets from plays and concerts. She picks it up, holds it to her face in both hands and tries to breathe in something, anything, of Kostya's smell. Are these his final thoughts? No, wait, they can't be. Somewhere, not here, there must be a diary for 1993 too. She pictures it, imagines Kostya's handwritten entries for the first six weeks of the year, and then, after that February evening, nothing but page after page of virgin white, untouched and unwritten on.

★

Early that evening, just as she's starting to prepare her borsch, she hears Galina coming in the front door. She hears her announcing, 'I'm back', putting on her slippers and shuffling down the hallway towards Viktor's old room. There's a surprised 'Oh', as if Galina expects to find her there, like she has been most afternoons these past few weeks, trying to sleep or lying motionless on the bed in an effort to stem the panic in her breathing.

'I'm in the kitchen,' she calls. Her hands grip the edge of the sink. Rather than making herself useful, she feels like she's imposed herself on another woman's territory. All the years she lived with Gennady and Kostya – then with Kostya alone – the kitchen had always been her turf, a place where she was in control.

Galina bustles in and drops a couple of shopping bags on a chair. Straight away, she starts to cluck and fuss, insisting there's no need for Tamara to be doing the cooking. 'Let me take care of that,' Galina says, reaching for her apron. 'Why don't you go and—'

'No, Galya.' It comes out more abrupt than she meant, so she turns and forces a weak smile. 'Please let me do something to help out.' A little shake of her head. 'I did a bit of shopping, that's all. On my way back from the cemetery.'

Galina stands next to her, puts an arm around her shoulder. 'And how did that go?'

She sighs. 'Fine, I suppose.' And turns back to the sink, pushes the plug in, starts to run the cold water. Should she tell Galina about bumping into Zhanna? No, that would only raise more questions. She tries instead to sound practical, saying, 'I'll have to replace that photo of Kostya, mind – there's damp under the frame, now the snow's melting.'

'Ah, yes,' Galina says, 'that always happens this time of year.'

She looks at Galina. Of course, her friend would know about that sort of thing: she's tended Viktor's grave, then her husband's, year after year, winter after winter. Galya too is like those women in the church; she'd never thought of her like that before, enacting a scene that's repeated the length and breadth of Russia.

As if reading her thoughts, Galina adds, 'Which reminds me – there's another protest in Moscow next week. Against our boys being sent to fight in the Caucasus.'

For a second or two she doesn't reply. She knows Galina is talking about the Mothers for Peace – but surely she's not asking her to go to the demonstration with her? To think that they had both once been so proud of Russia's soldiers, those selfless sons and brothers sworn to the defence of the motherland. At least they had been before Viktor was killed, before Kostya was called up. Again, she pictures the women in the church; then pictures Galina out marching. Which is better, prayer or protest?

She shakes her head. 'I'm not ready, Galya, not to go back up to Moscow—'

'No, I didn't mean that.' Galina hugs her tight around the shoulders. 'I just wondered, if I went, whether you'd be all right on your own here for a day.'

She thinks. A whole day here on her own – a day and two nights actually, since Galya would be taking the overnight train. Two nights on her own. But come on, only two nights, it's not that long, is it. She nods her head. 'You go – I'll be fine.'

She turns to the sink again, plunging the beetroot into the water, breaking off clods of earth that dissolve into mud between her fingers and turn the water black. Galina touches her shoulder and tells her all right, she'll leave her to it. Once Galina's gone, a few minutes pass in which she stands with her hands in the sink, water halfway up to her elbows. The water is ice-cold, and her fingers start to go numb. Still she stands there, letting the numbness eat into her hands and creep up her wrists. It starts to hurt, but it's only physical pain, nothing like the pain she'd really like to numb.

When she can stand the cold no longer, she lifts the beetroot from the sink, puts it on the chopping board and slices into it with a big kitchen knife. She stares at her hands. They're stained with patches of red, rivulets of red trickling between her fingers.

*

She glances at the photograph as if expecting to catch Kostya watching her. Impossible, of course – but all the same she turns the picture to face the other way so that even his likeness can't be a witness to the transgression she's about to commit. Then, lying back on her pillow and pulling the bedclothes up to her chin, she opens his diary and turns it to the light. I shouldn't, she thinks, but I won't properly read it, I'll just skim-read.

And so, at first, she pays no attention to what Kostya has written, only to the sight of his familiar handwriting, neat but densely packed, the same careful script in which he did the school homework that he would show her every time he got full marks for English or art or literature. But then her eyes alight on one entry. There's something about him going bald and getting treatment for it; how bizarre, did he really do that? She flips the page, and out falls a leaflet advertising a baldness cure, with the slogan *Your Hair is Your Face*, and an address in the outskirts of Moscow. A couple of pages later, she stumbles across a mention of some 'Discotheque for Sexual Minorities' – and there's that word again, the one she dreaded seeing: *gomoseksualist*. As if it needed confirmation. As if it matters, now it's too late.

Stop, she thinks. What might he have written about me? What if he resented me for following him to Moscow and yearned to get away from me, like Zhanna from her mother? What if her son's words rise from the page like an accuser? Once glimpsed, such words could never be wiped from her memory. She snaps the diary shut, drops it on the floor, then turns the photo back around and switches off the lamp.

★

A dim yellow glow filters into the room from the street lights outside. Her head turns on her pillow, rolling away from the wall to face the bedside table. She sees Kostya. His portrait, his face. Except something's different. His eyes. They were averted before, weren't they, gazing dreamily to one side — but now they're looking right at her, unblinking yet drilling into hers, not so much soulful as bottomless black wells of resentment.

She pulls the bedclothes over her nose. Still her son's eyes remain fixed on her. Must be a trick of the light. I'll switch on the lamp, she thinks, I'll turn the photo to face the other way. Her hand reaches for the bedside table. It hovers halfway, frozen in the shape of a claw, unable to flick the switch or turn the photo round. She stares. Dark liquid trickles between her fingers, onto her palm, down her wrist. Dark, no — red like blood. Don't be silly, she tells herself, it's only beetroot juice from earlier, when I was cooking. Why now though, now as I'm lying in bed? And Kostya's eyes, why are they staring at me? Why are they—

She wakes, panting, bolt upright in bed, scrabbling for the light switch. Then, all around her, in the blinding glare, is Viktor's room as it always was: his Moscow Olympics poster, his map of the USSR, his pictures of Soviet tanks and fighter jets. And there, on the bedside table, is her framed photo of Kostya, his eyes gentle and dreamy, looking to one side.

Her hands, look at them. They're shaking. But at least they're clean, no sign of blood. She lowers her face to her palms, half-expecting to feel a bloodstained stickiness. But no, it was a bad dream, that's all. Even so, her breathing is rapid and tight. She looks up. The clock says 10:30 p.m., not as late as she thought. Galina might still be awake. Pushing back the covers, she swings her legs out of bed and slides her feet into her slippers.

In the hallway, she sees light spilling from under Galina's door. She must be reading in bed. Thank God, she *is* still up. If Galina is as good a friend as she's always believed, she won't mind being disturbed at this hour. Not when she needs her most, when she needs to talk about Kostya. Recalling that moment in the church, she wonders whether it's a priest she should talk to, not Galina. Either way, she knows the time has come to make a confession.

13

MARCH 1993. Moscow

Dima

A man's bare torso hovers before his eyes, in and out of focus, sharp then blurry, muscles glistening with sweat – some image stuck in his head, no doubt, some memory imprinted from Yuri's porn shoots ... Only, no: those piercing, flinty eyes – they're exactly like Yuri himself. Even now, he's reeling from Yuri's punch to his jaw; even now, Yuri is raising his fists, ready to sock him one again. No, Yuri, please Yuri, no—

Blinking his eyes open, he wipes the sweat from his forehead and peers blearily through his fingers. A sigh. The torso is that of Jean-Claude Van Damme, the familiar poster above the bed on Oleg's side of the room. For a second, as he recognises their old pin-up, it's as if nothing has changed these past few weeks. As if he and Oleg were still at Valery Ivanovich's.

Outside, however, the corridor echoes with the shouts and laughter of the student dormitory. He hears doors being slammed, a snatch of pop music on a radio and the *slap-slap* of flip-flops on linoleum. Inside the room, four single beds are crammed into a space barely larger than their old bedroom. Across from him is Oleg's bed, tidy and looking somehow cold and still, like it hasn't been slept in. Nearer the window, separated by a table and pushed hard against the walls, are two more beds, those of Oleg's new room-mates, also empty.

He reaches for his rucksack, rummaging around until his fingers locate the envelope Jamie gave him when they met for a second time. Inside is the address of some apartment in Khimki – along with the wad of dollars and hundred-rouble notes he extracted from Jamie as his price. In the next day or two, he needs to keep his side of their deal and go check out this address. Jamie told him his newspaper's secretary had dug up something about bribes and contracts – how that's linked to Kostya's death, God knows. He counts the cash, making sure it's all there.

The door swings open. In comes Andrei, one of Oleg's three new room-mates, wearing a Soviet sailor's vest and blue tracksuit bottoms. Greasy cooking smells waft into the room from the frying pan he's balancing in one hand. An enamelled kettle hangs from the other. Kicking the door shut behind him, Andrei plonks the frying pan, kettle and two forks on the table.

Andrei looks at him. 'Want some fried eggs, Dima?'

'*Da, spasibo.*' He quickly hides the envelope, hoping Andrei didn't catch sight of the cash, then lowers his feet to the floor – clammy painted floorboards, same as in his old room at Valery Ivanovich's – and pulls on his sweatpants and T-shirt.

He knew Oleg's new room-mates, Andrei and Timur, before he dropped out of film school – not very well, since he was always skiving classes, but enough for Oleg to persuade them to let him crash here for a few nights. A bed has become available because Slava, Oleg's third room-mate, is away for the week at his new wife's parents. *Blyad*, Dima had thought, married by the age of twenty-two – how suffocating.

Pulling up a chair, he sits and watches Andrei tuck into the fried eggs, eating them straight from the frying pan. Andrei pours them both a glass of black tea.

'Where's Oleg?' he asks.

'Don't know.' Andrei shrugs, dropping three sugar cubes in his tea and starting to stir. 'Didn't come back last night.'

No smile, nothing conspiratorial. Andrei isn't *nash*, certainly no 'partner in crime', and knows nothing of the nocturnal exploits Oleg and he get up to. Or *used* to get up to; he for one hasn't been out in search of a hook-up since the news about Kostya – Oleg, however, had only last night gone back out cruising at Ploshchad Revolyutsii.

'He doesn't have classes today, does he?'

Andrei swallows some fried egg. 'Don't think so.'

Dima shifts awkwardly in his seat. It's the first time over these past few days that he's been with either of the roommates without Oleg. 'And Timur? Has he seen Oleg?'

Another shrug from Andrei. 'Don't know. He's out as well.' He points at the fried eggs with his fork. 'C'mon, eat before it goes cold.'

He picks up a fork and helps himself to a greasy mouthful of fried egg. At that moment, there's a hammering on the door. Andrei drops his fork and goes to answer it. Dima turns to look. Out in the corridor, obscured by Andrei blocking the doorway, he can just see the *dezhurnaya*, that rodent-eyed old babushka on duty at the reception desk downstairs. She has a message for one of the boys, she says.

Andrei says *spasibo* and slowly closes the door, keeping his face averted longer than feels right, then turns to thrust a piece of paper towards Dima. 'It's for you.'

'Me?' He takes the note and looks at it. Another address, scribbled in pencil, this time a street somewhere in central Moscow. 'What's this?'

'A police station,' Andrei says, still not meeting his eye. 'She says Oleg's been arrested.'

★

His nostrils flinch at the reek of urine, sharper and more rancid with each step he takes. Down he goes, down to the cells, until it's as if he can almost *see* the taint of piss in the jaundiced paintwork and yellow strip lighting. The cop on guard duty – sunken-eyed, scowling, grey fatigues and military boots – halts, folds his arms and points his chin towards the cells. 'Second on the right,' he tells Dima. 'You've got five minutes.'

God, the stench. Clamping a hand over his nose and mouth, he tiptoes past the door of the first cell, all heavy clanging metal cratered with rust and painted the same yellowy-brown as the walls. At face height is an aperture little more than six inches square; he hears a drunken burble of swearing from within.

At the second door, he peers in through the aperture and sees a figure on the bunk curled up under a blanket, facing the wall. In the corner of the cell is a rusting metal bucket. That'll be where the stink's coming from. He raps on the door. A tinny noise echoes down the corridor, prompting more swearing from the cell next door. He uncovers his mouth, trying not to inhale the piss fumes – '*Oleg?*' he whispers. 'Oleg! It's me, Dima.'

The figure stirs, shrugging off the blanket and looking towards the door. At first, he hardly recognises Oleg: his hair, usually so suave and slick, is matted and hanging over his face. He watches as Oleg staggers to his feet, still in his faded denims but with no shoes, and limps over, slumping against the door with a thud. His hands grip the sides of the aperture as if trying to prise them apart. 'Dimik,' he weeps, 'Dimik, it's you.'

'I came as soon as I heard.' He stares, eyes wandering from Oleg's face to his feet and his hair, and he reaches up to squeeze Oleg's fingers.

'*No touching!*' barks the guard. Oleg starts to sob, shoulders convulsing up-down, up-down, and drags a hand across his face to wipe away the tears. There are swollen purple patches around both of Oleg's eyes, worse than his own bruises from Yuri's trained fist.

'Bastards!' he hisses. 'Did they do this to you?' Fucking police . . . Might even have been this meathead watching them right now. He shoots a glance at the guard, who sneers back, arms folded, as if to say, 'Oh yeah, what you gonna do about it?'

Oleg's sobbing quietens, and he stammers his way through what happened, his speech hesitant, impeded by a bust lip. As Dima listens, he shudders at the thought of the risks they ran night after night, outside the Bolshoi or at Ploshchad Revoly-utsii station: the risk of getting beaten up, or of being hauled in by the police and still getting beaten up. This time, in their latest crackdown, the police had deployed a handsome young cop in tight jeans and a leather jacket. Oleg had fallen right into the trap.

'I can't believe we got away with it for so long, Dimik . . .' Oleg's lips quiver. 'Maybe they *let* us get away with it while waiting to nab us. Guess my luck ran out, didn't it?'

You and me both, Dima thinks. Kostya's death. Getting 'fired' by Yuri. Being evicted from Valery Ivanovich's. And now this. He feels a twinge of self-pity, and struggles to listen as Oleg tells him what'll happen next: after a spell in police custody, he'll be charged with 'soliciting for indecent acts', then he'll almost certainly get expelled from film school.

'Aw, c'mon.' He tries to put on a brave face for Oleg. 'They can't do that, not for a first offence. They can't send you . . .' he halts, balking at the word 'prison', not wanting to say it, 'to *stand trial*, not for this, can they?'

'Fuck knows.' Oleg sniffles. 'I'm gonna need a lawyer though.'

'A lawyer?'

'Yes, Dimik. Help me, will you. Isn't there someone you can call? Anyone?'

Anyone he can call? Like who? Slowly, reluctantly, knowing he's going to disappoint Oleg, he shakes his head. Not so long ago he could have asked Kostya, even Yuri – each of them, in their very different ways, would have known a lawyer they could get hold of – but now there's no one he can turn to. Unless, of course—

'I could try asking Jamie.'

Oleg blinks at him. 'What, the English guy Kostya was always on about?'

'I've got nowhere else to turn, Oleg.' He sighs, dragging his fingers through his hair. 'Look, he's a journalist, he's got contacts. Besides, he owes me a favour.'

'A *favour*? What're you talking about, Dimik?'

Another long sigh as he tells Oleg about his 'deal' with the English guy: about Jamie passing him some mysterious address in Khimki that's linked to Kostya's death, and about his own offer to go and snoop around there.

'So you see, Oleg, he owes me. I'll call him soon as I leave,

I promise.' He reaches to touch Oleg's fingers once more, and again the guard barks at him. Visiting time is up.

He manages a defiant squeeze of Oleg's hand before the guard escorts him out of the station. As he steps into the street, his face is whipped by a blast of wind, icy but bracing after the urine fumes of the police cells. He makes his way towards the metro, dodging puddles of melting snow that seeps into his crappy Soviet boots.

But where's he going to go? The worries resurface, crowding out any pity for Oleg. He has himself to think of now. Where will he sleep once Slava returns and he gets kicked out of the dorm? He doesn't even have Oleg to smuggle him in, and Oleg himself will lose his dorm room if he gets expelled. As for finding Oleg a lawyer, sure, he can ask Jamie, but hasn't the English guy given him money already?

He comes to a halt at a bank of payphones outside the metro. Turning out his pockets, he finds a fifteen-kopeck piece and stares at the coin, at the payphones, then at the coin again. If only Kostya were still here, he could perform his 'magic trick' for him, the one with the coin that had so enchanted Kostya the night they went to the theatre. If only he'd held onto Kostya . . . If only he'd never had to make that fifteen-kopeck call to Tamara Borisovna.

★

'And what about that place in Khimki?' Jamie's voice hisses down the line, sounding like he's trying to keep it down and doesn't want anyone else to hear. 'When are you gonna get around to going there? We made a *deal*, remember.'

'All right,' Dima says. He knows Jamie's got a point, having paid him – bribed him, even – so he blurts out, 'I'll go tomorrow.'

'*Tomorrow*? Can I count on you?'

Why the hurry? Sensing the English guy's desperation to solve the case and get a 'story', he wonders: might Jamie cave in to further demands? 'One condition,' he says. 'You promise *me* you'll get that lawyer for Oleg. Otherwise' – he grips the receiver in his frozen hand, reluctant to start issuing threats – 'otherwise you can have your money back and the deal's off.'

A silence follows, prolonged and tense, his ear clamped to the receiver and tuned into Jamie's breathing. In that moment, he thinks, shit, I've blown it, that Jamie's going to say 'Screw you, mate, I don't need your help as much as you need mine'.

Beep-beep-beep-beep ... His time's almost up and he hasn't got another fifteen kopecks to extend the call. The voice hisses in his ear again. Even down the line, he can sense Jamie's teeth gritted, up-close to the receiver: 'All right, all right,' he says. 'I'll make some calls. I know this Belgian guy, works for a law firm, he'll know what to do.'

He sighs with relief. '*Spasibo*, Jamie. I owe you one.'

'Damn right you do,' comes the reply. 'Now, please, get your arse to Khimki.'

★

The bus's steamed-up windows enclose the fug of bodies sweating in thick, dirty coats. He feels a judder, the grinding of gears as the driver slows down. Using the sleeve of his jacket, he wipes the condensation from the window to see where they are. The view remains murky, obscured by a film of mud on the outside. He can just see, stark against the snow, the Soviet war memorial marking how close to Moscow the Nazi invaders had come: a criss-cross structure of steel girders assembled, like giant 'X's, in the shape of three oversized tank traps.

The bus peels away from the traffic clogging up the highway towards St Petersburg. Some of the road signs still say Leningrad. In a few minutes, he'll arrive in Khimki; time to act on his deal with Jamie and get that lawyer for Oleg. Time to get this over and done with. Then he can clear off out of Moscow and back home to Latvia.

He wishes Oleg was with him. That this was one of their 'partners in crime' outings, a game of wits and deception. Last summer they'd taken the bus together on a similar route – but headed for Sheremetyevo airport, where he had been sent to bribe some officious little jerk in customs to wave through a consignment of videos that Yuri was sending to Germany.

'Don't you ever dream,' Oleg had asked him that sweltering July day, 'that one day you'll ride this bus to the airport and get the hell out of this country for good?'

Dima had snorted. He'd heard this kind of talk a hundred times before.

'Aw, c'mon, Dimik, think about it,' Oleg had persisted, 'you and me, buggering off to the West. How about Amsterdam? We could get work in a bar or a hotel – maybe even find ourselves a sugar daddy.'

A sugar daddy. Wasn't that what Yuri had been? A relationship that was little more than transactional, where the perks came at a price and he was out on his arse as soon as he fell from favour. *Transactional*, he thinks – the word now lodged in his head – but doesn't that sum up how I treated Kostya? A little flirting and routine sex, and I had him at my beck and call ... It was gratifying, that eagerness in Kostya's eyes, his endless *gratitude*, his endless wanting to see him – plus Kostya could have been his ticket to somewhere new to live ...

He gives himself a shake, trying to picture his mum back in

Latvia. Mum and Petya – there they'll be, ready to welcome him home. When he turns up and admits it didn't work out in Moscow after all, she'll hug him close and make everything all right. She'll have baked a cake. She'll smile and look at him like she knows he's been telling lies. But will she care that he screwed up? Will he himself care that he's 'failed'? No, he thinks, not any more.

He unfolds the crumpled map he's been carrying, but gets distracted by the man in the seat opposite picking at the cellophane wrapping of a pack of cigarettes. Marlboros, he notices, if only he could afford Marlboros. Or quit smoking outright, like Kostya nagged him to. His craving makes it hard to focus on the map and his gaze drifts outside, his hand shielding his eyes against the white-out of daylight bouncing off the snow. Up ahead, half-hidden beyond the forest, he spies a bronze-tinted building of squat, angular lines. A plane is coming into land. It's Sheremetyevo airport, tantalising gateway to the West.

The bus turns again, bumping its way down a muddy lane. His shoulder rubs and slides against the window. Outside, single-storey wooden houses roll past, painted in flaking blue and green, looking squashed by the weight of snow on their roofs. Icicles drip from their eaves. Before long, the houses give way to concrete and rusting fences, to factories, depots and the tyre tracks of heavy goods vehicles in the slush. This must be Khimki. He looks at the map and then at the address Jamie's given him.

*

On one side of the lane, an electricity pylon stands like a watchtower guarding the sheets of undisturbed snow beneath. His ears detect a faint hum from the cables overhead. In that muted, white-clad stillness, he savours one last drag on the cigarette he scrounged from the man on the bus. Since he got off, he's found himself walking alongside a wall of concrete panels topped with barbed wire. Set behind the wall, a few hundred metres back from the road, is a building of grey brick and blank, dark windows, six or seven storeys of them. It's hard to tell exactly how many floors because the lower part of the building is obscured by a thicket of fir trees dusted with snow. The upper-floor windows appear to have bars.

He shivers. Why, of all places, would Kostya have ended up out here? If he'd been beaten up in that ambush by the skinhead gang, as Oleg seemed to think, then surely they'd have taken him from the disco to the nearest hospital. Yes, the discos were always held in out-of-the-way places like this – but the address Jamie has given him isn't even that of a hospital but of a private apartment. Something doesn't add up.

Flicking his spent cigarette into a snowdrift, he squints at the map, wondering if he got off at the wrong bus stop. As if in confirmation, another bus passes, splattering him with slush. '*Blyad*!' he curses, and for the next half-mile he sticks close to the verge, weaving his way around mounds of snow that's thawing to reveal gashes of black soil and dead vegetation. No matter how carefully he treads, the meltwater gets inside his shoddy boots.

A vehicle approaches and he looks up, braced to avoid another splattering – this time it's a car, black, low-slung and sporty, heading in the opposite direction. As it tears past, he recognises it as a Western model, a BMW. Then he catches a glimpse of its driver, dark-haired and grinning.

Yuri ... *Blyad*, what's *he* doing out here? And some young guy in the front seat next to him, probably that 'Other

Kostya' . . . He stares as the car recedes into the distance, suddenly aware of his heart thumping. Steam puffs out of his mouth in short, agitated bursts. For a minute, alone on that muddy lane, he stands there, relieved that Yuri didn't see him, yet shaken at being reminded of him.

Eventually he arrives at a junction with a cluster of low brick buildings and kiosks. A dozen babushkas line the pavement, trying to sell the usual home-made scarves and jars of pickles. In the cold, their eyes are watery and suspicious. One of them is selling ten-packet blocks of Marlboros. Again it hits him, a craving for that slightly burnt but silky taste in his throat, the warmth and calm filling his lungs. After that unexpected sighting of Yuri, he needs something to steady his nerves.

'How much?' he asks, with a nod towards the bulging carrier bag sitting on the trampled snow at the old woman's feet.

'Four thousand a block,' she croaks. 'Cheaper than in Moscow, sonny.'

He knows it is: 4,000 roubles works out at about sixty cents a packet, well below the going rate. But don't go telling her she could charge 6,000, he thinks – I could buy at 4,000 and sell them on at 7,000. God knows I need the money, at least as much as she does.

'How many blocks you got there?'

Her eyes dip down towards the bag, then stare back into his. 'Twelve, young man.'

Whatever conscience he's got, he decides to swallow it. After all, Granny's probably got a roof over her head, unlike him. He haggles, offering her 35,000 for ten blocks. She shakes her head, but says she'll accept 40,000 for the whole lot. God knows where she got her hands on these Marlboros, but the old woman isn't shy about driving a bargain.

He agrees to 40,000 and takes the envelope from his inside pocket. The cash changes hands, the cigarettes too, and the babushka crosses herself, thanking him.

Shuffling off to a sheltered spot behind a kiosk, he rips open a packet – just one to myself, he thinks; the others I'll sell – and lights up. But as he inhales, he's trembling inside, shaken not only by the sight of Yuri driving past but ashamed of how he's wrung a discount out of an old woman on a Soviet pension. If Kostya were here, he'd be appalled; poor Kostya, who so disapproved of smoking, would've nagged him to cough up the full price.

His mouth is so dry, his fingers so cold that he doesn't even finish his cigarette but stubs it out on the side of the kiosk. As for all these other ten-pack blocks of Marlboros, well, don't think of them as cigarettes, he tells himself, think of them as currency.

★

Five more minutes of trudging through the slush brings him to the doorway of a nondescript block of flats down a side street. There's a grid of doorbell buttons, some with labels – and there it is, he's found it, the place he's been sent to look for. *Renaissance*, it says, second floor.

Sounds like some kind of *bizness*, the type that's been popping up all over Russia – new firms, co-operatives, consultancies, all marketing themselves with names like 'Revival' or 'Restoration'. What on earth they make or sell, he hasn't a clue. He presses the doorbell, along with four or five others, taking care to pick those from the uppermost floors – another trick he used to play with the coastal patrol lads whenever they gatecrashed a party. The door unlocks amid a chorus of buzzes and voices calling, '*Allo*?'

Inside, he finds a lobby like that of any Soviet apartment block, the standard-issue whitewash, painted metal mailboxes, the whiff of garbage chutes lingering in the stairwell. He feels nausea stir in his gut, then grips the railing and starts climbing the stairs. As he walks up, clutching his bag of Marlboros, his mind runs through what he's going to say: varying permutations of charm, lying, insistence or acting lost. He hears doors being opened on the floors above, and the shuffling feet of those whose doorbells he'd buzzed. On the second floor, before anyone can see him, he stops. In front of him is a door with a small plaque that reads 'Renaissance. Health and Wellbeing Consultancy'.

Wellbeing? Not what he was expecting ... But then, what *was* he expecting? A gay men's underground protest group? A hangout for gang members? Think, he urges himself, think. Then, before he has chance to knock or press the buzzer, the door opens. Just a crack, but it opens, and peering out at him from inside is a young woman with glasses and tied-back brown hair.

She eyes him suspiciously. 'Was that you who rang the bell downstairs?'

'Uh, yeah,' he says, truthfully enough. 'But it was open, so I—'

'Do you have an appointment?' she asks. A pause. 'Well? Do you?'

This is one where he can't lie. 'Uh, no – you see, I couldn't find your phone number.'

'Hmm,' she says, frowning. 'Well, we don't exactly *advertise* our services.' Another pause. 'So how did you find us then?'

Now he has an answer ready. 'Through an acquaintance,' he says, looking right at her. At least that's not a lie. 'In fact, you were *recommended* to me.'

She stares back, eyes narrow behind her thick lenses. 'Recommended for *what*?'

Think, Dima, think. 'For a check-up?' As the words leave his mouth, he can hear the doubt in his voice. But what does she mean by 'we don't exactly *advertise* our services'? That would fit with what Jamie said about the place being hard to track down.

'*Everyone* who comes here gets a check-up,' she says with a sniff, glancing at his bag full of Marlboros. 'If you're that worried about your health, you should stop smoking.'

She must be feeling surer of herself, however, because she opens the door a little wider and he sees that she's wearing a white lab-coat.

He hugs the bag of cigarettes to his chest. 'Oh, these aren't for me to *smoke*.' He raises an eyebrow, stopping short of a knowing wink or telling her that they're 'currency'.

'I see.' She stiffens. 'Well, we take payment in cash only here. Roubles or dollars.'

'Oh, I have roubles *and* dollars,' he replies. He notices a flicker of interest cross the woman's face, and takes out the envelope to show her. It's stuffed with cash, much of it from Jamie. Then, recalling his altercation with Jamie the day they walked to the metro, another idea occurs to him, one that might get him through the door.

He hangs his head in a well-rehearsed act of shame (albeit one that his mum would see right through). 'The truth is,' he says, adding a deliberate stutter to his voice, 'I'm not here for any old check-up. I'm here for something much more, well, *delikatny*.'

★

For the next half-hour, he sits in a waiting area with a row of plastic chairs set against the wall. He flicks through a copy of

Kommersant – though business news was never his thing – and looks around him. The apartment's interior has been converted into what looks like office premises, its walls painted a silky clinical white, purging any trace of this ever having been someone's home. Near the door is a desk with a telephone and filing cabinets. There are slender potted plants, shelves lined with academic-looking journals, and a low table with magazines, a jug of water and some glasses.

Lab-coat woman has left him alone, stepping out into the hallway for the second time since he sat down. Once again, he hears her knocking on the door to another room and talking indistinctly to someone, an older man by the sound of it, probably senior to her, with a voice that sounds inconvenienced, even curt. He can't make out what they're saying but a second later he hears her footsteps. He looks up, eyebrows lifted in a look of expectation.

'This is not a convenient time,' she says, positioning herself behind the desk and fidgeting with her files of paper, 'but Stepan Mikhailovich will spare a few minutes to see you now.'

Jamie

Jesus, that photo again. Framed, in black-and-white, the one he handled at Kostya's grave. He stares. Where did they get *that*? Off Kostya's CV? Surely they didn't ask Tamara Borisovna? Either way, here it is, a portrait of Kostya the would-be theatre director on the vacated desk of Kostya the downtrodden admin assistant. A vase of wilting white flowers stands close by, alongside a card edged in black, printed with the words: *In memory of Konstantin Gennadyevich Krolikov, from his colleagues at US-Care.*

A young woman – silk blouse, glossy fringe – rises from her desk and strides towards him. He turns to face her, averting his eyes from the photograph. Better not let on that I knew Kostik, he thinks. Judging by her tarty high heels, this must be Nastya, that bitch Kostya had told him about, the one always shit-stirring about his not having a girlfriend.

'Can I help?' she asks, glancing down at his scuffed Doc Martens.

That supercilious look. It's Nastya all right. 'James Goodier, *Moscow Herald*,' he grunts. He makes a point of not offering to shake hands. 'I'm interviewing Mr Waterson.'

'I'll let him know you're here.' She totters off and knocks on the door of an inner office with a polished brass nameplate. He steals another peek at what used to be Kostya's desk, at the framed photo, the card, the flowers. How long before US-Care decides enough, he wonders, and assigns the desk to a new employee?

'This way, please.' Nastya holds open the door to Waterson's office.

He's been here once before, of course. That time over a year ago, when he had a little swivel in Waterson's fancy chair and asked Kostya, '*What does he actually do, this boss of yours?*' Today he's here to ask much the same thing, only it's supposedly for a business article. Setting foot inside the office, he recognises the view, the Gothic skyward thrust of the Ukraine Hotel, its Stalinist spire almost at eye level up here and, twenty storeys below, the curve of the Moskva river, a splintered jigsaw of ice floes.

He barely has the chance to take it all in before Waterson rises from behind his enormous desk to greet him, hurriedly shoving something into his desk drawer at the same time and nudging it shut with his knee. The American pumps Jamie's hand in both of his, then touches him on the shoulder to guide him towards the black leather sofa.

Waterson is roughly fifteen years older than him, dark-haired and genial, and wearing a pale pink shirt and silvery silk tie. He finds it hard not to stare: a few months back, he had seen Kostya's boss at a party. It was the sort of bash he was keen to get invited to: a private party of gay expat businessmen thrown by a pal of Oliver Rutland-Kerr's, a moustachioed leather daddy from Finland. Like a lot of these expense-account expats, the Finn had a big swanky apartment – in this case with its own sauna and hot tub. There, at the party, he'd watched as the paunches and man-boobs of middle-aged expat men sank into the bubbling waters and rubbed – quite literally – against the sculpted chests and fake suntans of young Russian guys on the hunt for a ticket to the West. Waterson, he recalls, had sneaked off with one of them into a bedroom stocked with vodka and condoms.

Not that he'll remember *me*, he thinks. But God, how he'd ribbed Kostya at the time for not cottoning on that Waterson was gay. '*Kostik, you're so clueless,*' he'd said. It had seemed funny back then, something he and Artyom could have a laugh about. But not any more. Now, as he sits here inhaling Water-son's cocktail of cologne and corporate furnishings, it's not funny at all. Kostya's lost life of theatre and literature – a life contained and maybe, he thinks, even kept 'safe' until they met – was oceans apart from Waterson's jet-setting and hundred-dollar lunches. He'd heard there was a label for Waterson's type, a term that Oliver Rutland-Kerr and his expat buddies used to congratulate themselves on their life-style and status: the 'A-gays'.

Putting on his professional smile, he offers Waterson a business card. I'm here to ask about investment, remember, he tells himself. Not about Kostya, but about American trade prospects in Russia; 'emerging market', they call it, these types. At least that's what he'd said when he fixed up the interview. *'Tread carefully,'* Bernie had warned him after hearing about Kostya and his job with US-Care. *'Tread carefully – but get me a story.'*

Grinning, Waterson lounges in the sofa opposite him. 'Great view, eh?' He makes a sweeping wave towards the window, as if it were his personal fiefdom out there. Jamie allows himself another smile, relieved that Waterson seems not to recognise him.

As they wait for Nastya to bring them coffee, the American makes small talk, saying he was back in the States for Christmas with his 'folks'.

'Let me tell you something. It was as cold in Chicago as it is in Moscow.'

He forces a matey chuckle, a look of mock surprise. 'As cold as a Russian winter?'

'Yup, just as cold,' says Waterson. 'Only it sure ain't as *grim* as here.'

It's a relief when Nastya returns with the coffee and they can move on to the interview. Resting his notebook on his knee, he kicks off with a question about the recent US-Care investment conference. As Waterson holds forth, there's little he hasn't heard before – much of it from Kostya, who'd been disillusioned with the job for months – so the Yank sits there, giving him the usual patter about 'enterprise' and 'wealth creation'. As if all these American oilmen, fast-food chains and pharmaceuticals execs were drawn to Moscow out of the good of their hearts, to improve people's lives. Come off it, he thinks. But as Waterson reels off his list of success stories, he keeps nodding, repeating 'uh-uh' and 'oh, right?', acting impressed.

At one point, Waterson goes to his desk and brings Jamie a freshly printed document. He pretends to study it, glad of a prop for feigned curiosity, an excuse to break eye contact. It's a list, nothing remarkable, just a rundown of projects for which US-Care plans to grant funding. There's one column listing the recipients, another detailing their sphere of business. Before the interview is even over, he folds up the sheet of paper and shoves it in his bag.

Trouble is, talking to Waterson isn't giving him any pointers to how Kostya died, or anything that would make a story for Bernie. What would he write? *A 24-year-old man who worked on American–Russian trade deals* ... Only that'd make Kostya sound all business-y, not like him at all. How about: *A 24-year-old man who dreamt of becoming a theatre director –* that'd be more humanising to the reader – *has died after* ... After what, though?

His hour with Waterson is up, but as they head out the office door, he recalls what Larisa had told him and tries a different line of questioning.

'What sort of dealings do you have with the Russian Ministry of Privatisation?'

'What *sort* of dealings?' Waterson looks puzzled as he holds the door open. 'Why, pretty regular dealings. Most of the projects on that list I gave you get referred to us by the Ministry of Privatisation.'

'*Referred* to you?'

'Sure – the ministry wants American investment, right?

And boy, they have a list as long as their arm of new businesses wanting our know-how.'

'I see . . .' They're out in the open-plan area of the office now, near Kostya's old desk. 'And are any of these dealings especially *sensitive*?'

'Well, there's always commercial confidentiality, sure.' Waterson quizzes Jamie with a look. 'Whaddya mean by *sensitive*?'

'I mean, sensitive enough, for example' – how can he put this? – 'for a ministry employee to overstep the mark?'

Waterson shrugs. 'What would I know? You'd have to ask the ministry that.'

Hmmph, he thinks, fat lot of good that'll do. He tries another tack, coming to a halt by Kostya's old desk, acting like he's surprised by the sight of the photograph and the flowers. Before he even asks, Waterson is shaking his head, saying, 'Terrible business. Poor kid.'

'Oh yeah?' He searches Waterson's face for some clue. 'What happened?'

Waterson, to his surprise, looks genuinely bewildered: sighing, his expression falling and a discernible slump in his posture. The all-smiling, all-American front seems to be whipped away, like a veil, to reveal the person, not the persona, a man who might have known loss and pain after all. For a second or two, he's silent.

'We don't know,' Waterson says finally. 'Konstantin was a great kid, real smart. Spoke great English. Took on a lot of extra responsibilities. Then one day he didn't show up for work. Next thing we heard, he'd passed away.'

Jamie turns back to Kostya's portrait. That's what could work as the opening to his story – *A photograph, framed in black,*

sits on the desk of Konstantin Krolikov, a young man whose dreams
of acting and directing were cut short when ...

He hears himself ask, 'You've no idea how he, err, died, this
colleague of yours?'

Waterson's still shaking his head. 'Not a clue. Nothing from
the police. Zilch, *nada*. And nothing more than "natural causes"
in any official account. You're a reporter. You know how hard
it is to get to the truth in this country.'

He nods: he knows all right. That's why he needs Dima to
check out that address in Khimki. The cheeky twat had the
nerve to phone and demand *another* favour, saying he needed
a lawyer for his mate Oleg. He'd agreed too: he dreaded to
think of one of his own pals getting arrested by the Russian
police, and after all it was no skin off his nose to call Jules and
get someone from his law firm to go see Oleg.

Waterson adds, 'Weird thing is, Konstantin never took a day
off sick or showed any sign of being ill. He just stopped turning up to work. But that was more than a week before the
news. And during that time, not a word. He certainly didn't
call in sick.'

Looking round, Jamie sees Nastya at her typewriter, head
lowered but clearly watching him and Waterson. Their eyes
meet, a split second only, then she gives a shake of her head.

Time for one last question, he thinks, something businesslike. 'And your colleague' – he peers at the condolences card
in an exaggerated pretence of reading it – 'err, Konstantin,
right – what sort of work did he do for US-Care?'

Waterson frowns, as if snapped out of his reverie. '*What sort*
of work? Why, he did exactly the kind of work I've spent the
past hour telling you about.'

'Oh, right. Yes, of course, I see.' He reaches inside his bag for the list of US-Care projects that Waterson gave him.

'He helped assess those outfits who apply to us for funding. In fact,' Waterson nods at the list in Jamie's hand, 'the projects on that list are ones for me to sign off on. But before I do so, they have to be vetted. Some of them Konstantin vetted himself. Due diligence, we call it. And Konstantin, always working late, was *very* diligent.'

Dima

'Have we met before, young man? I feel sure I recognise you from somewhere.'

The question throws him off-guard. He finds himself staring back at the face on the other side of the desk: Stepan Mikhailovich has white hair combed back from a blotchy, pink forehead, his brows are knitted and bushy, and sunken eyes squint over the top of wire-framed spectacles. A face he doesn't recognise at all.

'I don't think so.' He shrugs. 'It's my first time here.'

Wait, was that the wrong answer? Should he be acting like he's familiar with this place, whatever they do here? Except that wouldn't fit with what he's rehearsed. Ironic, he thinks, how much he's longed to be in the movies, to have strangers come up and say they recognise him – but now that he's 'in character', facing this fifty-something man in a grey suit, what he needs, more than anything, is to remain unrecognised.

Stepan Mikhailovich smiles, showing ranks of tea-stained teeth. 'Must be my memory playing tricks on me.' He sighs. 'Now excuse me a moment – as you see, I'm having something of a clear-out, please bear with me ...'

Stepan Mikhailovich turns to open a filing cabinet, and Dima's eyes roam around the small office they're sitting in. On the walls he can see faint patches that he recognises, from his own experience of vacating his room, as the impression left by pictures removed in haste. The shelves are empty too, and on the floor a stack of books waits next to a suitcase. Hanging on the door behind him is a white lab-coat, but all that remains on the wall are two diagrams: one of the human brain, one of the nervous system.

'Well, there's no record of you in my files.' Stepan Mikhailovich turns back to Dima, clasping his hands together on the desk in front of him. 'Maybe I've seen you somewhere else ...' A puzzled frown. 'Now tell me, how can I help you?'

Dima swallows. It's one thing looking nervous, acting unsure of himself – that's part of the plan – but he now feels genuinely nauseous, unable to shake off the desolation and unease of this place: that icy road, the landscape blanked out by snow, the hum of electricity pylons, his sighting of Yuri's car. All this, at an address connected with Kostya's death; an address with all the trappings of a *bizness* – the plaque on the door, the office, the reception area – but where something, he can't tell what, remains hidden from view.

Again, he hangs his head. Partly to avoid Stepan Mikhailovich's stare, partly to put on his act once more, to inhabit the recognised body language of shame. 'It's *delikatny*,' he mutters – the same word he used with lab-coat woman, the same word Jamie used when he suggested that Dima ought to get tested for Aids. 'Thing is, Doctor, I've been sleeping around, taking risks.'

It sounds right, addressing the man as 'doctor'. Even if he isn't one, he looks the type who expects deference. He pauses for effect, then adds, 'I mean, with other men.'

'With *men*, you say?'

'Yes, Doctor.' Time for his killer line: 'I want to get tested to make sure that I haven't caught Aids.'

Stepan Mikhailovich presses his fingertips together and regards him, swivelling slowly in his chair, left to right, right to left. '*Aids*, you say?' There's a disapproving silence as he lets the word linger in the air.

The swivelling abruptly stops and Stepan Mikhailovich thrusts his face across the desk, confronting Dima with those tea-stained teeth. Under his bushy brows, the eyes are wide with scepticism. 'Young men don't come to Renaissance to get tested for *Aids*,' the doctor says. 'You should know that, shouldn't you?'

He can almost see himself go pale. Has he been rumbled? Could Stepan Mikhailovich suspect why he's really here? No, think, that's not possible, how could he? The doctor fixes him with his gaze, as if he's been thrown in front of a judge or a priest, forced to confess his sins. Licking his dry, chapped lips, he tries to think of what to say next.

But it seems there's no need for him to speak. Stepan Mikhailovich stands and turns to stare out of the window. Dima looks at the grey-suited back of his interrogator. Beyond that, beyond the street outside and out in the distance over the fields, he recognises the prison-like building he passed earlier.

Still with his back to him, the doctor speaks again: 'I take it you've been engaging in *unsafe* sex? With men too. *Sodomy*, in other words.' He turns to face Dima, narrowing those piggy eyes, his lips pinched tight with distaste.

Dima nods, letting his head drop. The shame feels real – induced not so much by Stepan Mikhailovich's stony stare as by his memories of cheating on Kostya: the nights he lied, saying Kostya couldn't come over because Oleg was ill, the nights he was out picking up strangers, the nights he was giving blowjobs to Yuri ...

'I could refer you elsewhere for testing,' the doctor adds. '*Or* I could report you to the police.' He leans heavily on the desk, and Dima looks up, alarmed. 'Let me be clear though: this is no Aids clinic. I don't run the sort of service that *condones* sexual deviancy by providing anonymous tests and kind words. If you want a sympathetic ear for your perversion, you've come to the wrong place.'

Silence. Stepan Mikhailovich returns to the window, staring outside once more with his back turned as if to let Dima know that he's dismissed.

I should give up, he thinks. Better call it a day and get out of here. He stands, scraping back his chair.

'Wait.' The doctor speaks again. 'I didn't tell you to *leave*, did I?'

Stepan Mikhailovich has stepped away from the window, but his eyes are averted towards some mid-air point between the floor and the desk. 'I may not be able to "assist" you when it comes to Aids,' he says; 'nevertheless your type of *deviancy* does form a substantial part of my research. In fact,' he gestures at the pile of books by the suitcase, 'I've been invited to speak at a conference in America, in the state of Utah.'

Warily, Dima sits back down. Looking him in the eye, the doctor goes on: 'Now, I could be away for some time – so you wouldn't be seen by me personally. However, there *is* help that we can offer for your condition. Let me explain what it is and how it works.'

14

SIX MONTHS EARLIER

AUGUST 1992. Moscow

Kostya

'Black Saturday' I called it. A day when bad things that had been waiting to happen seemed to tire of waiting and all happened at once.

That morning, Mama had for some reason decided that the apartment needed spring-cleaning. When I told her I was heading out, she was standing on a chair to polish the top of the display cabinet. She stared down at me, spluttering not so much from the dust as from the news that I wouldn't be staying in to help her.

'Going out where?' she said, coughing.

'I've made plans, Mama.'

'*Plans?* Can't it wait another day?'

'No, Mama.'

'Well, will you be back for dinner?'

'Yes, Mama, *yes.*' Before she could object any further, I grabbed my briefcase and made a run for the door.

Moscow was sweltering that day. Everybody, everything wilted in the sun's glare. People without dachas to escape to stumbled along, mopping their brows, looking wobbly in the waves of heat radiating up from the pavement. Dust hung in the air and leaves hung, lifelessly, on the trees. Yet despite the heat, I set off with a spring in my step. I was on a mission: I was going to call in on every theatre in Moscow that I'd not heard back from, and I was going to deliver, in person, my curriculum vitae.

I know: you thought I'd given up my dream of working in theatre. But Mama and I simply needed the money that kept me tied to US-Care. It was soul-destroying ... I soon cottoned on that the true purpose of US-Care's 'assistance' to Russia was to dish out contracts to American companies: a collective farm in need of new combine harvesters to make sure the wheat didn't rot in the fields would apply to US-Care — but the money ended up as sweeteners for American manufacturers of farming equipment.

Day after day, businessmen waltzed in to see Mario, reeling off sales pitches about Russia being their big new 'emerging market'. What did they think we were 'emerging' *from*? The Dark Ages? They didn't see the Russia that produced Tchaikovsky and the Bolshoi and *War and Peace*. They didn't see a land that was home to people who lived and loved, and laughed and cried. Once, when I explained my job to Mama, she'd snorted, '*Market*? Capitalist nonsense! All we are to them is another place to sell stuff.'

After work, I kept going to the baldness clinic, although its potions and 'healing energy' never produced the attractive head of hair I craved. Other evenings, I stayed late in the office, using work as an excuse to avoid sitting at home with Mama.

Worse, I never saw you any more. My vision of us in Moscow 'together' was an illusion. Once you'd met Artyom, our sleepovers and late-night chats came to an end. And when you'd invited me out with you as a couple, I was sullen and snappy, wincing at every touch you shared, every 'we', every kiss. As it happened, that very Saturday night Artyom was throwing a party to celebrate having his parents' flat all to himself. Out of the blue, you'd phoned me at work to invite me along. 'C'mon, Kostik,' you'd said – '*we'd* love to see you.'

★

At the Satire Theatre, they told me it was not the right day. At the Arts Theatre, it was not the right season. The Taganka didn't have any money. Other theatres had other excuses. Box office after box office, stage door after stage door, harassed stagehands glanced at my sweaty face and dusty shoes, took my CV without looking at it and said no promises of a job. Not once did I get to speak to a director.

After the last theatre on my rounds, I bought some lemonade from a babushka outside and drank it on a park bench at Chistiye Prudy. I sat watching husbands and wives stroll arm in arm with their children, eating ice-creams, and was stung by a yearning to be like those young couples whose lives were mapped out for them, approved of by society. There was one couple with a little boy of about eight; he reminded me of myself at that age, when I played for hours on end with the toy theatre that Papa built. And now I sat there, feeling that I would never get to play at theatre as an adult after all.

★

So *this* was what Mama was up to with her 'spring clean'. This was why she'd been ferreting around in Irina Efraimovna's display cabinet. She had polished the landlady's wine glasses and set them out on a tablecloth so crisply ironed that it fell into neat little folds at the corners. The table was laid with Irina Efraimovna's best cutlery too, and a roast chicken squatted on a china platter – also the landlady's.

'We have a guest tonight,' she announced as I eased my sweaty feet out of my shoes. She wafted the smell away with her hand. 'Now go get showered and freshened up for her.'

'Her' turned out to be Rita, a girl in her twenties who worked with Mama at Stockmann. She was educated, unaffected, not tarty or excessively made-up like Nastya, and with a disarming habit of tucking her blonde ringlets behind her ears. Rita was studying classical music. 'Kostya likes classical music, don't you, Kostya,' Mama kept saying. 'Tell Rita about those symphonies you like listening to.'

Like everyone in Russia, Rita needed money – hence her part-time supermarket job – but aspired to become a musician, practising the violin and going to auditions. 'Sounds like you, Kostya,' Mama prompted. 'Trying to get work in the theatre, I mean. Tell Rita about all those theatre jobs you've been chasing.'

At this point Mama excused herself, saying she needed to clear up in the kitchen. Rita stood too, eager to leave the table. 'Let me give you a hand, Tamara Borisovna.'

'I wouldn't hear of it!' Mama said. 'You're a guest. Besides, I should leave you two young people alone to chat, get to know each other.'

Rita sat back down. She fidgeted with her hair and forced a smile. Make conversation, I told myself, offering her another glass of wine. She clamped her hand over the glass – '*Nyet, spasibo*' – but asked me about my plans for a job in theatre.

I poured myself a bigger glass than I was used to and, as I talked, I sensed Mama listening in from the kitchen, the sound of clattering plates conspicuously absent.

When the time came for Rita to leave, we stood in the hallway to say goodbye. Mama put on a clown-like face of regret, head to one side, bottom lip pushed out. 'Such a shame you can't stay longer,' she pouted, but insisted that Rita must come over again.

Rita nodded hard. 'Of course, Tamara Borisovna, that'd be lovely.' I made as if to shake her hand but ended up in a clumsy exchange of kisses on the cheek. Out of the corner of my eye, I saw Mama watching our every move.

'Wait, Rita,' she said. 'Kostya'll walk you to the metro, won't you, Kostya?'

I shot a glance at Rita, who was shaking her head and saying that was very kind but really, it wasn't necessary. Mama gave me a shove, insisting we couldn't let a young woman walk alone to the metro in the evening, could we. So I escorted Rita down in the lift, a descent into silence punctuated by small talk about how hot the weather had been. By the time we'd crossed the yard with nothing else to say, Rita said she'd be fine from there.

Later, as Mama and I did the washing-up (she hadn't touched it earlier, when she was eavesdropping from the kitchen), she asked me what I thought of Rita. Her eyes were prying and expectant. I looked away, my gaze fixed on the plate I was towelling dry. Yes, I muttered, she seemed nice.

'Isn't she just!' Mama wittered on. 'And you've so much in common! Her music, your theatre. We got chatting one night after work and I thought, right, I'll invite her over—'

Perhaps I'd had too much to drink, but suddenly I couldn't

play along any more. Flinging down my tea towel, I said, 'Yes, Mama, I'm glad you're making new friends.'

She turned, still bent over the sink, and glared at me. 'Making friends?'

Silence. Mama put down the plate she was washing and straightened up. 'You know perfectly well,' she went on, 'that at *my* age I'm not looking for friends of *her* age to go to parties with, or whatever it is that youngsters get up to these days.'

'That bothers you, does it?' I said. 'What youngsters get up to these days?'

Mama sniffed. 'Most youngsters, no. But it bothers me what *you* get up to, Kostya.'

My throat tightened. I sensed the onset of another row, our first since the August coup a year earlier. And as I froze, weighing up the fallout of what I might say next, I could hear my pulse, my breathing, the sound of water gurgling down the plughole.

Mama turned off the tap. 'Your father's not here to have this conversation with you.' Her voice was shaky but cold. 'So, once again, it's down to me to pick up the pieces.'

Pick up the pieces. She meant getting me out of the army all those years ago; Mama could always play the martyr with that one. 'You're not a boy any more,' she went on, 'you're a young man – *twenty-five* next year – and still single. Don't you think it's time you found—'

'Found what?' I said. 'A girlfriend? A wife?'

She inhaled sharply. Then nodded. 'You do want to meet someone, don't you?'

Yes, I told her, I did want to meet someone – I didn't say 'a girl', I said 'someone' – but there was no need for her to match-make, she could stop interfering, I'd be fine.

She snorted, a bitter little laugh. 'Fine? You call this "fine", do you?'

I felt my hackles rise. What, I asked her, did she mean by 'this'? And what wasn't 'fine' about it? Wasn't I good enough for her the way I was?

She brandished a wooden spoon at me like a cudgel, her hand shaking as she launched into a lecture about how hard life could be on your own, how she didn't want me to end up like that. But I had no *intention*, I told her, of ending up on my own. What was this anyway, another sob story about how she'd had to cope since Papa left?

She shook the wooden spoon at me, then settled for prodding me in the chest with it. 'I've told you before,' she hissed, 'not to bring your papa into this!'

Then stop acting, I said, as if she cared about *me* ending up lonely. She started yelling: all right, it wasn't only me she was worried about. Hadn't I stopped to think of *her*? Did I have any idea how it felt to be a mother, to worry about her son's future? Then she came out with: 'And I'd hoped I might be a grandmother one day – doesn't that matter to you?'

I too found myself raising my voice. Oh, what a disappointment I must be to her. It'd be so much better if I were to *procreate*, wouldn't it? Then I could perpetuate her cycle of 'family values', couldn't I, a cycle of disappointment and divorce—

She threw down the spoon and raised a hand to slap me, just like a year ago. This time I caught hold of her wrist. She raised the other hand and I caught that one too. For a second or two, we tussled and grunted, and Mama lost her footing, staggering back against the worktop. One of the plates she had washed slid off the pile into the sink and cracked in two.

Irina Efraimovna's best crockery ... Mama turned and

gaped at it. I drew breath but then pressed on, saying, 'You don't need to be breathing down my neck.'

'Breathing down your neck?' Her chest heaved as she steadied herself against the sink. 'I suppose you'd rather have left me in Voronezh on my own?'

I fought to keep my voice down and reminded her that I had not, at any point, *asked* her to follow me to Moscow. She shot back: 'You'd like that, wouldn't you? Me hundreds of miles away, leaving you to get up to God knows what in Moscow.'

And what did she suppose I 'got up to'? Come on, I urged her, spit it out, what was she so frightened of?

There was a hiatus, but I felt it coming, what she was going to say. She went quiet, her fingers clinging to the edge of the sink, her gaze turned not towards me but towards that broken plate. It was me and 'that English boy', she muttered. Didn't I think she'd noticed? I was 'infatuated' with you, she said, 'obsessed'. You'd 'corrupted' me, she said.

I was dumbstruck. She was right about the first point: I *was* infatuated with you. But *corrupted*? If only I had been 'corrupted' by you, if only you had been my boyfriend ... When I recovered my voice, I told Mama she was being ridiculous, like she was spouting *Pravda*. How could one boy, however charismatic, overturn a lifetime's upbringing, everything society had drummed into me, and single-handedly 'corrupt' me into becoming a homosexual?

There, I'd said it: *gomoseksualist*. I couldn't believe I'd used the word in front of her. She let go of the sink and collapsed into a chair. 'Is that what you've decided you are?' She stared at the table. 'Listen to you, using *that word*. Doesn't it turn your stomach, the thought of it? What happened? Didn't I bring you up right?'

I sank into the chair opposite her, my head in my hands. 'How on earth,' I said, 'could my upbringing have anything to do with it?' I was brought up Soviet and conformist, like her. Raised by heterosexual parents, schooled in heterosexuality from day one at nursery school. Bombarded with role models such as soldiers and cosmonauts. How could I be 'turned' by one English boy I'd known for barely three years?

That was logical, right? Surely Mama would see sense? But all she did was shudder like she was going to be sick. 'Are you trying to tell me it's natural, this *gomoseksualizm*?'

Your words came to me, from that sleepover more than two years earlier. *It's natural for me*, you'd said. And that's what I told Mama: that it was natural for me.

She didn't answer. In that moment's silence, the sound of our breathing stabbed at the air. We could hear a radio in the flat next door. At this point in previous rows, she might have given in to tears and that would be the end of it. I would hug her and she would sob, shaking in my arms. Not this time. She turned her back on me and stared out of the window. It was still light outside but her reflection was visible, stony against the evening sky.

I recalled something else you said: that mothers always know, they just do – and I softened my tone, trying to tell Mama it was natural for her to worry, I understood that, but I wasn't alone, there were plenty of boys like me, even in Russia—

She shot to her feet, her chair crashing to the floor. 'I don't care about other boys! Not Jamie, not any of those *deviants*. You' – she jabbed with a trembling finger – 'are *my son*. And I'm not letting any son of mine be corrupted, turned into—'

I'd had enough of trying to reason with her. Enough. I

stood, walked out of the kitchen and snatched up my keys. I had to get out – and I knew where I could go.

Mama followed me into the hallway. 'Where d'you think you're going this time of night?' I turned and saw her standing there, fists shaking at the side of her apron. So I told her I might as well live up to her belief that I was 'corrupted'. If that's what she thought, I'd go and make damn sure that I got myself corrupted.

The idea came to me in a flash. There was no 'Discotheque for Deviants' (as you called it) that night, but there *was* the party at Artyom's. Any unease, any jealousy about seeing you and him together, I pushed to the back of my mind. To put me in the mood, I could down a shot of vodka from the kiosk near the metro. That would help loosen my inhibitions.

*

'*Kostya?*' Artyom's voice crackled down the entryphone, audibly puzzled. Didn't he remember me? I caught a snatch of music in the background, some frantic whispering, then: 'Oh, *that* Kostya! Jamie's Kostya!' He sounded drunk. 'Come on up! Top floor.'

The buzzer sounded and I entered the foyer of a distinctly grand apartment block. There was a porter's desk – unmanned at this hour on a Saturday night – and polished wood panelling instead of standard-issue whitewash. I tiptoed across the marble floor towards an old-fashioned lift, a cage of fancy metalwork cranked up and down on whirring pulleys.

Once at the top floor, I rang the doorbell, expecting it to be answered by Artyom. But it wasn't him, it was you. Even though I knew you'd be there, I was tongue-tied at the sight of you, suntanned in your white REM T-shirt and Converse All Stars, a bottle of beer in one hand, the other holding the door open wide as if you lived there. Maybe you *did* live there now? With Artyom's parents in the States, you might have moved in. *Shacking up*, you called it – like you and I had once talked about doing.

'Kostik!' you said, beaming. 'Kostik, come on in!' You flung your arms around me and hugged me, holding on for a few seconds longer than I dared to hope. 'We haven't seen you for *ages*! Bit late for you, isn't it? We thought you weren't gonna come.'

That 'we' again. For those few seconds, as I savoured the embrace of your arms and the warmth of your cheek touching mine, I sought some sign, some reassurance that we were still bosom buddies like we'd been in Voronezh; that we could get over my jealousy. But then I heard that 'we'. You were a 'we' person now, one half of a couple bonded at a level that was not only intimate but exclusive of others too. You weren't just Jamie any more, you were Jamie *and Artyom*. From inside the apartment came the hubbub of conversation and the *doof-doof-doof* of dance music. The party was well underway.

'Look at you!' I said, lamely. 'Where d'you get that suntan?'

'What, *this*?' You pulled a quizzical face, half grin, half shrugging it off. 'Weekends at Artyom's dacha, mainly – plus we just got back from holiday in Cyprus—'

'*Cyprus*?' I was gobsmacked – your word again – that you'd been *abroad* and could be so blasé about it. I hadn't even known you were going.

'Yeah, Cyprus!' you continued, almost shouting in my ear as you ushered me along the hallway to a room packed with bodies. 'Aeroflot flies to Larnaca, you know. And we got a flight for *roubles*! You should go – the place is full of Russians.'

In Cyprus, you rattled on, it had been 'proper hot, proper

sunny', and you'd found 'this cheap hotel where all the Eastern Europeans went, right near the beach ...'

I nodded but had stopped listening. Instead, I gazed around the room, trying to picture it without all these people crammed in. The lights were low and the cigarette smoke so thick that I could barely make out high ceilings, book-lined shelves, dozens of framed pictures. I recognised a few faces from the disco: tall, blond Rasmus sharing a joke with short, brown-skinned Jules; Oliver Rutland-Kerr talking to that paunchy Finnish guy in leather jeans. At one end of the room, a table spilled over with bottles and used glasses; at the other, Artyom, wearing headphones to play the DJ, stood at a smaller table with records and cassettes piled next to a large speaker. He saw us – or you, rather – and grinned, giving a thumbs-up.

'So, Kostik,' you were asking, 'what's it gonna be?'

'What's that? Oh, to drink ... err, vodka, please.'

After storming out on Mama, I had stopped only for a hurried shot of vodka from the kiosk on our street. Its soothing warmth had spread from my gut, a pleasant contrast to the cooling evening air, and helped to numb the barbs and blows of our row. Yet as I rode the metro, her words rang in my ears – as did what I'd said to her; I'd used the word *gomoseksualist*, I'd said it was 'natural for me'.

So yes, more vodka. You squeezed my shoulder and made your way out to the kitchen, stepping over the legs of couples sitting on the floor smoking and drinking beer straight from the bottle. Just then Artyom put on some American dance number I'd heard at the disco but couldn't put a name to – and two women in sleeveless black tops leapt to their feet and started dancing, pouting and beaming at each other.

You reappeared with a glass of vodka. I grabbed it and downed it in one.

Your jaw dropped. 'Bloody hell, Kostik! What's got into you?'

I'd thought of telling you about my showdown with Mama, but decided it could wait. A vodka-fuelled thrill of warmth shot up and down my back, and I had to exhale sharply. You noticed that I had my eye on the second glass of vodka in your other hand. 'Hands off!' you said. 'This is for the DJ!'

Artyom duly popped up at your side, lips puckered against your cheek and his arm slung around your waist. My gaze followed his hand down to your bottom, where it slipped inside your back pocket, then slipped out and fingered the hole in your jeans just below.

'Kostik!' he said with a grin, leaning heavily on you for support. 'Long time, no see!' He ran a hand through his long hair, a touch blonder after the sun of Cyprus, and I caught a glint of his silver earring. He raised his eyebrows. 'Now, what're you doing with an empty glass in your hand? C'mon, Jamie, get Kostya a drink, will ya—'

'I've just given him one!'

'Then get him another! Now, where's the vodka? In the freezer? Nah, tell you what, give him mine—'

He snatched the empty glass from my hand, grabbed the full one from yours and handed it to me, spilling half the vodka in the process.

I blushed. Might have been the vodka, might have been Artyom's rakish charm. 'Oh,' I stuttered, 'what about you?'

Artyom inserted his head between ours. 'Don't worry about me,' he hiccupped. 'I'm gonna have a smoke now.' And out came his shiny pouch and cigarette papers.

You shook your head, still grinning though. 'What about the DJ-ing, Artyom?'

'Ah, forget that!' Artyom carried on rolling up and nodded towards the two girls in black sleeveless tops. 'They don't need me, look! People are dancing!'

I looked again. One of the girls had dark hair in a pert, shiny bob, while the other was a spiky peroxide blonde. Each swayed in time with her partner, teasing one another with a little shimmy of the shoulders or a caress of the other's face.

As you excused yourself and went to the kitchen for some beer, I found Artyom's face up-close to mine, inhaling on his joint, then blowing smoke in my general direction.

'So, Kostya,' he asked, 'did you ever make it to Peter?'

Peter? Ah, yes, St Petersburg – that aborted conversation from the night he'd chatted me up ... I coughed and shook my head. 'Well, I'd love to' – I weighed up my reply – 'but it's not much fun without someone to go *with*.'

Artyom pulled a mock-serious face, head cocked to one side. 'Aw, c'mon, Kostik,' he said, putting a hand on my shoulder. 'No hard feelings, eh? I mean, about Jamie and me? We're all still *friends*. We're all still *cool*, right?'

I didn't know what to say. Artyom had articulated what neither you nor I had bothered to express all these past months, with me in a prolonged sulk and you giving up on me. On the one hand, I thought: no, we're not 'cool'. On the other, I felt almost gratified that he had acknowledged my feelings. Maybe I was even a little flattered by his attention, and I shrugged, saying, 'You know, it's just—'

'Hey, tell you what.' Artyom stuffed his joint between his lips and placed both his hands on my shoulders. Then, puffing out of one corner of his mouth, he said, 'I'm gonna introduce you to some friends of mine.'

Which was how I met Nina and Veronika. Yes, the groovy lesbian couple dancing right in front of me. Nina was the one with the bob – 'My Audrey Hepburn look!' she said, giggling – while Veronika was the spiky peroxide blonde. Like Annie Lennox, I quipped, emboldened by my fourth or fifth vodka and feeling another rush as my joke elicited laughter. I immediately warmed to the pair; they had a sense of togetherness without smugness, ready to stick two fingers up at the idea of needing a man. They reminded me of Zhanna.

Nina suggested that we go out on the balcony for some air. By now the sun had all but set, a band of orangey pink across the horizon, then purple above our heads where the stars were coming out. To the west, I spied a fiery ribbon of light where the sinking sun reflected off the Moskva river; to the north, beyond the mosaic of rooftops, dusky courtyards and lighted windows, I saw the towers of the Kremlin, floodlit and topped by glowing red stars.

Veronika lit a joint that she'd scrounged from Artyom and passed it first to Nina, then to me. I had never done drugs, but that night I thought: what the hell. Clumsily pinching the thing between my thumb and forefinger, I inhaled and ended up coughing and spluttering, my eyes watering. The girls laughed, but kindly, slapping me on the back. On my second or third attempt, its pungent herbal smokiness slipped easily into my lungs.

It must've loosened my tongue because I started telling Nina and Veronika about my thwarted dreams of working in theatre, about not having a boyfriend. And about my row with Mama. They nodded, squeezed my hand, made sympathetic noises, offered me more drags on the spliff. I accepted, I inhaled. And they told me how they'd been disowned by their parents after years of denial and, in Veronika's case, going through with a sham marriage in a bid to 'straighten herself out'. It was a story, they said, shaking their heads, that was repeated the length and breadth of Russia – and would be until gay people asserted their right to be. The discos were only a first step, they said: we should open permanent bars and clubs, then demand equality before the law. They talked of organising a 'kiss-in' outside Moscow City Hall—

'No way!' I said. My head was more than spinning: it felt like it was on some wonky orbit somewhere above my neck and below the sky. I wasn't sure whether I meant no way, it's never going to happen, or it's so outrageous, let's do it.

By then, I'd lost sight of you and Artyom. Others came out onto the balcony though – Jules cadging a drag on Veronika's spliff, and a ginger-haired boy in a flowery silk shirt who tumbled out from the living room, giggling loudly and singing along, in a grating Russian accent, to Mariah Carey's 'Can't Let Go'—

'Oh my God!' Nina span round to grab both my hands. 'That's a friend of ours who works in theatre. I've *got* to introduce you! You'll love him!'

My poor head, wobbling, circling, orbiting . . . Who was she talking about? I blinked. No, she couldn't mean this ginger-haired boy in the flowery shirt, not my type at all! Too short, too ginger, too freckly, too – but I felt Nina and Veronika grab me (holding me up, more like) by both elbows and manoeuvring me along the balcony towards him.

Right then, through the balcony doors, I saw you and Artyom. You were locked in a slow dance, a smooch to the warbling of Mariah Carey. You each had a hand tucked in the back pocket of the other's jeans. I wondered what that would feel like, my hand on your backside, yours caressing mine.

As Nina and Veronika introduced the ginger-haired boy, they were all so high and giggly that I didn't catch his name. Not that I was paying attention: I couldn't stop looking at you and Artyom. Next thing I knew, though, I was being bundled in through the balcony doors, stumbling over the threshold, and grabbing onto the ginger boy to stop myself falling. Without really meaning to, I put a hand on his waist. His hand reached for my shoulder and we found ourselves in a slow dance too. Side to side we swayed, in and out of focus went the boy's grinning freckled face, blink-blink went his batting eyelids.

I couldn't break free of him, not just yet, not with my head spinning and legs lurching from step to step – but at least I could let you see I'd found someone to dance with, someone else, not you. So I shuffled about until we bumped into you and Artyom. You winked at me as if in encouragement; if I'd been trying to make you jealous, it hadn't worked. I stared, my eyes narrowing with resentment – then felt myself being tugged back to my dance partner, this ginger-haired face full of freckles grinning inanely at me. He whispered something in my ear. Turned out he hadn't caught my name either. Kostya, I told him. His was Kirill.

*

I'm going to be a theatre director, I told Kirill. Not 'want to' be a theatre director, not 'hope to', but *going to*. That's what you say, isn't it, when you're trying to big yourself up? I'm sure it's what *you* did when you met Artyom.

We were out on the balcony again, leaning on the balus-trade, half-bottles of vodka in our hands. I made a sweeping gesture towards the Kremlin, as if to let Moscow know of my ambition. But I gestured with the wrong hand, and my bottle went flying, falling, falling until it landed in the courtyard below with a tinkle of broken glass.

Shocked silence. Then a fit of giggles, both of us convulsed with laughter and burying our heads in each other's shoulders. When Kirill looked up, his eyes were shining. 'And I'm going to be an *actor*!' he cried. He struck a theatrical pose, his hand miming a fluttering heart. 'Or, who knows, an *actress*!' More giggles, this time only his.

'I'm tired of being stuck behind the scenes!' he went on. 'I wanna be on stage, treading the boards!' He assumed an expression of mock solemnity and started bowing to an imaginary audience, then pressed his face close to mine. 'Tell me, Kostya. When you're a famous director, will you cast me in your play? Will you? Promise?'

I tried to inch away from Kirill, but my legs were slow to respond. As I shifted, he half fell, half lunged, dropping his bottle in a potted plant, and thrust his face at me. Before I could pull back, even a little, he had planted his lips on mine. His mouth tasted of the cranberry-flavoured vodka he'd been drinking.

As Kirill kissed me, I thought the writers and poets must have got it all wrong. In novels and operas, first kisses were magical, transporting their heroes or heroines to another world. Well, this was mine and it didn't. I squinted back at Kirill. His eyes were closed, his lashes fluttering, his freckles close up and blurred. His tongue slid its way into my mouth, poking and wriggling, and my own poked back like I thought you were supposed to, pushing his tongue away. I pictured two slugs wrestling.

Snogging, you called it. You taught me that. I pictured you sprawled on top of that boy at the nightclub in Birmingham, and attempted those same puckering, gulping shapes with my mouth. It wasn't enjoyable, not what I'd imagined. But it had better look convincing – not for Kirill's sake but because, out of the corner of my eye, I saw that you'd appeared at the door onto the balcony. I'll show you, I thought. I'll show you that I'm capable of 'pulling' too.

But as Kirill's cranberry-vodka-tasting tongue-slug slithered around mine, as saliva dribbled from my mouth, I saw that Artyom had joined you. I thought you'd look away, embarrassed. But no, you nudged him and whispered in his ear. You both started sniggering.

Kirill pulled back from our long, wet kiss and licked his lips. Leaning his head on my shoulder, he asked me if we could carry on at my place.

The bravado of my theatre-director persona evaporated. I can't, I told him, I live with my mother. 'Then come back with me,' he said. 'I live with friends.'

I tried to stand up straight but collapsed against the railing. The burning red stars atop the distant towers of the Kremlin appeared to drift apart, then swirl, reeling and dancing before my eyes. I tripped over the potted plant where Kirill had dropped his bottle and crashed to my knees. Then came the vomit. A thin, runny vomit that tasted of Mama's carrot salad gone sour, pickled in vodka and dope. Most of it landed in the plant pot.

I staggered to my feet, wiped my mouth on my sleeve and brushed off Kirill's helping hand. 'No, I can't come with you,'

I said. I had to get home. Mama was expecting me. 'I've got to go before it gets late—'

Kirill reached for my hand — but I was off, hobbling back into the room, tripping over Nina's and Veronika's legs where they sat on the floor. 'Kostya!' they called. 'Are you OK?' In the hallway, I saw you come out of the bathroom and barged straight past you, ignoring your calls of 'Kostik? Kostik?' I ran for the door, in as much of a hurry to get away from Kirill as I'd been to get away from Mama. The taste of vomit in my mouth affirmed my feelings of disgust. Ugh, that giggly little drama queen. No substitute for you ...

So much for that fairy-tale kiss. Not wanting to wait for the lift to crank itself into view, I blundered down the stairs, knowing the last metro had already gone and that I'd have to flag down a car. As I ran, a scene from my childhood toy theatre popped into my head, that of Cinderella fleeing the ball without a carriage to take her home. Now I was the one being a drama queen. But this was no ball and Kirill was no prince — and as for a glass slipper, I wouldn't even want to leave him my phone number.

Tamara Borisovna. Ten days later

The bus was nearly empty; most of the passengers had got off a couple of stops earlier. Yet she sat as if she'd been shoehorned into some distress position, legs clamped together, lips pinched shut. Her sunglasses hid half of her face, and even her shopping bag she hugged to her body like a barrier, as if she were still pressed up against the bodies and sweat of the crowd that had piled onto the bus with her outside the metro.

The bus bumped its way down a country lane. Rusting

Ladas and Moskviches rattled past, churning up clouds of dust. In the heat, the painted timbers of old wooden houses flaked and blistered, even under trees thick with leaves and shade. Further on, as the bus pulled up, she saw lines of babushkas selling bottles of water and lemonade, headscarves framing their wrinkles and squinting eyes.

At least I'm not reduced to that, she thought. Years ago, when she'd first travelled this route, she was still a head librarian, and you didn't see old women having to beg.

Her pity was fleeting, quickly trampled by the should-haves and what-ifs that crowded into her head, elbowing their way into every thought since her row with Kostya. What if her son caught Aids? What if he ran off to the West? Apart from phoning Galina, she'd had no one to talk to. If she tried calling Gennady, she might get his mistress on the phone – or worse, have it confirmed that Kostya's 'condition' was why her ex-husband had left her.

Maybe she was over-reacting? She cast about for crumbs of reassurance, for a reason to turn back home. Like her observation that Kostya hadn't mentioned the English boy for months. He'd stopped reading Jamie's articles out loud from the *Moscow Herald*. There were no more sleepovers. His 'phase', she'd hoped, had passed – hence her matchmaking with Rita. But what about the row they'd had? Kostya calling his condition 'natural' ... No, it wasn't natural. How could it be? She couldn't stand by and let her son slide into deviancy.

Her destination was further from the bus stop than she remembered. She had retraced the steps she'd taken along this very same lane when Kostya was a gangly seventeen-year-old in the army. It was quiet out here, with only the hum of the electricity pylons and distant roar of planes taking off from

Sheremetyevo. Her stomach churned, exactly as it did on that first visit. She recognised the perimeter wall: concrete slabs ranged three metres high around a six-storey block with small, barred windows. But the address she'd been given wasn't here, where she remembered it, but closer to Khimki town centre.

She was panting – I'm out of breath, that's all, she told herself, it's a long walk from the bus stop – and kept having to mop sweat from her brow. She stopped to shake out a stone that had lodged itself in one of her sandals. Come on, she thought, this is where I got help for Kostya before; surely I can get help again … Eventually she found the address, in an ordinary block of flats. Inside, on the second floor, a nurse ushered her into a waiting room in a space sleekly converted from an apartment.

The last time she came to Khimki, her mission had been simpler. To get Kostya out of the army, she had needed the doctor to sign certificates classifying her son as psychologically unfit. All she'd had to do was pay the bribe. Last time, she had known what to ask for; this time, she wasn't sure if salvation could be bought. Would the doctor even remember her after all these years? She hugged herself as she stared at the plaque on his door: 'Dr Milyukov, Stepan Mikhailovich, Psychiatric Director'.

*

The first thing she noticed as she entered his consulting room was that Stepan Mikhailovich looked sprightly and well-fed. But then he would, wouldn't he, all the money he was raking in. He remembered her too and, once the niceties were out of the way, asked her to sit and explain what was troubling her. She cleared her throat and fumbled for the right words, looking down at the floor, at the flowery pattern of her summer dress, at the medical diplomas and diagrams of the human brain on his wall. At times she looked up, hoping for the doctor to finish her sentences for her. He didn't. Instead he remained quiet, listening, fingertips pressed together. His grey eyes were hard to stare back at, as she searched for a glimmer of reassurance or even – God help her – warmth. When she came to the end of her explanation, he reclined in his high-backed swivel chair. There was a silence in which she heard a plane fly low overhead.

'Tamara Borisovna,' he said, 'you sound like you have every right to be worried. And Konstantin sounds like a somewhat deluded young man. But I can't simply write a certificate this time, can I?' He peered over his glasses at her. She looked down and shook her head.

'Especially,' Milyukov continued, 'if your son refuses to acknowledge his *condition* as being a problem.' He sighed, took off his glasses and polished them on the sleeve of his white lab-coat. 'There is, however, a course of treatment I can prescribe here. We call it "corrective reorientation". It works on the subconscious and other, more cognitive, reflexes too. It has to be applied in conjunction with medication – there's no magic pill, mind.'

He put his glasses back on. 'But it would require Konstantin's compliance. He would need to attend sessions, almost certainly overnight, possibly for several days. And as you know, Tamara Borisovna, you can lead a horse to water, but you can't make it *drink*, can you?'

15

MARCH 1993. Moscow

Dima

'How much longer are they gonna keep you in here, for fuck's sake?'

He shoots a glance along the row of cells. The same meat-head police thug is standing guard, eyes trained on him and arms akimbo as if to say 'Don't you try anything'. He presses his face back against the aperture in the door of Oleg's cell. The metal is cold on his cheek but at least the smell of urine inside has subsided, masked by a faint whiff of disinfectant.

Oleg looks down at his feet, shaking his head. 'Don't know. Couple of days? Maybe another week.' He looks up. 'Thing is, they might transfer me—'

'*Transfer you?*' The word 'prison' hovers, unspoken. 'But what for?'

Oleg shrugs. He looks thinner, his face ragged with stubble. Still, his bruises have faded and his hair is combed; the bastards must have let him scrub up before the lawyer arrives.

'The police could still charge me for loitering with intent – which I *was*, let's face it' – Oleg winces – 'but they don't have grounds to charge me with anything else. And because no actual sex act took place, Jules reckons that I—'

'*Jules*? Who's that?'

Oleg raises an eyebrow at him. 'The lawyer, of course. Jamie's pal.'

'Oh? He's been already?' He's surprised. Before his frantic phone call to Jamie, he'd not felt sure he could demand even more in exchange for going to Khimki – yet now it seems the English guy was willing to cough up after all . . . 'What was he like?'

'He's Belgian. Nothing like Jean-Claude Van Damme though.' Oleg's face cracks into a lopsided smile. 'A bit on the short side, but kind of cute, dark eyes, bronze skin—'

'Oleg! I'm being serious.'

'So am I, Dimik. I've seen him before, at the disco.'

'Really?' That's a good sign, he thinks. If this Jules is not just a mate of Jamie's, but also *nash*, one of us, he should be on our side. 'Did he come alone?'

'He had a Russian secretary with him to interpret.' Oleg gives him a wink. 'I didn't take much notice of *her* though.'

He manages a smile. This is the Oleg he knows, his old 'partner in crime'. They bump fists through the aperture, a gesture they've picked up from some American movie.

'OK,' he says, 'but can he get you out of here? What's this "transfer"? They can't mean *prison*, can they?'

Oleg shrugs again. 'Not if there's no evidence of a sex act – and not if Jules is right about this coming change in the law.' A pause. 'You know what change I mean, don't you?'

He nods. The rumours had been circulating on the gay scene for weeks now. Even Jamie mentioned it, last time they met. The news, if it could be believed, was that President

Yeltsin was going to repeal the old Stalin-era clause of the Soviet penal code that outlawed homosexual acts. Imagine it, no more threat of hard labour, no more criminalisation, full stop. Imagine Kostya's response, had he still been alive: '*See, Dima,*' he'd have said, '*we* can *set up home together, we* can *live like a couple* ...' Back in the real world, Yuri had greeted the rumour as good for business: more scope for his videos meant more viewers, bigger profits.

'Good old Yeltsin, eh?' Oleg attempts another smile but it crumples into a sob. 'Be sure to thank Jamie for getting Jules to come. If I wasn't in here, we'd celebrate, wouldn't we?' Another sob. 'Christ, I'm dying for a cigarette.'

'We will celebrate, Oleg. We will. Beers and Marlboros. Soon as you're out of here.'

Oleg wipes a tear on the cuff of his dirty denim jacket. 'Don't worry about me, Dimik,' he says, sniffling. 'You've got enough on your plate. Like, have you got anywhere to stay? Seriously, where are you gonna sleep tonight?'

*

'*Attention! Respected passengers, please vacate all carriages. Attention! Respected passengers, please vacate* ...'

Over and over, the announcement booms across the public address system. Must be the tenth time he's heard it, the tenth time he's ignored it. It's nearly 2 a.m. and he's done two complete circuits of the Circle line already. This time he's going anti-clockwise; all that's changed is the order of the stations – Taganskaya, Kurskaya, Komsomolskaya, instead of Komsomolskaya, Kurskaya, Taganskaya. The thing about the Circle line is there's no terminus, so if he can keep riding, he's in with a chance of staying on the metro all night. Even when the trains get shunted off to the depot, he'll be in the warmth and shelter. As long as no one turfs him out. He's heard it's going to hit minus fifteen on the streets.

The pensioners patrolling the stations are on the lookout for rough sleepers, red-faced *bomzhy* reeking of booze. Surely they can *smell* that he's not one of the *bomzhy*? Then again, he hasn't had a shower or a change of clothes for four days . . . Last night he'd avoided getting kicked out on the street when one kindly old soul – reminded him of Valery Ivanovich – fetched him a blanket and let him crash on a bench.

Oh, for an hour or two of oblivion. His body longs to slip into unconsciousness. He has to stay awake though, make sure they don't chuck him out. If only he had some Marlboros left, a good smoke might keep him alert – but he's sold them, the whole lot. At least he got a good price. His hand fingers the wad of roubles in his inside pocket.

There's his rucksack too. Three days he's been lugging it around. Aside from the clothes layered under his coat, it contains everything he owns. He digs around inside to make sure nothing's been stolen, and his fingers close on something hard-edged. It's the book Kostya gave him, an anthology of English plays translated into Russian.

He glances up. The train has pulled into Kievskaya, a station full of murals celebrating Russian–Ukrainian 'brotherhood', all garlands of flowers and dancing in folk costume. He hears a siren blast as the doors open, and ducks out of sight. Fortunately, no one looks into his empty carriage. The doors close again, and as the train heaves itself off into the tunnel, he flicks through the book, alighting on the front page. It's signed: *To my handsome prince, Dmitry, 'My Own Private' Superman, all my love, Kostya.*

He catches a glimpse of his reflection in the window. It stares back as the blackness of the tunnel roars by. Some

'Superman', he thinks. What sort of hero did Kostya take me for? Where did he get the idea that we could build a life of domestic togetherness? He flinches, recognising how much he'd actually prefer that right now. Even as a fallback in case of eviction, imagine being cuddled up with Kostya now, instead of being on the streets.

Outside in the tunnel he sees sparks fly and feels the train braking. There's a lurch to the side. It's pulling into a sort of yard to be parked overnight alongside lines of other empty carriages. He yawns and turns to a bookmarked page for a play called *Vizit Inspektora*. Now I'm no longer on the lookout, he thinks, I can bed down for the night and read it. I owe it to Kostya. But then, just as he's scanning the play's list of characters, the train gives a final shudder and the lights flicker off, leaving him in darkness.

★

The minute they meet, the English guy is in his face, full of questions. 'Did you make it to Khimki?' he's asking. 'What *is* that place, the address I gave you? And where've you *been*? I've been trying to call—'

'Give me a break, will you!' That morning, when he called the *Moscow Herald* from a payphone at Belorussky Station, Jamie had started firing questions at him, an impatient, half-whispered inquisition buzzing in his ear down the line. Now, an hour or so later, he's standing with Jamie on the steps outside the *Herald*'s building, too exhausted, too humiliated to look him in the eye.

'You *can't* call me,' he mutters. 'I'm on the streets. I've got nowhere to live.'

Looking up, he sees Jamie's mouth drop. 'What d'you mean, nowhere to live? What're you talking about?'

He hangs his head, ashamed to be confessing to this smart-arse foreigner what deep shit he's in. He tells Jamie about getting evicted from **Valery Ivanovich's**, then being turfed out of Oleg's dormitory room. And now Oleg isn't even there to smuggle him in – I could've had Oleg's bed, he thinks, if I'd known he was gonna spend all this time in a police cell … 'That,' he says, 'is why I've spent the last two nights riding the Circle line.'

'*Blyad!*' Jamie swears. 'I'm sorry, Dima, how was I to know—'

'Well, now you *do* know. I'm homeless. One of the *bomzhy*.'

They fall silent and he can hear their breath alongside the drip-drip of icicles melting from the gutters above. He looks at his feet. These shitty boots, letting in water again. And Christ, what he'd give for a hot bath …

He feels Jamie's hand on his arm. 'Dima, c'mon,' he's saying, 'let me buy you lunch. It's the least I can do. You look like you need it.'

He stares back, searching the English guy's face for signs of – what? Trust? Pity? But they don't seem able to hold each other's gaze. Besides, he's in no state to say no to lunch. He shuffles his feet and gives Jamie a barely perceptible nod.

They decide to go to McDonald's. 'It's the one place,' Jamie says, grimacing, 'where there'll definitely be something to eat.'

Through the snow and slush they make their way to Belorussky Station, where they flag down a passing Volga. But as he sees Jamie reach for the car's door handle, he steps in front of him, feeling a need to assert some remnant of the old, confident Dima. 'Let *me* do the talking,' he says. 'The driver'll charge double if he hears your foreign accent.'

They sit in the back seat, his rucksack forming a barrier

between them. Jamie peers up ahead, as if checking where they're going, while his own gaze shifts between his hands in his lap and the view rolling by outside the car window, the parade of new fashion shops and privatised banks along Tverskaya Street. In the absence of conversation, he tunes into the *vroom* of passing cars. He shudders, struck by an unwanted flashback to that night in Yuri's BMW, the last time he'd been in a car, the last time he saw Yuri. Except no, that wasn't the last time; he *has* seen Yuri since then, driving his BMW out of Khimki and looking pleased with himself . . .

He hasn't been to McDonald's since that day with Kostya nearly two months ago, the day he told Kostya he was planning to leave Moscow. He didn't realise it then, but that would be the final time they ever saw each other. As Kostya had run off, in tears, he'd been left in the queue outside, cold and hungry – though not as hungry as right now – debating whether to run after Kostya. If he'd done that, he thinks now, if he had run after Kostya, he would have kept his hold on him; Kostya couldn't have resisted him, not for long.

They pull up at Pushkin Square and he lugs his rucksack out of the car into the cold. The air is sharp with diesel fumes. Jamie pays the driver and they cross towards McDonald's. The queue, unlike that last-ever time with Kostya, is short today.

Once inside, while Jamie heads to the counter, he bags a table beneath a man-sized model of Big Ben. England, he thinks, looking at the famous clock face. How Kostya used to prattle on about his trip to England, about his special English friend Jamie and how Jamie had invited him to England. He's never been to the West himself – but he recalls the opening, three years earlier, of this McDonald's, the first in Russia. From day one, the queues had stretched onto the street, looping around Pushkin Square. The crowds had stood and shuffled and waited for up to two hours, oblivious to the stony gaze of Russia's revered national poet whose statue dominates the square. That's how tantalised they were by this glimpse of Western life. Some life, he thinks, casting a cynical glance at the counter staff bouncing up and down in their eagerness to serve. Some of them are probably wannabe actors, like him. Even so, at every table he sees couples and families puffed up with smugness. Look at us, they're saying, we're consumers now.

He watches Jamie return, carrying a tray laden with burgers, fries, milkshakes, tea and deep-fried apple pies. With a mutter of '*spasibo*', he bears down on his burger, taking a bite so big that he can barely chew. Out of one eye he catches Jamie staring at him. 'My God,' the English guy says, 'are you *that* hungry?'

His mouth's almost too full to speak. Swallowing what he can, he begins describing to Jamie what Stepan Mikhailovich – Dr Milyukov – had told him in his consulting room. He chews and talks, talks and chews, all table manners forgotten, letting grease dribble down his chin. He stuffs fries in his mouth, afraid of letting them go cold, not knowing where his next meal will come from. Unexpectedly, he feels Jamie's hand on his – 'Slow down, mate,' he's saying, 'take your time.'

He sees Jamie has taken out a pen, started taking notes. Oh, so he doesn't care if I make myself sick, he thinks, he just wants to pump me for answers to his goddamn questions. Questions like what is it, this 'corrective reorientation' that Milyukov prescribes? What is his *korrektirovka* supposed to do? And the worst question of all: how could anyone die of it?

'What I mean,' Jamie says, 'is, it's not exactly invasive surgery, is it?'

'Surgery?' It's a thought that occurred to him on his way to Khimki, that maybe Kostya had died during a conventional operation, on his brain or heart or something. As for the *korrektirovka*, there's no certainty that Kostya was even prescribed the treatment, let alone went through with it ... Wiping his mouth on the back of his hand, he shakes his head. 'No, not surgery – it's a psychiatric treatment.'

'Psychiatric?' Jamie raises an eyebrow.

'I'm telling you what Milyukov said.' He swallows another mouthful of burger and repeats what Stepan Mikhailovich told him: that the *korrektirovka* was designed to *act on the subconscious, as well as on cognitive reflexes* – then adds, like an afterthought, 'He had these diagrams of the human brain on his wall.'

'*Psychiatric*, though? Are there still places here peddling that shit?'

'Of course there are. D'you seriously believe we've put it safely behind us, all the crap from Soviet times?' He pictures Oleg, beaten and bruised in his police cell. 'D'you think *nashi* get treated any better nowadays than they did back in the 1950s?'

Jamie shrugs. 'Look at yourself, Dima. There's shitloads of stuff you wouldn't have got away with before *glasnost*. You're free to travel abroad, to flaunt your black-market gear, free to go to gay discos—'

'Gay *discos*?' He spits out a piece of burger gristle that's stuck in his teeth. '*Blyad*, look at 'em, those discos. Hiding in some godforsaken factory out in the sticks where no one can find us.' He thinks of Igor and Kirill, beaten senseless, hospitalised, cracked ribs. 'Except they still find us, don't they? They still come and beat the shit out of us.'

Discos and shops, jeans and trainers, BMWs and McDonald's – what's it all worth if none of *nashi*, not him nor Oleg nor Kostya, can ever kiss the guy they love or hold hands without getting beaten up? What good is it all? As if by way of an answer, another queasy flashback pops into his head: Yuri again, boasting about his expanding porn video sales.

He swallows the last of his burger and scrunches up the wrapper. 'You know, those discos haven't magically turned Russia into some "cool" place to be gay, in case that's what you think. All it means is that someone's now got a licence to make money out of us.'

A few seconds' silence. He sees the English guy squirm in his seat, fidget with the spoon in his tea. 'OK, Dima,' Jamie says, 'but I still need to ask you about this *korrektirovka*. Is that "corrective" as in it's supposed to turn a gay guy *straight*?' A snort, shaking his head. 'Well, it wouldn't work on me, I tell you that.'

'Nor on me.' He wipes his fingers on a paper napkin, frowning as Jamie scribbles in his notepad. 'But why would *you* ever have to worry about that? You're from the West.'

Jamie stops writing. 'I'm not *living* in the West.'

'That's still your home though, isn't it? You can get back there anytime you like. Being in Russia, that's just some big adventure for you.'

The English guy looks taken aback. 'What the hell's this got to do with Kostya?'

Dima meets his eye. 'Kostya was in the closet before he met you, wasn't he?'

'Yeah ... And?'

'It must've been quite the challenge for you, daring him to come out, then having him follow you to Moscow.'

'*Daring* him?' Jamie snorts. 'Now you sound like his mother. Are you saying he should've stayed in the closet?'

'Course not! I don't know ... Maybe it just all happened too fast for him.' He feels faintly nauseous – not only because of scoffing his burger and half a deep-fried apple pie, but at the thought of what the *korrektirovka* involved. He looks at Jamie again. 'What d'you *want* out of being in Russia, anyway?'

'Want?' Jamie stiffens. 'I want to be a foreign correspondent, don't I? And Russia is where some of the world's biggest news stories—'

'A news *story*? Is that all this is to you?' He grabs Jamie's notepad and brandishes it at him across the table. 'Is that why you're taking all these fucking notes?'

'Dima, give me that back.' Jamie stands, trying to snatch the notepad from him, but he yanks it out of reach, then tosses it to one side, where it lands, pages flapping, on the abandoned table opposite them, barely missing a discarded burger wrapper smeared with tomato ketchup. Jamie goes to retrieve it, then defensively stuffs it in his bag. 'What the hell?'

Still glaring at the English guy, he jumps to his feet. 'Admit it, you didn't come back to Russia for Kostya, did you?' he says. 'You're here because we're like an exotic species to you, so you can get your name on the front page of some lousy newspaper—'

'Dima! I've been doing you favours, haven't I? Big favours. I got a lawyer to see your mate in the police cells, didn't I? And *this* is how you thank me—'

'*Thank* you? You foreigners pitch up in Russia and expect us to be grateful for your *bizness* and your money and' – he gestures at the counter, where the staff are still bouncing up and down, ever eager for the next customer – 'and your McDonald's. Fuck, I've had enough of this. I'm out of here.'

He grabs his rucksack from the seat next to him, hauls it onto his back and turns to go.

Jamie reaches for his arm. 'Dima, wait! Where are you going?'

He looks back and sees the English guy's hands raised, as if in surrender, trying to placate him, and says, '*Domoi*.'

'Home?' Jamie repeats. 'But you said you didn't have anywhere—'

'I mean home to Latvia. I'm going to the station. I'm going there *now*.'

This time, unlike his last time at McDonald's, it's not just a plan, it's the only option he has left. There's nothing to keep him here, no job, no roof over his head, no Kostya – and since he's got his rucksack with everything he owns, he might as well head straight to the station. With any luck, there'll be a spare ticket for tonight's train to Riga. This time tomorrow, he could be home with Mum and Petya.

Jamie

Another evening in the office, alone. Now the others have gone, he can properly concentrate and get on with writing his story. He stares at his computer screen, at the cursor blinking in the dark where his opening sentence tails off: *A photograph, framed in black, sits on the desk of Konstantin Krolikov. He was a young man who dreamt of acting and directing but—*

He stops to think. What has he found out from Larisa, from Waterson, from Dima? There's got to be a link, somewhere out there, between post-Soviet privatisations, bribes paid to secure contracts and that address in Khimki ... He tries writing again ... *acting and directing but was drawn into a murky world where even his own death appears to be the subject of a cover-up* ... Hmm, not bad, he thinks, but I'll need to back it up—

The phone rings. Artyom? Nah, he's meant to be at a party with Nina, Veronika and that crowd. Unless he got bored and left early? Probably doped-up and horny, knowing Artyom. He picks up the phone. '*Moscow Herald*, James Goodier.'

He hears the *clunk* of a coin forced into a payphone. '*Allo? Dzheymz?*'

Bloody hell ... it's Dima. Only, how come? A whole day's gone by since the ungrateful twat flounced out on him. After all he's done for Dima too. '*Dima?*' he says. 'Shouldn't you be on a train to Latvia? Or are you calling to have another go at me?'

The voice at the end of the line is fuzzy but audibly snarky. 'I'm at Rizhsky Station right now, since you ask. And it's not too late for me to catch that train.'

As if to confirm Dima's words, the distant blare of a public address system booms out in the background, indistinct but strident as it echoes round the station concourse. There's even what sounds like the hoot of a train.

'Oh, calling to say goodbye, are you?'

'Fuck you,' comes Dima's voice. 'You should count yourself lucky. I've had a rethink.'

'A rethink?'

'Yeah.' A pause. 'I'm not ready to leave. Not while Oleg's still in custody.'

He sits up in his office chair. 'Really? So you're prepared to—'

'Listen, if I stay, I'm doing this for Kostya and Oleg, not for you.'

'D'you mean—'

'I mean I'll go back to Milyukov. I'll help you get your story.'

'You will?' He scrabbles for his notepad.

'I will,' Dima says. 'I already spun the doc some tale about needing treatment – I can get back there in the next few days and act the willing patient. That's what you need, isn't it, if you're gonna make the front page?'

Gripping the receiver, he takes a deliberate slow breath. 'This is more than a *story*, mate. We're doing this for Kostya, right?'

'Whatever. But I'll need two more favours from you.'

'What now? More money? Another lawyer?'

'Of course I need more money. But not for me – it's a down-payment for the treatment. That'll be at least 50,000 roubles.'

He almost drops the receiver. 'Fifty thousand!'

'Oh, c'mon, James, that's only about 200 dollars, isn't it? If you get a story out of this, you can claim it as expenses.'

What a nerve, he thinks. But Dima's right: pull off this story and he could claim more than that from any editor ... 'OK, OK,' he says, sighing. 'And what's the second favour?'

He grits his teeth, wondering what Dima's going to demand this time. Help finding a job that pays in dollars? Or worse, an invitation to England? That'd be out of the question – think what Artyom would say. But the voice buzzing faintly in his ear sounds unexpectedly sheepish, nothing like those earlier demands. 'I've spent two nights on the metro' – Dima's voice drops, almost mumbling – 'and unless I catch that night train to Riga, I don't have anywhere to sleep.' A long, drawn-out sigh. 'A few nights is all I ask. When this is all over, I promise I won't ask anything of you ever again.'

*

It's more than a year since anyone slept on his sofa; Kostya's final sleepover – that would've been the last time, months before the two of them fell out. To be honest, he'd lost patience with Kostya sulking, playing the spurned lover. But right now, as he opens the sofa out into a bed, he wishes Kostya could be sleeping here tonight.

And what happened to the promised visit from Wag, Davy and Sanjay? On his trips back to England, he'd cajole them, saying, '*It'll be like old times. Just book a flight, I'll sort your visas out, I've got a sofa you can crash on.*' Not one of them has visited though. Not one of them has booked that plane ticket or applied for a visa, let alone crashed on this flea-bitten Soviet contraption that groans and catapults dust into the air as Dima helps him unfold it.

Dima, of all people, staying the night. But then he can hardly let him sleep rough on the metro ... Watching Dima look around the room, he regrets not making the place more homely. When he'd found this flat, over a year ago, it had been a bargain, the rent less than a hundred dollars a month, and he has only the furniture it came with, including this crummy fold-out sofa. Pinned to his wall are smiley, sunny photos of Mum, Dad and Lisa, even of Bessie, the family's Labrador; there's Davy, Sanjay, Wag and him outside their student house; and there he is with Artyom, beers in hand, at some party. There's also that photo of him and Kostya, the one with their arms around each other's shoulders at Voronezh station that summer evening.

'I recognise that photo,' Dima says. 'Kostya had the same one.'

He nods. 'Yeah, that's three years ago nearly. In Voronezh – that's where—'

'I know, James, I know. He was always talking about you.'

He doesn't reply. Dima lets the silence hang, then adds, 'He was in love with you.'

Another silence. He can't exactly deny knowing that, and the only reply he can think of is, 'He was in love with you too, Dima.'

Dima doesn't even blink. 'He loved you more. For a long, long time too. Even when he was with me, I sensed he was still in love with you.'

They look at each other, then at the photo, then at each other again. Their gazes meet mid-air. He detects a look in Dima's eyes that seems to say, 'You're thinking the same as me' – and that's what he *is* thinking too: that Kostya deserved love. A love that even they didn't know how to give.

'Yes,' he says, feeling a combination of wretchedness and something like relief as the words come out. 'Yes, I know he was.'

Silence. A moment passes, then Dima asks, 'D'you mind if I take a bath?'

'No, that's fine.' He turns away, glad to break eye contact, and crosses the room to close the curtains. Outside it's been dark for hours, an inky cloak blotting out the ashen skies of daylight and lending a bluish flush to the concrete of neighbouring apartment blocks. Windows glow, warm and yellow, like openings on an advent calendar: glimpses into the kitchens and living rooms of families and couples and friends. He gazes out, feeling, for some reason, almost as lonely as Dima must do.

When he turns back, he catches a whiff of body odour. Dima has undressed, his clothes lie in a pile on the floor and he is standing there in nothing but his boxer shorts, clutching a T-shirt to his chest. If it's meant as a gesture of modesty, it still confronts him with the sight of Dima's physique: hulking shoulders, the sculpted curve of his pecs, and, unusually for a Sov, a tattoo of an anchor and chain on his right bicep.

'I, err, don't have a washing machine,' he says, trying not to look – not too much – and nodding at Dima's clothes on the floor. 'But there's a launderette down the street – you could go tomorrow.' A nod from Dima. 'Right, well, I'll go and run the bath.'

When he comes back from the bathroom, Dima has changed into an Adidas tracksuit, the sort worn by every Russian black-market spiv. He also sees that Dima's studying the poster on his wall that Kostya gave him – Kostya's own poster advertising *An Inspector Calls*, the production that Kostya had worked on. *Vizit Inspektora*, it says, in fractured black capitals above an image of a detective's magnifying glass and red rivulets trickling down the walls of a grand house. He never told Kostya, but he always found that poster a bit corny.

He runs a finger down the edge, where the poster has come unstuck. 'A present from Kostya,' he says. 'It was his favourite play.'

Dima kneels to rummage in his rucksack. He takes out a book and holds it under Jamie's nose. 'And this was *my* present from Kostya,' he says. '*Vizit Inspektora* – that's one of the plays here, see? I've just started reading it.'

He tells Dima about taking Kostya to see the play in England. Dima smiles, recalling how Kostya had dragged him along to see *The Cherry Orchard* and how he'd fallen asleep during the performance; it wasn't his thing, really.

The gurgle of the running bath nudges its way into the silence. 'I'd better go check that bath,' he says to Dima. 'I'll get you a towel and sheets and then' – he forces a deliberate yawn – 'I'm off to bed.'

★

Come the morning, just as he's pulling on his old studenty overcoat and is about to head off to work, he sees Dima, awake and sitting up from the sofa, wrapped in the duvet. They have a bleary-eyed exchange of *dobroye utro*, good morning.

'There's tea in the teapot,' he says, nodding towards the kitchen. 'It'll still be hot.'

Dima nods. '*Spasibo*, Jamie. I'm getting up. Are you off to work?'

'Yeah – I'll leave you my keys.' He buries the thought of not trusting Dima – after all, he's got nothing worth stealing – and fumbles in his pocket, pulling out a notebook, his woolly cap and a piece of folded paper. What's this? he thinks, unfolding it. Oh yes, Waterson's list of US-Care funding projects, ones that Kostya might have worked on. He is about to fold it up again or chuck it in the bin when something catches his eye.

'Jesus Christ . . .'

Staring at the list, he wanders over to the sofa in a daze.

Dima looks up at him, mid-yawn. 'What's the matter?'

He sits, almost dropping onto the sofa at Dima's side. 'This list,' he says. 'It's from Kostya's boss at US-Care, that American organisation he worked for.'

Still wrapped in the duvet, Dima rubs his eyes and squints. 'What about it?'

'It's a list of Russian outfits that have applied for investment – you know, factories, farms, co-operatives, all that crap about transitioning to a market economy. But look at this one . . .' He runs his finger down the list and jabs it against the paper. 'Recognise it?'

Dima stares; then their eyes meet, wide with bafflement, their lips parted as if frozen in the act of trying to speak. Again they look at the paper, but neither of them seems to know what to make of it. Right there, on US-Care's list of projects, lodged alphabetically between the Rainbow co-operative and a catering firm called Restauservice, is an address in Khimki for Renaissance – a 'health and wellbeing consultancy' headed by a Dr Stepan Mikhailovich Milyukov. The place that's pre-scribing 'corrective reorientation'.

16

THREE MONTHS EARLIER

NOVEMBER 1992. Moscow

Kostya

'Everyone calls me Dima,' you told me. 'No one ever says "Dmitry", apart from our landlord.' A little chuckle. 'Oh, and my mum, sometimes.'

You flashed that sideways grin of yours at me. Even on that dark wintry night, the patches of street light flickering by outside the car window allowed me a glimpse of a wayward streak that your mum must've known only too well and had long since given up trying to tame. Lucky you. You seemed to love your mum *and* to have broken free of her; you hadn't spent your life being a good boy, always anxious to please.

'Is that when she's cross with you' – my attempt at a joke – 'that she calls you Dmitry?'

'Aw, c'mon, why would anyone ever be cross with me?' You laughed, nudging Oleg in the front passenger seat.

But then, for a second, your laughter subsided, the sparkle in your eyes dimmed. You looked away, out of the car window, and muttered, 'There's my boss, though – he calls me Dmitry. When he's "cross" with me.'

So brief was the twitch of unease across your face that it barely registered before you'd changed the subject, asking the driver if he needed directions. Just then, *that* song came on the radio. Like almost every car radio in Moscow in those days, it was tuned to a non-stop playlist of Western pop hits. 'I *love* this one!' you said, and asked the driver to turn it up loud. I didn't know the song at the time, but since that night with you I've never been able to get it out of my head: 'Rhythm is a Dancer . . .'

★

But let's rewind to how we met. That Saturday night in late October; me waiting in line outside the Bolshoi Theatre, the jostling of the queue for *Sleeping Beauty*, the box office seemingly hours away. There was no way I'd get tickets for *that* night – but I could, perhaps, get my hands on tickets for another night, and invite Mama. It would be a peace offering of sorts.

Eight o'clock had come and gone, and I gave up on the box office altogether, deciding to take my chances with the ticket touts. I had dollars from my US-Care pay packet, hard currency being the only way to get tickets to the Bolshoi these days. Sure enough, a few *muzhiki*, young men in tracksuits and chunky torso-bulking coats, were lolling against the massive columns outside. One of them saw me, approached, and a furtive exchange ensued.

So there I was, tickets in hand, walking towards the metro. Suddenly I heard footsteps behind me and a call of 'Young man! *Molodoy chelovyek!*' I turned to see two other *muzhiki* – two I didn't recognise – hurrying after me. We were in a badly lit part of the square, between the bushes and the subway, out of sight of the theatre's floodlit entrance, but I could see that both men were stubbly and well-built. I froze.

The fatter one demanded, 'What tickets d'you buy back there?'

Not daring to say it was none of his business, I stammered, '*Sleeping Beauty.* Why?'

'Pay in dollars, did you?' The slimmer one this time, taking a step closer.

'OK, yes,' I said, now afraid that they might be police. 'But why?'

'Cos the guy who sold you them was on our patch.' The fatter *muzhik* took a step closer too. His eyes were sunken and unflinching. 'And they're probably counterfeit.'

'Counterfeit?' I took the tickets out for a closer look. 'How can you tell?'

In that dim light, I could barely read the small print, but as I inspected the tickets, the slimmer *muzhik* moved in and snatched them out of my hand.

'Like I said' – his eyes bulged, daring me to snatch them back – 'counterfeit. Not worth the paper they're printed on.'

My eyes darted to one side, then the other, but there was no one to call on for help; any passer-by would simply think I was engaged in the kind of black-market trading that took place on every street corner.

'Please,' I said, reaching for the tickets, 'there's some mistake here, let me—'

'No point,' said the slim one, waving them in front of me. 'They're worthless, these. Just make sure you buy from *us* next time.'

And before I could do anything, he tore the tickets in two.

I stepped forward in protest, but the fatter ticket tout shoved me in the chest and I fell backwards against a tree. I felt my throat and gut tighten, the beginnings of a panic that I recognised from my ordeals in the army. I cowered, abruptly aware of every heartbeat, every speeded-up breath—

'Guys, what's going on? Is there a problem?'

It was a third voice. Behind the *muzhiki*, I saw that two more young men had appeared.

'He's buying fake tickets,' said one of the touts. 'Bad for business, that is.'

'Fakes, eh?' came a sarcastic reply, a fourth voice. 'Who says?'

The *muzhik* again: '*We're* taking care of this, all right?'

'Oh, gotta buy *your* tickets now, has he?' came the first new voice. 'I know your game.'

The fat *muzhik* span round. 'Fuck off, this is none of your business.'

'We're making it our business. Now leave the boy in peace.'

Before it could sink in, my astonishment at two strangers coming to my rescue, I saw, in the semi-darkness, that all four young men were tensed for a fight. Fists were clenched, chests puffed out. But what happened next came fast and confused, a flurry of flailing arms and scuffling feet. A punch might have been thrown, a kick might have been aimed. The fatter one of the two touts lost his footing, and I only just got out of the way as he stumbled into the tree where I stood. Leaving him no time to recover, one of the newcomers moved in on him and landed a kick between his legs. The fat guy doubled up in pain, momentarily unable to speak, and I caught a glimpse of the newcomer, a tall blond guy, broad-shouldered in his silvery quilted coat, as he pinned my assailant against the tree, holding an elbow to his throat and a knee to his groin.

The two of them exchanged threats: loud, sharp whispers spiked with expletives, *blyad* this and *pizdyets* that – but I didn't get to listen too closely because the second newcomer took me by the arm and pulled me to one side. He was tall too, with dark, slicked-back hair and wearing faded denims under his coat. The other ticket tout, the slim one, was limping away, stopping to lean against a lamp post and nurse his head in his hands.

A moment later the blond guy came over. He gripped me by both shoulders, looked me right in the eye and asked, 'Are you all right?'

I nodded and stared at the face of my rescuer. You, Dima. It was the first time I got a good look at you. Despite the fracas that had just taken place, your eyes were steady and piercing, holding my gaze with an urgency that overlaid a promise of playfulness. Your eyes were the first thing I noticed – then the grip of your hands on my shoulders, consoling yet forceful, letting me know you had it all under control. Months later, I came to see that moment as a foretaste of my desire to stay like that; for you to always maintain your hold on me.

'C'mon, you,' you said. 'We'll get you home. And don't worry about your tickets' – you tilted your head towards your friend with the denims and slicked-back hair – 'my partner in crime here will get you some new ones, won't you, Oleg?'

★

By the time you'd flagged down a car, you and Oleg had smoked a Marlboro each and given me a shot of vodka from the flask in Oleg's pocket. 'A drink'll do you good,' you said. 'It'll help steady your nerves.' You were right, it did: my shaking subsided, my breathing slowed, warmth spread from my chest to my fingers.

So there we were, riding in a stranger's Moskvich, one of the newer 1980s models, when 'Rhythm is a Dancer' came on the car radio. The driver turned it up loud, just as you'd asked, and you started nodding your head to the beat. The vodka got passed around again, including to the driver. I relaxed still more, slipping into the music that boomed out inside the car.

Leaning close, you whispered, 'D'you fancy a change of plan?'

'A change of plan?' This time my blushing wasn't the effect of the vodka.

A grin. 'Yeah! Not doing anything else tonight, are you?'

I thought. Not for long, just enough to picture another evening sitting in my room with Mama next door sewing or watching TV. 'No,' I said, smiling, 'nothing special.'

Nudging Oleg at the back of his ribs, you asked, 'How about you, Oleg? Would you be up for it tonight?'

Oleg turned around from the front seat. 'OK!' he said, grinning. 'Let's do it. *Davai.*'

'*Davai!*' you said, stretching your arm along the back seat and draping it around my shoulder. 'We're going dancing.'

*

I hadn't been to the disco for nearly three months. The gay 'scene' in Moscow was so tiny that ever since I embarrassed myself at Artyom's party, I had dreaded bumping into him and Jamie – or, worse still, Kirill, after our fumbled 'snog', after running out on him. Tonight, however, with *you* to take me there, things felt different.

The organisers had hired a disused sports hall about a mile south-east of Pechatniki. An indoor basketball court over-looked by rows of plastic seats served as the dance floor, and the DJ had set up shop underneath the hoop at the far end.

With no space for tables, the front-row seats were thronged with boys smoking and clutching bottles of beer or Pepsi, their eyes wandering from side to side, ever on the lookout.

I sensed their eyes on you as we walked in. Who could blame them? You sauntered onto the dance floor in a black leather biker jacket bristling with zips and studs. Under it, a plain white T-shirt stretched across your chest, and glistening blond hairs showed through the frayed rips in your jeans. A vision popped into my head: a comical scenario of taking you home to Mama, and of Mama scurrying off to get out her sewing machine, anxious to patch them up.

At the bar, you bought us all beer, clutching your bottle by the neck and resting your other hand in the small of my back; it was the lightest of touches, but enough to lay claim, to say 'you're with *me* now'.

We'd only half-finished our drinks though, when the DJ started playing 'Rhythm is a Dancer'; I recognised it from the car radio. In one gulp, you drained your beer, grabbed my hand and said, 'How about a dance' – it wasn't a question: more like an instruction that wasn't to be resisted, a statement of the next stage in your seduction of me.

You shrugged off your jacket and handed it to Oleg. My God, how I gawped at you in that tight white T-shirt ... those muscles! I'd never pictured any gay boy having a body like yours – only tough guys had muscles, didn't they? Tough guys like – well, *you*, seeing off those ticket touts. I couldn't stop staring at your arms, wondering if I'd get to be held in them. You even had a tattoo, looked like an anchor and chain.

As you led me to the dance floor, I saw heads turn, stares of curiosity and envy. I looked around, hoping to spot Jamie or Artyom, hoping they'd see me with you. But I didn't see them, not at first – instead, there among all the faces in the crowd, I spotted a head of ginger hair and eyes that were trained jealously not on you, but on me. It was Kirill, standing close to Nina and Veronika, yet apart from them, stock-still as the pair of them danced.

Soon though, his face was lost amid the clouds of dry ice and the shifting, crammed-together silhouettes of bodies. But despite the crowd, you made space for us, keeping me close, barely a foot away: I could feel the heat from your body. And how it danced, that body of yours, hips that circled and thrusted, your boots stomping on the painted lines of the basketball court, your shoulders and arms pumping in sync with the beat.

In my stiff flared jeans and a shirt that was too small for me (one of Jamie's cast-offs), I bopped along as best I could. Only twice did my gaze leave you – once, when I spied Kirill's ginger head behind you, his face stony but his eyes seeking mine. He shot me a look, then turned away. The second time was when I saw Jamie squeeze past, trailing behind Artyom. He did a double-take and stared at us, his mouth falling open: his turn to be 'gobsmacked'.

★

It was 3 a.m. when we – but without Oleg – left the disco together. We stood in a pool of light under a street lamp on Volgograd Prospekt as you flagged down passing cars. My head swam with giddiness and vodka; my ears were ringing with 'Rhythm is a Dancer'. Before long, a mud-streaked white Lada veered towards the kerb. 'We're going to my place,' you said, and bundled us into the back seat. As we rode back into the city, you took my hand, in the dark, and held it. Up front, I glimpsed the driver's eyes, framed in the rear-view mirror, watchful and suspicious. Could he see our hands touching? Suppose he kicked us out? But with you at my side, I felt as though I needn't fear anything ever again.

★

'*Sshh*!' you said, pressing a finger to your lips, 'my landlord'll be asleep.'

You unlocked the door and steered me inside, your hand cradling my bottom. Then, inside the darkened hallway, you bumped into something and couldn't stop yourself laughing. Switching on the light, you laughed even more when you saw me tiptoeing past, shoes in hand like a scene from a bedroom farce.

'Don't worry!' you whispered. 'Valery Ivanovich is as deaf as a post. And he never comes into our room.'

'Our room' meant a room shared with Oleg, who didn't come home to his messy bed that night; I wasn't aware, at the time, of your 'arrangement' for giving each other space ... As my eyes did a sweep of the room, taking in the adverts plastered across his wall, the poster for *My Own Private Idaho* on yours, and a small TV and video player, I felt you kiss the back of my neck. Just a quick kiss, over in a second. Your lips were warm, making me tingle, and while I stood waiting for the next kiss, you switched from the overhead glare to the bedside lamp – 'That's better, more intimate' – then excused yourself while you went to the bathroom.

I sat on Oleg's bed, seeking out a spot away from the lamp-light to hide my pitiful un-muscled body and began, hands trembling, to unbutton my shirt. Was I dreaming? Was this really happening? From down the hallway, I could hear the noise of you peeing, and my mind conjured an image of you standing there in the open doorway, legs planted wide apart, your jeans unfastened. My heartbeat quickened and I scuttled over to your single bunk, clutching my shirt to my chest until I was safely concealed under your bedclothes. On the wall by my head, underneath the *Idaho* poster, was an old black-and-white photograph of a woman with long blonde hair, smiling as if she knew we were up to no good. Your mum, of course. Your only other picture was of Jean-Claude Van Damme, some movie actor I guessed, posing bare-chested with his fists raised.

When you came back in the room, you bolted the door. Then, pulling your T-shirt over your head, you stood over me in the lamplight, which cast upwards ripples of shade over your abdomen and chest – you looked rather like Jean-Claude Whatsit. Your jeans slid to the floor. Under the bedclothes, my heart was racing; the erection I'd had since I entered the room felt like it would burst.

I had wondered how to tell you this was my first time. You see, I hadn't given much thought to what this would be like, actual sex. Even on nights when I lay alone in bed dreaming about whichever boy I'd fallen for, my desire for him had been a swooning, abstract kind of thing. My yearning for Vasily or Jamie had been a yearning to *be around* them, to be liked by them, to bask in their glow. Nothing more carnal than a smile or a touch or an arm around my waist ... Only I didn't need to tell you: when you pulled back the covers and clocked the swelling inside my underpants, there was an upward curl to your lips, a raising of an eyebrow, a smile that said you'd read me like a book.

In the end, I did little more than lie there. You had me pinned down, straddled between your thighs, and it was all I could do to reach up and run my fingers over your arms and chest. Up and down went my hands, relishing your warm, downy skin, trembling in awe of the power contained in those muscles. One of your hands crept inside my underpants; with the other, you cradled the back of my neck, lifting my head to meet your eyes. Your breath brushed my cheek, your tongue flicked at my earlobe – then you let my head flop back on the pillow, teasing my chest with your fingertips as you drew them down towards my crotch. Your touch sent convulsions through my body, a kind of electricity that sent my back arching, my breath speeding, my head leaping off the pillow until I cried out for release. Yours was a practised touch – the result, I should have realised, of seducing many a boy before me.

You were the first to fall asleep. I wanted to watch you as you slept but you held me tight from behind, the two of us squeezed into that single bunk, your breath hot on my neck and a muscly, tattooed arm wrapped around my chest. So I stayed as I was, tuned into your snoring, and was only once startled in the middle of the night by a sliver of light appearing under the door when Valery Ivanovich got up and shuffled to the bathroom.

I thought of all the nights I'd shared a bed with Jamie. That was intimacy of a sort too, but it hadn't come close to this; I wasn't even sure if *this* was what I'd wanted from him. But what I *did* want – a desire thwarted by the fact that Jamie and I were barely speaking any more – was to tell him about you. Not so much to make him jealous (after all, he had Artyom) but because now I could feel equal to him. Who knows, he might even be proud of me.

★

It was nearly eleven when I woke. Through blurry eyes, I watched you doing press-ups: you were wearing a white singlet and silky blue tracksuit bottoms that clung to your backside as your arms pumped up-down, up-down. Next to me, on the bedside table, was a tray with a breakfast of tea, bread, cheese and jam.

It was a morning I didn't want to end. Like waking up to Christmas or the day you're setting off on holiday. A morning of kisses, caresses and of scuttling comically to and from the bathroom while trying to avoid Valery Ivanovich.

After I'd showered, I sat wrapped in your oversized towelling bathrobe, with its smell of expensive German shower gel, and you brought the phone into the room so I could call Mama. She wanted to know where I was, would I be home for lunch? I told her no, I wouldn't. She sounded relieved. I spun her the familiar story about staying at Jamie's. I doubt she believed it, but the only thing on my mind was to spend that Sunday, all of it, with you.

★

The sky was turning purple. Behind us, the skyscraper spire of Moscow University cast a long, long shadow creeping its way down avenues of lawns and flower beds; as the sun set, the shadow stretched and stretched until it was longer than the spire was tall. Ahead of us spread a view over Moscow: running down to a loop in the river was a slope thick with trees, clumps of bronze and gold that rustled in the wind. On the far riverbank sat Lenin Stadium; beyond that the red-and-white walls of Novodevichy Convent and, more distant, pinpricks of gold from the bell-towers of the Kremlin.

How fast it went, that day. It seemed only moments since we had bumped into Valery Ivanovich in the hallway as we left. 'My friend Konstantin,' you'd said, without missing a beat. 'He borrowed Oleg's bed for the night.' I shook hands with him, anxious to play along, but he didn't seem too surprised. On our way down in the lift, you'd kissed me to stop me laughing, kissed me long and hard – pulling away with only a split second to spare as the lift doors opened at ground level to reveal a waiting babushka.

We'd been for a stroll on Red Square, and as you pointed to the domes of St Basil's, your hand had found an excuse to fondle my waist. In the autumn sun, the domes glowed like multi-coloured sweets, those 'humbugs' they eat in England. You told me that old story about Ivan the Terrible having the architect blinded so that he could never again create the like of St Basil's; the tsar, you said, had never seen such beauty.

Ah, that blissful Sunday. The fried doughnuts we ate on Arbat Street. Our trolleybus ride up to Lenin Hills. You, striking a pose at the foot of the Gagarin monument, chest thrust out as you mimicked the cosmonaut being launched into orbit. We talked, we laughed, my face glowed whenever you smiled at me. You wanted to be a movie actor, you said. And I want to be a theatre director, I told you. My dad left us, you said. Mine too, I said.

Of course, we were hopelessly different. I knew that. I could never have pulled off your don't-give-a-damn attitude – like on the trolleybus, when that babushka scolded you for your ripped jeans and you gave her the finger. As we ran off at the bus stop, my shock gave way to laughter and a thrill of admiration. If only I could be like you. One consolation: you told me I was 'cute'. 'It's no big deal losing your hair,' you said, running your fingers down the back of my neck. 'Just shave it off, like they do in the army.'

All too soon, the end of our first day together was upon us. Resting our forearms on the balustrade of the viewing platform, we gazed across the Lenin Hills and the river below. To my side, I saw other couples – husbands with wives, boyfriends with girlfriends – all taking in the same view, but hand in hand, arms around waists. I felt you press your shoulder up against mine and I pressed back; it was as intimate as I dared to get, in public.

Turning up your collar, you squinted at the sky. 'First snow's on its way.'

You were right. The clouds were low and smothering, pregnant with a wintry whiteness that would soon descend on the city and leave it transformed. By mid-November, the snow would be here to stay. They are cold and long, our Russian winters – but what I didn't know at the time was that the winter would outlast our relationship.

The wind blew from the north, right at us, making me shiver. 'Now that it's the season,' I ventured, 'perhaps we could go to the theatre together? Maybe even the Bolshoi?'

As soon as the words left me, I feared sounding like I was rushing things.

But you simply shrugged and lit another cigarette. 'You know what, movies are more my thing. That's why I wanna act in them.'

'Ooh, cinema!' I gushed. 'You know Mosfilm's studios aren't far from here – have you tried auditioning?'

'Nah, not Mosfilm.' You were shaking your head. 'That Soviet stuff is finished. Films like they make in the West, that's where it's at – television too, and pop videos.'

'So will I get to see you in a pop video? I'd love to—'

Suddenly a fit of coughing overcame you. I thought you'd inhaled too much cigarette smoke. Then your coughing turned to laughter. 'No, Kostya! Not yet, anyway. This film I'm in, we're still shooting – it might not even get released.' You tilted your head towards me. 'Besides, why bother watching me in some video? You can see me in real life.'

I swallowed. 'Does that mean ... Do you mean, I can see you again?'

Another shrug. 'As long as I stay in Moscow. But I'm busy a lot of evenings on shoots. And it's not every night' – a wink – 'that I can get rid of Oleg and have the room to myself.'

I never did get to watch you acting in the end. Unless, of course, you count the act you put on the whole time, in real life: your excuses about Oleg being home, the nights you said you couldn't see me. But back then I didn't pick up on any of this, least of all those casually uttered words, '*As long as I stay in Moscow.*'

Tamara Borisovna

That tale Kostya had spun her about staying over at Jamie's – it didn't wash, not this time. She ought to have felt relief; at least he no longer wittered on about that English boy like he used to. Yet where Kostya had previously made no secret of his infatuation, now he was hiding something from her, maybe something worse. Since their row in August, since he'd stormed off to go get himself 'corrupted', she'd been haunted by visions in which she pictured her son naked, slimy with sweat, being kissed or groped or even, God forbid, penetrated.

My imagination's getting the better of me, she thought. And no wonder, now there was such a vacuum to fill. Since the end of August, Kostya had avoided her as much as possible, always out, always working late, always in another room. When he couldn't avoid her, they exchanged the bare minimum of words about their working hours and mealtimes; he would even skip dinner some evenings to avoid sitting with her.

They became too much for her, these toxic silences. In September, a couple of weeks after her visit to Dr Milyukov, she had gone down to Voronezh to spend a weekend with Galina, seeking out the comfort of her old friend. But how could she persuade Kostya to go and see Dr Milyukov and try his 'corrective reorientation'? How, given his insistence that he was a *gomoseksualist*? Arguing with Kostya would be useless, as would telling him straight out that she wanted him to undergo treatment. She would have to think of some other way.

Kostya

On a damp autumn evening four days after I met you, Mama announced that she was going to move back to Voronezh. Our flat there was sublet, of course, so her plan was to stay a while with Galina Sergeyevna. 'I can't be living all alone,' she said, giving me a pointed glance, 'not since your father left. But I can't go on being a supermarket skivvy in Moscow either.'

It was the most words she and I had exchanged in weeks. I ought to have been stunned. But the thing is, her announcement came barely an hour after I'd phoned you from work, a furtive call from my desk in which I'd confessed that I couldn't stop thinking of you. My heart leapt when you said yeah, you'd been thinking of me too. Could we, I asked, meet again? To my joy, you'd said Oleg would be out on Saturday night and I could stay over. I was so lightheaded with excitement that I struggled to summon up the response Mama expected.

Was I supposed to say, 'No, Mama, don't do that', when in truth I would prefer her gone?

Somehow though, uplifted by the prospect of seeing you again, I managed to channel the warm glow inside me, translating it into kind words. Hugging her, I made us tea and sat with her at the kitchen table. It's probably for the best, I told her – only, why now? She gave me another pained look; I saw tears well up in her eyes. It's all too much for me, she said, and I nodded – not too hard, trying to look sympathetic rather than impatient for her to move out. She missed Voronezh, she said, and let's face it, we hadn't been getting on, had we, she should give me my space. I nodded more, perhaps a little too eagerly.

She reeled off a litany of calamities that I'd heard her lament so often: Papa leaving us, losing her library job, the demise of her beloved Soviet homeland. She cast her eyes down at the cup of tea gripped in both hands. 'It's been terrible for my nerves.' A long pause. 'In fact, before I leave, I'm seeing a doctor about treatment – for depression.'

Why, I should have asked, *before* she left? Why not move back to Voronezh first, then seek treatment there? But I didn't ask. It didn't occur to me. I was so consumed by giddiness and relief that a wave of compassion towards Mama washed over me. Giddiness, Dima, at the thought of a second night with you. And relief at the thought of life without Mama breathing down my neck; a life that now promised the shelter of your arms and nights out dancing in front of envious eyes. I squeezed her hand and said I was sorry, I wished I could help. To which she replied, 'Well, Kostya, there is one way you can help.'

I thought she meant help with her packing – but no, she wanted me to accompany her to an appointment at the doctor's.

'Please, Kostya,' she said, looking up from her teacup, 'I'd simply like you to be there.'

★

I was too distracted to guess where Mama might be leading me. Especially when it was the Saturday of my date with you, a night I'd been counting down to. Oleg would be out, we'd have the room to ourselves, we'd eat, drink, watch a movie and make love; I'd be spending the entire night with you and the whole of Sunday too. It was all I could think of.

Even so, I was baffled – frustrated too – by the long trek to Mama's appointment. We took the metro to the end of the line, then a stinking, crowded bus all the way to Khimki, of all places. We were packed in tight with other passengers, me squashed up against a man with a sack-load of video tapes and Mama squeezed into the last available seat, her bag on her knees. Couldn't she see a doctor somewhere in the city centre? I asked. Near work or near home? 'He's been recommended to me,' she muttered, staring out of the window.

It was a rainy day, and the bus bumped along a country road cratered with potholes full of mud. Autumn's final leaves, a limp yellow against the grey, clung to trees on both sides. Eventually we reached the town centre, where the remaining passengers got off, including the man with the sack of video tapes. We crossed the road to an ordinary-looking block of flats, where Mama's appointment turned out to be at a 'mental wellbeing consultancy' on the second floor. The place had been converted from an apartment, and had had money spent on it, like a business that was doing its best to look Western and profitable. All the while, Mama was tense, saying little, reluctant to look me in the eye. The wave of kindness that had washed over me was receding, and now I was itching to go home, to get ready for our date. We didn't have to wait long, though, before a dark-haired woman in a lab-coat emerged and said, 'Stepan Mikhailovich will see you now.'

*

'How you've grown since last time.' Stepan Mikhailovich looked me up and down. 'Quite the young man now, aren't you? You've put on weight, even started losing your hair a bit — all normal developments for a boy maturing into adulthood.'

Last time? When had I seen him before, this Dr Milyukov? It took me a while to recall who he was — of course, the same doctor Mama had bribed all those years ago to get me out of the army. He even showed me an old photo from his files: me in my Young Communist uniform, looking thinner and spottier than now but with thick, greasy curly hair.

'Now you do understand why you're here, don't you, Konstantin?' he asked.

'Why *I'm* here? What do you mean?' I frowned at the doctor across his desk, then at Mama in the seat next to me.

'Kostya,' she said. She half-turned towards me, eyes trained somewhere between me and the floor. 'Listen, it's true that I've been suffering from depression. Really it is. But that's not why we're here.' Her chin and lower lip quivered as she looked up at me. 'I mean, it's not *me* who's here for treatment.'

The realisation hit me. This was Mama's idea of how to deal with my 'condition' . . . Looking back, I should have left there and then, but the shock of having fallen into a trap was like a weight that pinned me to the chair.

I stared at her. 'You lied to me. Why? Tell me why you've brought me here.'

'Kostya,' Mama said, 'I *am* going to move back to Voronezh, that much is true, it *is* too much for me. All I lied about was getting help for you.'

Help, she called it. Her deception made me nauseous, all my goodwill towards her now exhausted. Still, I didn't walk out, not yet. The doctor started talking again, explaining the psychology behind his treatment. I had, he claimed, suffered a 'deviation from normal male development' – not physical or hormonal, he said, pointing to my hair loss and facial stubble, but psychological and emotional. He talked about 'phases', about the mother–son relationship, about the 'absence of appropriate male role models'. Then he came right out and asked me, 'Do you acknowledge feeling attracted to members of your own sex?'

Mama was staring at her lap, then looked away, around the room, at the certificates and diagrams of the human brain on the wall. Anywhere but at me. So I addressed my answer to Dr Milyukov. 'Yes,' I said. 'I do. I'm gay.' It was only the second time I'd spoken that word to refer to myself. I saw Mama flinch.

'And don't you regard this as a delusional attraction, a temporary, passing phase?'

I thought of you then, Dima. I thought of Vasily too, and Jamie and Artyom, even Kirill. But mainly, in an effort to summon up all the conviction I could muster, to banish any wavering or doubts, I thought of you on the dance floor, you in the car holding my hand, you astride me in bed. The strength you transmitted to me. And I said, 'No, Doctor, I don't think it's delusional or temporary.' And again, Jamie's words: 'It's natural for me.'

Dr Milyukov was peering at me over his glasses, but then lowered his eyes and wrote something on the notepad in front of him. 'And you don't think,' he asked, without looking up, 'that this deviation might be a consequence of your traumatic experience in the army?'

An abrupt chill. The warmth I'd summoned, thinking of you, drained away. Oh God, the army. He was right, it was traumatic, it still gave me nightmares. All those times I got cornered in the barracks or the shower-room. Those boozed-up lads given free rein to bully and abuse. The blind eyes turned as they strove to prove their manliness ...

For a moment, I couldn't manage a reply. I had to reach back into other memories and hopes, recalling the skip of my heartbeat and the adolescent yearnings I'd recorded in my diary or had dreamt of acting out on stage. Thoughts of Vasily, of Jamie, of you.

I swallowed hard. 'No,' I said. 'I've always been this way.'

Mama looked up now, eyes pleading. 'Kostya,' she whined, 'I can't stand by and let this happen to you. You're my only son. Please, won't you at least—'

Dr Milyukov interrupted. 'Perhaps I could talk to your son alone, Tamara Borisovna?' He smiled at her. 'That might be more productive. Hmm?'

Obediently, she nodded and picked up her bag and coat. Mama had always deferred to authority figures. She tiptoed out of the office as if some delicate psychiatric procedure were already underway. And, for all I knew, it probably was. I watched her close the door behind her, then returned to face Dr Milyukov. He was leaning back in his chair, fingertips pressed together and a smile of encouragement spread across his pinkish face.

'Why don't you tell me what it's like, this, err, *attraction* you feel,' he said. 'I'd really like to know. And it's just between us, now your mother's out of the room.'

For a moment, I hesitated. Then, taking a deep breath, I told him. I left out the details of sleeping with you, Dima, anything that would expose us to accusations of sodomy. Instead, I spoke of crushes and yearnings. About my schooldays infatuation with Vasily. About feeling nothing for girls. About Jamie, about the sleepovers, my gazing at him as he slept. And I told him about you, Dima, how you made me feel protected, made my heart skip a beat. It was a relief to unburden myself, to let my desires pour forth to someone who listened and seemed able to read how I felt.

That spell was soon broken. The doctor leaned forward, made a note on his pad and said, 'But Konstantin, what you describe is not part of the healthy male development I alluded to earlier.' He sighed. 'Far from it. You're labouring under the delusion that this is a "natural" way of being. I'm not saying you're immoral – no, all I'm saying is you've become confused, unbalanced, sick even.'

I was silent. He put his pen down and stood, pacing over to the window, peeking out through the blinds, then turning back to me. 'Let me explain how I can help you, Konstantin. You don't have to stay this way, but you have to *want* to be helped—'

'Why do I need "help"?' I grappled to find some counter-argument. 'Isn't it possible for a man to *love* another man? Look back through history: there have always been men, some of them great men – look at Oscar Wilde, look at Tchaikovsky—'

'No, no, no, Konstantin.' The doctor was smiling again – but as if at some mental patient having a hallucination. 'Those are exactly the kind of delusions you're suffering – thinking that you're exceptional, that you're like one of these "artists", someone who needn't conform to the rules the rest of us live by.'

Rules the rest of us live by ... That made me think of you, Dima. You didn't conform, you didn't live by 'the rules' – you'd even given the finger to an interfering babushka. But there was nothing enfeebled or sick about *you*. As I thought of you, Dr Milyukov was describing something called 'corrective reorientation'. It involved 'erotic stimuli', he said, applied in conjunction with medication to help 'realign subconscious and cognitive reflexes'. I wasn't sure exactly what this meant – all I knew was that he was proposing to 'cure' me.

I stood up. Which took some effort; like Mama, I'd always deferred to authority figures. I felt unsteady on my legs, almost faint. Yet somehow I stood – it was the prospect of my date with you that evening that gave me a nugget of strength – and I walked out, pausing only to steady myself against his office door.

'No, Doctor,' I said. 'This "cure" of yours ...' – I felt my resolve falter – 'No, no, that's not what I want ... I don't want to be told I'm *sick*, I—'

In the waiting area, I saw Mama jump to her feet as I made for the exit. She ran after me, calling, 'Kostya, wait—'

'No, Mama,' I told her, 'I'm not subjecting myself to that treatment.'

She followed me, still calling, 'Kostya, wait,' struggling to keep up as I bounded down the stairs two steps at a time.

Outside it was still raining. People bustled by under their umbrellas, taking no notice of us. 'Kostya, wait!' she called, again. But I didn't wait, not even to accompany her home. No, I was in a hurry for my date with you. Recalling how you'd flagged down a car that night, I stuck my hand out, waving a

1,000-rouble note for good measure. It worked: the first car to pass, a rusty old Moskvich, screeched to a halt, splattering the kerb with mud.

Behind me, Mama had caught up and grabbed my hand, but I turned to her and said, 'Mama, let me go. I have a date tonight, I don't want to be late—'

'A *date*?' Her eyes were wide, tinged with red.

'Yes, Mama,' I said. 'A young man. You'd actually *like* him if you met him, if—'

'Oi!' The driver of the car had wound down his window. 'Where are you headed?'

I told him and got inside. I didn't ask Mama to get in too. No, let her take the bus. As I closed the car door, I saw her face crumple and heard her wailing, 'I'm trying to *help* you, like I helped you before—'

Yes, she'd helped get me out of the army. But I didn't want her 'help' now. Now, I had you, Dima; I had finally stepped over the cliff edge that Jamie had invited me over, falling head-first into the love I had long craved. And as I was driven off in that stranger's car, I glanced back – a sight that has stayed with me ever since – and saw Mama in her frumpy blue anorak, standing on the street corner in the rain, getting smaller and smaller, then disappearing as the raindrops obscured the back window.

★

I was seventeen when it happened. They had tripped me up in the showers and I was on the floor, naked, slippery with soap, shaking so much that I couldn't get to my feet. They kicked me in the ribs and globs of spit pelted my face. Their faces were contorted with hate, raining down insults like the water raining from the shower. *Faggot. Poofter. Nancy boy*. I couldn't even cry; my throat had seized up and I could hardly catch my breath, let alone form the words to beg for mercy. Their faces crowded in from above, then a pair of arms held me from behind − I didn't see his face − one arm hooked around my neck, the other twisting mine behind in an armlock. Another kick, this time to my stomach. I howled, the only sound I could manage, a cry that echoed through the shower-room. I don't know if anyone else in the barracks heard it. Or cared. A hand was clamped over my mouth. *No more screaming, faggot,* they said and dragged me upright, my feet slip-sliding uselessly, and rammed me up against the wall, pressing my forehead hard to the tiles, my back now under the running water. '*Davai! Davai!*' they yelled, 'Go on, give him one!' Another lad behind me grabbed me by the hips, asking for the soap. Why soap? I thought, clueless. I soon found out, feeling his hips thrust against my backside, then something fleshy but firm and rubbery sliding up between my buttocks.

★

I heard a voice cry out. My voice. I woke, finding myself in the dark, sitting bolt upright in an unfamiliar bed. Where was I? What was happening? I sensed a fumbling behind me, and the bedside lamp came on. It was you, Dima, at my side, stroking the back of my head.

'*Tikho*, Kostik,' you said, 'Shhh, Kostik, it was only a nightmare.'

Still shaking, I turned, and you stroked my cheeks, shushing me all the while. Your face was bleary-eyed with sleep, yet gently smiling as you ran your fingers under my chin. Even in the half-darkness, with only the light of that feeble bedside lamp, your face shone with kindness − handsomeness *and* kindness. Nothing like the faces in my nightmare. Those faces were far behind me, weren't they? It didn't ever have to be like that again, did it? Your words gave voice to my thoughts: '*Tikho*, Kostik. It was only a nightmare. I'm here. You're with me now.'

★

All around us came bursts of laughter, whoops of excitement – some close by, others distant and muffled by the snow – a clamour that circled and swirled, jostling with the carnival music blaring out from the loudspeakers. We were in Gorky Park, a Sunday in late November, a few days after the first snow, the air sharp and laced with frost. The sun was out, the sky above us blue, the snow blinding and unsullied.

That was our fourth Sunday together, two weeks after I went to Khimki with Mama. As I'd left the flat the day before, I told her the truth about where I'd be sleeping: *At my boyfriend's place*, I said. It was strange, hearing myself utter that word 'boyfriend' – but I wanted Mama to know about you. She looked up from her sewing machine, frozen in the middle of repairing a blouse, and let the clatter of the machine die away.

She said nothing to break the silence.

'He's a wonderful, kind young man,' I pressed on. 'You say you don't want me to end up on my own – and I don't either, Mama.'

More silence. Even then, I'd wanted to win her round, to *see* her offering to patch up your jeans on this very same sewing machine. 'If only you met him' – I pictured you charming Mama with your smile, just as Jamie had with his – 'you'd like him, I'm sure.'

Still more silence. She lowered her eyes and sniffed. 'It's your life,' she said, then ploughed on with her sewing, the hammering of the machine even louder, more determined now.

So there we were in Gorky Park, on the ice rink. Through

those grand Stalinist gates we had marched together – not, of course, hand in hand, but taking our place alongside the other couples in a space built for the Recreation of the Soviet People. You had your own skates, a snazzy brand-name pair that your dad had sent you years ago from Sweden; the ones I'd hired were tight and pinched my feet. And unlike most other kids at my school, I'd never learnt to ice-skate; without you there, I would have slipped and fallen flat on the ice.

I didn't fall, though. Not once. You didn't let me. As I tottered onto the rink, clinging for dear life to the railing, you whooshed up to my side and performed an about-turn that sent a little shower of ice crystals onto my feet. I looked up. You were beaming at me under your ski cap, cheeks red with the cold. 'Take my hand,' you said. 'Don't bother with gloves.' And you held me around the waist with your left arm, gripping my right hand tightly in yours; it was warm and a little sweaty. Then, without further warning, we were off – your legs powering us ahead in long, sweeping strides, my own skates barely seeming to touch the ground. My nerves dissolved into laughter, into shrieks of elation. Tighter still you held me, surefooted as we overtook other couples, weaving in and out around them. It felt like we were flying – in fact, it reminded me of a scene in *Superman*, that silly American film we'd watched on a pirate video the night before, the scene where Superman takes Lois Lane on a flight over night-time New York. Without him, Lois would fall, helplessly plummeting to her death … but like me with you, she stays aloft, safely in the arms of her hero, airborne, love-struck and soaring above the earthbound masses.

17

MARCH 1993. Moscow

Tamara Borisovna

She steps off the train and stares along the platform. Up ahead, rising out of the smoke and steam, are the giant metallic letters astride the station roof that spell out 'MOCKBA'.

Moscow ... She hadn't counted on finding herself back here so soon. It's been only four weeks and five days since her sleepless overnight journey taking Kostya to be buried down in Voronezh. Days that she's counted since that night she watched the porters loading the temporary coffin that contained her son's body, fearing they might slip on the icy platform.

The ice is all melting now, the platform awash with slushy puddles that reflect the grey of daybreak. People bustle past, as indifferent as they were that February night. She steadies herself on Galina's arm. She wouldn't be here if it weren't for her old friend talking her into it. Galina was planning a trip to Moscow anyway, to join her Mothers for Peace demonstration – and now she's here herself too, with Galina. But not for the demo. She is here as a result of her late-night confession a few days earlier.

She had sat, that night, on the edge of Galina's bed, shivering with remorse. Her hands shook, fidgeting with her hair, her sleeve, the bedclothes. She'd felt like she was being sick, words spilling from her mouth that were half-chewed, too bitter to swallow. But her confession was clear enough: it was she who had taken Kostya to Milyukov in the hope of getting him 'cured'. That 'cure', she said, must be what killed him.

The shock had hovered for several frozen, silent seconds before Galina recovered that decisive head of hers. Or maybe it wasn't shock, maybe Galina was just listening. The odd thing was, Galina never questioned the actual idea of Kostya being 'different'; instead she gripped her by the shoulders and told her, ordered her, not to blame herself. Focus on the facts, Galina said – like the fact that Kostya had *refused* the treatment. He walked out of the clinic, didn't he?

Yes, she thought, pausing mid-sob. She could hardly forget Kostya flagging down a car, leaving her in Khimki, in the rain. But then, how did he end up going back there?

'Besides,' Galina added, 'Milyukov's a charlatan. We knew that. It's one thing signing certificates to get lads out of the army' – here Galina had flinched – 'God knows, if I'd heard about Milyukov earlier, I would've paid him to get Viktor out . . . But it's another thing claiming to be able to cure boys of these "urges". If anyone's to blame, it's Milyukov.'

Even as Galina tried to calm her, she had broken down again. 'It was *me*, though,' she sobbed, '*me* who took Kostya to Milyukov that time in November.'

Galina gripped her hand and took a long, deep breath. 'You've got to come with me, up to Moscow. You won't have any peace of mind until you get answers.'

★

The minute they get on the metro, she sinks into a seat. Galina stays standing, trying to assemble the hand-painted placard she's brought with her from Voronezh – *SAVE OUR SONS!* it says.

Save my son, she thinks. That's all I tried to do, wasn't it? Not from war, like Galina's boy, but to save him nevertheless ...

She had dreaded being left alone for two nights while Galina went away – a dread compounded, again, by her should-haves and what-ifs. What was worse, knowing what happened to Kostya or not knowing? The answer, surely, would be in her son's final diary, his 1993 diary: that's where any written account of returning to Milyukov would be. But again, because she couldn't find it, she'd been drawn back to last year's diary.

Looking over what he'd written in the later months of 1992, she had flicked rapidly from page to page, afraid of dwelling too long on any entry. Anything that shocked her made her snap the diary shut, as if to blot out what she'd read. But no, it all sticks in her mind – especially Kostya's account of their 'Black Saturday' row, of his storming off to get 'corrupted' and 'snogging' some ginger-haired boy at a druggy party. Even Kostya had sounded disgusted.

But then came that more recent entry, in November. This time, far from being disgusted, Kostya had penned a breathless description of a brawny blond lad who'd taken him dancing, and later to bed; of the 'electricity' that had shot through his body. She could never quite airbrush from her mind a vision of her son lying naked, straddled by that other boy, being masturbated by him. Dima, that was his name. And yet – even she had to admit it – Kostya's effusive tale of falling in love made him sound happier than she'd seen him since, well, since he'd met Jamie.

They change lines at Ploshchad Revolyutsii, hurrying past bronze statues of battle-ready soldiers, then head to Arbatskaya, the metro nearest the Ministry of Defence. She used to admire it long ago, this Soviet riposte to the Pentagon, a fortress of white marble proud with sharp-edged verticals and giant military stars.

It is here on Znamenka Street that the Mothers for Peace have gathered for their protest, a crowd of about a hundred held back from the gates by a line of policemen in fur caps and long grey overcoats. The police seem embarrassed, the ones she gets a good look at, wearing a stony officiousness at odds with their youth – after all, they're only in their twenties, like Kostya, like the soldier sons these mothers are here to shout about. She scans the faces of the other women: like her, middle-aged, hair bundled under woolly hats and, below those hats, eyes full of fight as well as pleading. The air is chilly, and clouds of steam billow from their mouths as they chant, '*Shame on Grachev! Bring our sons home!*' She holds back from chanting but Galina links arms with her and joins the chorus: '*Shame on Grachev! Stop killing our sons . . .*'

The plan is to surround the defence minister, to flood the media with images of Grachev amid a sea of placards demanding an end to the bloodshed. He can't ignore the grief of a hundred mothers, can he? But she sees no sign of Grachev, and as the police corral the women well away from the steps, she wonders if anyone in authority has ever truly cared.

Jamie

He'd stayed late at work again the night before and had finally been about to leave, around 8 p.m. it must've been, when the phone on his desk started ringing. Thank God, he thought, that'll be Artyom, ready to kiss and make up.

It had been three days since Artyom stopped returning his calls. All because of the row that blew up when Artyom called his flat and Dima had picked up the phone. '*What the fuck's* he *doing there?*' Artyom had demanded to know. It's a row he keeps replaying in his head. For Christ's sake Artyom, he'd said, nothing's going on. The guy's homeless, he's got nowhere to stay. Besides, he's helping me investigate what happened to Kostya. '*Oh yeah,*' Artyom sneered, '*you and Dima, I forgot how much you both care about Kostya. You didn't tell me he'd moved in with you.*' Dima hasn't 'moved in', he protested, he's just dossing on my sofa.

Anyway, he wanted to tell Artyom, Dima was gone now, gone to pose as an overnight patient at that 'health and well-being consultancy' linked to Kostya's death. Only he couldn't explain that to Artyom because Artyom wouldn't answer the bloody phone.

But the call wasn't from Artyom. He'd heard the unexpected *beep-beep* of a payphone, then the clunk of a coin being fed into the slot. It must be Dima, he'd thought, calling from Khimki already. But no, it was a woman's voice, panting as if she were in a hurry.

'*Dzheymz?*' she said. 'This is Galina Sergeyevna, from Voronezh.'

Galina who? He'd had to think for a second, then quickly recalled, yes, of course, that battle-axe who's got Tamara Borisovna staying with her, the one from the cemetery. She must have kept the business card he'd given her.

'*Galina Sergeyevna?*' he said, surprised. 'Oh ... how can I help you?'

'You can help,' she'd said, 'by meeting me at our Mothers for Peace demonstration outside the Ministry of Defence tomorrow.'

Mothers for Peace? Was that it? Nothing about Kostya or Tamara Borisovna? He started explaining how the *Moscow Herald* had already reported on the Mothers for Peace and that he had another appointment the next day, but Galina interrupted him.

'I'll have Tamara Borisovna with me,' she said. 'No time to explain now – we're just catching the night train to Moscow – but you and she need to have a serious talk.'

★

Still no call from Artyom the next morning. No call from Dima either. He wonders where it's going, his 'investigation'. If he wants this story to get him noticed, he should sell it to a bigger newspaper, not confine himself to the crummy little *Herald* . . . He shakes his head at the sight of the empty desks vacated by Josh and Patsy last week. Josh has been offered a contract at the embassy, while Patsy's landed a job at the *Moscow Times*, wouldn't you bloody believe it.

Pulling on his coat, he glances into Bernie's office. His editor has his head down over some paperwork, probably more bills that the *Herald* can't pay. And with all the Western business advertising going to the *Moscow Times*, how can Bernie afford to keep him on? There isn't even a replacement for Larisa. One night, he'd overheard Bernie on the phone to the States: 'These ad revenues, the circulation,' he was saying, 'the investors ain't gonna like it.'

★

That makes two meetings this morning, one of them unplanned. I'm gonna be pushed, he thinks, but for a story like this, it'll be worth it. First, ahead of his rendezvous with Kostya's mother and Galina, he has an appointment he'd fixed up before Dima set off for Khimki.

The first thing he notices on arriving at the offices of US-Care is that the little shrine to Kostya has gone. No flowers on Kostya's old desk, and no framed photograph. How long did they keep them? One week? Two? The desk is now occupied by a young man about Kostya's age, only with a full head of pale blond hair, who's sitting there in an ill-fitting suit, typing up spreadsheets on the computer.

Once again, it's that Nastya who ushers him into Waterson's office. Over the phone, the American had sounded surprised at his request for a follow-up interview, so soon after last time – but now he's pumping his hand, all big toothy smile and 'great to see you again'. Feeling a scruff next to Waterson in his designer shirt and fancy silk tie, he lowers himself onto the sofa, glancing at his battered Doc Martens and looking away, out of the window. A dozen storeys below, the snow is melting and the sweeping black curve of the river is now free of ice. Nastya asks if they require coffee. Getting out his notebook, he unfolds Waterson's list of US-Care projects and lays it on the coffee table.

Waterson kicks off the interview with the usual business-speak bollocks about Russia's 'emerging market potential'. He nods, pretending to listen, but feeling his pulse rate quicken as he prepares to ask the question – *the* question – that has brought him here.

'What can you tell me' – he runs his finger down the list to point to Milyukov's so-called consultancy – 'about this outfit in Khimki?'

Waterson looks at the list. 'Renaissance? Can't say I'm

familiar with that one.' A shrug and another big toothy smile. 'You know, we facilitate nearly a hundred projects in Russia. Farming, healthcare, public services. What's the big deal about this one?'

Here goes. 'I'm conducting an investigation' – sounds good, he thinks; let this Yank believe I'm on to something – 'and have reason to suspect that this clinic, the one here on your funding list, is prescribing an unsafe form of treatment.'

Waterson furrows his brow, leaning back in his chair with a dismissive shake of his head. '*An unsafe form of treatment*?' he repeats. 'What d'you mean?'

A deep breath. Time to lay his cards on the table. 'One of my sources,' he says, 'has been to this clinic, posing as a patient, and he was offered a treatment that is widely discredited in the West – something that they're selling as a "cure" for—'

Waterson cuts him off. 'Wait. Let me tell you something, James – can I call you James? – the projects that US-Care funds in Russia have to comply with strict criteria. Are they enterprise-based? Do they promise material or healthcare or law-and-order benefits to the local population? And they all get vetted, all subject to our due diligence.'

He looks at Jamie, nodding towards his notebook. 'Ain't you writing this down?'

What a load of corporate claptrap, he thinks. Still, he takes his notepad and writes 'due diligence'. He pauses, pen hovering above paper, thinking he can throw Waterson's words back at him. 'OK, so this "due diligence", as you call it – is that something I can take a look at? Could you show me how this clinic was *vetted*?'

Waterson's smile fades. 'I don't know where you're going with this "investigation" of yours,' he says, starting to loosen his tie. 'But sure. We have nothing to hide.' He stands, then adds: 'It's all on file – in fact, I'll get Nastya to dig it out for us.' He buzzes on the intercom, dictates from the list and returns to his seat opposite Jamie.

He returns Waterson's stare. 'I get it, Mr Waterson – I know this is sensitive stuff. But this really could add up to a matter of life and—'

'And *death*?' Waterson pulls an unconvinced face.

'Yes, life and death.' He sees Waterson staring at him, one eyebrow raised ... How can he persuade the Yank to give him more? 'Look, Mr Waterson, we can go off the record if you like, but these are questions we need to get to the bottom of.'

'*We*?' Waterson frowns, then sighs. 'OK, go on. And call me Mario, will ya?'

Another deep breath. 'OK, Mario. My *sources*' – he stops to think of Larisa and now Dima – 'have uncovered a link between this clinic' – another pause, here it comes – 'and the death of your former employee Konstantin Krolikov.'

For a second, maybe two, the Yank doesn't reply but keeps staring at him, visibly taken aback, his tie still not quite removed. He wonders whether Waterson is about to terminate the interview and boot him out.

'Now you listen to me.' Suddenly Waterson is on his feet, flinging his tie on the table, his accent turning all Midwest Bible-basher. 'Konstantin's death came as a terrible shock to us at US-Care. A *terrible* shock.'

The American looks away, towards his desk. 'I happen to have been real fond of that kid,' he says. He swings back round. 'And you come in here suggesting that his *death* could have been linked to a project we're supporting?'

'Mr Waterson' – he holds up both hands in a plea to be heard – 'Mario. I'm trying to alert you to a bogus "cure" for homosexuality. One that might've killed Kostya.'

Arms folded, Waterson looks down at him. 'Are you *that* desperate for a "story"? I've heard that little newspaper of yours is going through hard times. Losing advertisers, losing readers. But *this*? I'd be surprised if anyone ever gets to read your "investigation".'

Wasn't he thinking the same thing about the *Herald* only an hour earlier? He's got his answer ready: 'Forget the *Herald*' – he grabs the US-Care document listing Milyukov's clinic and waves it at Waterson – '*this* is a story that *any* newspaper would want. I could even sell it to radio or TV. Think how they'd love a scandal like this—'

'Scandal? Now it sounds like you're making *threats*.' Waterson glares at him. 'I think you ought to leave before I have you—'

'Kicking me out won't fix this, will it?' he blurts out, gripping the arm of Waterson's sofa as if to resist being forcibly ejected. Shit, he thinks, better keep the Yank talking. 'Listen, if you've nothing to hide, then fine, let's see your files. Prove me wrong. But if I'm right, you'd be supporting a totally discredited practice.'

Shaking his head, Waterson averts his eyes, but only for a second, then looks right back at him. 'OK, James,' he says, 'but first I'm gonna show you something.'

He watches Waterson go to his desk and take something out of a drawer – an object that the Yank then thrusts in his face. It's a framed colour photo of an American-looking guy in his thirties – perfect teeth, blow-dried blond hair, polo shirt – being embraced from behind by a darker, swarthier man, also in a polo shirt. It takes him a second or two to recognise the darker man, the one embracing his boyfriend from behind, as a younger Mario Waterson.

'That,' Waterson says, 'is my partner Doug. Or rather, my *late* partner Doug. That's *late* as in, he died four years ago. Aids, in case you hadn't guessed.'

A memory flashes up, a recollection of seeing Waterson hide something in a drawer the last time he was here. 'I'm sorry, Mr – I'm sorry, Mario,' he mumbles. 'I had no idea.' Sensing a lull in their confrontation, he asks, 'How long were you together?'

'Ten years,' says Waterson. 'Ten years with the man I loved.' He fixes Jamie with a stare and jabs a pointing finger at him. 'So don't *you* come in here accusing me of helping to finance some "gay cure" bullshit.'

'But isn't that what US-Care does? You dish out grants to bring in contracts for American companies. Kostya himself told me that.'

Waterson folds his arms. 'That's the second time you've called him "Kostya". Did you *know* him, by any chance?'

'Yeah, I did.' He nods, confidently, feeling bolder now than when he approached Larisa. This is all going to come out when he publishes his story, so why pretend otherwise any more? 'What if I did? It's a small world, isn't it, the gay scene in Moscow?' He returns Waterson's stare. 'I'm sure you know that.'

Before Waterson can reply, Nastya comes in, bringing the coffee and the requested file. The Yank grunts, swiftly returning the photograph to his desk drawer, then waits for her to leave. As soon as Nastya has closed the door behind her, he says, 'All right then, James, well, I'll show you something else I've been keeping.'

Now it's *his* turn to frown, puzzled as Waterson opens another drawer, takes out another framed picture and stands it on the coffee table.

'Oh my God.' He can't hide his surprise. It's Kostya's portrait, the duplicate of the black-and-white one he saw at his grave. He picks it up, holding it in both hands, staring into Kostya's eyes, always familiar, always averted and faraway.

'I kept this on his desk for nearly two weeks,' Waterson says. 'Any longer, and it'd have looked like I was *too* fond of him.'

Whatever anger the Yank was venting seems to have turned to bewilderment. 'You tell me,' he says, offering Jamie a gesture that's part shrug, part plea, 'why I would approve funding for *aversion therapy*? That shit messes with gay men's lives. I should know: we have it in the States.'

'Good question,' he shoots right back, standing Kostya's photograph on the coffee table in front of them. 'Knowing what you know, *why would you*? But here it is' – he picks up the piece of paper again – 'on your list, in line for a cash handout.'

Waterson grunts again and sits down, this time on the sofa next to him, and opens the file that Nastya brought in. He spreads a batch of letters, faxes and other paperwork across the table and starts sorting through them.

Then, out of the blue, Waterson says, 'Jesus! What the fuck . . . ?'

He cranes his neck to look over Waterson's shoulder. The American is studying a print-out dated January 1993 – just two months ago – a table of costs in roubles and dollars, then details of Milyukov's 'facilitating partners': North Temple Pharmaceuticals, Gospel Bank of Utah, the Theological Investment Foundation, all with addresses in Utah.

'What? Are you telling me you didn't know about this?'

'I didn't.' Waterson is shaking his head; he looks genuinely rattled, only with confusion now, not anger. 'I swear to God, I am seeing this for the first time—'

'So who *are* those "facilitating partners"?' He grabs his notepad and starts scribbling.

Waterson drags a hand down his face. 'I don't know. Some religious nuts who must've lobbied head office direct. The kind that say Aids is God's punishment on us fags . . .'

Now *this* is a story . . . Scribbling in his notepad, he turns to Waterson, feeling emboldened, feeling ever more like an investigative reporter. 'How come *you* didn't know about this? Doesn't sound like US-Care has done a proper job of that vetting—'

'I told you before, I left a lot of that work to Konstantin.'

'I see' – still scribbling in his notepad – 'you took your eye off the ball, then?'

Waterson casts a glance at the notepad. 'I thought we were off the record?'

'I'll be quoting what's in that file, not what you say.'

'Hold your horses. You think you've got a story, but I can make amends—'

'Amends? Too late for that, isn't it?'

Abruptly, Waterson stands and goes to his desk. He buzzes on the intercom once more. 'Kid, could you step in here a minute?' A timid knock at the door follows, and in tiptoes the young man with the ill-fitting new suit, the one at Kostya's old desk.

'Sasha, an urgent job for you,' Waterson says. He hands the young man the print-out. 'You've taken over this project, right? OK, I want you to contact these *institutions* here' – he stabs the paper with his finger – 'and let them know we're withholding any grants they're expecting from us. Got it?'

Sasha looks at the document. 'All of them?'

'All of them. Phone 'em, fax 'em, do it by telex, but they need to know they're not getting any money until –' Waterson shoots Jamie a glance – 'we've tied up our investigation.'

He watches Sasha leave and faces Waterson again. 'OK, I get it, you want to do some "damage limitation". But how did this even get past you in the first place?'

Waterson sits back down beside him, landing heavily. A sigh. 'Thing is, US-Care has partners all over the States – and they're hardly all liberal types. I mean, *Utah*?'

'But you said Kostya checked out these applications here' – he gestures around him – 'in this office. You delegated that vetting to him, right? So how could—'

Just then there's another knock on the door. It's Sasha again.

'Excuse me,' Sasha says, 'I don't know if this has any connection with the place in Khimki you asked about, but *this* arrived in the post for Konstantin last week. I didn't open it—'

Waterson stands. 'Well, we'd better open it now.'

Sasha hands his boss an A4-size brown envelope. As Waterson sits, Jamie sees that it's stamped 'private' and addressed, in Russian, to Konstantin Krolikov, administration assistant, US-Care. The postmark is three weeks old, but that doesn't surprise him: that's how long the local post can take, even within Moscow.

Waterson turns to him. 'OK, *you* open it, James. You're the Russian-speaking foreign correspondent, ain't you? My Russian's pretty non-existent.'

He looks up to check that Sasha's closed the door and runs his finger under the envelope flap. Out slides a cheaply produced black-and-white magazine, also in Russian, ten or so pages thick and titled *Tema*. He instantly recognises it from the 'Discotheque for Deviants': *Tema* is the underground gay newsletter founded a couple of years earlier by gay activists, the likes of Nina and Veronika. This edition, for some reason, is an older one, dated May 1992.

'I'm just guessing,' he says to Waterson, 'but Kostya wasn't out of the closet to his mum. Maybe that's why he had it delivered here. Unless there's some other reason?'

An inside-page illustration of a half-naked man seems to confirm his theory – but then he finds a slip of paper in the envelope. He reads it out loud for Waterson's benefit: *'Dear Konstantin – We hope our investigative exposé in this issue will be of assistance in your inquiries, best wishes from the editorial collective.'*

Dima

He was driven here in the back of an ambulance, manhandled by two male orderlies in green smocks. They'd held him, one arm each, as they bundled him through the rear doors, and they'd kept hold of him all the way. Inside was one other patient, a young man with dribbling lips and sunken, rolling eyes; he moaned and slobbered but didn't actually speak, his arms twitching uselessly in stitched-together sleeves.

Earlier, when he'd presented himself at Renaissance, there had been no sign of Milyukov. 'Stepan Mikhailovich is at a conference in Utah,' lab-coat woman reminded him, barely looking up from the reception desk. She counted the cash in his envelope – some from Jamie, plus what he'd made reselling the Marlboros – asked him to sign something, then placed a phone call. He sat there, alone, for an hour, dying for a smoke.

To pass the time, he read the copy of *Vizit Inspektora* that Kostya had given him.

When lab-coat woman announced, 'They've come for you', some instinct told him to hide the book. That was when the orderlies showed up. That was when he realised he wouldn't be treated here, on the premises of Milyukov's 'consultancy', with its businesslike furniture and fancy brand name. No: this place they've driven him to is nothing more than an old Soviet psychiatric hospital – the same six-storey block that he'd seen on his way here, then glimpsed from afar inside Milyukov's office.

How could Kostya, brainy English-speaking Kostya, have fallen for this? After all, it was Kostya, during another whinge about his job at US-Care, who'd once explained to him the concept of 'outsourcing' – one company paying another to do its dirty work, saving money, maximising profits. That must be what's going on here: Milyukov sells a 'cure' to his patients, then dispatches them to this 1950s mental institution.

They've put him in a room by himself, a cell-like space with an iron-framed bed and a bucket that he hopes he won't need to use. So far, they've allowed him to use the toilets at the end of the corridor. But there's no phone, not on this floor. How's he going to let Jamie know that he's in this place, not at the clinic? Otherwise, he's free to roam past the communal ward. It reminds him of the police cells where he last saw Oleg: strip lighting and walls painted in whitewash and green sludge; only here the synthetic ether of disinfectant masks the whiff of piss. He screws up his nose. They're not allowed to open the windows – they even have bars, these windows up on the top floor. Still, unlike the inmate from the ambulance or the other vacant-eyed men on the ward, he has clearly been singled out as a 'special' patient, one of Milyukov's. The order-lies watch his every step, but he hasn't been restrained. Not yet.

It's his first morning here. Must be 8 a.m. or thereabouts. He doesn't have his watch but hears a plane fly overhead, its roar filling the sky before fading into the distance. He's slept barely a couple of hours, kept awake half the night by bursts of wailing, by shouts and curses from the orderlies.

And by the question: what is it they might do to me here?

Lowering his legs out of bed, he slides his feet into babushka-type slippers of coarse blue felt. They're loose and itchy, like the stripy grey pyjamas the orderlies made him change into. He wonders what they've done with his clothes, how far he could get without them.

Out into the corridor he goes, looking left, then right, where a babushka is mopping the lino with a sodden rag. He says good morning. She doesn't answer. He shuffles – the only way he can walk in those slippers – to one end of the corridor.

Near the door to the stairs, an orderly sits at a desk, eyes trained on him. It's the same green-clad jerk who said he couldn't leave this floor, let alone the building – 'Walk up and down as long as you don't shit yourself.' And shit himself is exactly what the young man from the ambulance did as he was dragged, twisting and screaming, into the ward.

The orderly snaps at him, 'Where d'you think you're going?'

Without bothering to answer, he turns back the way he came. The orderly jumps to his feet. 'Keep away from the stairs, I told you! We'll be taking you down there soon enough, when it's your turn.'

His turn for *what*? He glares back at the orderly, a scrawny guy a head shorter than himself. Listen, mate, he wants to tell him, you know as well as I do that I'm sane. There's nothing wrong in the head with me. Nothing 'wrong', except I like cock.

And what about Kostya? Did he get sent here by Milyukov because he ... Only, Kostya would never have put it that way, would never have said, *I like cock* ...

Reaching the other end of the corridor, he stops to gaze out of the window. A few miles away, above the snow-dusted forests stretching to the horizon, a plane climbs into the sky – it must've taken off from Sheremetyevo. He's dying to lean outside and have a smoke. He peers past the bars, trying to identify an escape route from this place; but all around the grounds of the hospital is a concrete wall with barbed wire and, beyond that, the muddy road he'd walked along into Khimki that first time.

He shudders at the thought of Kostya roaming this very same corridor. If he'd known, he would have stopped Kostya going to see Milyukov. Like that hair restoration clinic Kostya used to go to – what a bunch of charlatans. He'd managed to talk Kostya out of that, hadn't he? *Just shave your hair off,* he'd told him, *like they do in the army.*

But he didn't save Kostya. He wasn't there for him in those final weeks. His plan had been to leave Moscow and dump him. Again, he pictures Kostya that day on Pushkin Square, the last time he saw him, face pink with cold, eyes red, shoulders convulsed by sobbing. He turns from the window and plods back along the corridor. The babushka looks up from her mopping and spits, pointedly, into her bucket.

It's been light for the past hour but he notices, as he passes the ward, that the six men there are all still snoring or moaning in their sleep. The guy from the ambulance is muttering and drooling from one side of his mouth. The quiet strikes him as eerie, not like any hospital he's been in before. No urgency, no bustle of doctors and nurses. As if the place is in a state of suspension or waiting, holding its breath for something that's going to happen.

In that unnerving silence, the creak of his bed feels isolated and amplified as he climbs back in. From under his pillow he pulls *Vizit Inspektora*. Just a few pages to go. He reads, the only sounds being the odd plane in the distance, the rattle of the babushka's mop-bucket, the turning of pages. His eyes come to a halt. There, in the inspector's sermon to the wealthy Birling family, are some words Kostya had underlined, maybe a translation query, yet giving voice to a guilt he's been trying to dodge. '*We are responsible for each other.*'

Jamie

Thank God the metro's not busy this late in the morning. He flops onto a seat, resting his bag on his knees, and fishes out that old edition of *Tema*, still in its A4 envelope.

This isn't going to be easy, seeing Kostya's mum. '*You and she need to have a serious talk,*' Galina had said. What, after Tamara Borisovna accused him of leading Kostya 'astray'? Was she sure?, he'd asked. Isn't she still angry with me? Galina had gone quiet for a moment, then said, 'I've persuaded her. You're a journalist. Help us to expose what killed Kostya. God willing, that might make amends in her eyes.'

Make amends? Not if he tells Kostya's mum what he's just discovered. *Oh, by the way, Tamara Borisovna, when Kostya worked for US-Care, he handled the funding application for some bogus 'corrective' facility* ... So what *can* he tell her? How about blaming Kostya's job for steering him in the direction of the clinic? How else could he have ended up going to Milyukov? That way, he'd be able to present it to Tamara Borisovna as the fault of those meddling capitalists, looking for dodgy shit to invest in.

As he flicks through *Tema*, one article in particular catches his eye. He tears the page out – I can't go showing the magazine to Tamara Borisovna in its entirety, he thinks, not with all these pics of half-naked guys ... But then, as he reaches the station where they're due to meet, his eyes alight on one sentence on that page, on a word that Dima used after scoping out Milyukov's clinic: the word *korrektirovka*.

Tamara Borisovna

Within minutes of Grachev being chauffeured away in his ministerial car, the protest begins to disperse. After all this waiting, all this chanting and stamping of feet. She'd even joined in at one point, just to pump some blood into her frozen fingers. She had felt Galina at her side, on tiptoe, brandishing her placard, screaming, 'Save our sons!' But the minister didn't stop, didn't even look at them; he just emerged in his finery, his coat weighed down with medals, and headed for his car, shielded from the crowd by his bodyguards.

It strikes her, not for the first time, just how much Russia is a country run by men but held together by women. How women keep the home fires burning, raising families, queuing for rations, cooking, feeding – even doing men's jobs while men go off and die in the wars started by men. She watches Galina go around hugging her fellow Mothers for Peace, telling them to stay in touch, that their voices will be heard some day.

Then, amid the huddle of reporters and onlookers on the pavement, she spots a familiar face, a boy's face, pink and shivering, bundled up in a scarf. She knew he'd be here, of course – he was part of Galina's plan to persuade her to come back to Moscow. 'We need him,' Galina had said, 'to help us nail the bastards for what they did to our sons.' Yes, she'd said '*our* sons'. Whatever the differences between Viktor and Kostya, both were victims of a system that crushed souls. Hadn't they both died in the name of turning boys into what 'Mother' Russia deemed to be men? And this English boy – he's someone's son too, isn't he? She lets Galina take her hand, steering her across the street, and as she gets closer, she sees he looks different, without that impertinent twinkle in his eye.

Jamie

He keeps his head lowered, almost bowed – like he did the last time he saw her. Her head is lowered too, as if she's reluctant to look at him. He speaks. 'Tamara Borisovna?' And removes his glove, holding out his hand for her to shake.

She looks up. A glance at his outstretched hand, then her eyes meet his. He sees her gaze flicker with the tiniest movements, taking in his eyes, his hair, his head exposed to the cold. There's a red tinge to the rims of her eyes, which widen as they look into his, bloated with pain, or defiance, or both, and God knows what other feelings he can only guess at.

Without removing her gloves, she takes his hand and for a second cradles his fingers in hers as if she's not accustomed to handshakes – then suddenly, her arm is wrapped around his back, her head on his chest, and she's sobbing, 'Oh, Jamie ...'

Unsure of himself, he returns her hug. It's not like those

hugs they exchanged in Voronezh, summer-days hugs that came as easily back then as the comings and goings between him and Kostya, from theatre to ice-cream parlour to Kostya's home and Kostya's bed. They pull slightly apart and she wipes her eyes on her coat sleeve.

He's still wondering what to say when Galina says, 'Let's get out of the cold, shall we, and warm up with a cup of tea. Do you know anywhere, James?'

The nearest place is Café Prague, but they'd need a reservation to get in. He thinks. 'How about the Conservatory? It's not far from here.'

Both women nod in agreement, Tamara Borisovna still red-eyed and sniffling. He leads them under the main road, through a subway echoing with traffic noise, and as they leave the bustle behind, they enter the stillness of back streets where shovelled piles of snow stand waist-high. It's quieter here. He tries to breathe in time with the crunch of their feet in the slush and the drip-drip of ice melting from the eaves.

As they reach the Conservatory, he comes to a halt by the statue of Tchaikovsky outside. Bouquets of flowers are still piling up in the leftover snow, exactly as they were that day of his 'vox-pops' on attitudes to homosexuality – that day he still thought Kostya was alive. Glancing at the dates on the pedestal – 1840–1893 – he remembers that it's the composer's centenary, an event that Kostya would surely have wanted to—

'He would have been here laying flowers, if he were still with us.'

Tamara Borisovna has quietly crept up to his side and is gazing past him, at the statue. Her voice sounds strangled as she asks, 'So, do you like Tchaikovsky's music?'

He fidgets with his scarf. 'To be honest, I haven't listened to that much.' An embarrassed shrug. 'Apart from, you know, what Kostik used to play for me.'

It's the first time since they met today that anyone has uttered Kostya's name. He sees that she's biting on her lip, making long, forced ins and outs with her breathing.

'Yes,' she says. 'That would've been the *Pathétique* Symphony.'

'That's right. I remember it.' He can picture it now, the well-thumbed sleeve of Kostya's old vinyl record, a Melodiya LP with a glowering portrait of Tchaikovsky on the cover; it was the music whose despairing finale had moved Kostya to tears.

Tamara Borisovna looks away, down at the flowers in the snow. She says, 'I could hear it from his room, the *Pathétique*. He kept playing it. So loud too. Over and over he played it, especially before ... especially those last few ...'

As her voice trails off, he recalls something that Kostya told him about that symphony. 'It was Tchaikovsky's final work, wasn't it?'

'Yes,' she replies, still transfixed by the flowers. 'Composed just before – well, you can see.' She gestures at the date on the pedestal, the year of Tchaikovsky's death.

The wind on his neck makes him shiver. *A swansong ...* That's what Kostya told him – that the symphony was the composer's swansong, a dying lament. Some instinct tells him not to mention that to Tamara Borisovna, but she speaks first anyway.

'He was hounded to his death.' She looks round at him. 'Tchaikovsky, I mean. Such terrible things they said about him. I never used to believe them – it wasn't what the Party taught us. But now I don't know, I don't know what to believe any more ...'

He hears footsteps in the slush as Galina takes Tamara Borisovna by the arm, saying, 'Come on, let's go inside now.'

In the tea-room they find a little round table, one of the old Sov types where you have to stand, and hang their coats on the hooks underneath. As he and Galina go to the counter to order tea and cake, he watches Kostya's mum survey the room, its fake chandeliers and ornate plasterwork. Like most of the other customers, she keeps her hat on.

Thankfully, he doesn't have to steer the conversation; Galina takes care of that, asking him questions that Tamara Borisovna, as he can see, is in no mood to ask. So he talks, glancing at Kostya's mum for her reaction even as Galina tries to hold his attention. Seems they've already heard of Milyukov, so he tells them about Dima snooping around, posing as one of Milyukov's patients – and then steels himself to pull the page from *Tema* out of his bag.

He'd barely had time to skim-read the article before they met. Its gist was that past 'cures' for homosexuality – including in Britain and America, as well as Russia – had left patients traumatised, brain-fried, even at risk of dying. Side-stepping the detail that Kostya had sent off for this copy of *Tema*, he says, 'I found this article. I warn you, it's distressing stuff.'

Galina frowns. 'Where's this from?'

'From an underground newspaper.' He lowers his voice. 'It's a kind of *samizdat* for sexual minorities.' Turning to Kostya's mum, he sees her eyes widen with shock. 'I really think you ought not to read this, Tamara Borisovna—'

'I'll read it.' Galina puts on her glasses and motions for him to pass the page to her. He slides it across the table.

Galina takes a sip of her tea and starts reading. The article clearly shocks her so much, however, that she can't stop herself muttering out loud, phrases such as 'erotic stimuli', 'chemical-induced nausea', 'choking on vomit' – and that's when he sees Tamara Borisovna totter sideways, grabbing on to the edge of the table as if she's about to faint. He's just in time to put out an arm to catch her by the waist.

Galina stops reading and grabs Tamara Borisovna's elbow. 'Quick, James, a chair!'

He fetches one from by the wall and slides it under Kostya's mum, who folds into it rather awkwardly, her face sinking to the level of the table-top. Her gaze seems to settle on her untouched slice of cake. Galina puts an arm round her, urging her to take a sip of tea.

'I'm sorry, Tamara Borisovna.' Hesitantly, he touches her on the shoulder. 'I shouldn't have shown you that article. That stuff it describes goes on in other countries too – it doesn't mean that it's the same thing that Milyukov—'

He feels his hand being gripped by hers, right where it is, on her shoulder. Keeping her eyes fixed on the cake, she says, 'It sounds close enough to what Milyukov described to me.'

'*Described to you*, Tamara Borisovna? What do you mean?'

'I wouldn't have taken him there if I'd known all this,' she goes on, shaking her head. 'He made it sound so scientific, so reassuring.'

He stares at her, pulling his hand free of her grip. Wait ... so, Tamara Borisovna took her own son to get 'cured'? What a thing for a mother to do. Which means that it wasn't at work, through US-Care, that Kostya found out about Milyukov's clinic – he must've made his inquiries into *korrektirovka* afterwards. As if he'd wanted to know more.

He moves round the other side of the table to face Tamara Borisovna. She's trembling, scarcely lifting her head as she speaks, as she owns up to taking Kostya to see Milyukov back in November, shortly after he'd declared himself to be gay.

'I wanted to *help* him,' she says. Her hands jitter, turning her teacup in the saucer, making it clink and scrape. 'Like you, Galya, with your mothers' peace protests. Being "that way" isn't *natural*, is it? Or so we've always been taught. But you know what he said?' She looks up. 'He said it was *natural for him*.'

He stares, recognising the words he used with Kostya during their late-night heart-to-heart three years ago. *It's natural for me*, he'd said back then.

His face flushes warm with indignation. 'Well, what if it *was* natural for him?'

Tamara Borisovna sniffles. 'I don't know how my son turned out that way. It doesn't matter any more, it doesn't—'

'Shush!' Galina looks at them both in turn. 'What about Milyukov?'

'I thought I could trust Stepan Mikhailovich,' Tamara Borisovna persists, 'after he got Kostya out of the army.' She faces him. 'He certified Kostya as mentally ill, you know. He must have told you about that?'

More shushing from Galina. 'Yes, Milyukov's a fraud, we know that. Taking honest people's money for—'

'I *didn't* pay him though,' Tamara Borisovna says. 'Not this time.'

'So who did?' Galina asks.

The question lingers, over their tea and untouched cake. He knows Renaissance is out to make a profit, so *someone* must have paid Milyukov; if it wasn't Kostya's mum, then who? He watches her clutching her cup in both hands: she too seems genuinely puzzled.

Then, as if her thoughts have taken her elsewhere, she stops turning the cup in the saucer and looks up at him. 'You're the only boy of "that sort" I know ...' He sees her swallow, as though the words left a bitter taste in her mouth. 'Does *your* mother accept the way you are?'

He glances at Galina for a cue as to how he should answer. But instead of following the conversation, she seems distracted, her gaze turned towards the doors leading outside.

'Yes,' he says. 'She does accept me.'

'And didn't she ever try to *help* you?'

No, she bloody didn't, he thinks, but limits himself to saying, 'You know how mums are – she worried at first, but she got used to it—'

'Stop!' says Galina. Her hand is clamped to her mouth as if in shock. 'What did you say about some boy going to the clinic? Your friend? Posing as a patient?'

He freezes. 'You mean Dima. What about him?'

'Well, is he there now?'

He can feel the blood start to drain from his face. 'Well, yes, he is—'

'You did read this, didn't you?' Galina jabs her finger at the *Tema* article, still on the table. '"Chemical-induced nausea", "choking on vomit" – does that boy know the risks?'

Shit, he thinks, what can they do now? Sure, he'd counted on streetwise Dima being able to look after himself – but he couldn't possibly know about the methods described in the *Tema* article. Nor has he heard from Dima yet. He's been so caught up with Tamara Borisovna and the evidence trail linking Milyukov to US-Care, that he's lost sight of Dima. And after he's bribed Dima to go to Khimki ... There's no way of contacting him either.

'We have to go there,' he says. 'To Khimki. We have to go now.'

★

First, however, he stops at the payphone in the foyer of the Conservatory. 'We can't do this on our own,' he tells Galina, frantically gesturing at her to wait as he dials.

Mercifully, the phone isn't out of order and he gets straight through to Waterson's office. 'You've gotta help us,' he tells the Yank, and explains how his 'source' might be in danger at Milyukov's clinic. The police didn't 'give a shit,' he says, 'about investigating Kostya's death, but they might give a shit if *you* get them involved.'

'*Me?*' Waterson's indignation is audible, even through this crappy Sov receiver. 'You're asking me to put my position on the line by—'

'It's already on the line, isn't it? You want to make "amends", don't you? You know, "damage limitation"?'

'I cancelled that funding. What more d'you expect me to do?'

'I've seen that list – I know US-Care's been bankrolling equipment for the local police. Well, you're the American big-shot, aren't you? Call in some favours. Surely they *owe* you.'

Dima

Morning morphs into afternoon. Eventually, a cold-eyed nurse in starched whites wheels a trolley into the room. 'Food,' she says, without looking at him. She plonks a glass of fizzy water and a cracked enamel plate of meatballs at his bedside.

'Excuse me,' he says, 'how long will it be until—'

Ignoring him, she walks out. He prods the meatballs with

his plastic fork. They're vile, full of grease and gristle, but he's so hungry that he swallows a few mouthfuls, washing them down with the fizzy water. That tastes odd too, vaguely metallic and powdery, like something's been dissolved in it.

Hours drag by. He's finished reading *Vizit Inspektora* and has grown tired of walking up and down the corridor. His throat and gut feel queasy, and not only because of the meatballs. He tries to sleep, first on his side, then on his back. What else can he do? Wait his turn for the treatment? From outside comes the hum of distant traffic.

At one point a woman in a white coat, a doctor this time, comes back with the nurse and takes a blood sample. No small talk, just instructions to roll up his sleeve and do as he's told. The nurse produces a syringe and spears his vein.

Sleep, that's all there is to do. Ignore the nausea. Try not to think what they might have done to Kostya here. Just sleep, he tells himself, close your eyes, let the tedium wash over you. Breathe in, breathe out. Chest rises, chest falls. A plane buzzes overhead. Mumbling from the corridor. Ignore it, just sleep. In a few hours the sun'll be setting.

*

He stirs, not quite awake but aware of movement close by. Two blurry figures, not in white but in green, are standing over him, positioned on either side of his bed.

The orderlies. They've come for him. It's time.

'I told you your turn would come,' one of them says.

It's that weasel-faced jerk from the corridor; but the other orderly is a man he hasn't seen before, a bear-like *muzhik* with a black beard and bottomless eyes.

Next thing he knows, he's being hoisted out of bed. He tries to stuff his feet into his slippers, but his legs won't respond as they should; they're like jelly. His head, too, sways and spins as though it's becoming detached from his neck. So hard to stand . . . The room circles before his eyes, a whirl of bed, piss-bucket, wheelchair, half-eaten meatballs . . . Wait, *wheelchair*? There wasn't a wheelchair in here before.

On both sides, the orderlies grip his arms. Their fingers dig into his flesh as they haul him into the wheelchair. He tries to resist, tries to stand, but the room seems to tilt onto its side and the bear-like *muzhik* pushes him back down. He feels his neck cradled by a high, rigid head restraint that makes it hard to turn or look to either side. His head falls back; he sees the ceiling roll by as he's wheeled out of the room. Where are they taking me? he thinks. What are they gonna do to me? Or should I act like I'm expecting this? He tries to speak – 'Hold on, lads, wait, I'm not ready' – but his voice is a feeble croak he can hardly recognise as his own.

Down the corridor they wheel him, past the ward. A long, agonised moan bellows out from one of its inmates. He pictures their eyes following him as he's taken away. The strip lights in the ceiling streak past above his head. This is it, he thinks, this is what they did to Kostya, this is what I'm here to see. But fuck, how can he be a witness *and* get out of here? His thighs and feet twitch. They must have drugged him – that fizzing water, the syringe. Even if he were capable of making a run for it, there'll be more orderlies, maybe even guards.

'Wait,' he croaks again, 'I'm not ready, not today—'

They reach the stairs, the ones he's been barred from going down. Weasel-face gets out his keys and unlocks the door. A whiff of distant cooking wafts up the stairwell: those meatballs again, cutting through the smell of disinfectant. Another door, sliding open to reveal a lift, and he's wheeled inside. The doors close. The lift whirrs and descends, down one floor – or is it two? Out through another set of doors and into another corridor, a silent one. No groans or cries, no patients, no sign of activity.

It's darker down here, even more cut off from daylight than upstairs. He tries to speak, but the orderlies ignore him, wheeling him along the corridor and talking about him like he's asleep or not even there. Their voices come and go, floating into and out of his consciousness, one minute an indistinct babble, the next minute ringing loud inside his head.

One of them – he can't tell if the voice is Weasel-face or the other guy – sounds like he's asking, 'Is everything in place?'

His eyes fall shut and he tunes out, not hearing any answer; then comes another question, something about 'the usual drill', asking, 'Should we change it? After last time—'

'A one-off,' says the other voice. 'Won't happen again.'

His eyelids flutter open, then shut again. What 'one-off'? What are they talking about? He catches another fragment: 'The doc's not here now to take the rap . . .'

They stop at an unmarked door. A jangling of keys as the door is unlocked and opened, then the blinding glare of lights flickering on inside. He screws up his eyes, blinking and fighting to keep awake. They're in a small laboratory, with a door to an adjoining room and a large internal window between the two rooms. On the worktops there's an array of bottles and test tubes, a rack of syringes and two electrical monitors, plus a sink and what looks like a TV set.

The lights bear down on his eyes, the walls of the room seeming to drift apart, then close in on him. He can still feel the lurch and rattle of the wheelchair being hurried along the corridor, yet realises that they've come to a halt, that the orderlies have parked the chair in the middle of the lab. As they adjust the head restraint, he tries to listen in. But their muttering is indistinct and they've turned away from him, back towards the door.

'Should we wait for Semyonovna?'

'Relax, she'll be on her way.'

'I don't know. I'd better go and phone.'

Who's Semyonovna? he wonders. A doctor? Yes, I'll talk to *her*, tell her there's been some misunderstanding. He tries to turn his head but it's heavy and stiff, held tightly in place by the head restraint.

It was stupid coming here, so stupid. Again, he attempts to speak, another croak he can barely hear. 'Please, lads, there's been a mistake, get me the doctor—'

He hears the door being opened and another muttered exchange. 'We do nothing till she gets here ...' 'Just follow procedure ...' 'Leave him, he's not going anywhere ...' The lights are switched off. Darkness. He hears them lock the door; they're back in the corridor, their voices now snuffed out completely.

He tries again to stand, using his arms to press down hard and lift his body, like he does in his gym workout. It's no good: his arms are shaking and his legs almost numb. He falls back into the wheelchair. His skull sinks between the two hard wings of the head restraint – at least that'll stop his head spinning – and his gaze comes to rest on a blinking light in front of him, on a shelf below the TV screen.

Tamara Borisovna

By the time they reach Khimki, the grey of daylight has turned a faint, pinkish-violet. Out of the taxi window, she watches the passing silhouettes of trees, looking like fragments of black forked lightning crackling skywards. To her side, lights glow in those little wooden houses along that bumpy road into the town centre. They must be getting close now.

In her head, she can't stop repeating the words the English boy used to describe his own mother's reaction. '*She got used to it.*' Jamie's mother accepted him for what he was. Could she have done that? 'Got used to it'? Could *she* have said to Kostya, 'You're still my son'? Those few little words. If only she had said them. If only she'd known the dangers of Kostya ending up in Milyukov's hands. Some instinct stirs inside her, reinforcing what she's always known but never voiced out loud: that a gay son is better than a dead son, and that those few little words might just have spared his life.

She's sitting in the back seat, her hand in Galina's, looking left, then right, to check where they are, and peering ahead at the slush-filled potholes looming up in the glare of the headlights. Jamie sits up front, next to the driver, chewing his fingernails. In their hurry to get to Khimki, he insisted that they take a taxi all the way out here. 'It'll take too long by bus,' he said.

In the failing light, she recognises the block of flats that houses Milyukov's clinic; it's darker now than back in November when Kostya left her standing here in the rain. She tells the driver to stop, and Jamie hands him a wad of hundred-rouble notes.

She remains in the taxi with Jamie while Galina hovers by

the entrance to the apartment block. The driver turns off his engine. Silence. Eventually someone comes out. Galina catches the door and motions to them. Her stomach is knotted and, once inside, her legs feel on the point of giving way; she needs Galina and Jamie to support her as she leads them up to the second floor, to the door marked 'Renaissance'.

The door is opened by that young woman in the lab-coat and glasses whom she recognises from coming here in August and November. The officious little madam might even have been there when Kostya died – she ought to wring the girl by the neck and demand to know what happened to him, but part of her, the scared part, holds back and lets Galina do the talking.

As agreed, Galina tells lab-coat girl that she's Dima's mother: 'I've travelled all the way from Latvia to see my son Dmitry,' she says. 'I wish to speak to Dr Milyukov too.'

The young woman shakes her head, clutching a file of papers to her chest. 'They're not here, either of them. In any case, you'd need an appointment.'

She senses that lab-coat girl is about to shut the door in their faces. In that moment, she forgets the scared part of her; in its place, she feels herself channelling the collective fury of the Mothers for Peace, a rage now at boiling point, anything but 'peaceful'. Elbowing past Galina, she barges into the clinic and launches herself at the young woman, who staggers backwards, dropping her file. Pages scatter across the floor. This is so unlike me, she thinks, as she makes a grab for the girl's lab-coat lapels, so far removed from that orderly librarian I used to be. But this is what it's come to.

She finds herself flailing her hands after the girl, whose glasses fall to the floor and then go *crunch* beneath their feet.

She hears herself screaming. She can't believe that's her voice out there. '*What did you do to my son? Tell me what happened to Kostya!*'

She feels the restraining touch of two hands, both Galina's, one on her shoulder, one on her arm. Galina speaks, firm, no-nonsense, yet somehow motherly too. 'I just need to see my son Dmitry, understand? Now please take us to him.'

The girl's eyes flit from side to side, from her to Galina, dilated with panic. She starts to nod. 'He's not here, not now, but I can give you directions—'

'No,' Galina says, 'I want you to *take* us there. And may I ask your name?'

'My name? Emilia Semyonovna. Why d'you—'

'Very well, Emilia,' says Galina, gentler now, but still in charge. 'And what about this mother's son? Konstantin? What happened to him?'

Semyonovna's eyes avoid hers, looking at Galina, then at the floor. 'Konstantin?' she blubs. 'I don't *know*. I wasn't there at the time, I swear. We don't understand what went wrong, no one had suffered such an extreme reaction before—'

'Can't Milyukov tell us?' asks Galina. 'He's the esteemed expert, isn't he?'

'He's cleared off to the States,' Semyonovna says, sniffling. 'And I don't think he'll be coming back. What do you hope to achieve anyway, barging in here like this? I can't tell you any more than I have. Now please leave, or I'll . . . I'll call—'

'The police? You won't need to. They should be on their way by now.'

It's Jamie speaking. He's crouched near the floor, scooping up some of the papers from that young madam's file. But before she can ask what he means about the police, he brandishes two pieces of paper, one in each hand. One of them is that article he showed them earlier; the other is one that's fallen out of the file.

'This is what you've been prescribing, isn't it?' She sees his eyes bulging, nostrils flaring at Semyonovna. 'Have a read of this: "chemical-induced nausea", "erotic stimuli", "electric shocks". You've even got your fancy name for it, "corrective reorientation".'

She stares, wondering who he's most angry with. With Semyonovna? With Milyukov? Or with her, the mother who brought Kostya here in the first place.

Dima

One more heave, pushing with both arms, and out he stumbles, sprawled across the floor. Come on legs, he thinks, come on. But they're still half-numb, too unsteady to stand. He drags himself on his hands and knees to the door and grapples with the handle, even though he knows it's locked. Unable to reach the light switch either, he slumps against the door, in the dark.

Think of something, he tells himself, they'll be back soon. But to do what? He tries to recall how Milyukov had described 'corrective reorientation' – something about manipulating the subconscious. Right, so they've drugged him once, they'll probably drug him again. Can't let that happen. He looks round the lab and his eyes alight on the syringes. Break them, some inner voice tells him, don't let them inject you.

Hoisting himself up with his arms and propping himself on the edge of the worktop, he hauls his body across the room. Still on his knees, he grabs one syringe and smashes it, sending splinters of glass skittering across the worktop. Better still, he thinks, just break the needles. He picks up the others – five more to go – and stabs each syringe hard against the wall.

On the other worktop sits a monitor with trailing wires that lead to electrical clips. He tugs at the wires until they snap loose, then turns to the TV set. Edging closer, he sees it's plugged into a video recorder. What's that for? Do they film their patients? Or were they going to make him watch something? What did Milyukov say? '*Erotic stimuli*', some crap like that. Sure enough, there's a VHS cassette poking out of the machine. He's about to take it out and smash that up too – but how can *that* be harmful, it's not like drugs or electric shocks, is it? But wait, what if they filmed Kostya during treatment? He hesitates, switches on the TV and presses 'play'.

He watches. Only one minute, maybe less. It's enough. Enough for him to wish he'd destroyed that videotape straight off. He hits 'eject', pulls out the cassette and brings his fists down on it, hard, tearing at the casing, ripping out the tape until it's all over the floor. But it won't help, not now. He'll never be able, ever, to erase from his mind what he's just watched. It was a scene to make his heart stop beating.

★

He sits, motionless, in the wheelchair. Through a high window to his left, he sees the sky turning dark. Which matches his mood. What was the point of all this? What good can come of it now? Let them drug me, he thinks, or whatever they do.

He hears footsteps in the corridor. That'll be the orderlies, coming for him. What next? There's no getting out of here now. But wait, there's a bit of a commotion – raised voices and the sound of shoes, not the orderlies' slippers. Next thing he knows, someone's rattling at the handle from outside, then there's a man's voice shouting, 'Unlock this door!'

Lights come on in the adjoining room. He blinks, momentarily dazzled by the square of brightness blazing through the interconnecting window, and there, staring at him, are Jamie and the lab-coat woman from Milyukov's clinic. Standing beside them are a young, uniformed police officer and an older, Russian-looking man in a well-worn parka. There are also two middle-aged women, both wearing knitted berets, and a suave, dark-haired guy in a business suit but no tie – looks like an American. He can't hear a thing – the glass must be soundproof – but sees Jamie and the two women shouting and gesticulating.

More commotion, followed by a shout of 'Coming in!' and the laboratory door flies inwards. The lights come on. In steps the Russian-looking man in the parka, his face lined and his eyes like they've seen it all before. 'Dmitry?' he asks.

He nods. Outside the door, he sees Weasel-face and the other orderly being restrained by another policeman. Behind them stand Jamie, the American stranger and the two older women. He recognises one of the women now, those drawn, sullen features glimpsed months ago on a photo Kostya showed him.

The man in the parka flashes an identity card at him. 'Inspector Shustov, Moscow region police. We've come to get you out of here.'

*

He never imagined he'd be so glad to be inside a police station. Not after what the bastards did to Oleg. But at least he's got his own clothes back on – his jeans, his hoodie – and the steadiness has returned to his legs. Cradling a mug of tea, he tries to concentrate on the questions Shustov is asking. How weird, he thinks, an inspector really *has* called . . . An inspector every bit as resigned to the injustices of the world as the one in Kostya's beloved play.

He's left Jamie in the waiting room with Tamara Borisovna, that woman Galina who'd posed as his mother, and the American guy – Kostya's boss Mario, it turns out. The orderlies and lab-coat woman are elsewhere in the station. In the cells, he hopes.

From Khimki it was a short drive here, a little off the highway to St Petersburg. As the drugs wore off, he couldn't help noticing that the police cars in which they were driven to the station weren't clapped-out Ladas or Volgas but big American Fords, as new-smelling as Yuri's BMW. That's odd – he'd thought the cops were short of cash and equipment. He clocks the brand-new IBM computer on Shustov's desk, and watches the inspector typing slowly, painfully, with one swollen finger, like he's unsure how to use the damn thing.

But whatever relief he feels at being rescued is drowned out by the hallucinatory scene playing out in his head, those indelible images from the video.

Tamara Borisovna

They were still at Milyukov's office when the police showed up. Semyonovna had been making excuses, saying she couldn't take them to Dmitry, that visitor access was restricted. Then the inspector arrived with a pair of officers. Jamie was right, the police really had been on their way – and, for some reason, Kostya's boss Mario was with them. The American came up to her, head lowered, hand on his heart, and mumbled his condolences in English.

They were all escorted down to two waiting police cars and driven a short distance out of Khimki. Of course, she thought, recognising the psychiatric hospital where she'd first met Milyukov, years before he got his fancy business premises. Back then, he'd convinced her he was doing a good deed by getting boys out of the army. Wasn't it the same with his 'cure'? So deluded by her quest to 'do good' that she'd been prepared to risk doing harm.

★

Galina excuses herself to use the bathroom. Jamie and the American, meanwhile, get called into Shustov's office, leaving her alone in the waiting area. Out comes that boy Dima. The one in her son's diary – the one, she recalls, who phoned the week after Kostya's death. She watches him slouch, head bowed, towards a seat; he's handsome, square-jawed and with broad shoulders that fill his sporty hooded top. Nothing like her idea of a *gomoseksualist*.

He sits, a few seats away from her, his head in his hands. They are both silent. He must know who I am, she thinks – is he ashamed? That scene from the diary pops into her head, a vision of this boy seducing her son.

After a moment, Dima looks up and turns to her. His eyes are big and grey, almost blue, but tinged with red. He speaks. His voice is cracked. 'Tamara Borisovna, I'm so sorry' – his face screws up as if in pain – 'I should've made sure your son didn't go through *that*.'

He drops his head again, and she watches him rubbing his wrists in the palms of his hands, as though trying to wash them clean. *Go through what*? What's he holding back?

She glances to the side, where a policeman stands by the door, watching over them, and edges a few seats closer. Her lips twitch as those unnatural-sounding words come out. 'You were Kostya's *boyfriend*, weren't you?'

'Yes,' he says, without looking up. 'I was.' He buries his face in his palms, digging his fingers into his forehead. 'He deserved better though. Better than me.'

Silence. 'Oh,' she says, thinking she's understood. 'Weren't you ... *faithful* to him?'

She sees a tear slide down his cheek, and he shakes his head, shakes it hard, as if he's wishing something would go away.

'Why not?' Her words sound angrier than she intends. 'Don't you *believe* in love and settling down? Like *normal* people?' Immediately, she regrets saying that. What about her ex-husband? He was 'normal', but he wasn't exactly faithful.

Dima rubs away the tear with the back of his hand. 'Kostya did,' he says. 'He believed in love and settling down, I mean. Shouldn't be so hard, should it? But our sort' – *nashi*, he says – 'aren't allowed to love. We don't even get to try. How can we learn to love when people don't *want* us to? When all they want is to change us?'

She's dumbstruck. *People don't want us to*. That's people like her. *All they want is to change us*. That's her. She drops her eyes towards the dirty, cracked floor tiles. But she feels like this boy can read her thoughts; when she dares to look up, Dima's face is fighting back spasms of pain, or rage, his eyes are drilling into hers, bloodshot, and he's asking her, 'Tell me *how* though, Tamara Borisovna. Tell me how *your son* ended up in a place like that.'

Jamie. Six days later

The minute he enters the office, he knows from the sight of Bernie clearing his desk that the *Herald* is finished. 'We've been let go,' Bernie tells him. 'You probably saw it coming.'

Casting a final look around the vacated reporters' room, he wanders over to check the fax machine and there it is, what he's been expecting: an invitation from the *Moscow Times* to come in for a job interview.

Yes, he thinks, *yes*! As soon as he'd fitted the final piece in the jigsaw, he'd contacted the *Moscow Times*, knowing they'd jump at the big story he had nailed: the story of a young gay Russian guy dying in a Sov psychiatric ward after treatment to 'cure' his homosexuality. It's a story of Stalinist medical practices, dodgy financial backers in the States, a negligent US-Care boss who would now be obliged to resign and a doctor who took thousands in bribes to turn his practice into a respectable-looking business.

He rummages in his bag. There, still in Larisa's envelope, is that news bulletin: *A hospital statement blames 'natural causes' for the death of Konstantin Krolikov* . . . Rummaging some more, he finds the photo he'd thought he could use for his story: the one of him with Kostya three years ago, arms round each other's shoulders, grinning and looking to their futures.

18

ONE MONTH EARLIER

JANUARY 1993. Moscow

Kostya

'You're obsessed, Kostik!' you teased me. 'All this keeping count and making lists – what's that all about?' I know, Dima, I replied, I know ... And still I kept on counting:

Tchaikovsky concerts I'd been to: sixteen.

Theatre productions I'd seen: fifty-five. (Productions acted in: none.)

Nights sharing a bed with Jamie: lost count (but times we made love: also none).

Nights you and I had made love: (so far) seven.

Or should I include that one time you couldn't get rid of Oleg for the night? That would make eight. What a performance! You silent and stealthy, me trying to stifle my moans, all that pointedly heavy snoring from Oleg ...

But Oleg wasn't there the morning I'm thinking of. You were still asleep beside me as I rubbed my eyes, turned to the wall and studied that photograph of your mum. She was younger than Mama, with stylish blonde hair falling to one shoulder and a knowing smile that seemed to say, 'You can't fool me, Dmitry, I know what you've been up to.' I was still looking at her when you woke five minutes later. That, you said with a sleepy grin, was the expression your mum wore every time she caught you telling lies.

Every time she caught you telling lies. Cruel, isn't it, the way I never picked up on the warning signs? Your mum had known you your entire life, while we had only been 'dating' for two months; I hadn't yet cottoned on how much I was being lied to. 'I can't see you tonight, Kostik,' you'd say, 'I've got a film shoot.' Other times it'd be: 'A friend from out of town is staying over.' Or: 'You can't come around, Oleg's in bed with the flu.'

Number of times you've made excuses to not see me? Nine – and counting.

My suspicions intensified that evening I returned to the Bolshoi Theatre – this time to buy tickets for you and me, to *Swan Lake*. It seemed fitting to invite you to the Bolshoi, the place we first met. It was ten days before New Year's Eve, and Moscow was garlanded with lights and baubles, with scenes of Grandfather Frost and his sleigh laden with presents. Snow was falling, a slow-motion cascade of flakes drifting to earth and settling on every surface, rounding off every hard edge in the city. *Hush*, the snow seemed to say, like a spell that transformed Moscow into a place of stillness, gentle and soft-contoured.

Tucked into my inside coat pocket was an envelope full of dollar bills, my US-Care Christmas bonus. You were worth it – however much I had to pay; this would be my surprise gift. And one more night of not seeing you because Oleg was too ill gave me the chance to go buy the tickets. There was a spring in my step as I trod through freshly fallen snow on Theatre Square. Just imagine your face when I tell you. Picture it, you and I going to the Bolshoi! It'd be an occasion to dress up, to toast each other with *champanskoye*.

Amid that veil of falling snow, the theatre loomed before me. Its portico and mighty pillars were floodlit and glowing against a velvet sky, a portal to a magical world. Taking care to avoid any ticket touts, I stopped to drink in the sight of it. As I did so, there, right by the steps up to the heavy main doors, I saw a familiar figure leaning against a pillar, smoking. He had dark hair and no hat, just his collar turned up against the cold. I pulled my own hat lower to avoid being recognised by him. It was Oleg. But how could that be? You'd told me Oleg was at home, bed-ridden. I squinted as snowflakes blew into my eyes. Yes, it really was Oleg.

My stomach tightened. Were you lying to me? Or had I misunderstood? Perhaps you meant Oleg was going to be home *later*, if not now? But no, it was two hours since we spoke on the phone and here he was, out in the snow with no hat, loitering by the Bolshoi.

Instead of going to the box office, I ducked behind a pillar and watched Oleg. He soon seemed to have had enough of the cold; I saw him shiver, drop his cigarette and trot down the steps. Forgetting all about my tickets – or the risk of running into the wrong touts again – I started to follow him, partly to check if he was going home, where you'd said he would be. Some gut fear of embarrassment, or of deceit, prevented me simply going up to him and saying hello.

He crossed the square, heading into the underpass opposite the Karl Marx memorial, and I followed, keeping about ten metres behind. The underpass was crowded, dimly lit and awash with slush underfoot. We emerged on the other side of the road by the entrance to Ploshchad Revolyutsii metro station, and in I followed him, merging into the tide of snow-speckled hats and coats. The escalators were heaving, funnelling passengers into the bowels of the station, disgorging them onto the platform.

But rather than running for a train, Oleg loitered by one of the station's many statues, a bronze cast of a soldier with a machine gun. He unbuttoned his coat and shrugged off the hunch of his shoulders against the cold, then hooked his thumbs in his jeans and leaned against the statue, looking from side to side as if he was waiting for someone. Hovering out of sight, I noticed that at every corner, every archway, other young men were hanging around like him, trying to look casual, clearly in no hurry for a train. Eventually, one guy approached Oleg; I saw the two of them smile at each other, while looking around to check they weren't being observed.

I'd seen it at gay discos, what these boys were doing. A word popped into my head that Jamie had taught me that night at the club in Birmingham – *cruising*. That's what Oleg was doing; *this* was where he came when you got rid of him for the night. But if Oleg was here, if he wasn't ill like you'd told me, then what were *you* doing? And who with?

★

Don't be silly, I told myself the next time I was in your bed a couple of nights later. I'm being paranoid. There must be some explanation.

You'd lit candles, bolted the door, and were now tugging off your jeans to show off your new Calvin Kleins. It was an intimate moment, the wrong time to ask questions. But I did: 'So where *does* Oleg go when you get the room to yourself?'

You frowned, pulling back from me. 'Why d'you wanna know?'

For a second, I regretted asking. But instantly you arranged your face back into a smile, stroking me under the chin: 'We've got the room to ourselves, that's all that matters, isn't it?'

★

Of course, I saw how all the boys at the disco looked at you, Dima. If it made me feel insecure, it made me swell with pride too. Just as I'd felt being seen with Jamie in Voronezh.

I wanted to show you off. Like at that disco before New Year, the one where I got giddy on *champanskoye*. I was so eager to flaunt my being with you that when I spotted Jamie and Artyom, instead of avoiding them like I'd done for months, I swanned up to the bar, dragging you by the hand. *Look who I'm with*, I wanted to tell them, laying my head on your shoulder. *Look*, I wanted to say, *isn't he gorgeous?* That'll show them, I thought, as I took in their baffled stares, so taken aback that they couldn't manage a hello or a handshake.

And there was another warning sign I should have spotted: you hanging back, reluctant and — let's face it — embarrassed, as I paraded my 'boyfriend' in front of them.

★

Mama had started packing. Before long, she would quit her supermarket job and move back to Voronezh. Some days, her departure felt like a promise; other days, like a threat. Some days, I couldn't wait for her to be gone so I could have you staying over. Other days, her moving out felt like she was rejecting me, and I wished she could hug me and say

335

she'd love me no matter what, that she'd like to meet my boyfriend.

But now she was leaving, it occurred to me that I could set up home with *you*. I could move out of Irina Efraimovna's flat, you could finally move out of Valery Ivanovich's, and we could live together, like a couple! In my head, I'd started planning it all: the apartment we'd look for, how we'd decorate it, the dinners we'd cook each other – and, if I carried on working for US-Care, I could pay for you to take up your studies again.

Yes, that's what we'd do! I felt emboldened. So much so that I went to the barber's and told him to shave my head. Enough of my losing battle against baldness! As you'd said, 'Why don't you shave it off, like they do in the army?' I watched as the clippers sheared away at the few remaining curls; the new head-shape that emerged was sharp and defined, bold and sexy, even. I couldn't wait to show you.

But something was wrong. On what turned out to be our final date, we stood for an hour in the cold, queuing to get into McDonald's. You wouldn't talk, wouldn't look at me and kept staring down at your Timberland boots, stamping them in the snow, kicking the kerb. Finally, you spoke. We were still in the queue and hadn't even made it inside. You told me you wanted to move back to Latvia. For a second, only a second, it sounded logical. Mama was leaving Moscow, why shouldn't you? Lots of people, me included, found it hard to succeed here. But no, Dima, I said, not you, you're my boyfriend, we're going to live together, aren't we?

The alarm bells to which I'd been so deaf rang clear in your reply, the same words you'd used on our first date: 'I told you we could see each other – *as long as I stay in Moscow*.'

I don't recall much else of what you said. Something about getting citizenship in Latvia before they closed the borders, about being a small fish in the big pond that was Moscow.

I tried to protest. 'But I'm your boyfriend—'

My words, emerging as steamy breath, evaporated and died in the sub-zero air. Yours were of more solid stuff, a harsh whisper, penetrating like a knife. '*We live in Russia*,' you said, turning away from me. '*Men can't have boyfriends here.*'

As you spoke, the chill in the air seemed to solidify into an icy spear that struck deep inside me. I shook, not just shivered, feeling as if my legs would give way. It wasn't only my plea that evaporated, words dispersed as steam on gusts of Arctic air, it was my hopes for you that evaporated too. So much for being seen with you at the disco, for going to the Bolshoi with you. And as for setting up home . . .

It was hopeless trying to argue. You turned cold and callous, beyond persuasion. All I had the strength to do – my legs were shaky – was to walk away. It was melodramatic of me, I know; I wanted you to run after me. I heard you call my name, but you didn't come rushing to my rescue like you had on the ice rink. As for the new haircut that I thought you'd so approve of, my freshly shaved head stayed covered, and I never even got to show you it.

*

The minute I got home, I flung myself face-first on the bed. I buried my head in the pillow, willing it to stifle the pain, the heaving, drawn-out howl that rose from within me. The pillow soon turned hot and damp with tears. An hour passed. As my wailing subsided, I tuned in to the stillness of Irina Efraimovna's flat around me. I staggered to my feet and looked next door. Mama was out, her suitcase and trunk sitting on the floor next to piles of books and clothes. I caught myself wishing she were there to comfort me.

I went back to my room and lay down again. Eventually, out of exhaustion, I fell asleep. And once more I had that nightmare. The barracks. The shower-room. The kicks and jeers. The faces crowded round me, spitting and hurling abuse. Me, cowering naked under the running water. Only this time, when I glanced up at my tormentors, one of their faces was different. Among those barracks thugs was a new face. A face that joined in the torrent of jeering and spitting. Your face. And through the sound of running water and insults, your words came to taunt me – *shave it off, like they do in the army . . . like they do in the army . . .*

*

I made myself stay late at work, offering to take on tasks that Mario should have been handling himself. No more rushing round to your place as soon as you gave the word. But once Mario had gone, along with Nastya and the other staff, once I was alone in the office, the temptation to call you was unbearable. I lost count of the times I picked up the phone on my desk and dialled your number, only to clamp down the receiver before the last digit.

It was on such an evening that I came across a folder buried at the bottom of my in-tray. There were faxes, letters and lists of figures in dollars, all submitted by a trio of companies from Utah. Their 'mission statement' was all about mental health-care, claiming that their investment would '*shore up family values at a time of upheaval for post-Soviet society*'. I realised that Mario probably hadn't yet seen this project, but they had lined up the finances, the medical expertise and a proposal that appeared to match US-Care's criteria for assistance grants.

But then I saw the name of their Russian partner. I froze in my seat. It was Renaissance, Dr Milyukov's clinic in Khimki. I could hardly believe the coincidence – and yet it made sense, the way Milyukov had remodelled his practice as a business. Nearly three months had passed since I walked out of there; after meeting you, I'd almost forgotten about the place. Mario would never approve funding – after all, as Jamie pointed out to me, Mario was gay. I ought to warn him – but first I should do some 'vetting'. I needed evidence, perhaps an exposé by gay activists of how aversion therapy didn't work. That magazine *Tema* would be a good starting point.

★

Maybe you'll call, I kept thinking. Night after night, I stared at my office phone, willing it to ring. At home, the first thing I did was check the answering machine. If you had called, we could make it work. Let's find some compromise, I would have said. We could both move to Latvia, why don't I suggest that? Days passed. You didn't call. And neither did I.

But I did go to the disco again. Somehow, I found the will – or more truthfully, it was the thought that you might be there. Even if you were 'cruising', you couldn't ignore me.

The venue was the canteen block of the Red Hammer Cement Works. It was the usual set-up: way out of town, secretive directions to get there, and disco lights blazing against a backdrop of Soviet industrial decay. Inside, carried on the heat of men's bodies, wafts of cheap cologne cut through stagnant air stale with the whiff of canteen cabbage. I screwed my eyes up against the flashing lights and looked for you, squinting into dark corners, scanning the dance floor from every angle. I even looked in the women's toilets.

Then, near the bar, I spotted the back of a tall blond guy,

broad-shouldered and in a tight T-shirt. It was you, it had to be. I pushed through the crowd to get close, ready to tap you on the shoulder. The DJ was playing another Western hit from last summer, 'Please Don't Go' – and yes, like the lyrics of the song, I *would* beg, I'd be begging you to stay.

But it wasn't you, just some stranger who turned and looked right through me.

I bought vodka in a plastic cup and looked around for a seat. Through the crowd I could see Jamie and Artyom smooching on the dance floor, arms wrapped around each other. Artyom was smoking a joint. This time I didn't have *you* to show off to them. I couldn't bear it, Jamie's grin and that smirk of Artyom's. *Look at us*, they seemed to be saying, *we'll be making love later*. I lowered my head and skulked past, pretending not to see them.

I should have left then. But as I dawdled by the canteen's shuttered serving hatch, I sensed someone sidle up to me – 'sensed' because it was too loud to hear and because the dark was such that the disco lights made only the briefest, flickering incursions.

I felt a hand touch my arm and a voice buzz in my ear. 'Hello? Kostya?'

I turned to see a head of ginger hair and a face full of freckles. Kirill.

Before I could say anything, he rushed to speak, his words tumbling out in haste. 'Wait – don't go. Please. You're not going to run off again, are you?'

I dropped my head, ashamed, then shook it gently. I saw his face relax into a smile.

He spoke again. 'Look, I'm sorry I, err, forced myself on you last time. I'd had too much to drink. Did I come on too strong? Is that why you won't talk to me?'

I was half a head taller than Kirill, and he seemed to shrink before me as he spoke. He was all nerves and apologetic shrugs, which elicited in me a surge of pity for him.

'No, Kirill,' I said when I found my tongue. 'It's not that, it's not you – I'm the one who should be sorry.'

He smiled, a wide grin this time, and suggested, 'Shall we get a drink?'

I nodded. I might even have managed a smile. 'Yes, I'd like that.'

Five minutes later we'd found a pair of seats well away from the dance floor. Kirill had had a few drinks but wasn't tipsy or giggly like last time. Once or twice, he hiccupped and put his hand to his mouth, as if holding himself in check. And like the first time, we talked about the theatre. His dream, he said, was to see the big musicals in London. I've been to London once, I said, proudly. But the boom and wail of the disco made it hard to catch what he said next.

He bellowed in my ear, 'I said, let's step outside for a few minutes.'

I nodded. He was right: it was too noisy, too smoky where we were – and as we collected our coats from the cloakroom, I thought of suggesting that we leave the disco altogether. That way, I could stop looking for you and put you out of my mind, if only for that one night. But then I didn't want to encourage Kirill too much either.

Outside, the night was clear and freezing; in the blackness above us, the stars had a piercing, icy quality. I was on the point of asking Kirill which constellations he could name – a game I'd played once with you – but no, that might sound like I was getting romantic. So we walked around the block, shivering in the fierce chill, close to one another but not enough to project any bodily warmth. The windows of the canteen block blinked with the disco lights inside, and a layer of snow clothed the branches of the bushes by the factory gates.

Kirill smiled at me. 'I like your new haircut.'

'Oh, this?' My hand went to my head, instinctively stroking the stubble above my neck. I felt Kirill staring at it and thought that I really should put my hat on. 'I've got no choice, really,' I said. 'I'm going bald, so—'

'It suits you,' he insisted. 'It looks sexy—' He stopped himself, and even in the pale bluish moonlight, I think I saw him blush. 'Sorry, I don't mean to—'

'No, no, thank you.' I wanted to put him at ease. 'I'm flattered.'

And I was. I'd never been told I looked 'sexy' before. It made me wonder, again, how *you* would like my new haircut? Could it reignite your interest in me? It was silly to think that appearances could matter so much. Yet wasn't that what turned me on about you? (And had turned me off about Kirill?) Bodies, haircuts, the labels you wore: it was all part of packaging yourself, selling yourself – here at the disco, at the cruising area where I'd seen Oleg, even in the workplace. I recalled Jamie's words, two years earlier, about surviving in a market, about being a product waiting to be picked from the shelf.

Kirill seemed to read my mind. 'It's such a meat market in there, isn't it?' He jerked his head back towards the entrance. We had strolled some way by now, and the *thud-thud* of disco music was faint. We could hear the sound of our feet crunching in the snow.

We passed an older guy – mid-forties, I'd say – standing in a doorway, smoking. He was shivering under a coat thrown on top of a silky purple shirt, and was balding but with lank, straggly hair at the sides. He should put a hat on, I thought, or shave his hair off like I had. There I go, judging appearances again ... Two other boys passed us and nodded in greeting. They had the same idea as us and were getting some fresh air. We heard them stop and talk to the guy in the doorway.

'Hi, Igor,' one of them said, 'you out on the pull again?'

Kirill picked up where he'd left off. 'Hear that? *Out on the pull* – surely there's more to gay life than being out to cop a one-night stand?'

I thought about it. 'Yet how else are we to meet each other? How else can we find love?' The words 'find love' sent my thoughts back to that day outside McDonald's, with you. Again, as my breath turned to steam, I watched the words evaporate.

Kirill shrugged. 'Find *love*? There's finding *friends* too. We all need friends, don't we? Especially *nashi*. Friends to be there for us when lovers let us down.'

I dropped my gaze to my shoes as they trod through the snow. Maybe he was right: I needed friends more than I needed what I'd been chasing with you or Jamie.

A sad smile came to my face. Kirill was eyeing me expectantly.

'We could be friends, couldn't we, me and you?' he said. 'I don't expect you to *fancy* me – I know there are hotter guys in Moscow! But friends can still talk, go out dancing – we could even go to the theatre if you—'

'Hey, lads! Got a cigarette for us?'

We halted. I swung round and saw a pack of young men, six of them, I think, striding through the snow towards us – not strolling like Kirill and I, or like the pair we'd seen two minutes earlier, but gaining on us with a pace that bristled with intent. And they were coming from the other direction; not from inside, but from the bushes or from the street.

I opened my mouth, intending to say, 'We don't smoke, ask that guy in the doorway', but Kirill gripped my arm. His voice came out somewhere between a gasp and a whisper.

'Run,' he said. '*Run!*'

What? Why? Run where? Which way? Those few seconds, or however long it lasted, went into slow motion: Kirill tugging at my arm, pulling us towards the canteen block's back yard; me pulling the other way, to get past these lads and back the way we came. Then six faces advancing on us, shaved heads and scars, tight black knitted caps, breath issuing from bared teeth, eyes narrowed and pitiless. They were almost upon us, barely two metres away ... Then Kirill's voice again: 'Run, Kostya, run for it!'

I pulled away and ran. One of the lads, the one in front, lunged at me, his arm raised behind him, and I heard a distinct *whoosh* of something whipping past my head, something hard that cut through the air. He missed and swore – 'Fucking faggot!' – and slipped on the ice. I saw a long pole-like object fall from his hand and land in the snow – a baseball bat, I later realised. But that was out of the corner of my eye – I didn't turn to see if he'd got back on his feet, or if any of the other lads were chasing me, I just ran as fast as I could. My feet skidded, my heart raced. I ran until I was back at the main entrance where we'd be safe, where the doorman would let us in—

But wait. I'd lost Kirill. From the moment I ran, I'd lost him. He wasn't behind me, as I'd thought. Not even five, ten yards behind me. Oh God, he must've gone the other way ...

I pressed the buzzer. The doorman recognised me, opening

up straight away, and I found myself clutching his arm in both hands, pleading with him. 'Help! There's a gang out there, some kind of ambush—'

Clearly expecting something like this, he shook me off and shouted to the other doorman just inside. Both of them ran out, brandishing truncheons, their boots crunching in the snow. I followed, too late now to be thinking of my own safety, and heard a scream echo across the yard. I came to a halt. The doormen had rounded the corner now and there was a commotion – shouts of 'Die, faggots!' and 'Fucking scumbags!' and the scuffle of running feet. It was over as quickly as it had erupted.

That man I'd seen earlier, Igor, the balding guy smoking in the doorway, staggered past me and fell, sprawling across the floor of the lobby. A sleeve hung half torn from his coat, and his silky purple shirt was soaked with blood. He was howling in pain and as he fell, he wrapped his arms around his ribs.

A minute later, both the doormen burst in, shouting, 'Call an ambulance! Quickly! Call an ambulance!' I looked. They were carrying Kirill. His arms were draped around their shoulders, his feet dragged along the floor. I called out his name, but he was unconscious, his head hanging to one side, his ginger hair matted with blood. I ran over, calling, '*Kirill!* Kirill?', but the doormen told me to get out of the way. I staggered towards a chair and fell into it. I heard the disco music being cut off. A voice boomed out from the DJ's booth, telling everyone to stay calm, that there had been an ambush and no one was allowed to leave.

I sat in the lobby and felt it spinning around me. My ears rang with the aftershock – still I heard the *thud-thud* of the dance floor, the shouts of the doormen, the screams of the victims. The grey floor tiles and wilting potted plants and the factory's charts for cement production whirled and tilted, all jumbled in my head – all so dull and solid and yes, even safe.

Just in time, I grabbed the waste bin by my seat and threw up into it. I was nauseated. Not just by the ambush – what had we done wrong, other than come here to dance and make friends? – but nauseated by my cowardice too. Why didn't I check that Kirill was with me as I ran? Why didn't I go back for him?

Twenty minutes later, I watched as an ambulance crew carried Kirill out on a stretcher. Again, I trotted alongside them. He was motionless and splattered with blood. Still alive, they said, but he needed to be in hospital. I begged to go with them. No, they said, victims only, and I watched as Igor was helped inside after Kirill.

I turned to the doormen and pleaded with them. 'Please, which hospital are they taking him to? How do I get there?'

'No one's allowed to leave,' they reminded me, arms folded and blocking my path. I looked around. Most of the other boys, those who weren't standing in a daze, were starting to bed in, slumping in their seats or sitting on the floor. They would be stuck here until dawn.

It took more pleading – and a last-ditch 5,000-rouble bribe – to persuade one of the doormen to escort me to the road to flag down a car. Luckily, a driver stopped within minutes. I offered another 5,000-rouble note and asked him to hurry.

*

When we reached the hospital, I was made to wait in a corridor. I sat on a wooden bench and stayed there all night. I didn't sleep a wink.

The following day, they allowed me five minutes. I stood at Kirill's bedside and stared in disbelief at the new friend I'd now lost. He was asleep, motionless, and didn't even blink – I could see only the up-and-down of his chest. I almost envied his oblivious state.

I returned to the hospital the day after, and the day after that. On the fourth day, however, Kirill had been sent home. They wouldn't tell me where he lived – that's confidential, the nurse said – and I had no way of contacting him. What would I have said anyway? The first time we met, I'd run out on Kirill; this time, I'd run and left him to be beaten within an inch of his life. Why would he ever want to see me again?

*

I sat in my room, listening to the *Pathétique* Symphony. When it came to the final movement, the *adagio lamentoso*, I played it loud, beyond caring whether it disturbed Mama. Towards the end, the violins wail in anguish as the music's slow, funereal lament descends into despair – I told you once how the finale, at its first performance after Tchaikovsky's death, had the audience on their feet, in tears. And me? I cried like I had the day you broke up with me.

The music ended. I sat in the long, still, ringing silence and stared at the cover of my Melodiya LP; it was a portrait of Tchaikovsky, painted in the year of his death, that I'd seen in the Tretyakov Gallery. His face glared back at me out of the blackness, a face haunted by the persecution that drove him to his death. I slid the LP back in its sleeve and stood it on my shelf, with my books, photo albums and last year's diary.

I made another of my lists. I was a coward for leaving Kirill behind. I wasn't good enough for Jamie. I wasn't good enough for you. I was a downtrodden admin assistant, not a theatre director. I couldn't stand up to bullies like Nastya. I needed someone like you to rescue me, or even Mama, rescuing me from the army. I certainly wasn't man enough for the army. Or man enough for Papa. I was the reason he left us . . .

At work too, I endured more of Nastya's taunts: '*Why so glum? Still not found a girlfriend?*' I tried to ignore her, burying my head in the file on my desk. And there it was again, right under my nose: Milyukov's funding application to US-Care.

*

I packed an overnight bag, not telling Mama where I was going. Let's see if she misses me, I thought. Even then, I hoped she would. I could phone the next day and say, 'I've done what you wanted, Mama. I've gone to get myself cured.' She would be sorry for wanting to change me. Or she'd be pleased that I was giving it a try. Either way, I'd get through to her.

That evening, I left work early. I took the metro, then that stinking, crowded bus to Khimki. Snow was falling again, and in the diffuse glow of the street lamps, I recognised the stop where I had to get off. I checked the address against the one in Milyukov's application to US-Care. Yes, this was the place.

I'd phoned Milyukov from work the day before, and he'd sounded only too happy to fit me in for treatment. 'Ah, Konstantin,' he said. 'I'm so glad you've reconsidered.'

Once I was inside his consulting room, he was all smiles of encouragement and knowing nods of his head. As I sipped the herbal tea brought in by his assistant, Emilia, he applauded my courage in seeing the error of my ways. He reminded me – making it sound like a release from my obsessions – that I didn't have to be exceptional, I didn't need to emulate Oscar Wilde or Tchaikovsky. 'Come now, you're not some tortured artist, cut off from reality, are you?' He leafed through his files. 'You work as an administrative assistant, it says here – a good, sensible career. Now why ruin your chances of a normal life with these delusions?'

Yes, suppose I wasn't exceptional after all? Why all the torment I'd put myself through over Jamie and you? It was a relief to contemplate Milyukov's promise of an easier life. And it would be easier, wouldn't it, being straight? Easier than being *goluboy*. What did I stand to lose? What sort of life could I look forward to? A life of relentless hatred ... think of that gang putting Kirill in hospital. I couldn't go on living that life, could I? No, I had to change.

I signed some form without reading it and paid Milyukov, in dollars, handing him the unspent Christmas bonus with which I'd meant to buy tickets to *Swan Lake* for you and me. It was still in the same envelope.

As I watched him stash the money in a safe, he cleared his throat and explained that he'd arranged overnight 'accommodation' for me in a hospital nearby. 'You'll have a room all to yourself,' he said, smiling. 'Then, in the morning, we proceed to your first session. Now, the therapy simply entails exposure to, shall we say, "erotic" stimuli.' He cleared his throat again. 'It's really nothing to worry about.'

*

Throughout that night, the moaning and wailing of the patients on the ward was little more than background noise; I wouldn't have slept anyway. I lay in that cramped, stiff-sheeted bed, wearing hospital-issue striped pyjamas, and stared at the ceiling, watching as the passing of the night was marked by the slow slide of shadows cast by moonlight through the window.

My head seethed with images of Jamie and you – those nights of talk and shared beds, our bodies touching, your faces grinning on a disco dance floor, my heart skipping a beat at the sight of you, my tears when it came to say goodbye. I saw Mama, stroking my face and holding me tight that day she came to the barracks to take me home. I saw Kirill's goofy, freckle-faced smile, the disco lights, the teeth and eyes of the thugs laying into him, their baseball bats making contact with his meek, defenceless little body. I heard echoes of Milyukov's sugar-coated voice too, assuring me he could put right all these wrongs, that I no longer had to go on suffering.

*

By now, of course, you'll know what happened next. Or most of it.

A nurse entered my room and gave me an injection; I drank some metallic-tasting fizzy water. Soon I felt sedated; nauseous too – drowsy but with my senses sharpened, every breath more acute, every heartbeat tighter, my guts on edge with the lingering sourness of the cabbage soup I'd forced down at lunchtime. I fell asleep until the orderlies came, took me downstairs in a wheelchair and positioned me in the laboratory.

The lights flickered on in the adjoining room, and through the interconnecting window I saw the nurse and another doctor, one I hadn't seen before. They seemed to be monitoring me. But Milyukov wasn't there – no, he'd 'outsourced' his 'cure', washed his hands of me. Two orderlies in green smocks came in. What were they going to do?

I tried to speak. My voice was slurred and my words garbled. 'Want to stop … Fetch Stepan Mikhail'ich … call Dr Milyukov …'

I had of course been drugged. Not so heavily as to be oblivious to it, but enough to be unable to act. The orderlies ignored me, turning the wheelchair so that I faced a TV screen. I tried to move my head, but it was clamped in place by a head restraint. I saw them switching on what looked like a video player. My voice was feeble, barely a moan. 'Stop, I've changed my mind . . . Mama, where's Mama? Dima, where are you, Dima?'

Yes, you, Dima . . . A vision sprang before my eyes: you, bursting through the door, here to rescue me! You, knocking those orderlies out cold! I saw you lifting me out of the wheelchair in your big strong arms, I heard you saying you'd changed your mind about leaving. You'd tell me you'd come to take me away with you! That we would build a life together . . .

The orderlies switched off the lights and left the room. In the dark, the TV screen flickered into life. The images were fuzzy, badly shot, yet with a burning intensity that imprinted them on my mind. I was watching two young men, naked and peachy-coloured. A pair of buttocks filled the screen. A driving, electronic soundtrack juddered and climaxed in the background. The camera circled and zoomed in on an erect penis, shiny along its shaft, tender at the head . . . then up the camera travelled, up towards a firm, rippling stomach, a pumped-up chest, and finally pausing on a familiar face, a familiar grin, a familiar pair of eyes.

I stared, my eyes dilated but unable to look away. My heart-beat grew faster, too fast, and louder, too loud. My stomach began to heave and regurgitate. Vomit rose, sticking in my throat. To the side, I saw alarm in the adjoining lab, the doctor and nurse rushing round, the door thrown open, shouting, lights coming on. But by now the vomit was choking off my breath and a spasm, like something about to burst, hit my chest.

The video had stopped, the image frozen on screen. And that was the last thing I ever saw. You, Dima, grinning at me.

19

TWENTY-ONE YEARS LATER

FEBRUARY 2014. Epilogue

Dmitris

Kneeling, he picks at the grain-sized splinters of glass still embedded in the carpet, the fragments missed by his hoovering. Some lie scattered far from the window. Got to make sure no one treads on them, he thinks. The guys who attend his group like to leave their shoes at the door, pad around in their socks, make themselves at home. For some of them, his weekly basement session is one of few places they *can* feel at home.

On the other side of the room, Karlis unstacks the plastic chairs that they will shortly arrange in a circle for tonight's meeting. 'At least they didn't want to nick our telly!' Karlis chuckles, with a nod towards the bulky old 1990s TV set squatting in the corner.

He gets to his feet – ow, that twinge in his knees – and frowns at Karlis. His assistant is skinny, not yet thirty and with a neat beard of the type that's fashionable among young guys these days. 'What are you talking about, Karlis? This wasn't a *burglary*—'

'Duh, I *know*!' Karlis puts down the chairs and mimics his frown. 'I'm joking! Trying to find a funny side to it, that's all. Honestly, Dmitris!'

Dmitris. Even now, twenty years after moving to Riga, it gives him the occasional jolt to hear himself called 'Dmitris'. It's a reminder, having finally completed his acting studies here, that he's built this 'new life' around a role he's playing; a role he is stuck with year after year, never straying out of character. Everyone in Riga – everyone except his mum – calls him by his Latvian name. It's an assumed identity, a bid to disown the old, Russian-speaking Dima. Years of Latvian language classes have paid off too. Most of the time, despite a hint of an accent, he manages to set himself apart from the Russians who make up so much of the population here.

He looks around the basement room, at its strip lighting and reproduction artwork, all shots of beaches at sunset and close-ups of pebbles. He pictures the faces, some men, some still boys, that will sit in a circle facing him that evening, hanging on his words of wisdom and opening up as they find themselves among their own kind. His gaze returns to the plywood that's been hastily nailed over the broken window.

'There isn't a funny side, Karlis.' He runs a hand through his hair, what's left of it. 'We're not gonna be able to stay here. Not if we get another brick through the window.'

There had been one brick already, a few months earlier, just before he hired Karlis. It was lobbed through the window late one night as he was stacking the chairs and locking up. Thank God everyone else had gone and no one was hurt. After the crash and the shock, after the dull *thud* of the brick landing on the carpet, came a shout of 'Death to faggots!' In Russian, which didn't surprise him.

'We'll get the money for a new window, won't we?' Karlis says. He switches on the TV, fiddling with the DVD player they use to show videos on relationship role-play. 'I mean, we are insured, right?'

Dmitris flicks a chunk of broken glass into the bin. A splinter has stuck in his fingertip, drawing a drop of blood. 'A new window?' he says. 'It'll only get smashed again. New premises – that's what we need. Up on a top floor where they can't find us.'

He sucks at the drop of blood. He knows they can't afford new premises, not with Riga's astronomical rents these days. His support group has already gone over budget. If need be, he thinks, I'll host the sessions at home – as long as Aivars doesn't mind their little flat being taken over one night a week. But it'd be a step back, a return to hiding away, like the shifting venues of those very first gay discotheques in Moscow.

We shouldn't be *hiding*, he thinks. This is Latvia, we're in the European Union. Yet gay men have, he knows, been suffering more abuse, more beatings of late. Even here, outside Russia but unnervingly close to its borders, Putin's ban on 'homosexual propaganda' has emboldened local gay-bashing gangs. He shivers. There's a draught from the boarded-up window.

His smartphone vibrates in the pocket of his jeans – that'll be a reminder to take his medication. He goes into the kitchen, a poky alcove smelling of damp and bleach and used teabags. By the sink is a rack of mismatched mugs for the men in his group to sip tea as they open up during exercises on Learning To Love And Be Loved. He pours himself a mug of water and swallows that day's pills, one white tablet and a blue capsule.

Checking his phone, he sees that the reminder is in fact to send some flowers to Jules in Brussels. *Blyad*, he thinks, ten years since Oleg died . . . Oleg and Jules had ten years together, and now it's been another ten. It makes him wonder, sometimes, whether he would've been wiser to stay unattached: if steering clear of relationships – as he had with Kostya all those years ago –would inoculate him against the grief and heartbreak that tore Jules apart during his vigils at the side of Oleg's hospital bed. Even living in Brussels, after emigrating there to shack up with Jules, Oleg wasn't diagnosed in time, and it was too late, even with the same medication that's prolonged his own life, his life as Dmitris, not Dima.

He gives himself a shake, thinking, come on, that's not the attitude. After all, it was a love story that Kostya would have applauded, with Oleg falling head over heels for his handsome, smiley lawyer. A classic case of Learning To Love And Be Loved.

Back in the main room, he looks across at the TV. On screen is a sultry shot of a young man pouting in a singlet. It fades into the next image, then the next, all athletic boys – like he once was – bare-chested or in tight T-shirts bulging with biceps and pectorals, and all flashing the now-obligatory exposed waistbands of their brand-name underwear.

'Is that your DVD?' he asks Karlis. 'Did you put that on?'

Karlis grins. 'Bit of eye-candy, eh? Thought it'd lift the mood. Isn't that our message tonight? "Embracing Your Sexuality"?'

A muscly, dark-haired youth appears, staring right out of the screen. His fists are raised and he's wearing boxing gear: padded gloves, shiny shorts, lace-up boots. He shudders. The image is gone a second later, but the flashback lingers in his head, a vision of Yuri, mean and sweaty in his gym kit.

He starts to object. 'Sorry to sound prudish, Karlis, but I'm not sure these images are' – he fumbles for the right word – 'well, *appropriate* for the kind—'

His phone vibrates again. What now? Probably Aivars, texting to ask when he'll be home, and should he save him some dinner? What a fusspot. After four years together, Aivars should know how long these evening workshops can go on for.

He looks. It isn't from Aivars though, but a Facebook update from Jamie – another of the photos and video clips he's been bombarded with since they reconnected online a couple of years ago and became 'friends'. So Jamie's messaging again to show off that he's on TV. His instinct is to ignore it – except this update appears to be addressed to him alone. *Hi Dima – Make sure you don't miss this. Tune in 6:30 p.m. Moscow time, 5:30 p.m. in Riga. Jamie.*

He looks at his watch. That's only ten minutes away. He rarely bothers responding to Jamie's messages – let's face it, it's not like they're real-life friends – but the fact that Jamie has gone to the trouble of messaging him personally, so close to his on-air time, makes it sound urgent. It's an excuse to grab the remote control and switch over from Karlis's DVD.

Karlis protests. 'C'mon, Dmitris, I'm just trying to lighten the mood.'

He shushes him. 'There's something I need to catch on the news.'

'The *news*? But the group starts in half an hour—'

'I'll only be a few minutes. Why don't you make us a cup of tea, eh? Before the guys start to arrive.'

Karlis slopes off to the kitchen, leaving him to fiddle with the remote control until he finds MWV, the channel Jamie's on. The Winter Olympics logo sits in one corner of the screen, but this isn't a report from the Games in Sochi – it's from Voronezh. Kostya's home town ... He stares. There's footage of the Olympic torch being paraded down the city's main avenue – then of a young man getting arrested for brandishing a rainbow flag. His English is too rusty to understand much, so he turns up the volume, but catches only the tail end of the young female reporter's words, 'a flag that promotes homosexuality ...'

Voronezh, of all places. Is this what Jamie wants him to see? He sits, turning one of the plastic chairs to face the TV. Kostya, he thinks. Another anniversary ... Twenty-one years this month. If only ... if only *what*? If only, perhaps, Kostya had lived to have the benefit of a group like this one, or if only he, Dima not Dmitris, had Learned To Love And Be Loved. If only he had practised what he's preaching tonight.

He's only half-listening as the news report ends and switches to the TV studio. 'And now,' says the presenter, a young woman, blonde and slick, 'we go live to Sochi ...' – and there, on the TV screen, is a face familiar to him from Facebook but that he hasn't seen in the flesh for nearly twenty years: the hair now grey, the forehead lined, TV make-up masking a drawn look under the eyes – 'where we join our correspondent James Goodier.'

Jamie

Despite the cold, sweat trickles down the back of his neck. Must be the lights blazing down on him from behind his cameraman Sergei. A wintry breeze blows in off the Black Sea, through Sochi's Olympic Park. He glances over at the floodlit bulk of the ice-hockey arena, emblazoned with the Olympic rings. Pulling himself up straight, he turns to face the camera.

'OK, *Dzheymz*,' says Sergei, 'you're on air in ten seconds – ten, nine, eight ...'

★

Finally, or so he'd thought, he had it all. Everything he set out to achieve. Using his Russian, reporting from Moscow, getting his face on the news ... Back in Manchester last year, at his dad's funeral, some bloke had even come up to him and said, 'I've seen you on the telly!' He'd blushed, a bit, and tried to sound modest about it.

Still, he knew what he was signing up for. Moscow World View pays well but its news output – all in English – is dictated and bankrolled by the Kremlin, a slick, Western-looking propaganda riposte to the alleged 'Russophobia' of CNN or the BBC. He can't say he wasn't warned. Yet his ego couldn't resist this chance to finally be a foreign correspondent.

On days like this, he regrets not following Artyom to New York back in the 1990s. Who knows, they might still have been together. Plus, if he'd relocated to the States, he'd have been able to cover the long-running story about efforts to extradite Milyukov for manslaughter. This time round in Moscow, he's not met anyone like Artyom – and certainly no one like Kostya. Just a series of short-lived flings with younger guys, usually ones who recognise him off the telly. There's a new suspicion of Westerners too, only without any of the old Soviet-era curiosity or the effusive invitations to home-cooked feasts like Tamara Borisovna's.

He was preparing to trot out a routine to-camera piece on Sochi welcoming the influx of athletes and dignitaries when, out of the blue, he heard the news from Voronezh. News that he can't stop thinking about: an arrest in Kostya's home town, on the same street he'd strolled along with Kostya on their way to his weekly sleepovers. What happened to the hopes of which they had talked late into the night? He can still smell that cramped bed, see the theatre posters on Kostya's walls, can replay in his head the talk they had when he'd urged Kostya to come out of the closet. Some good that had done; Kostya might've been better off staying in the closet. And now, under Putin's paranoia-fuelled crackdown, a young man has been arrested right where he and Kostya had walked, shoulders touching. For what? For waving a rainbow flag. Jesus, he thinks – just as he'd thought twenty-odd years earlier – I despair of this country.

Tamara Borisovna

The tip of her walking stick glances off the icy kerb. She stumbles, almost falling into a gutter flooded with melting snow. Just in time, she manages to steady herself on the back of a parked car. She stops for breath and rests her heavy shopping bag on the car's rear bumper. It's one of those high-off-the-road Western models with big wheels that she's noticed all over Voronezh; it's sad how you hardly ever see any Soviet cars these days. A sudden *whoop-whoop-whoop* blares out and the car's tail lights start flashing. She's so startled that she clutches her hand to her heart and drops the walking stick altogether.

'Babushka! Babushka? Are you all right?'

She looks up, panting, her hand still on her heart. A young man in a wolfskin hat and long camel-hair coat is running towards her through the snow. What cheek, she thinks, calling her 'babushka'. She's not *that* old — and she's wearing her smart woollen beret, not some peasanty headscarf. The man points with his keys, and the car alarm stops as abruptly as it started.

Studying his face, she catches a waft of expensive cologne. 'I just lost my footing on the ice,' she says, looking down and bending to retrieve her walking stick.

'Here, let me.' Quick as a flash, he's picked up the stick and hands it to her. He smiles, breath billowing between perfect teeth. 'Babushka, are you going to be all right?'

Stop calling me babushka, she thinks — but says, 'I'll be fine, *spasibo*. I'm only going to that doorway there.' She nods across the whiteness of the snowy courtyard. A gaggle of girls are smoking by a bench, their giggles echoing off the surrounding blocks of apartments.

'Come on, let me give you a hand,' the man says. She protests — '*Ne nado, ne nado*' — but he's already hoisted her shopping bag off the car bumper and offered her his arm.

As they cross the courtyard, she glares at the girls in their garishly pink anoraks with big fur-lined hoods. Two of them are transfixed by the smartphones in their hands, but another two nudge each other and snigger as she waddles past.

Young people these days, she thinks. No respect. But then, hasn't she always said that? And it's not the case with her Maksim, is it? Now there's a nice young man for you. Goes to show, you can't always pre-judge. And she does appreciate having him around. 'You should get a lodger in too,' she's been telling Galina for the past year. 'He's ever so helpful, is Maksim. A lovely lad, despite what they say.'

The man in the camel-hair coat escorts her to Galina's block of flats. Once inside, he stamps the snow off his shoes, waits with her until the lift arrives, then hands her the bag of shopping and says goodbye. Thankfully, he doesn't call her babushka again.

She wrinkles her nose at the whiff of garbage chutes in the lift. Most of the flats in the block have been privatised and sold – some of them for a fortune – but the smell of the lift shaft hasn't changed. She's grateful for little things like that, things that stay the same. And thank God she managed to find a new flat, just around the corner, before they all started being snapped up at sky-high prices. At one point, after she'd lived at Galina's a whole year, Galina had asked her if she wanted to stay for good. That wouldn't have been right though, would it, taking over Viktor's old room? And besides, the pair of them were starting to get dirty looks from some of the neighbours. Honestly, how ridiculous. As if anyone could get the wrong idea about the two of them living together, two women of their age.

Galina doesn't get out of the flat much these days, at least not in winter. Too hard on her joints, she keeps telling her – which is why she's been out to get Galina's shopping again. She lets herself in – she still has a key – and plonks the shopping down by the kitchen door.

A shout from down the hallway: 'Tamara? Is that you?'

'Of course it's me, Galya! Who d'you think it is?'

She finds Galina in bed, where she left her, sitting upright in her nightdress and with the pillows plumped up behind her. Her eyes are watery and her hands trembling as if she's had a fright. 'Oh dear,' Galina's saying, 'you're not going to believe who was on the news.'

'On the news?' She's taken aback by the catch in Galina's voice.

'You'd better sit down.' Galina nods towards the bedside armchair.

She sits. She's only just got her breath back and can already feel her heart rate starting to rise again.

'It's your Maksim,' says Galina. 'He's got himself in trouble with the police!'

'*Maksim?*' She frowns, half incredulous, half irritated. Galina does tend to get confused of late, bless her. Here she goes again, imagining things.

Galina must have sensed her scepticism because she reaches for the remote control and switches on the TV. 'It's been on the local channel three times already,' she says. 'It'll be on again, I'm sure. Just watch – give it five minutes, you'll see.'

★

She's got into such a flap about what's happened to Maksim that she hasn't left quite enough time to tend to Kostya's grave. If I don't hurry, she thinks, it'll be dark soon. She could go tomorrow instead – but she's been carrying around that newly framed photograph that Maksim has printed off. Besides, today is the twenty-first anniversary.

The gravestone is mouldy now, the old photograph faded and warped. Kostya's eyes still gaze to one side, as dreamy as they always were, oblivious to passing years of rain and wind; bleached by the sun, frozen by the snow. He is streaked with damp down one side and creased round the edges. At least he doesn't get any older, she thinks, picking up the old photograph and creaking with stiffness as she hauls herself up straight again.

The cemetery is quiet, muted by the snow blanketing every headstone, every patch of ground. The wind tickles the back of her neck, making her shiver. Bells peal at the church up the hill – thank God the church is still there, something else that's unchanged. But downhill, towards the river, the view across to where she and her family once lived is obscured by a cluster of new apartments decked out with balconies and satellite dishes.

One last look. She's placed fresh flowers alongside the new photograph – the same old image, just a new print in a new frame, a fresh incarnation almost. She stares, deep in thought. Twenty-one years on, she can still feel the body blow that felled her. And they say time heals. How she wishes, even now, that she could alter the past. People are trying to revive the Soviet Union; they might succeed. But there's no turning back the clock on Kostya's short life.

★

Maksim's rent money helps, of course, her pension being what it is. And, like she keeps telling Galya, it's good to have company, a young man under the same roof. But that's not the main reason she took him in. He doesn't tell her everything – why should he, the boy's got his own life to lead – but she can put two and two together. She knows his parents have kicked him out, that they've disowned him for being 'the way he is'. If only she could talk to them and persuade them to avoid making the same mistakes she'd made.

He's out most of the time, at university, with his friends, at his meetings. Some nights he doesn't come home at all. She doesn't ask where he goes. But sometimes she and Maksim have breakfast at the kitchen table together; he might even get the shopping in or bring her flowers, and she leaves him a pan of borsch in case he's hungry. One day it'll come to an end though. He'll move on. Only to be expected, isn't it. Handsome boy like him, he'll meet some other handsome boy and they'll move to Moscow together, or abroad if they've any sense.

★

Thank goodness, they've let him come home. He looks pale after his night in the cells – and what's that on his face? A bruise? A cut? Maksim tells her not to worry, but she scuttles off to the bathroom to look for some ointment. She can't help herself. She likes having someone to fuss over again, likes to feel needed. And how she does wish he'd let her patch up those jeans of his! It's the fashion, he tells her. But look at them, all ripped at the knees – and far too tight, can't be healthy.

She catches sight of herself in the bathroom mirror. The eyes staring back at her are milky and fretful, but look all the more mobile amid the wrinkles sagging beneath them. But as her idea takes shape, the corners of her mouth crease upward into the beginnings of a smile.

When she goes back into the kitchen, Maksim is sitting at the table with his head in his hands. He looks up, brushing his strands of lank, dark hair out of his face. She sees that his eyes are red. 'I suppose you'll want me to move out, Tamara Borisovna?' he says. 'You must have heard. About the police arresting me for—'

'Oh, Maksim, why would you think that? I wouldn't hear of it!' She clasps her hands together. 'On the contrary, I think you're very brave.'

'Really?' he says, wiping his eyes. He stands and gives her a hug. Her face barely comes up to his chest. 'Aw, Tamara Borisovna,' he's saying, 'how can I thank you—'

'There's no need to thank me,' she says. 'But you can do us a little favour.'

And with that, she hands him the shopping list she wrote out after hearing the news. She talks him through it, telling him exactly what to buy, how much of it, the measurements and where to buy it — that little fabric stall near the local market.

She hobbles off to the living room, then stops, transfixed by the corner where her other photograph of Kostya stands. Above it, behind the television, there's the cupboard where she keeps his old books and classical records. She's kept his diaries too, but in a sealed shoebox, and she's never wished to look at them again. Stroking the photo, she thinks: I wish I'd found it in myself to do something like this for *you* ...

She starts to unfold the table that houses her sewing machine. The same old Soviet-made contraption she's had for thirty-odd years still works as well as any new-fangled Japanese gadgetry. Something else that hasn't changed. Better put my glasses on, she thinks, I can't be sewing without them ...

She looks up to see Maksim standing there, his mouth agape and eyes wide as he stares at the shopping list in his hand. 'Tamara Borisovna, is this what I think it is?'

She smiles. A tear wells up behind her glasses. Has he guessed? It's only the tiniest of gestures, it won't change the world. But she's made up her mind. To hell with the police and whatever people think, to hell with Putin's nonsensical law banning 'gay propaganda'.

'You just hurry down to the shop before it closes,' she says. 'And make sure you get all six colours — one metre each. Should be enough for a new flag, shouldn't it?'

ACKNOWLEDGEMENTS

They say writing is a lonely business. And truly it can be. For hours on end, day in day out, year after year, I've often sat alone, staring at a blank page or blank screen, either typing away or mired in writer's block, thinking I could have been out doing something more fun.

Yet it would be untrue to say that I've been alone on this journey. More than anything, what all would-be novelists need is *encouragement* – and indeed this novel could not have come into being without the encouragement, support and friendship of so many people.

For starters, my husband Laurent urged me to take the first steps, then bore patiently with me over the years whenever I 'was writing' instead of doing housework. Then there was Faber & Faber's Writing a Novel course, which brought me under the nurturing you-can-do-it tuition of Esther Freud and Tim Lott, and gave me confidence to Get On With It. No less valuable was the peer support and constructive criticism of my Faber cohort: Jill, Kate, Richard, Neil, Jo, Jackie, Rebecca, Jude, Bernadette and Mike, all of them talented writers.

For turning my dream of publishing a novel into a reality I am indebted to my agent Gordon Wise, who not only took a risk on an unknown, but then devoted so much time to reading and re-reading the manuscript. Thank you, Gordon, for your belief in me.

More of that 'you can do it' encouragement came from early readers Helen Smedley, Dan Evans, Garry Britton, Sophie Hanscombe, Piero Bohoslawec, Kate Taylor and Richard Cooper. I'm also grateful for the warm welcome (and occasional free coffee) I enjoyed from Sean, Genty, Magda and Paul, the staff of The Larder café in Wanstead, east London.

Obviously too, I'm not only thrilled to be published by Unbound, I am also moved and awed and inspired by the warmth, enthusiasm and professionalism of its editors and publicity team Aliya Gulamani, Alex Eccles, Anna Patterson, DeAndra Lupu, Faiza S. Khan, Rina Gill, Sophie Griffiths – and for the brilliant, evocative cover design by Mark Ecob. Warm wishes to them all, and to Solange Burrell, whose novel Unbound is publishing alongside mine.

A special word of recognition is due for my old friend and fellow student of Russian, Will Maciver, who (exasperated by my failure to get writing) once said, 'Why don't you write a gay murder mystery and set it in Moscow?'

This is a novel that is very much about friendship, and writing it has made me reflect on all the friends – all of them – who have helped me through life, many of whom I've lost touch with, neglected or, lamentably, fallen out with.

There are too many to name here, but they make up a veritable cast of hundreds (perhaps for some future 1,000-page novel): friends from Fartown High School, Greenhead College and Sainsbury's, all in Huddersfield; from a term at Heriot-Watt University; friends from the French and Russian departments and various flatshares at the University of Birmingham; from my student years abroad in Voronezh and Clermont-Ferrand; from working (and partying) in Moscow; colleagues from United Press International; all the wonderful gang of *The Baltic Observer*; London gay scene friends; colleagues and fellow novelists at the *Financial Times*; friends from various yoga and gay men's groups; friends from Madrid; and, last but not least, our much-valued friends in Brighton and Paris.

Unbound is the world's first crowdfunding publisher, established in 2011.

We believe that wonderful things can happen when you clear a path for people who share a passion. That's why we've built a platform that brings together readers and authors to crowdfund books they believe in – and give fresh ideas that don't fit the traditional mould the chance they deserve.

This book is in your hands because readers made it possible. Everyone who pledged their support is listed below. Join them by visiting unbound.com and supporting a book today.

Martha Adam-Bushell
Claire Adams
Viccy Adams
Keith Adsley
Tony Aitman
Neil Alexander
Sally Allen
Rhona Allin
Lulu Allison
Shelley Anderson
Kirk Annett
Sidra Ansari
Emma Antonova
James Aylett
Nicola Bannock

Vikki Bayman
Helen Bennett
Elizabeth Bentley
Senay Bereket
Maud Blair
Piero Bohoslawec
Emily Bolton-Hale
Fran Bongard
Kate Boulton
Susie Boyt
Sarah Brazier
Catherine Breslin
Stephanie Bretherton
Carolyn Brina
Garry James Britton

Brian Browne
Marti Burgess
Leroy Burke
Lydia Burke
Natalie Burke
Paul Burke
Grassarah Burrell
Sophia Burrell
Ana Calbey
Jennifer Campney
Grace Carter
Holly Cartlidge
Rosemary
    Chamberlin
Bruce Clark

Rocane Clarke
Mathew Clayton
Sarah Clement
Lara Clements
Anastasia Colman
Jude Cook
Nick Cooper
Richard Cooper
Deborah Crawford
John Crawford
Emoke Czako
Peter Dalling
Ben Dare
Rishi Dastidar
Nick Davey
Eileen Davidson
Laura Davis
Stephen Dixon
Ashley Elsdon
Emily & Tabitha
Ayla Chandni Estreich
Mary Jane Fahy
Patric ffrench Devitt
Paul Fulcher
Carmen Gayle
Claire Genevieve
Catherine Gent
Eva Georgiou
Terry Georgiou
Rina Gill
Richard Gillin
Carl Gordon
Paul David Gould

Robert and Cynthia
    Graham
Jo Gray
Emma Green
Joanne Greenway
Katy Guest
Aliya Gulamani
Daniel Hahn
Cris Hale
Eleni Hamawi
Sharon Hammond
Sophie Hanscombe
Chloe Hardy
Becca Harper-Day
Clay Harris
Elspeth Head
David Hebblethwaite
Paula Hedley
Anna Hepworth
Jerome Hering
Sean Hickman
Jan Hicks
Robin Hill
Tony Histed
Emily Hodder
Damian Hornett
Katy Hoskyn
Vicky Howard
Helen Hubert
Joe Huggins
Chris Hulbert
Iqbal Hussain
Cassara Jackson

Mike James
Amanda Jenkins
Jill Johnson
Alice Jolly
Margaret Jones
Nikki Jones – The
    Bookish Mindset
Sheila Jones
Adrian Justins
Diana Kahn
Steven Keevil
Kathryn Kerr
Dan Kieran
David King
Emily Kyne
George Kyriakos
Pierre L'Allier
Jane Lamacraft
Elizabeth Larkin
Capucine Lebreton
Lena Lee
Anastasia Lewis
Jennifer Lewis
Johanna Linsler
LJ
Jose Miguel Vicente
    Luna
Sabrina Mahfouz
Rachel Malik
Melanie McBlain
Megan McCormick
Marie McGinley
Joe Melia

Radojka Miljevic

Verna Milligan

Alastair W Monk

Daniel Monk

Paul Monteith

Martin Morrison

Janet Morson

Jo Murphy

Jamie Nash

Antony Nelson

John New

Emma Newell

Chris Newsom and
    Jasmine Milton

Iain Newton

Sue Norris

Jenny O'Gorman

Mark O'Neill

Karen O'Sullivan

Melody Odusanya

Wayne Olson

Jo Ouest

Camilla Marie Pallesen

Ryan Patrick

Alex Pearl

Jennifer Pierce

Chantelle Pierre

Yvonne Plummer

Justin Pollard

Patricia Pollock

Steve Pont

Tolulope Popoola

Janet Pretty

Tina Price-Johnson

Joanna Quinn

Daniel Rafferty

Amanda Ramsay

El Redman

Heidi Rees Williams

Leroy Reid

Emma Rhind-Tutt

Charma Rhoden

Linnette Rhoden

Jacqueline
    Rhoden-Trader

Jane Richardson

Pamela Ritchie

Jane Roberts

Bernadette Rodbourn

Janet Rutter

Caroline Sanderson

Emily Sandovski

Sarah

Lucy Shaw

Mom-Veronica Shaw

Isobel Sheene

John Simmons

Balmeet Singh

Andrew Smith

Valarie Smith

Kerriann Speers

Josh Spero

Ruth Stanier

Hannah Stark

Gabriela Steinke

Leoni Sterling

Mark Sterling

Susanne Stohr

Pamela Strachman

Ander Suarez

Pauline Subran

Kirsty Syder

Katie T

Celina Taylor

Jane Teather

Andy Telemacque

The Development
    Team Unbound

Kate Tilbury

Sabine Tötemeyer

Zach Van Stanley

Alaina van Thiel

Mark Vent

Steve Walsh

Chee Lup Wan

Anjunette Washington

Cassie Waters

Carole Watters

Andy Way

David & Natalie Willbe

Jenny Williams

Catherine Williamson

Phil Williamson

Keeley Wilson

Martin Wroe

Shereen Yala-Callum